D0019906

BAD KITTY
Kitten Trouble

WITHDRAWN

NICK BRUEL

SQUARE
FISH

ROARING BROOK PRESS
NEW YORK

For Robert
and all the dashing Daciws

SQUARE
FISH

An imprint of Macmillan Publishing Group, LLC
120 Broadway, New York, NY 10271
mackids.com

Our books may be purchased in bulk for promotional, educational, or
business use. Please contact your local bookseller or the Macmillan Corporate
and Premium Sales Department at (800) 221-7945 ext. 5442 or
by email at MacmillanSpecialMarkets@macmillan.com.

Library of Congress Control Number 2018944870

Originally published in the United States by Roaring Brook Press
First Square Fish edition, 2019
Square Fish logo designed by Filomena Tuosto

ISBN 978-1-250-23328-8 (Square Fish paperback)
1 3 5 7 9 10 8 6 4 2

ISBN 978-1-250-75281-9 (special book fair edition)
1 3 5 7 9 10 8 6 4 2

LEXILE: GN560L

• CONTENTS •

•PROLOGUE•

EIGHT YEARS AGO

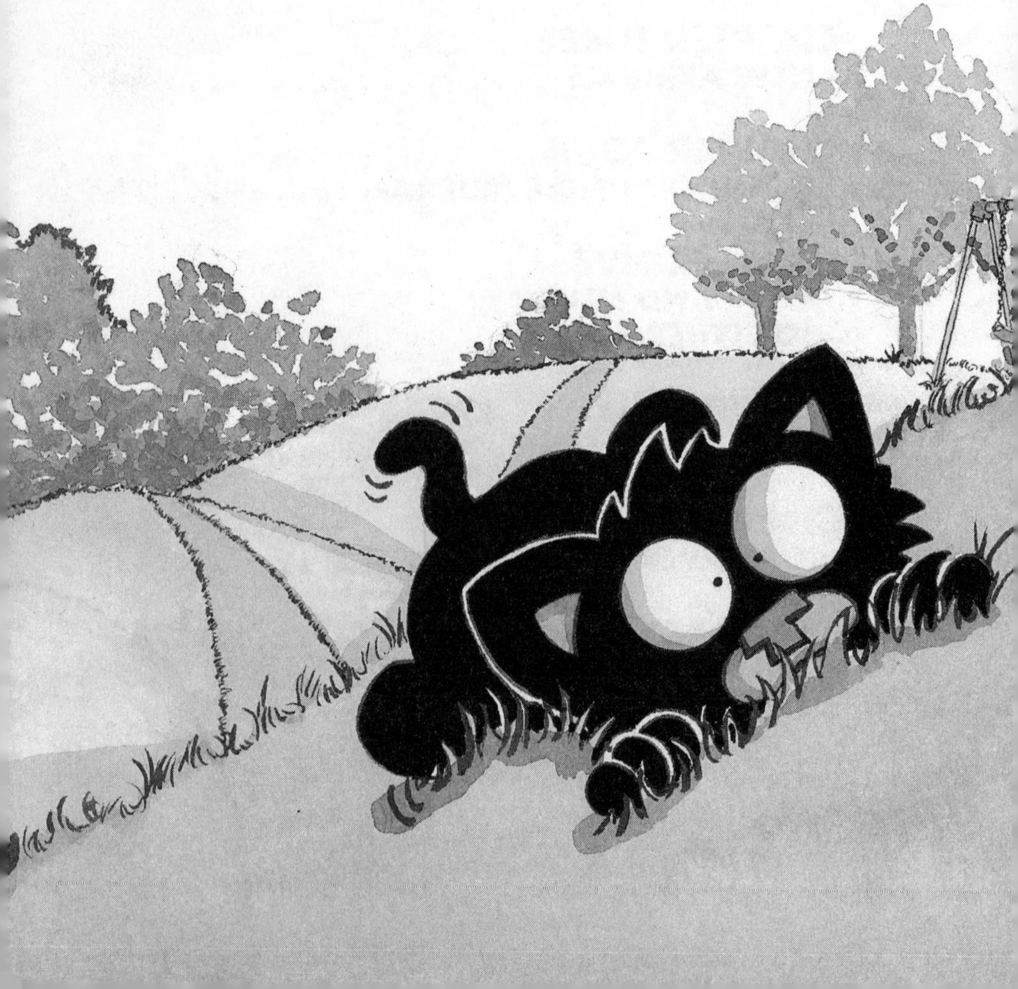

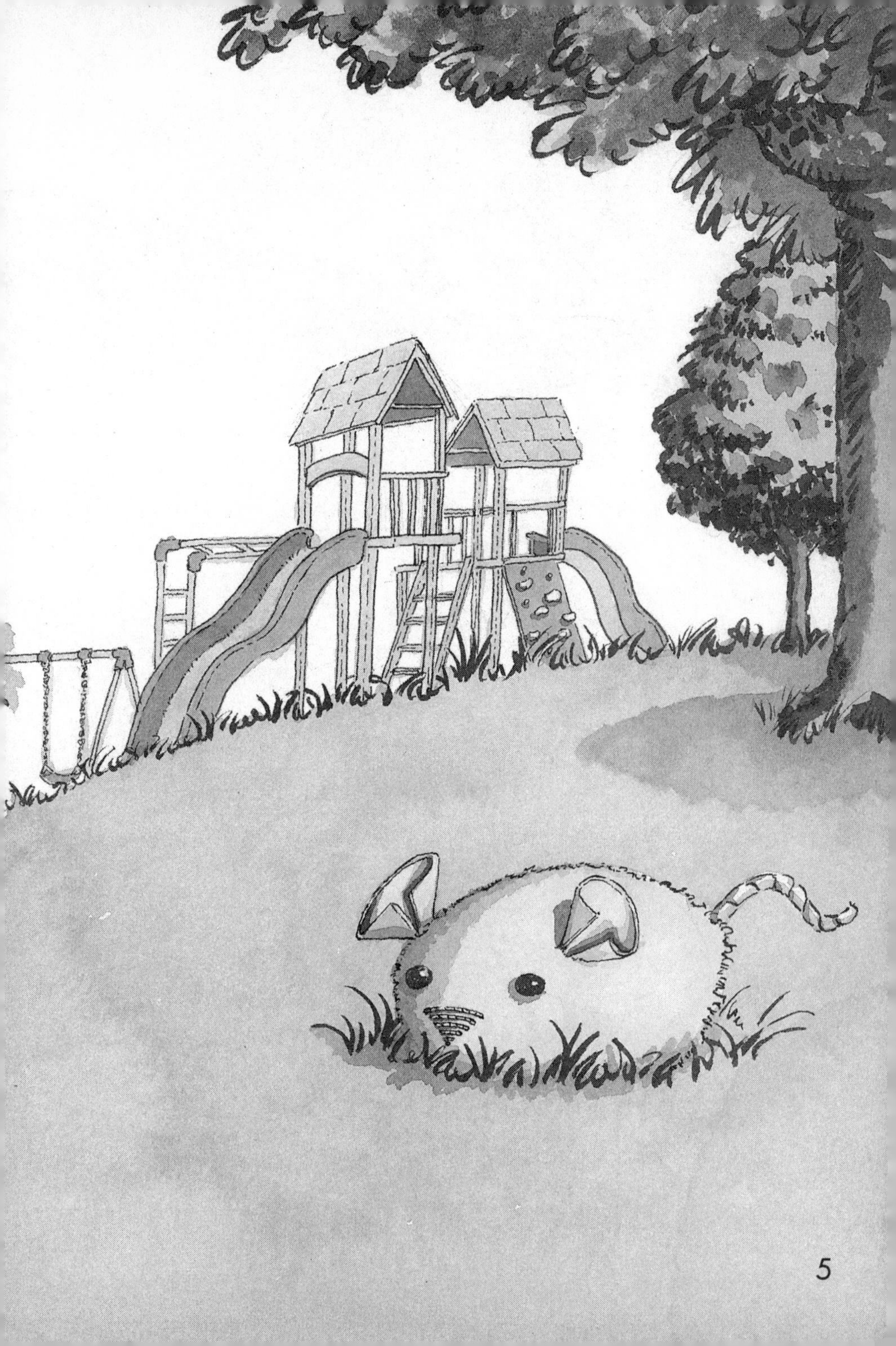

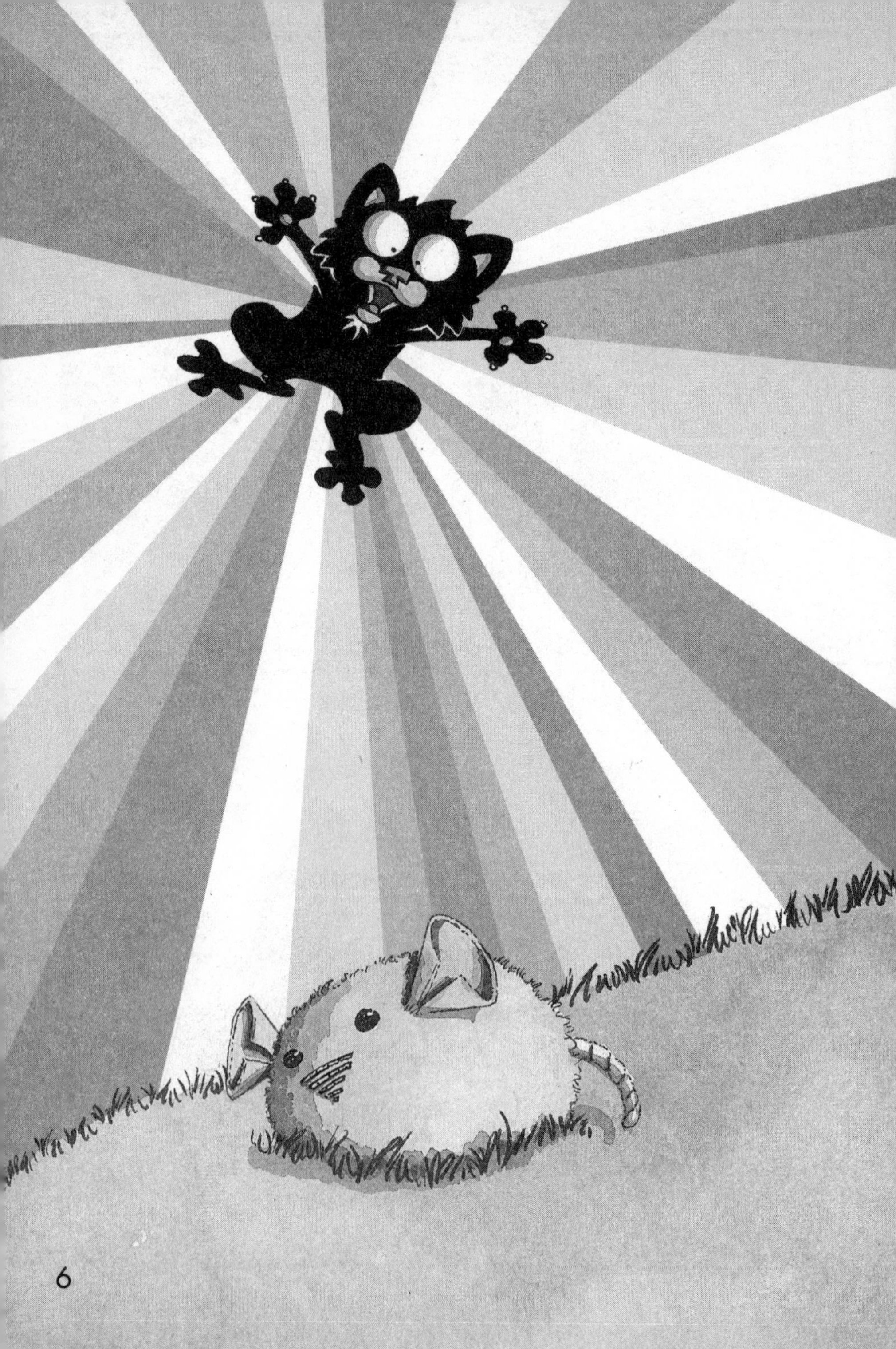

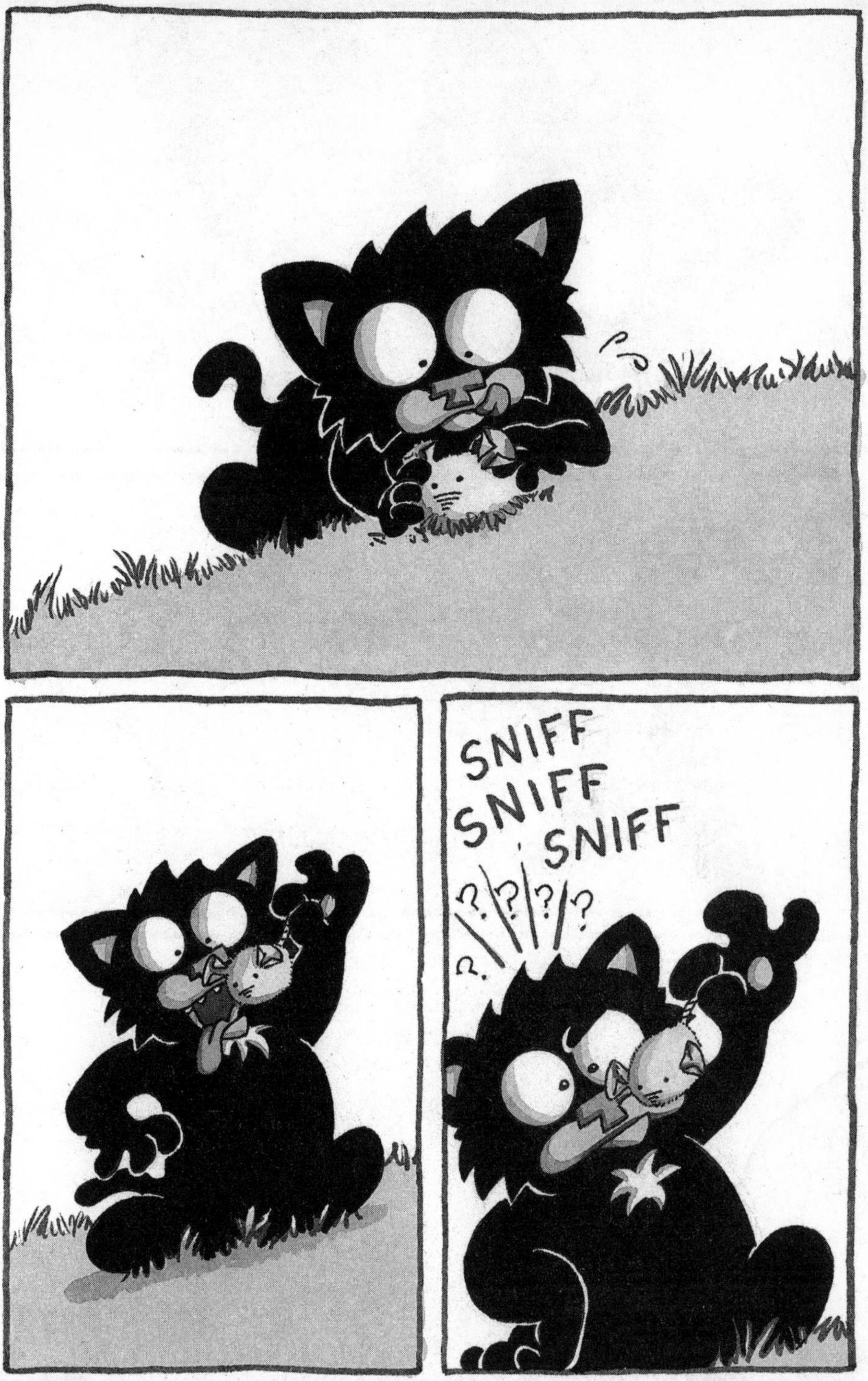
SNIFF
SNIFF
SNIFF

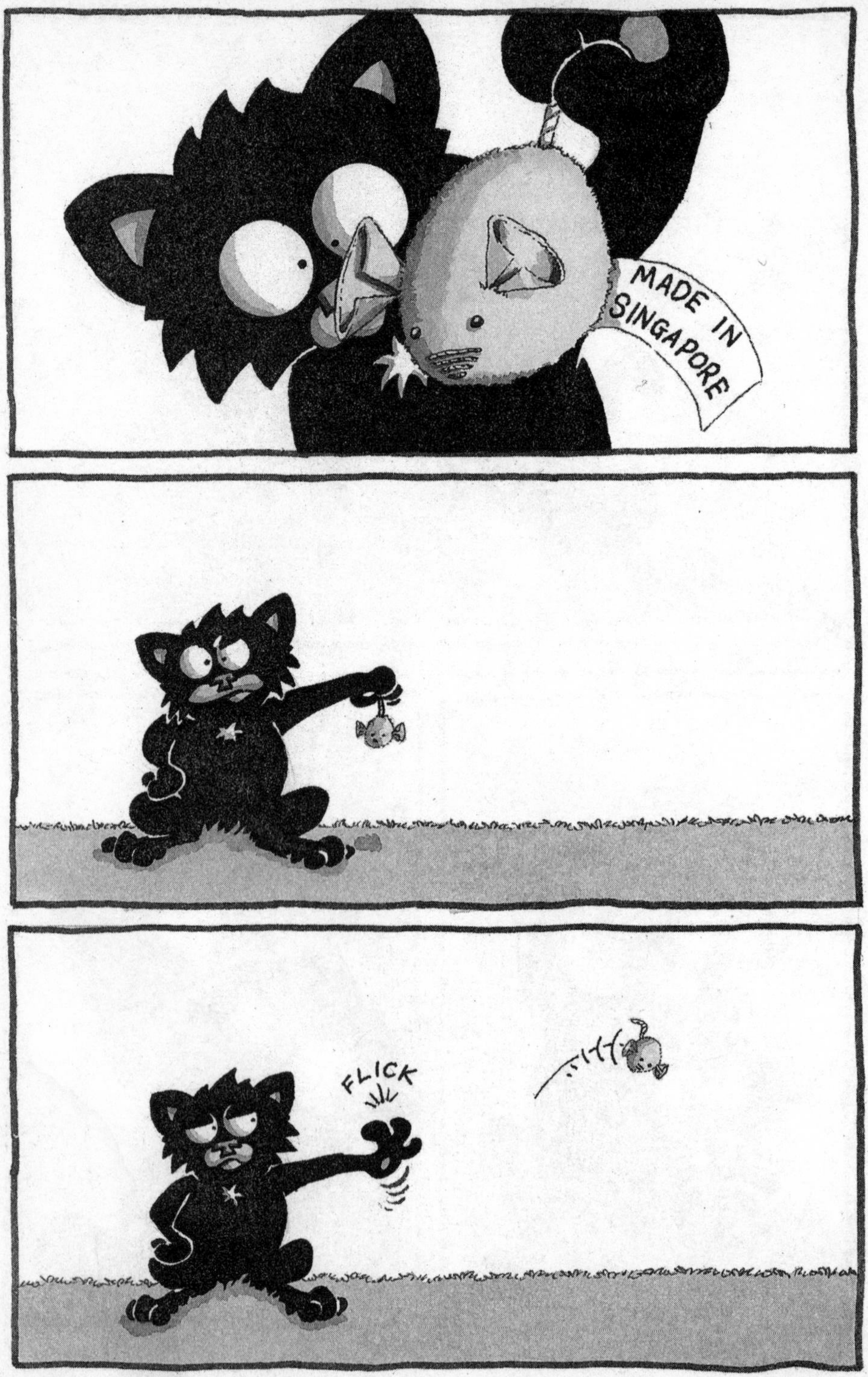
MADE IN SINGAPORE
FLICK

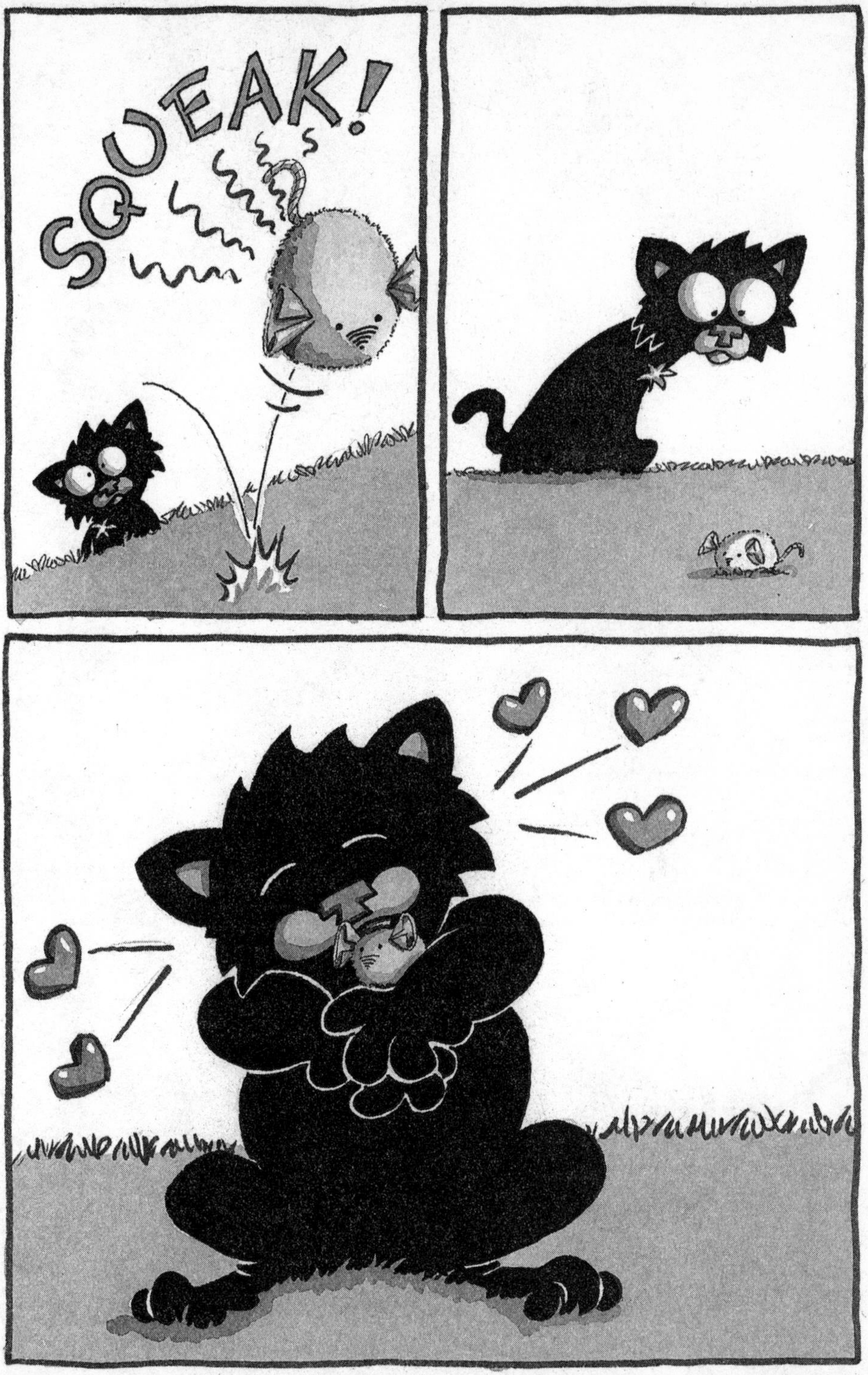
SQUEAK!

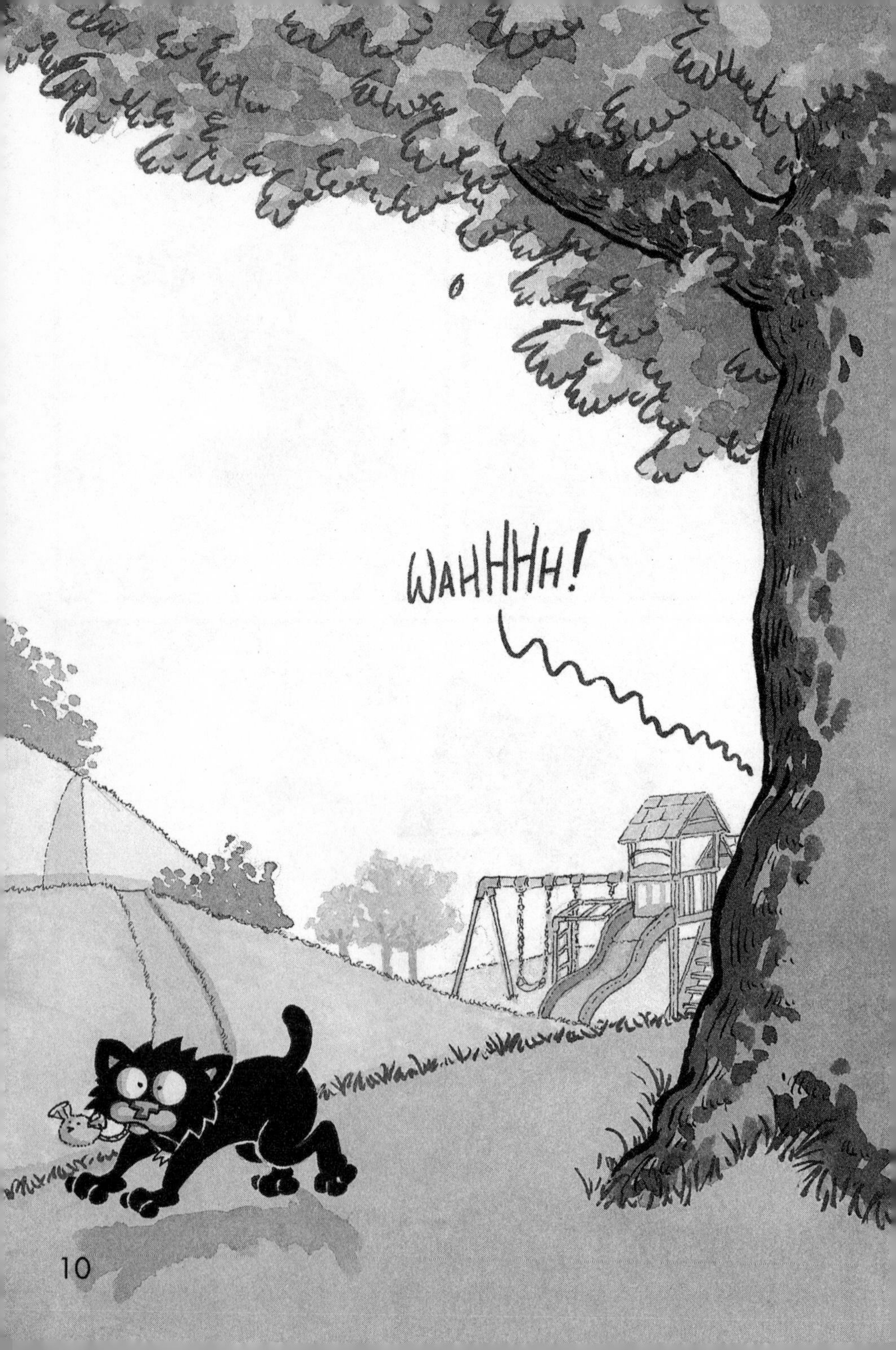
WAHHHH!

•CHAPTER ONE•

TODAY, MONDAY

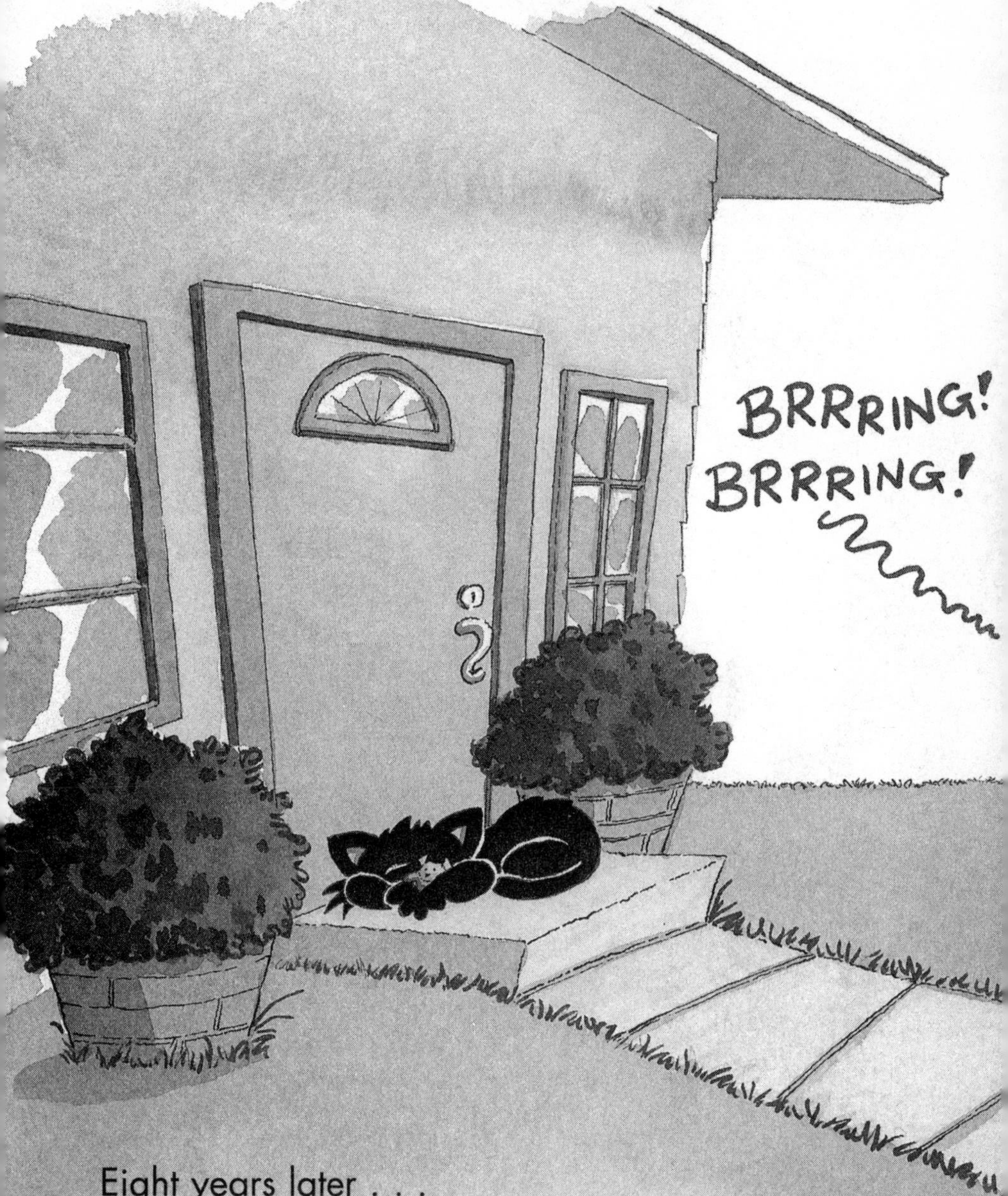
BRRRING!
BRRRING!

Eight years later . . .

Kitty doesn't like that kid who delivers the newspapers.

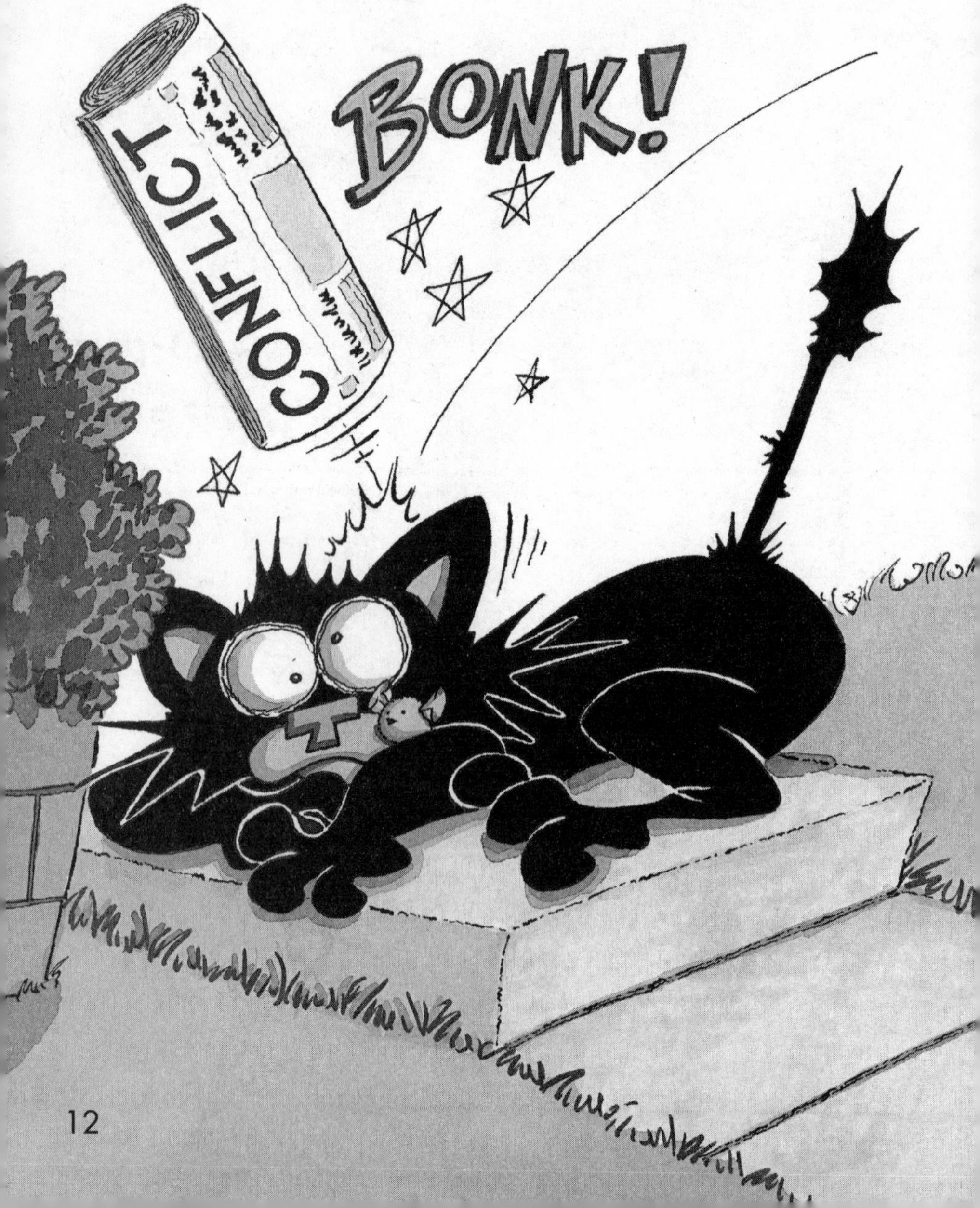
CONFLICT
BONK!

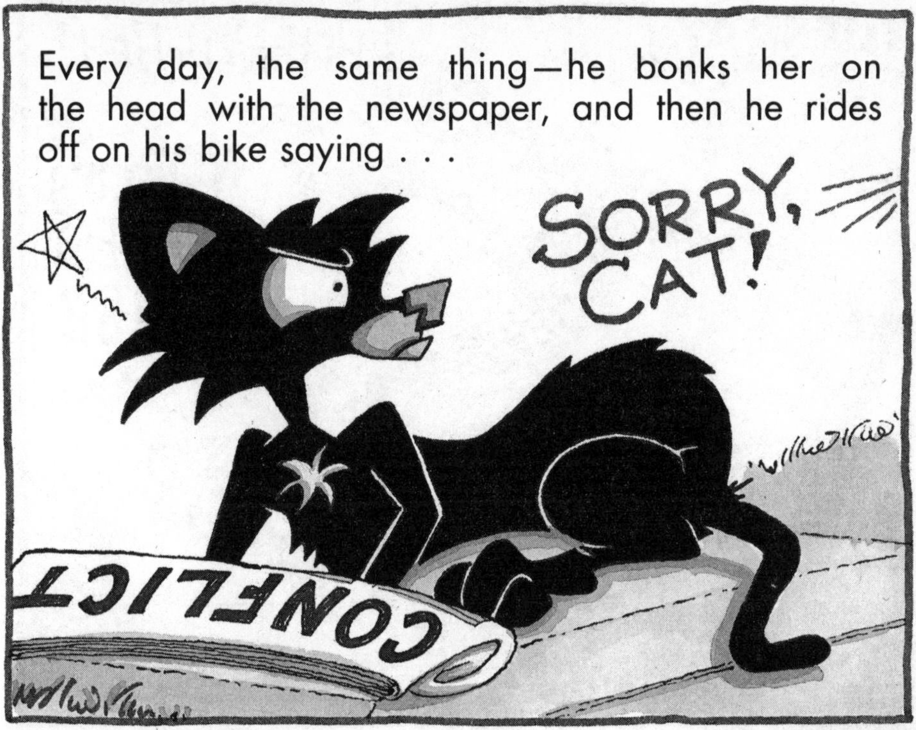
Every day, the same thing—he bonks her on the head with the newspaper, and then he rides off on his bike saying . . .
SORRY, CAT!
CONFLICT

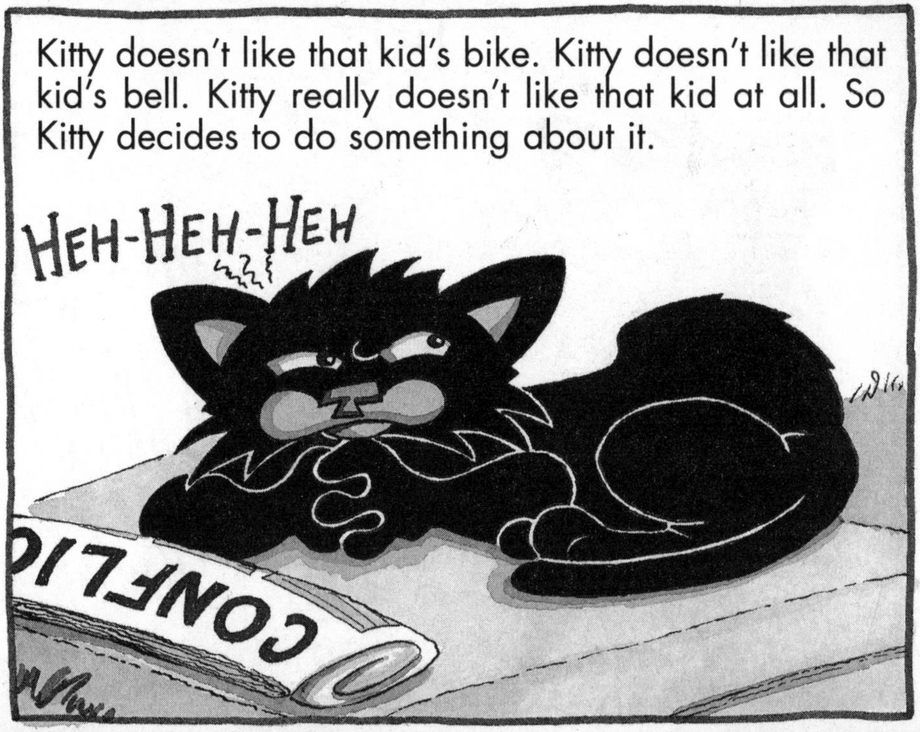
Kitty doesn't like that kid's bike. Kitty doesn't like that kid's bell. Kitty really doesn't like that kid at all. So Kitty decides to do something about it.
HEH-HEH-HEH

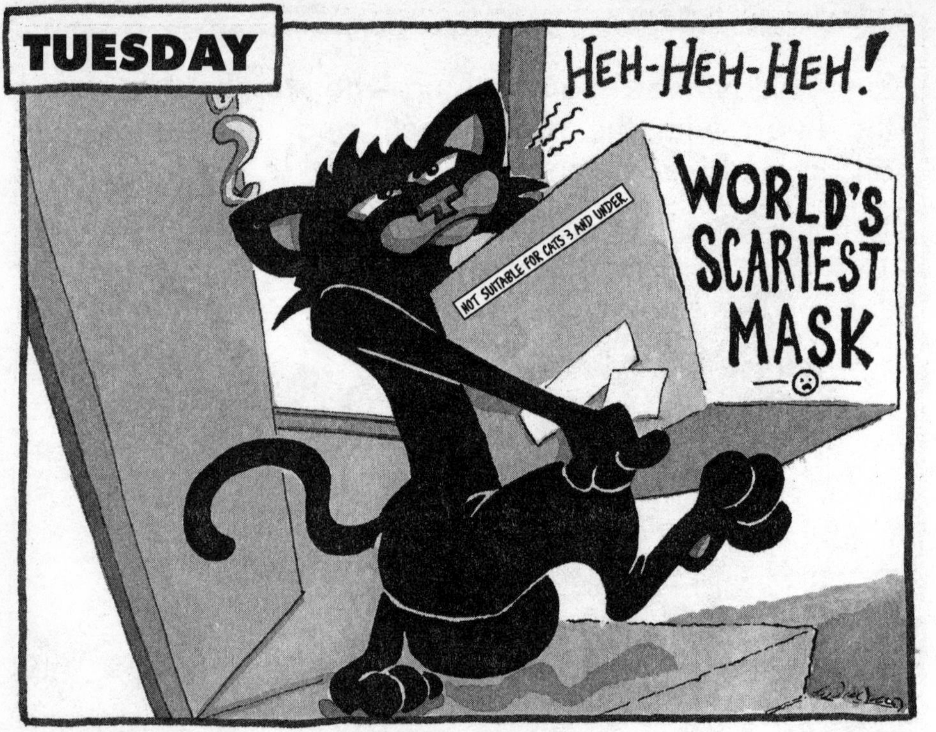
TUESDAY
HEH-HEH-HEH!
NOT SUITABLE FOR CATS 3 AND UNDER.
WORLD'S SCARIEST MASK

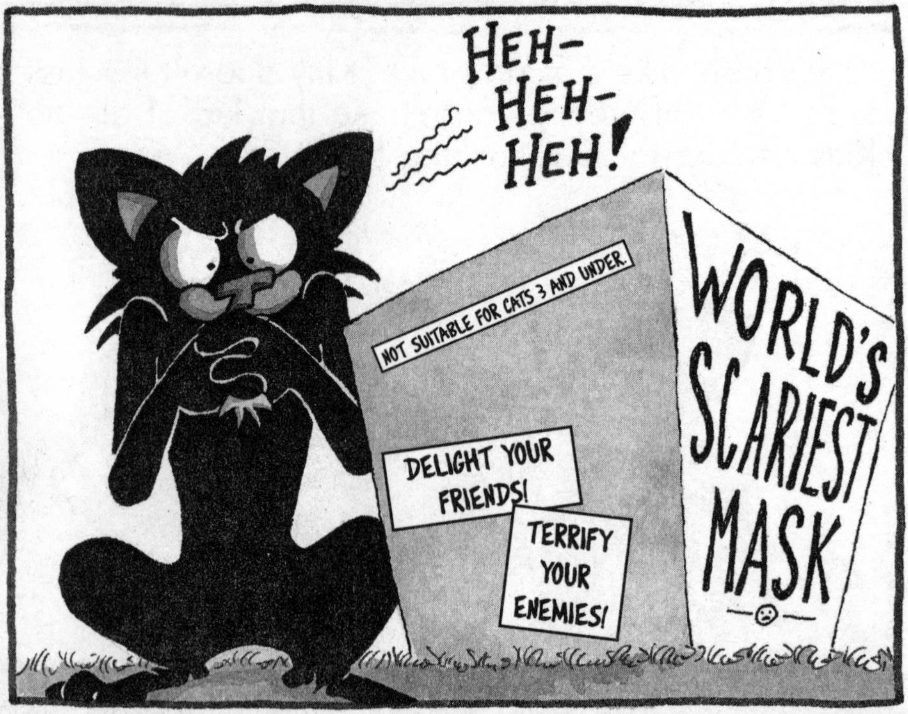
HEH-
HEH-
HEH!
NOT SUITABLE FOR CATS 3 AND UNDER.
DELIGHT YOUR FRIENDS!
TERRIFY YOUR ENEMIES!
WORLD'S SCARIEST MASK

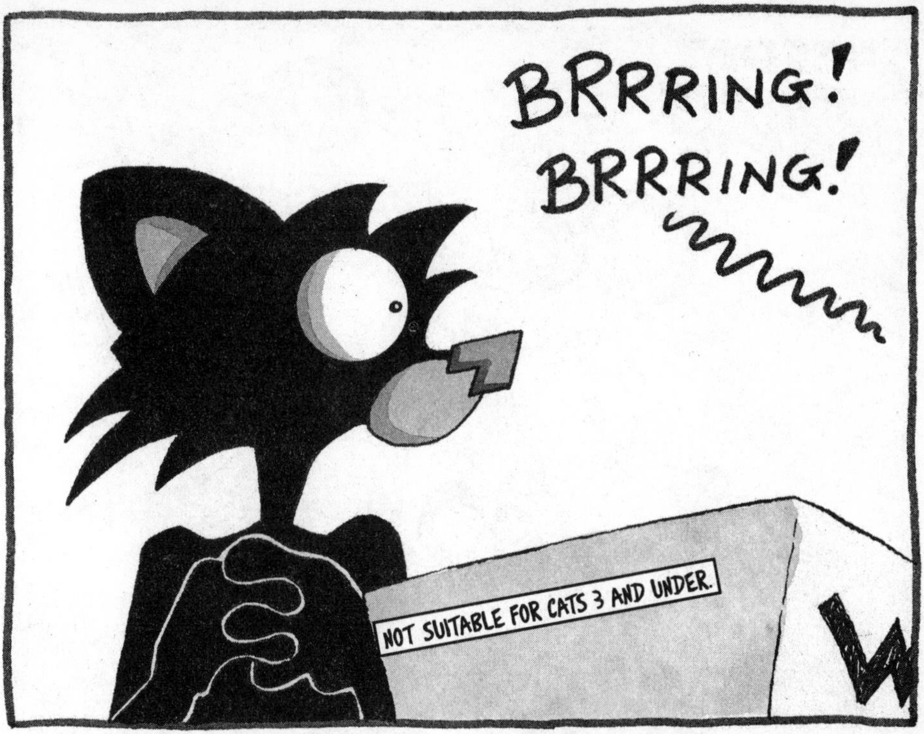
BRRRING!
BRRRING!
NOT SUITABLE FOR CATS 3 AND UNDER.

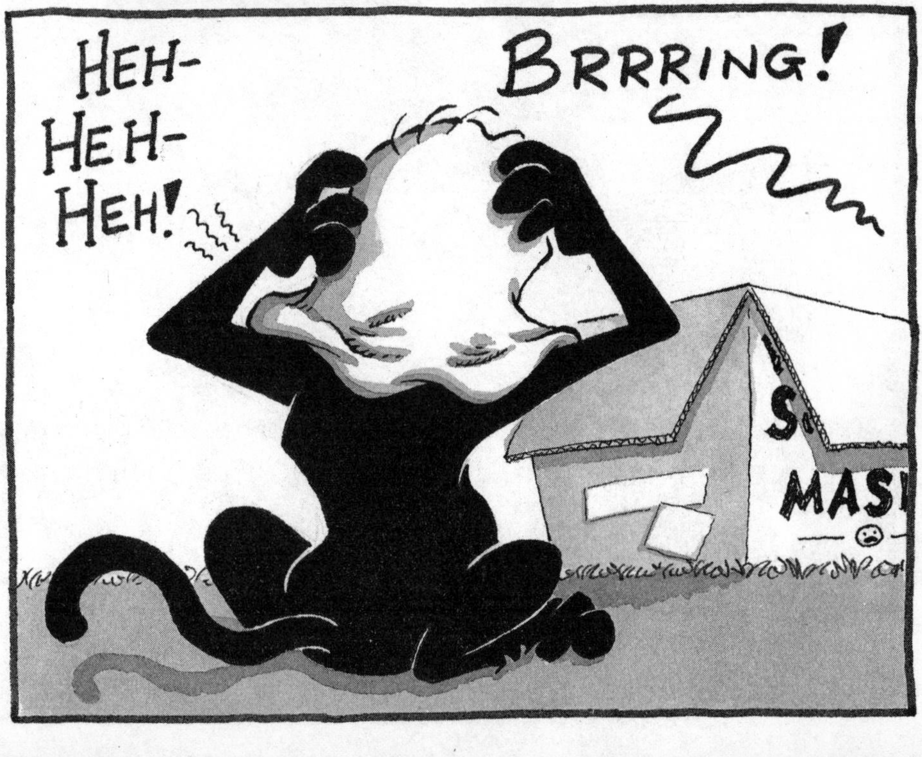
HEH-
HEH-
HEH!
BRRRING!
MAS

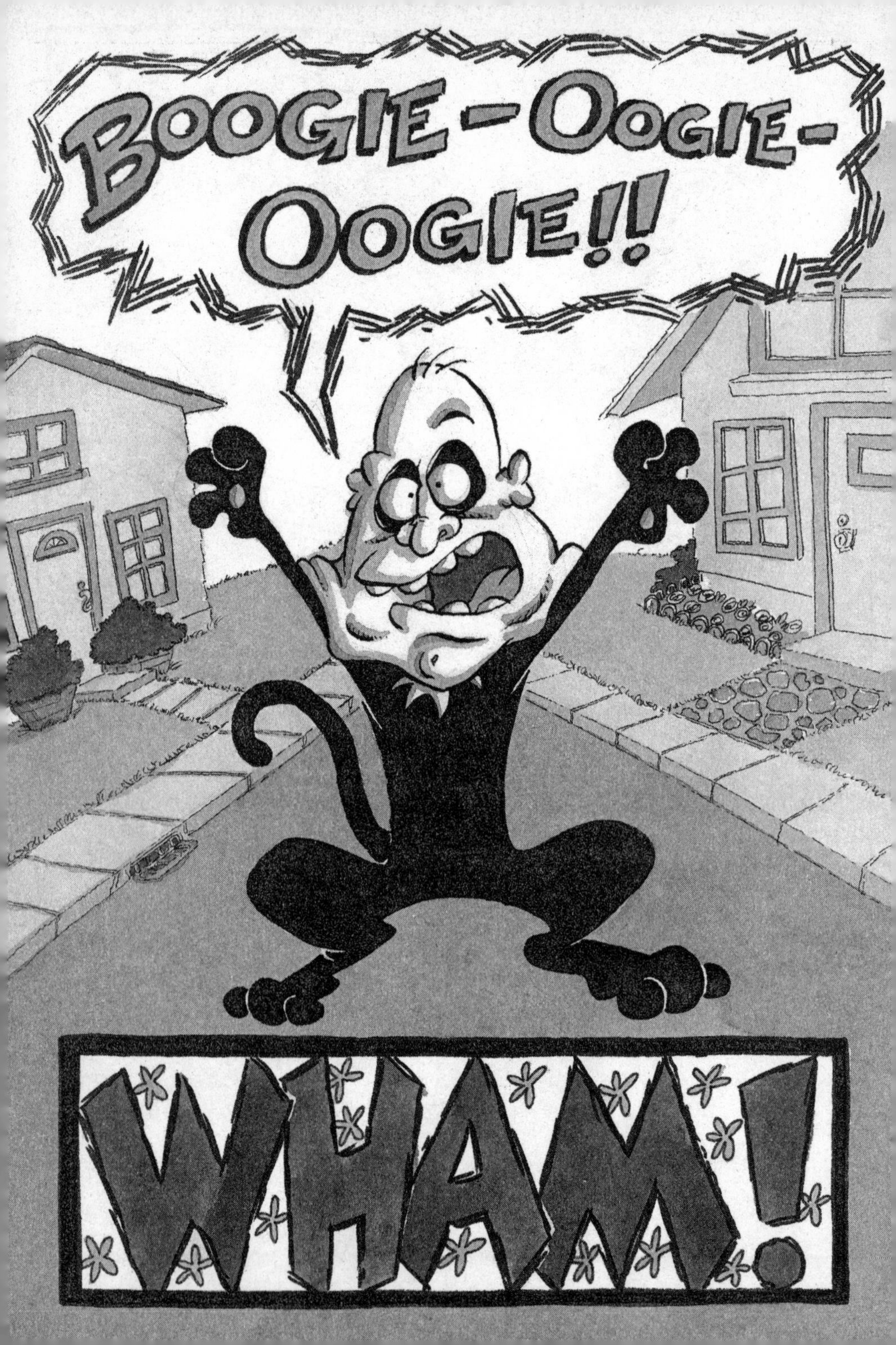
BOOGIE-OOGIE-OOGIE!!
WHAM!

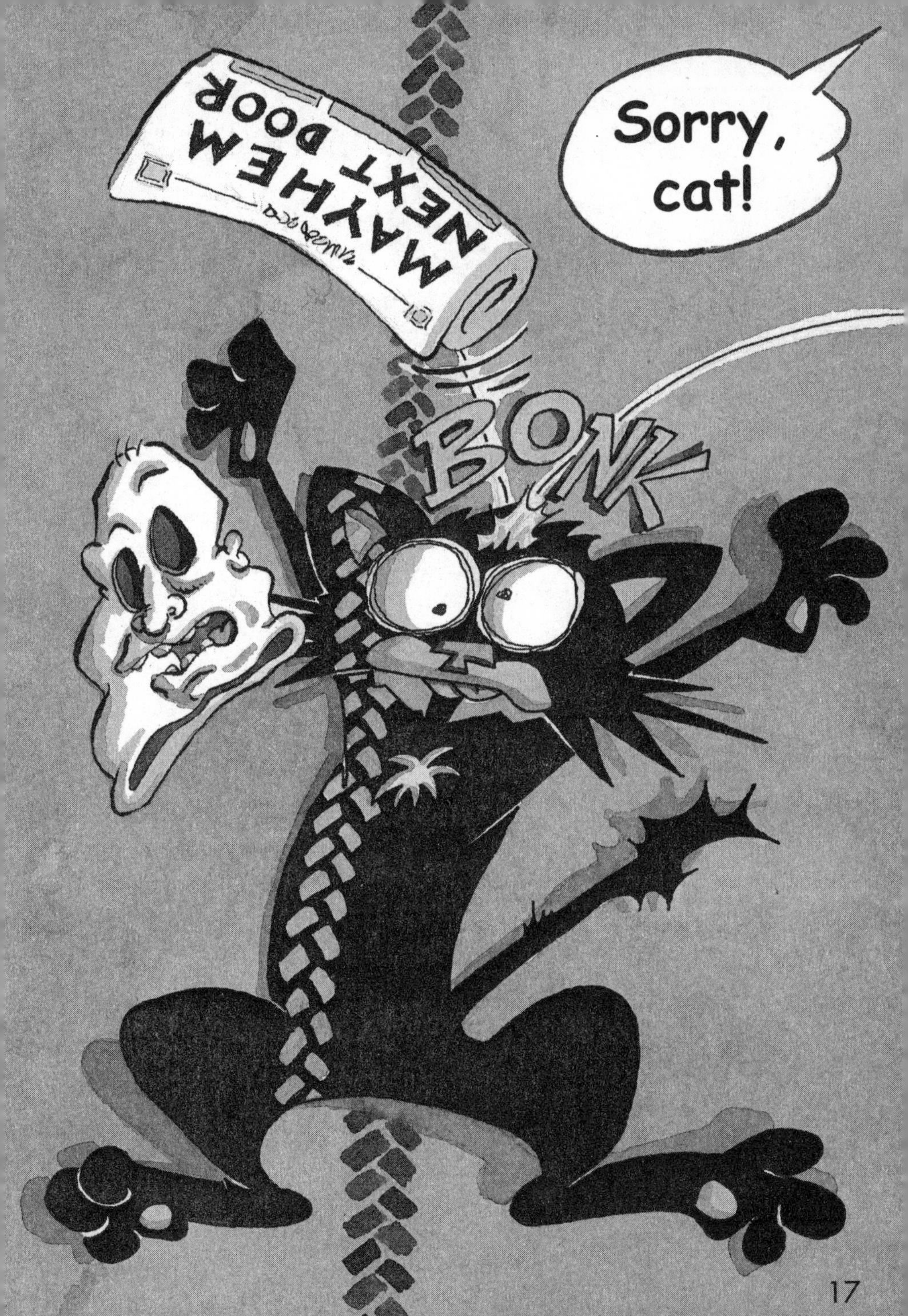
Sorry, cat!
MAYHEM NEXT DOOR
BONK

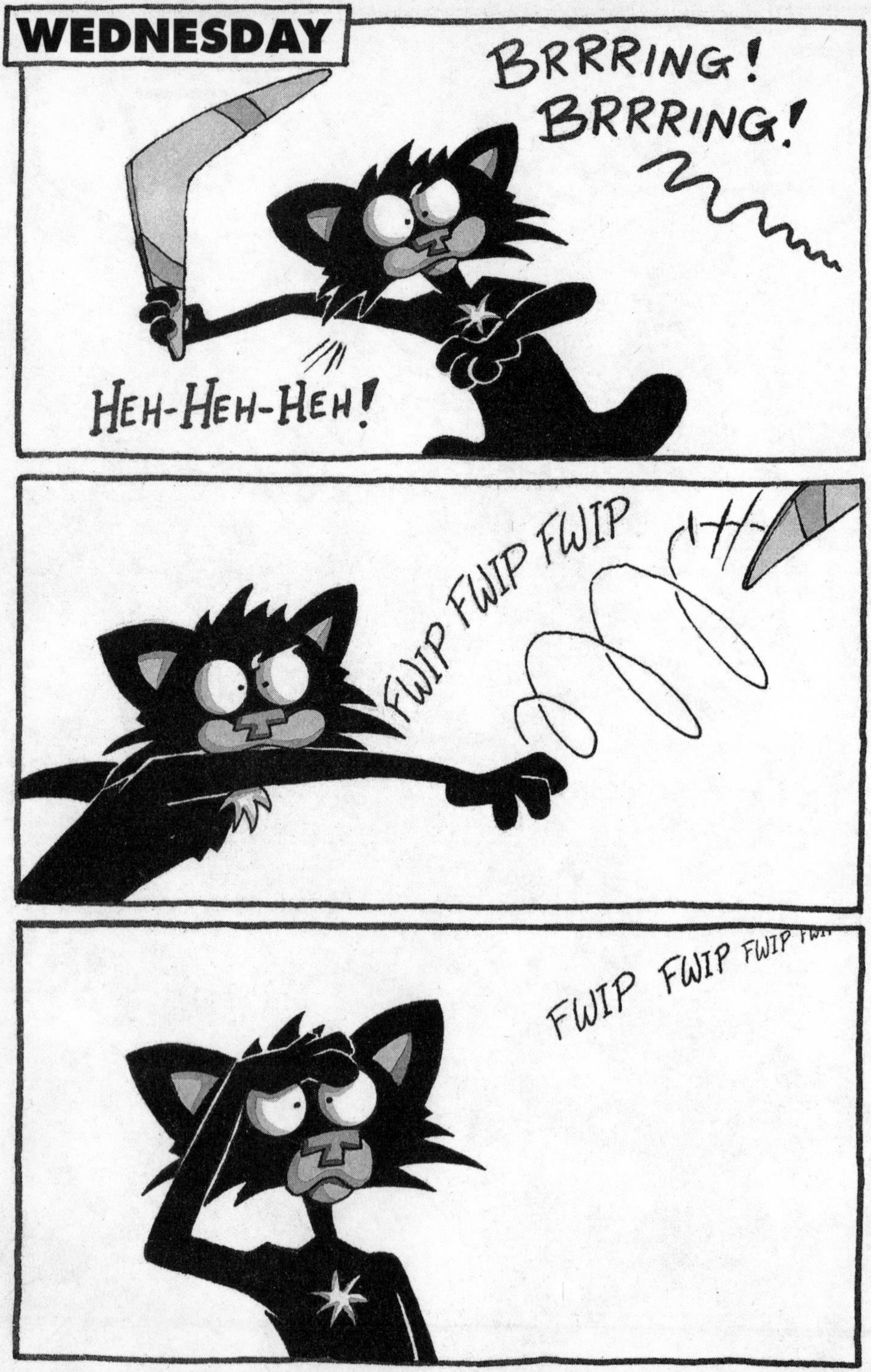
WEDNESDAY
BRRRING! BRRRING!
HEH-HEH-HEH!
FWIP FWIP FWIP
FWIP FWIP FWIP

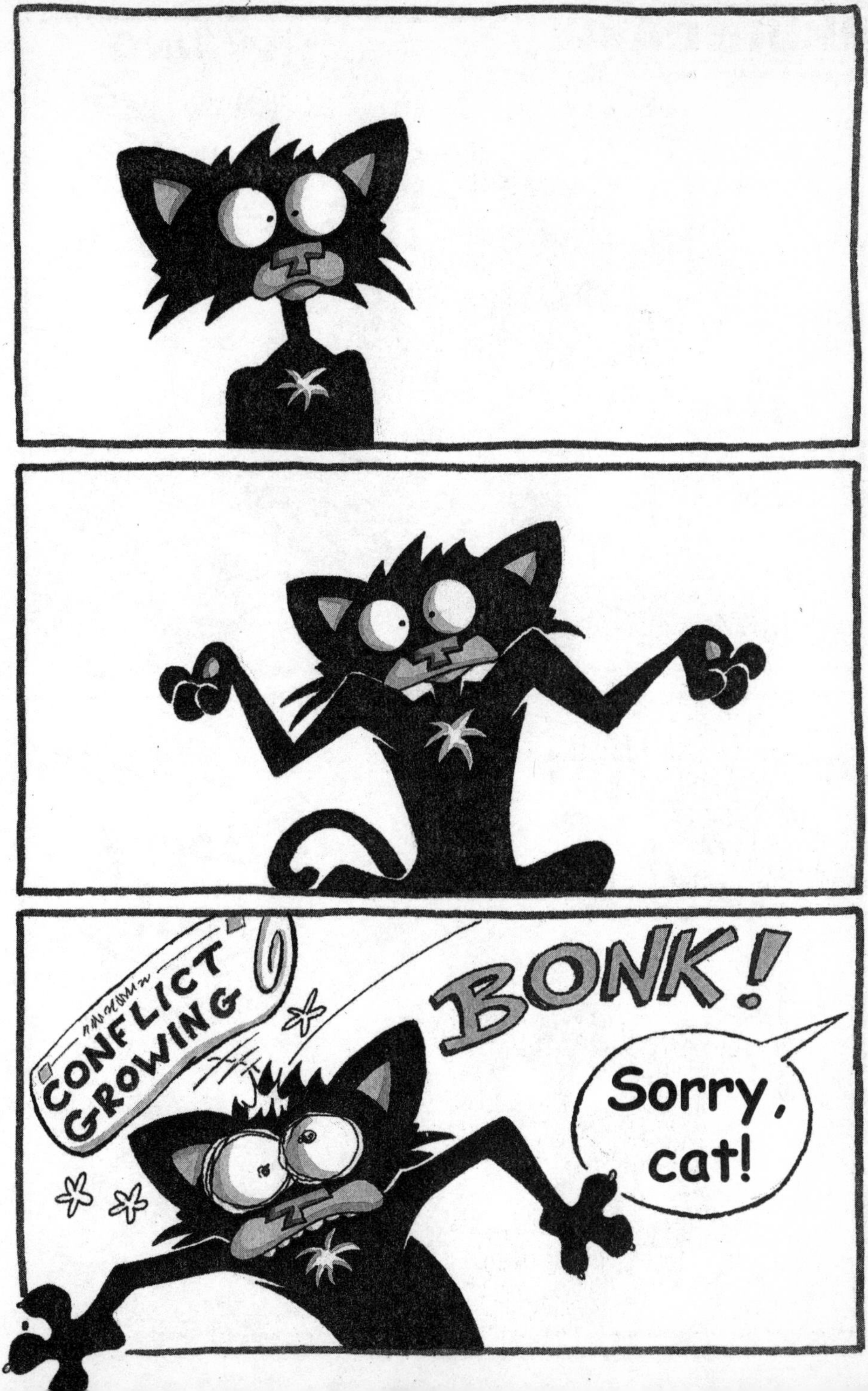

CONFLICT GROWING
BONK!
Sorry, cat!

THURSDAY
BRRRING
BRRRING
HEH-
HEH-
HEH!
GETTING
WORSE
BONK
Sorry, cat!

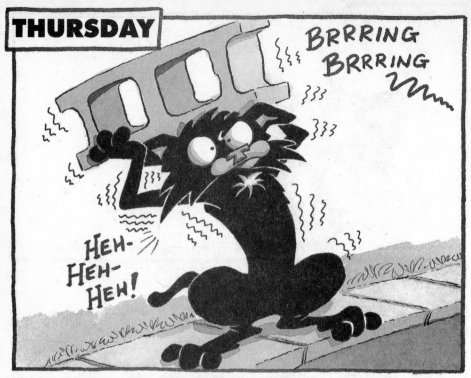

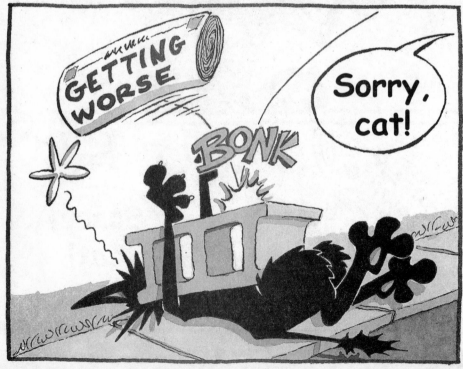

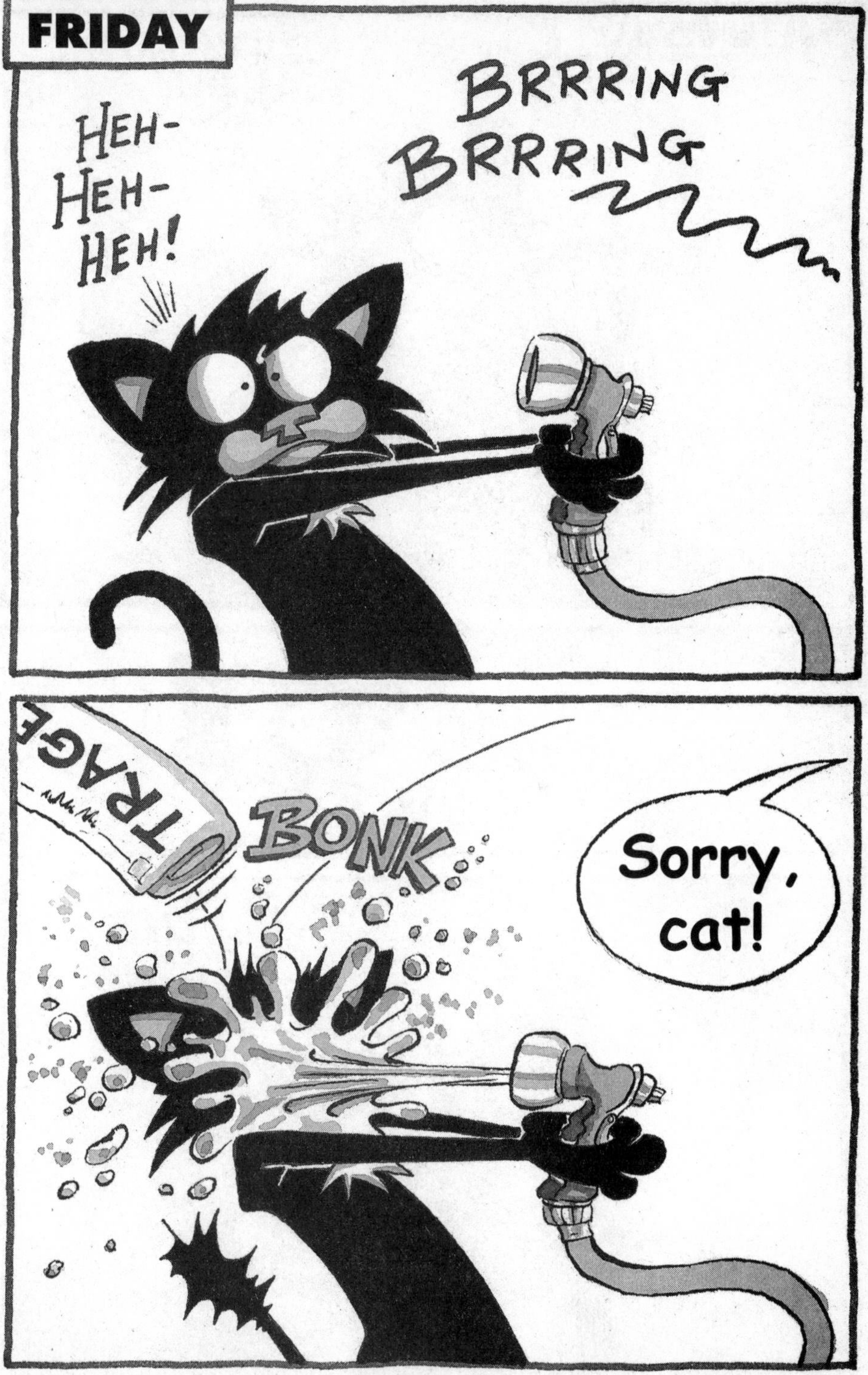
FRIDAY
HEH- HEH- HEH!
BRRRING BRRRING
BONK
Sorry, cat!

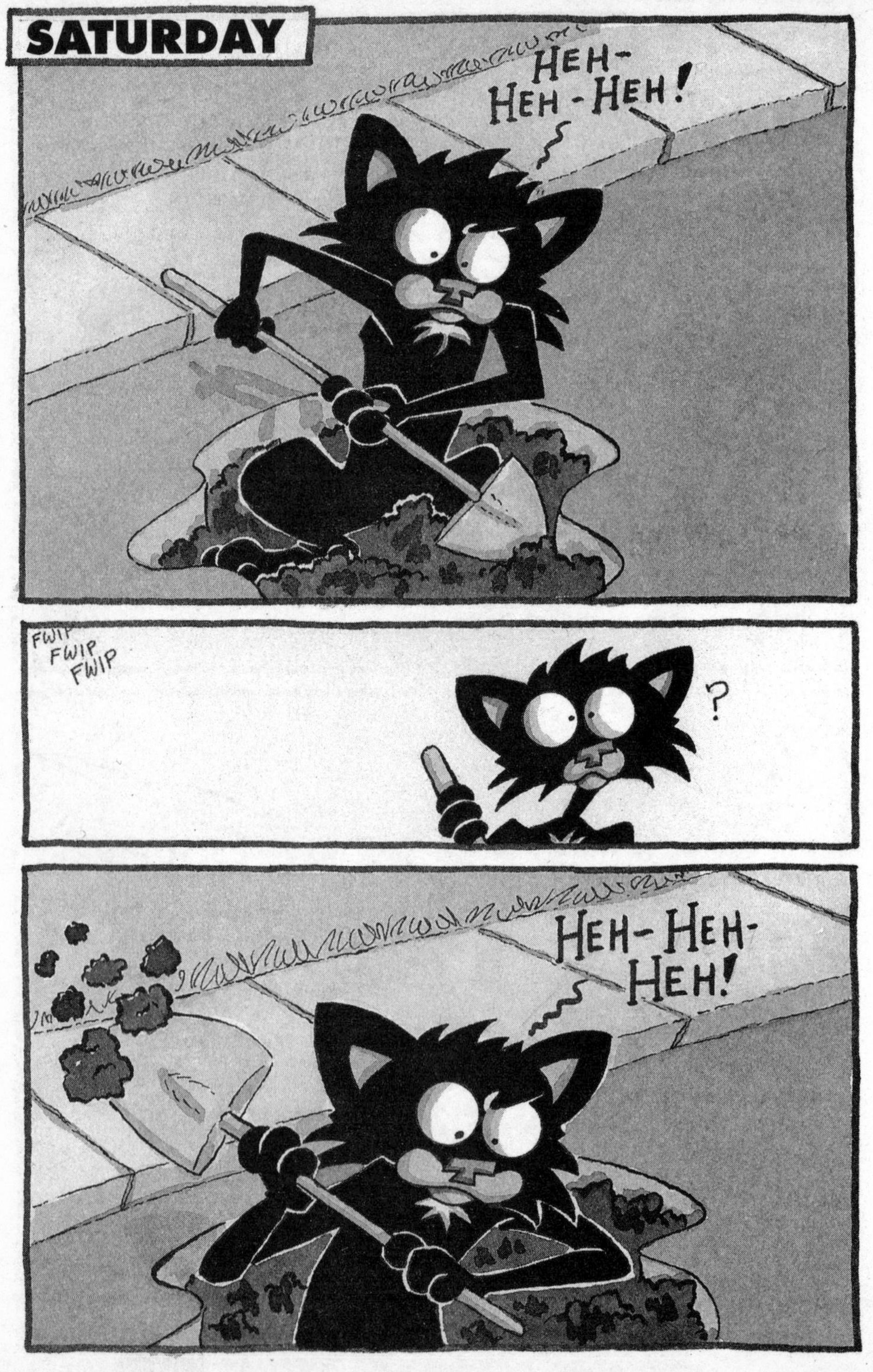
SATURDAY
HEH-
HEH-HEH!
FWIP
FWIP
FWIP
?
HEH-HEH-
HEH!

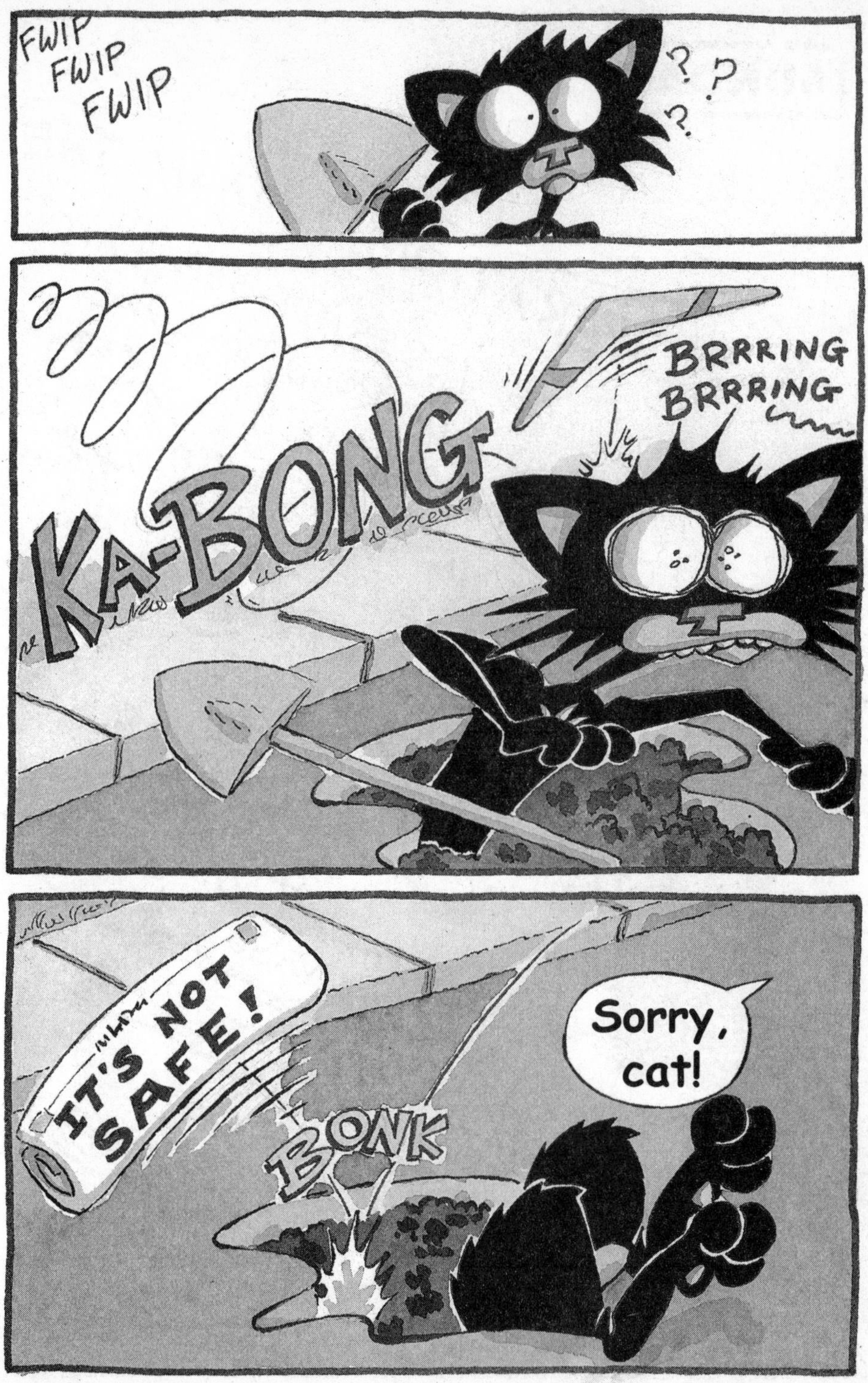
FWIP
FWIP
FWIP
? ? ?
KA-BONG
BRRRING
BRRRING
IT'S NOT SAFE!
BONK
Sorry, cat!

SUNDAY

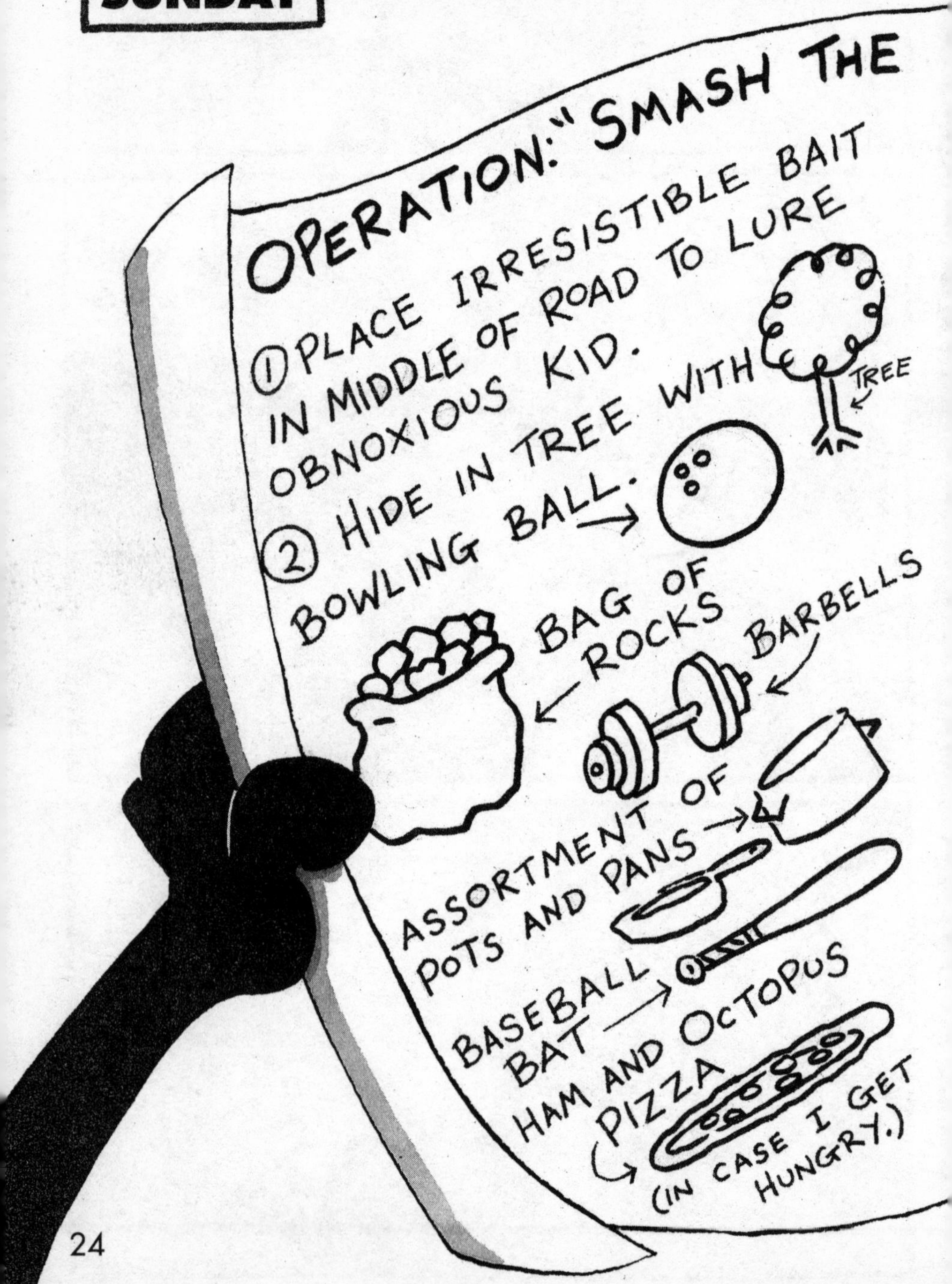

OPERATION: "SMASH THE
① PLACE IRRESISTIBLE BAIT
IN MIDDLE OF ROAD TO LURE
OBNOXIOUS KID.
② HIDE IN TREE WITH
TREE
BOWLING BALL.
BAG OF
ROCKS
BARBELLS
ASSORTMENT OF
POTS AND PANS
BASEBALL
BAT
HAM AND OCTOPUS
PIZZA
(IN CASE I GET
HUNGRY.)

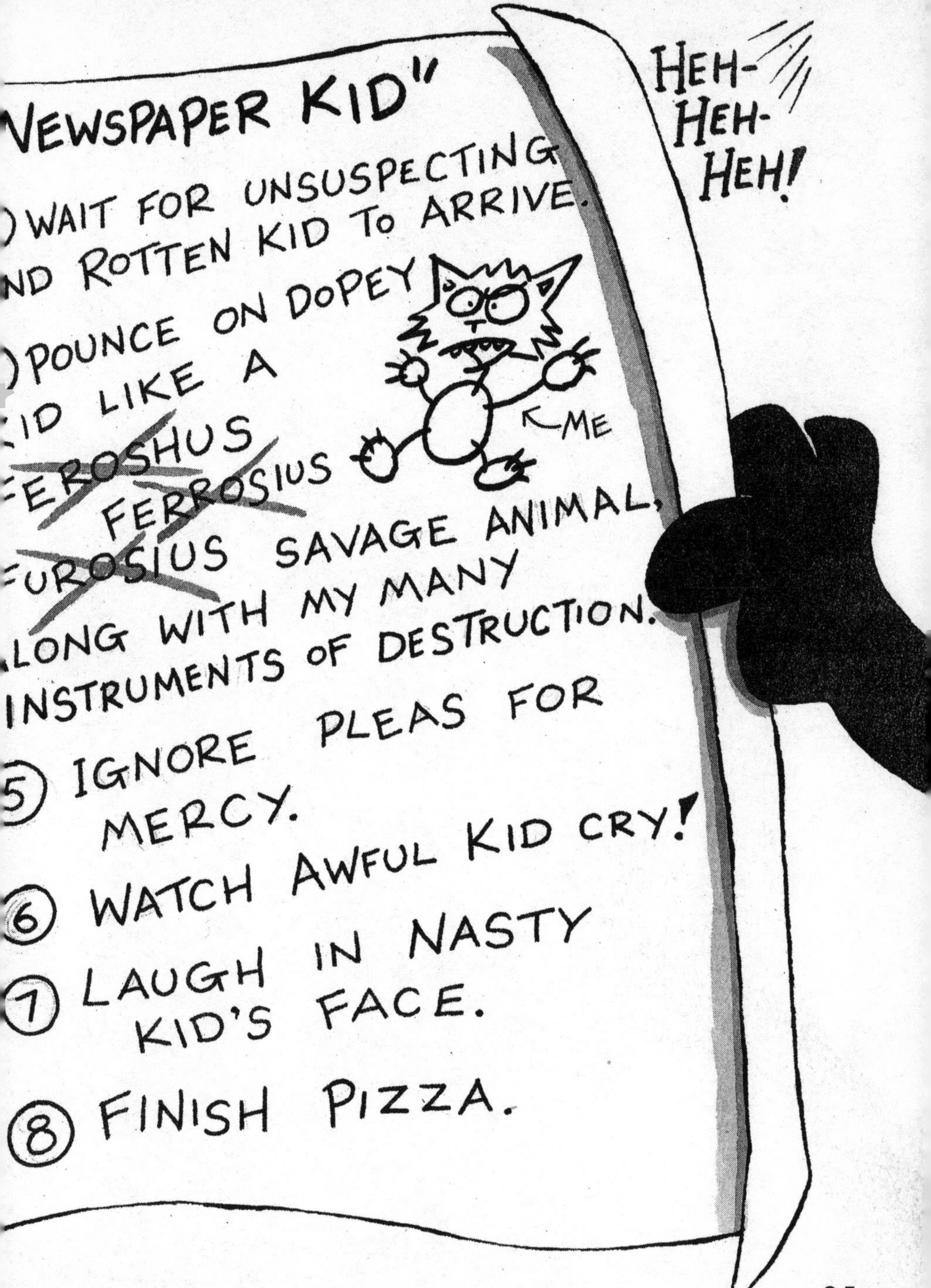

NEWSPAPER KID"
) WAIT FOR UNSUSPECTING
ND ROTTEN KID TO ARRIVE.
) POUNCE ON DOPEY
ID LIKE A
EROSHUS
FERROSIUS
UROSIUS SAVAGE ANIMAL,
LONG WITH MY MANY
INSTRUMENTS OF DESTRUCTION.
5) IGNORE PLEAS FOR
MERCY.
6) WATCH AWFUL KID CRY!
7) LAUGH IN NASTY
KID'S FACE.
8) FINISH PIZZA.
ME
HEH-
HEH-
HEH!

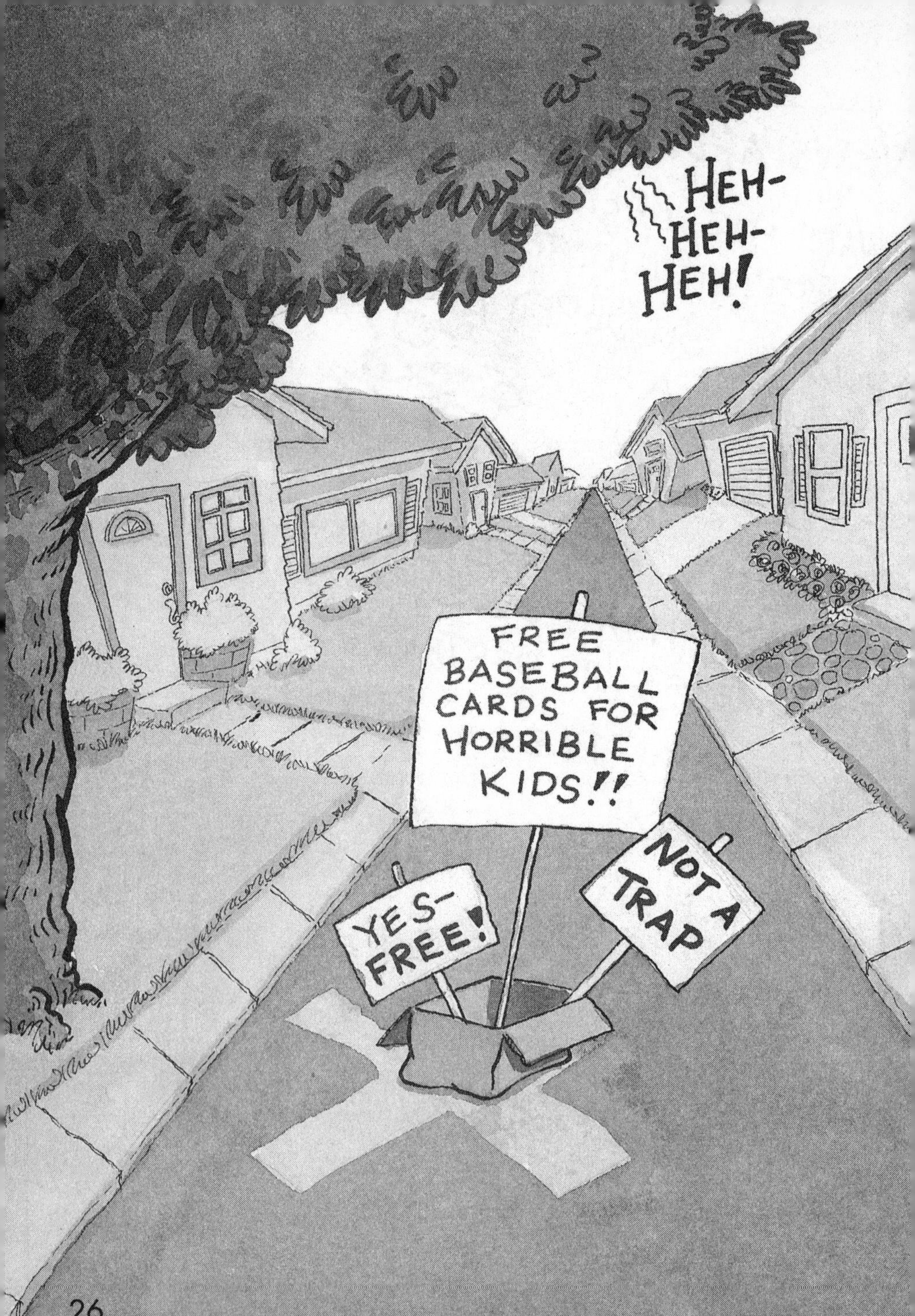
HEH-
HEH-
HEH!
FREE BASEBALL CARDS FOR HORRIBLE KIDS!!
YES-FREE!
NOT A TRAP

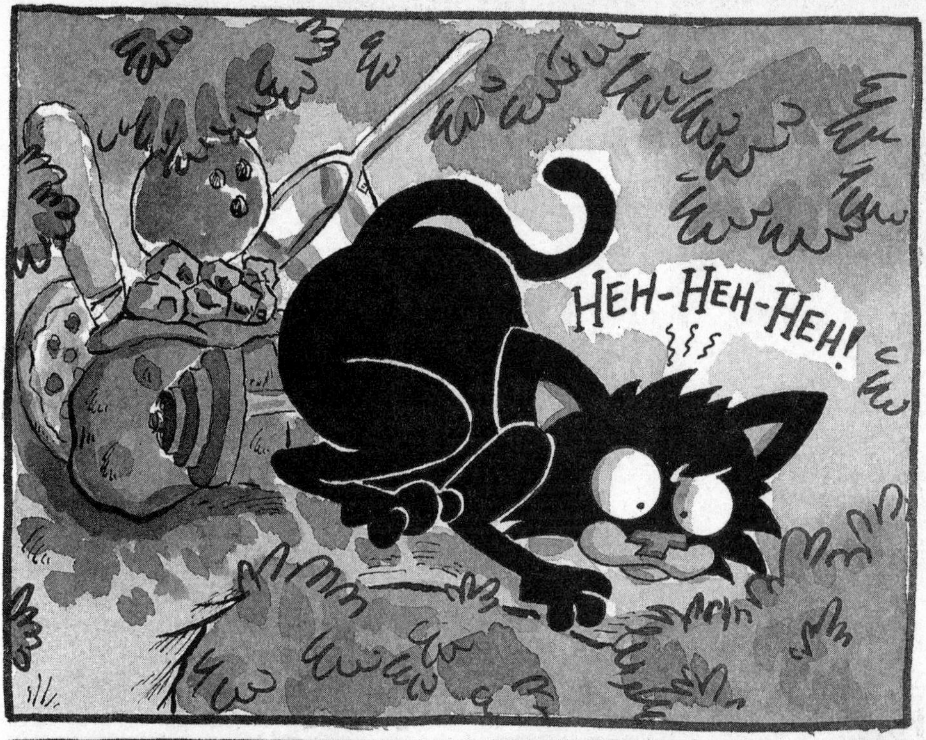
HEH-HEH-HEH!

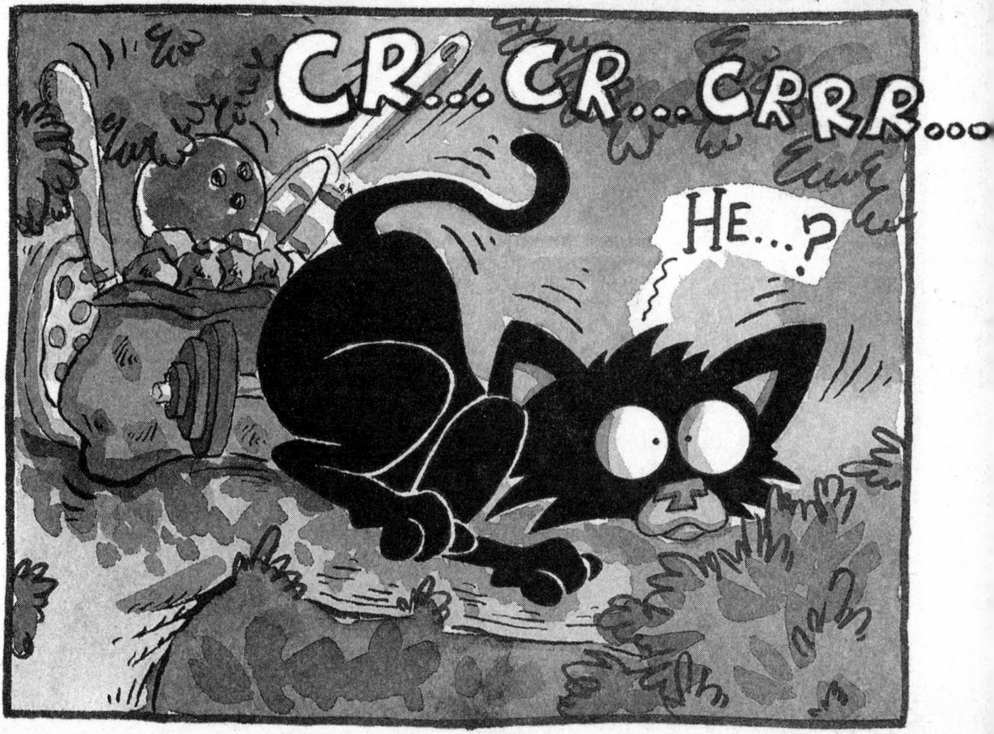
CR...CR...CRRR...
HE...?

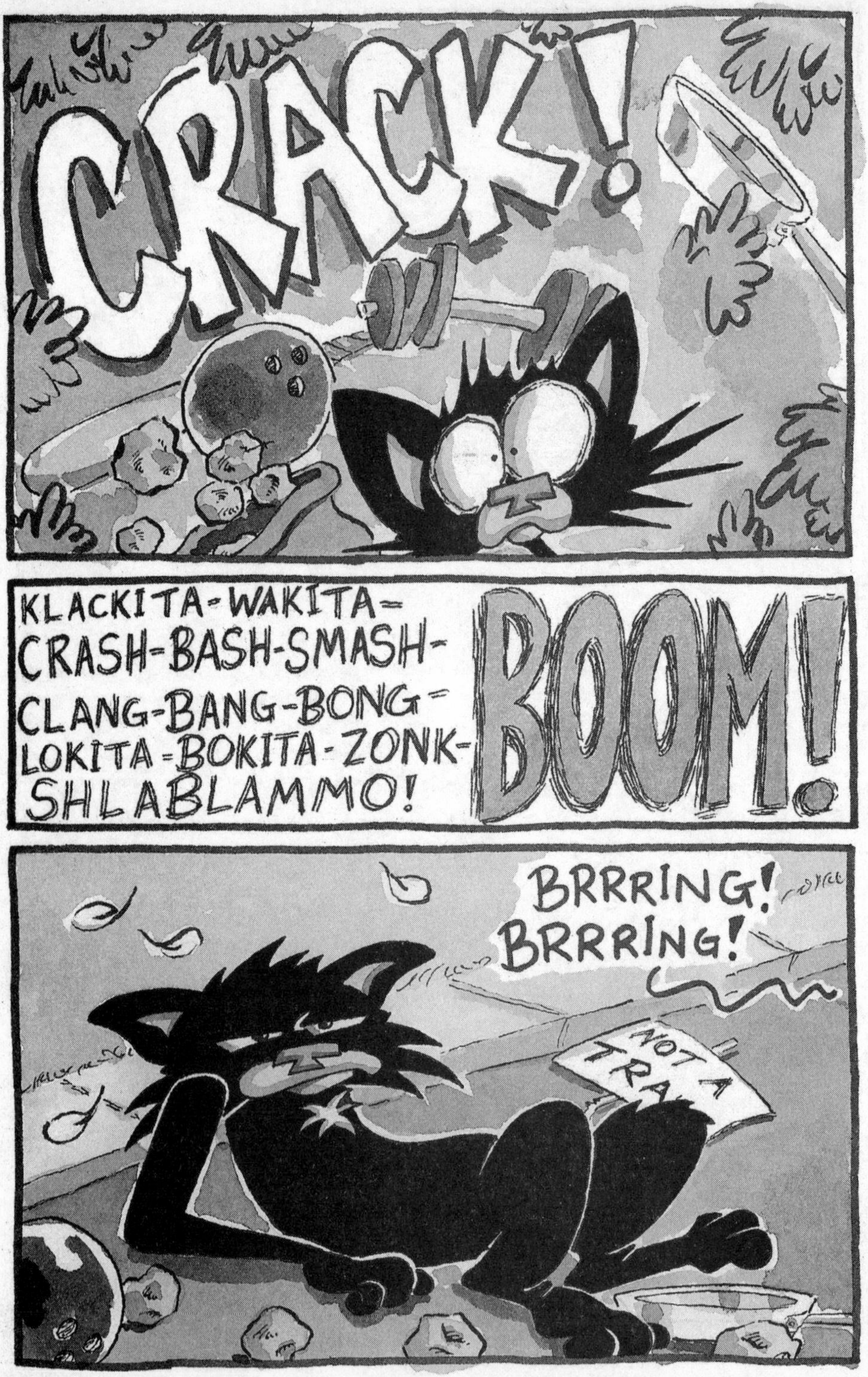
CRACK!
KLACKITA-WAKITA-
CRASH-BASH-SMASH-
CLANG-BANG-BONG-
LOKITA-BOKITA-ZONK-
SHLABLAMMO!
BOOM!
BRRRING!
BRRRING!
NOT A
TRA

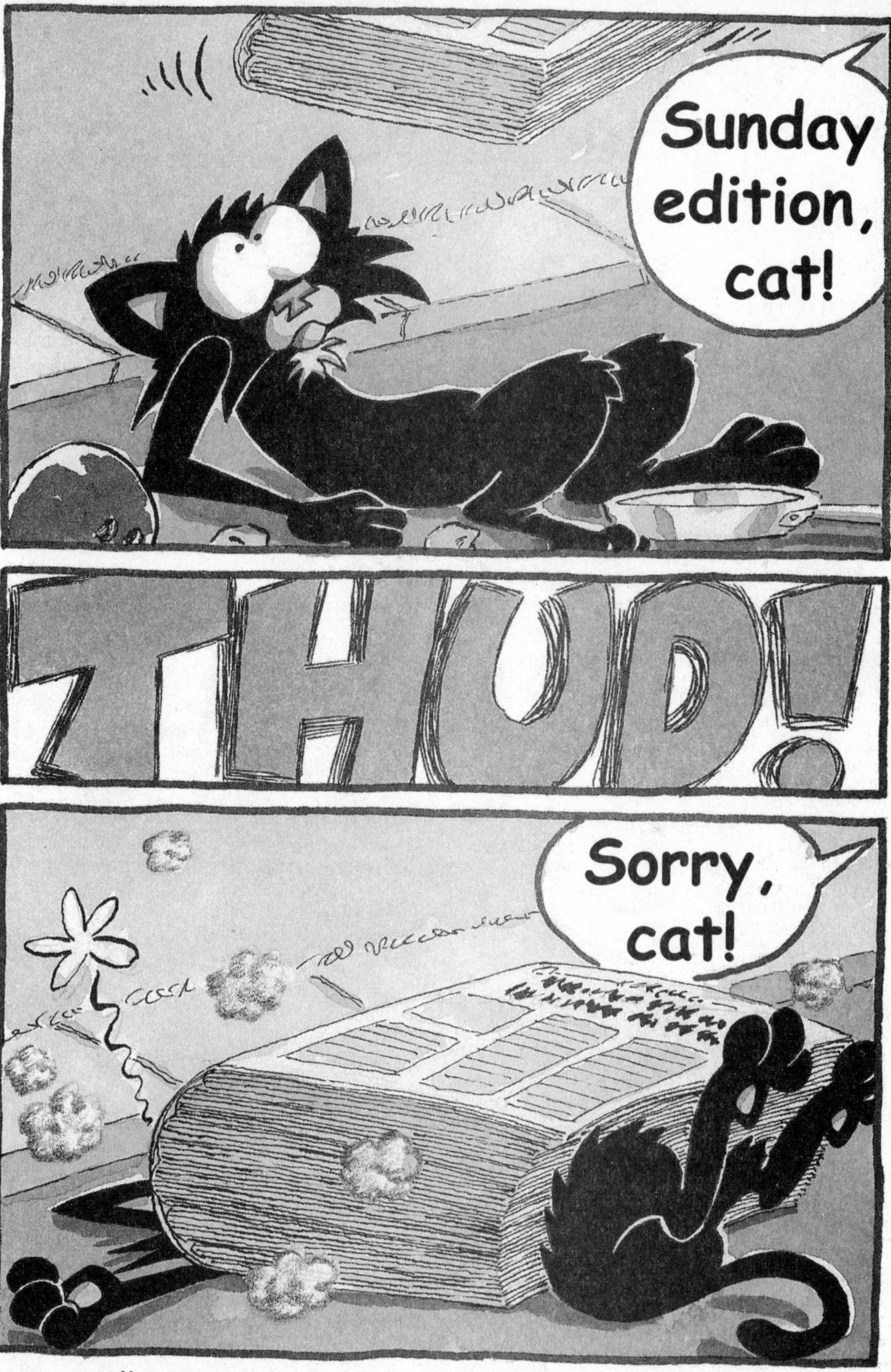
Sunday edition, cat!
THUD!
Sorry, cat!
Kitty really, REALLY doesn't like that newspaper kid.

•CHAPTER TWO•

THE BIG PLAN

Thanks for bringing in the newspaper, Kitty. Is there anything more peaceful than spending a quiet Sunday morning reading the news? I don't think so.

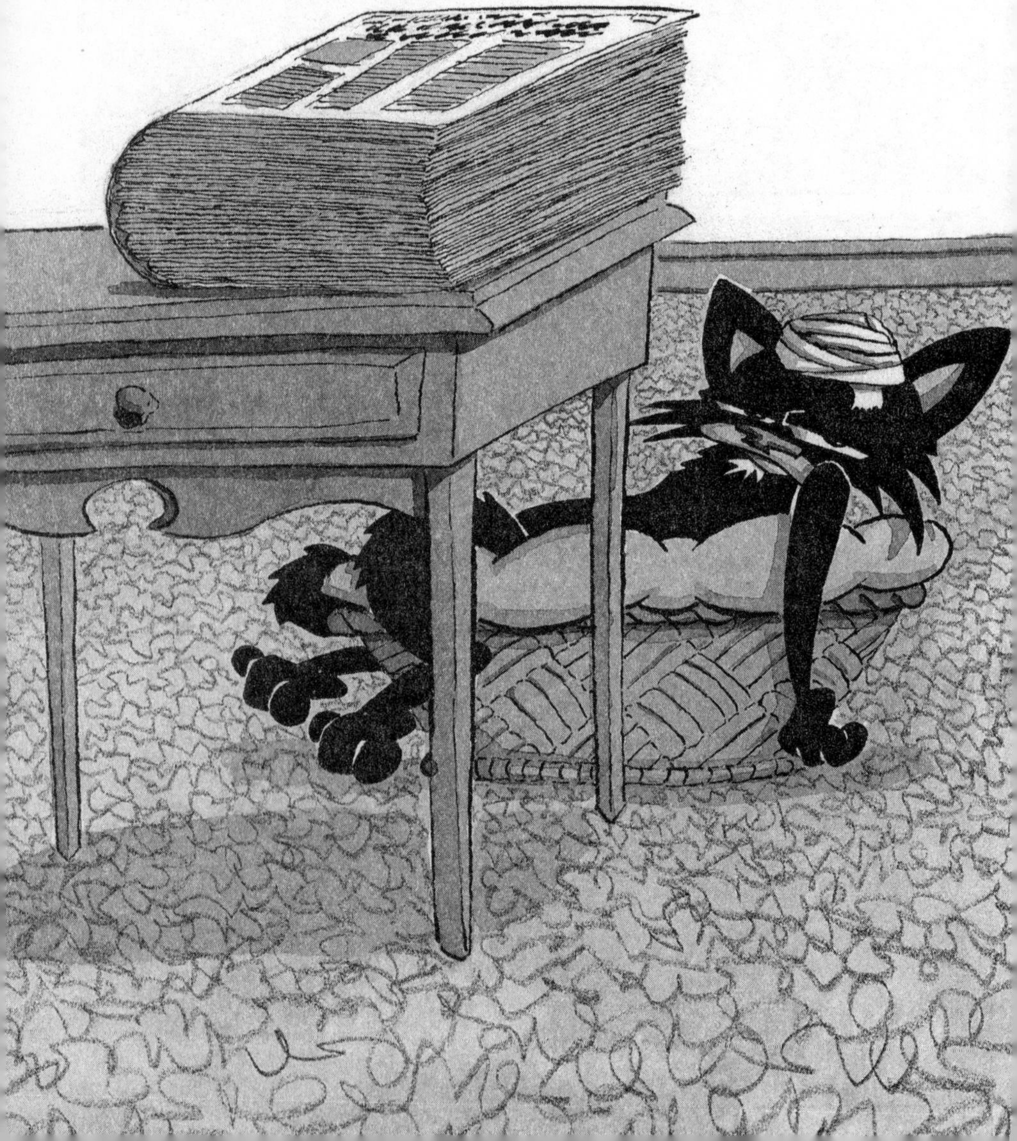

Now let's see . . . news, news, news. Where is the news? It's got to be in here somewhere. Hmmm . . . Ah-ha! Here it is!

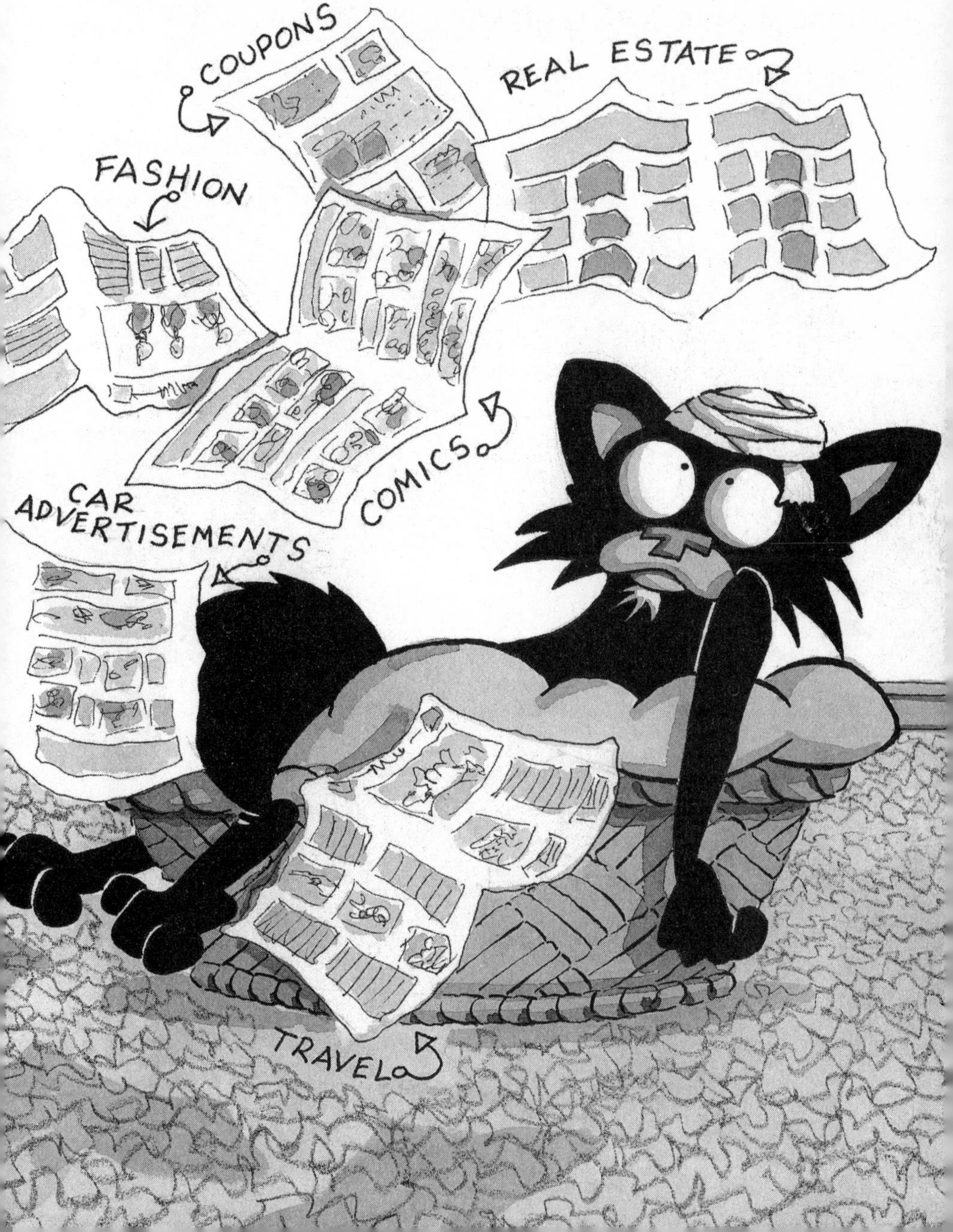
COUPONS
REAL ESTATE
FASHION
COMICS
CAR ADVERTISEMENTS
TRAVEL

Oh, dear! This is terrible news!

According to the paper, the conflict in the neighborhood next to ours is growing worse and worse!

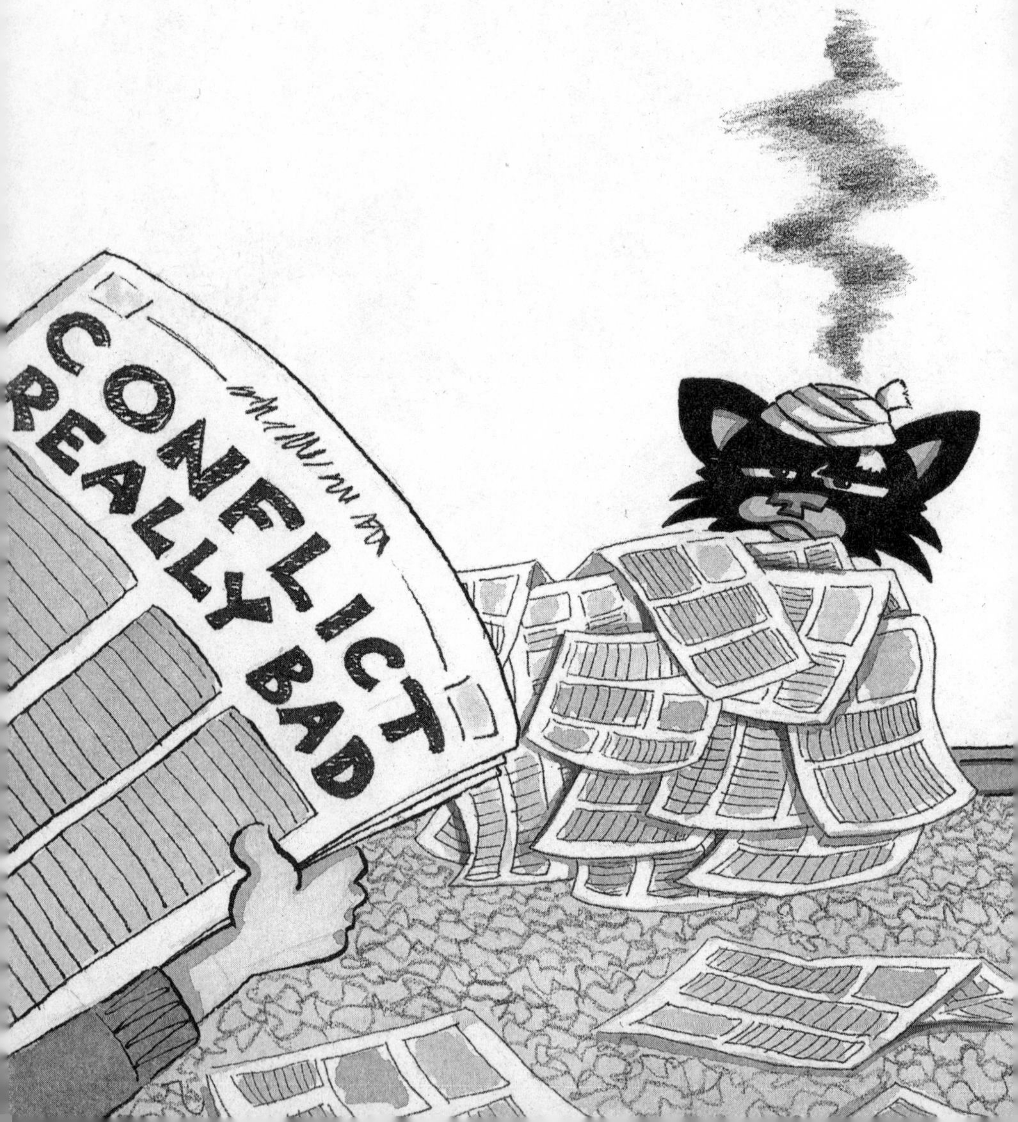
CONFLICT
REALLY BAD

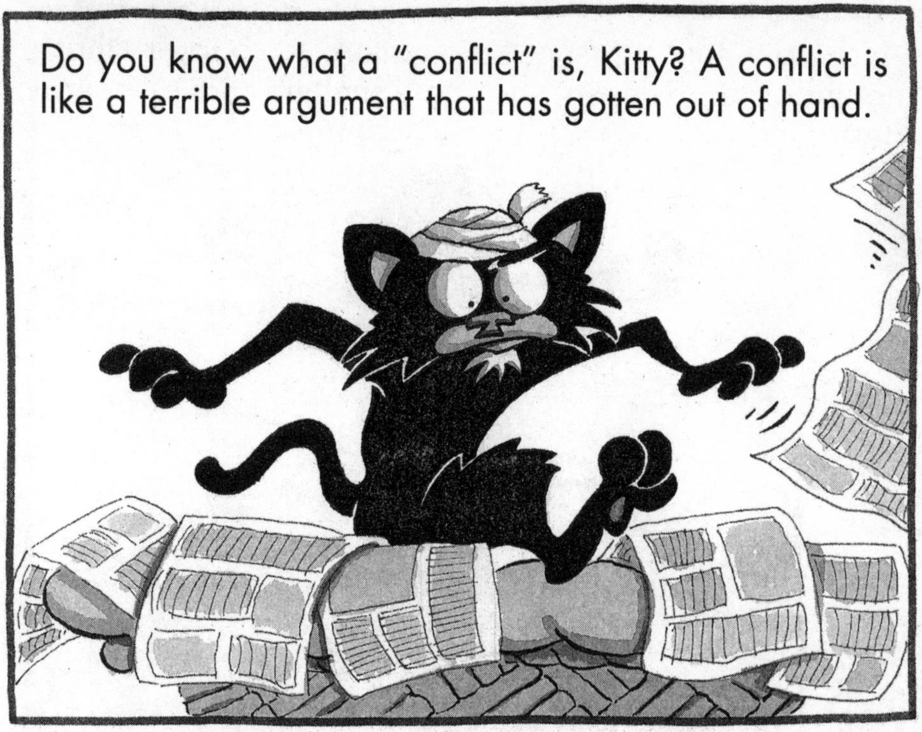
Do you know what a "conflict" is, Kitty? A conflict is like a terrible argument that has gotten out of hand.

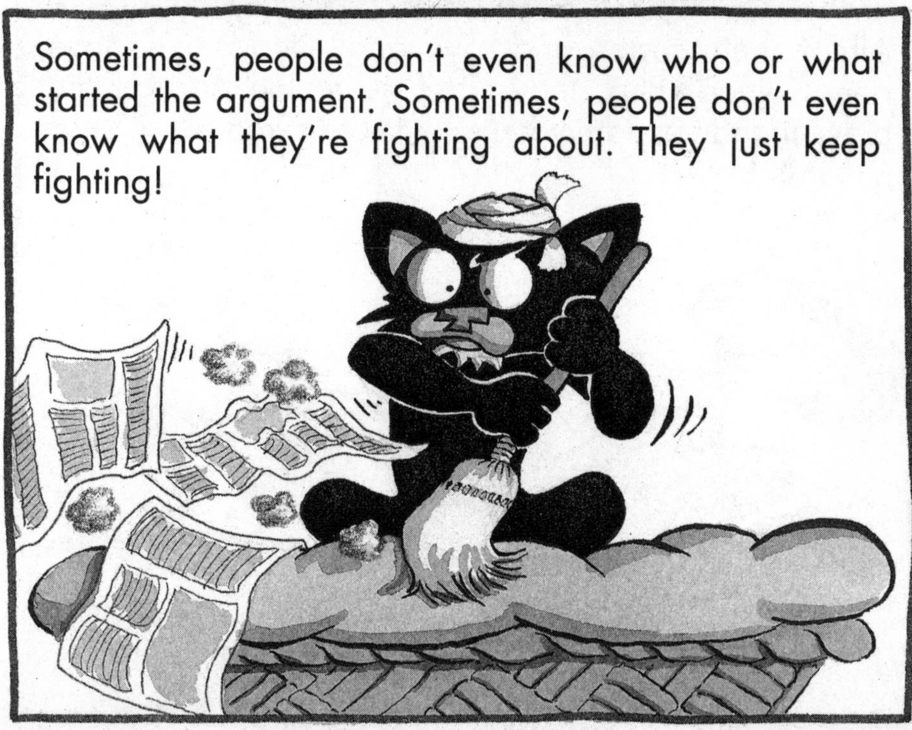
Sometimes, people don't even know who or what started the argument. Sometimes, people don't even know what they're fighting about. They just keep fighting!

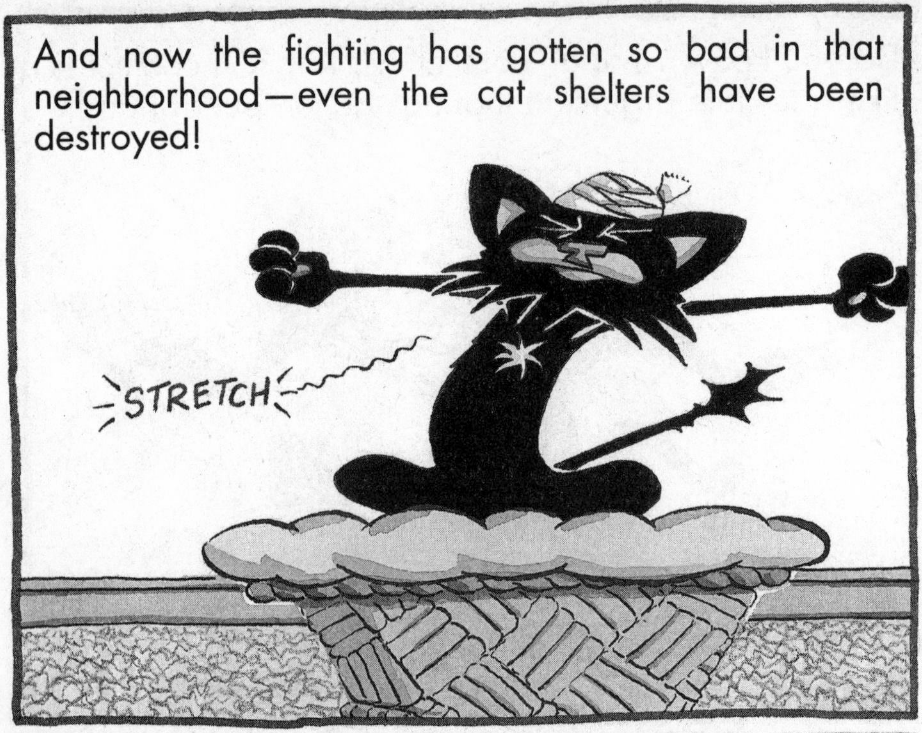
And now the fighting has gotten so bad in that neighborhood—even the cat shelters have been destroyed!
STRETCH

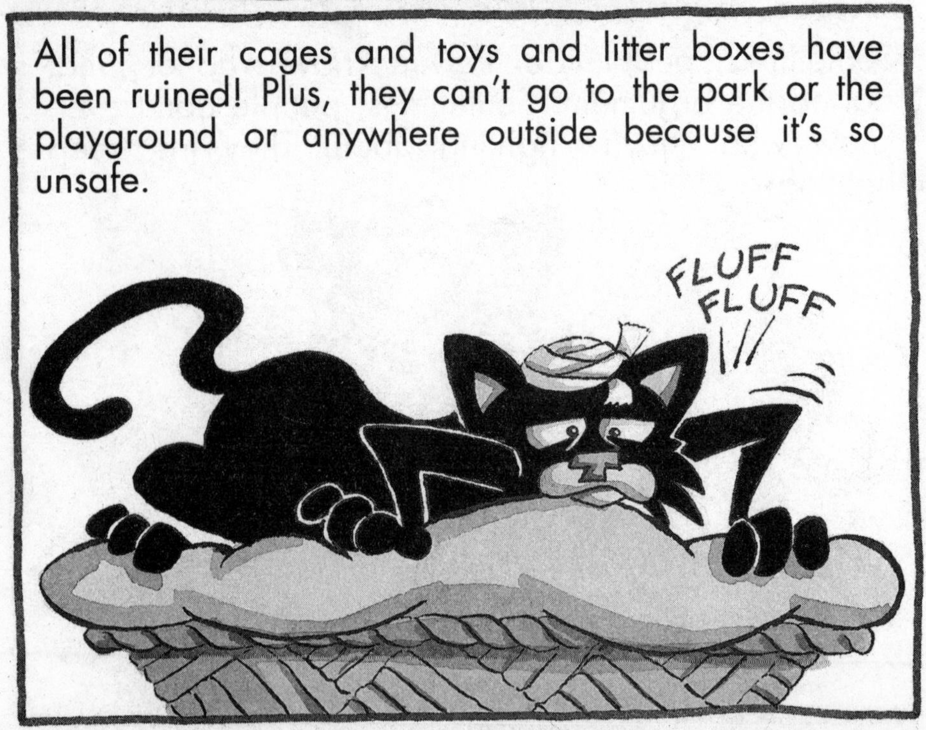
All of their cages and toys and litter boxes have been ruined! Plus, they can't go to the park or the playground or anywhere outside because it's so unsafe.
FLUFF
FLUFF

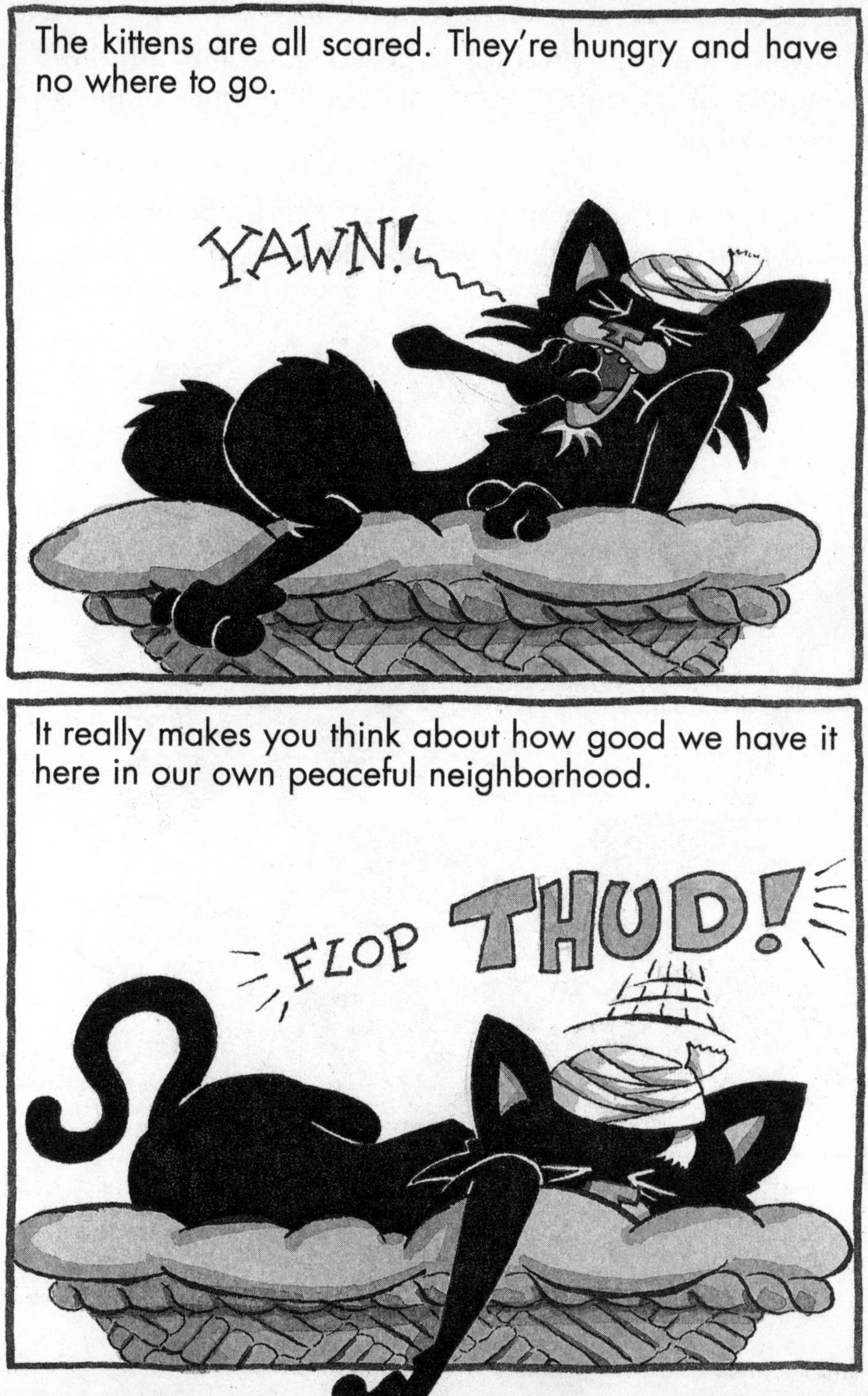
The kittens are all scared. They're hungry and have no where to go.
YAWN!
It really makes you think about how good we have it here in our own peaceful neighborhood.
FLOP
THUD!

Well, I think it's time for us to so do something. We might not be able to end this conflict, but I think we can still help.

There are oodles and oodles of KITTENS who have lost their homes. I think we should bring some of them HERE.

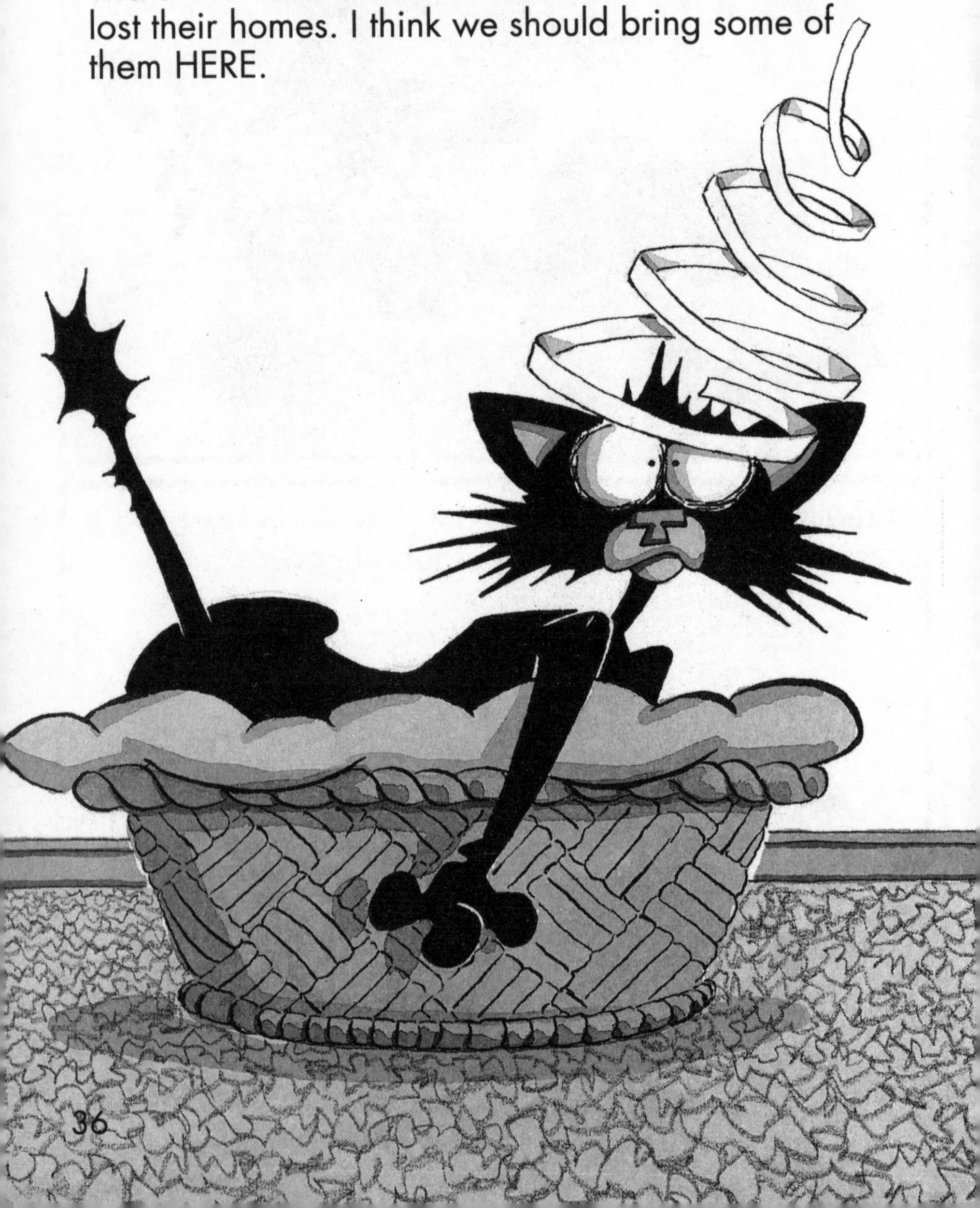

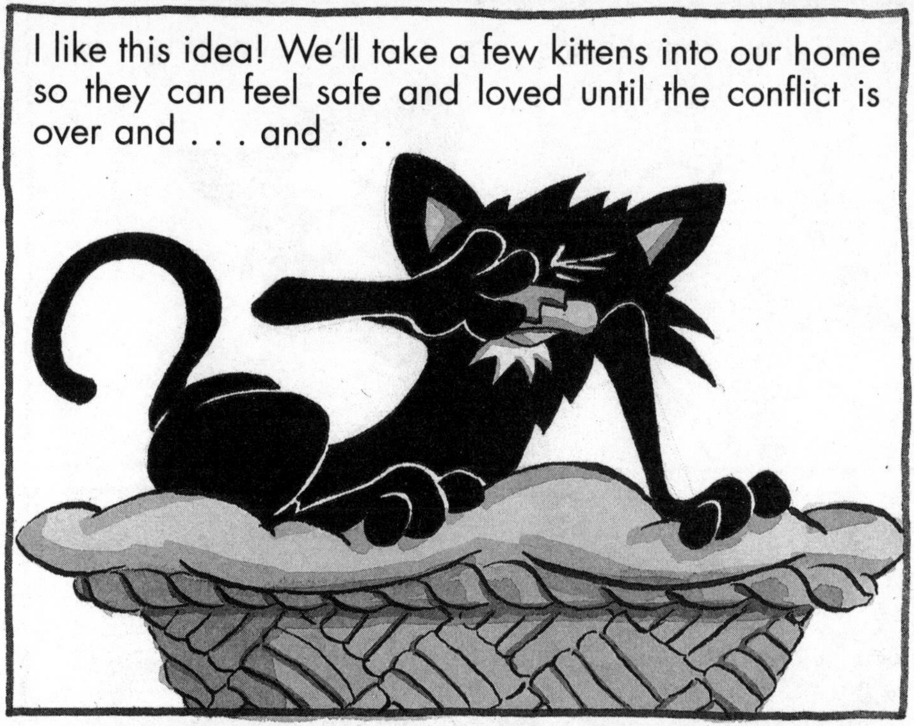
I like this idea! We'll take a few kittens into our home so they can feel safe and loved until the conflict is over and . . . and . . .

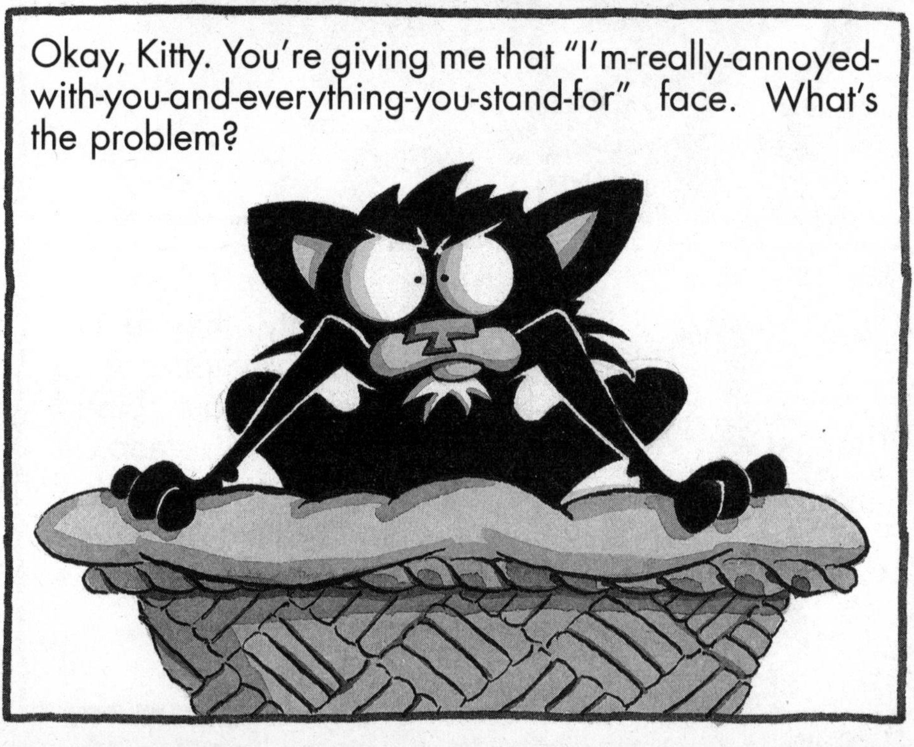
Okay, Kitty. You're giving me that "I'm-really-annoyed-with-you-and-everything-you-stand-for" face. What's the problem?

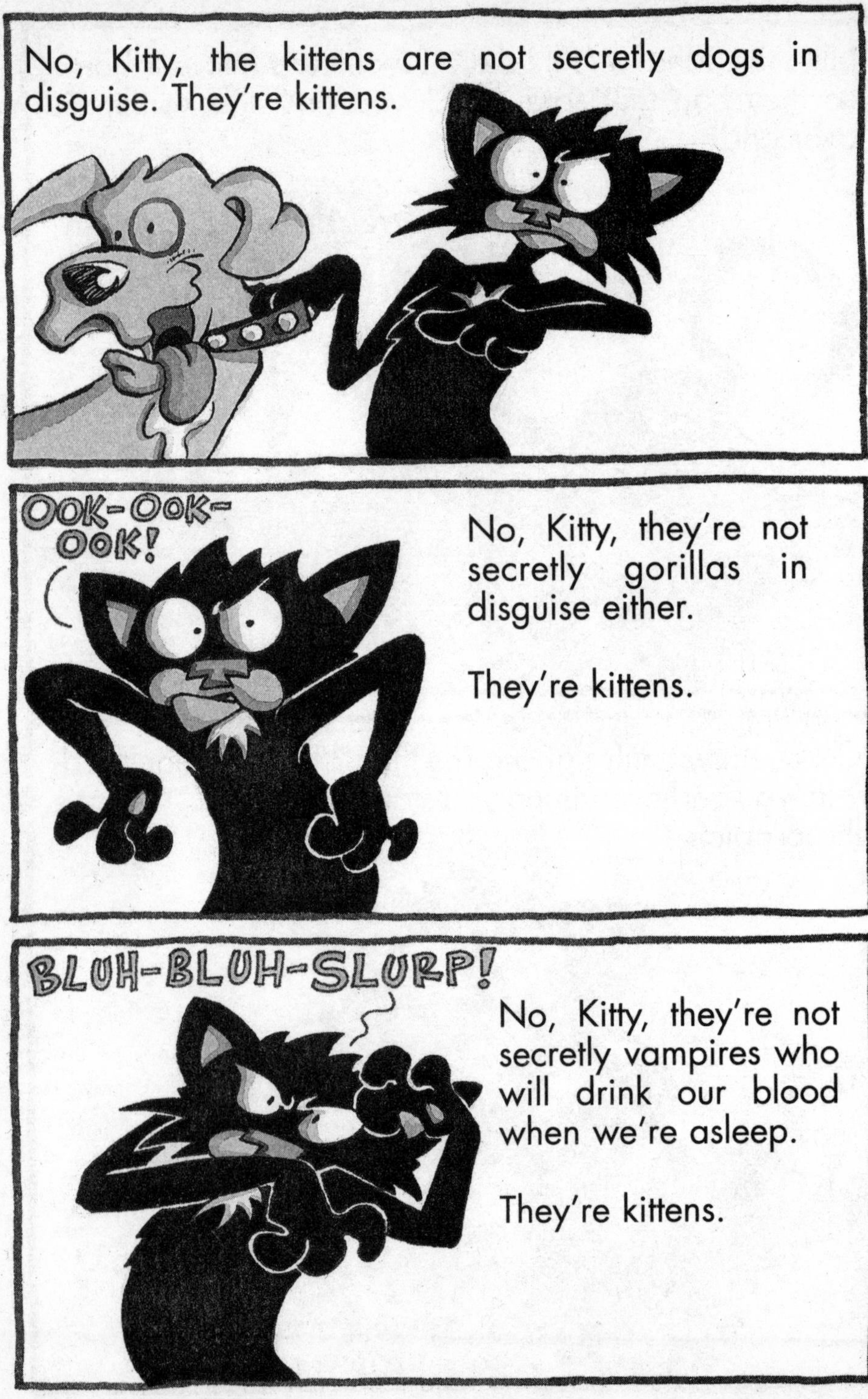
No, Kitty, the kittens are not secretly dogs in disguise. They're kittens.
OOK-OOK-OOK!
No, Kitty, they're not secretly gorillas in disguise either.
They're kittens.
BLUH-BLUH-SLURP!
No, Kitty, they're not secretly vampires who will drink our blood when we're asleep.
They're kittens.

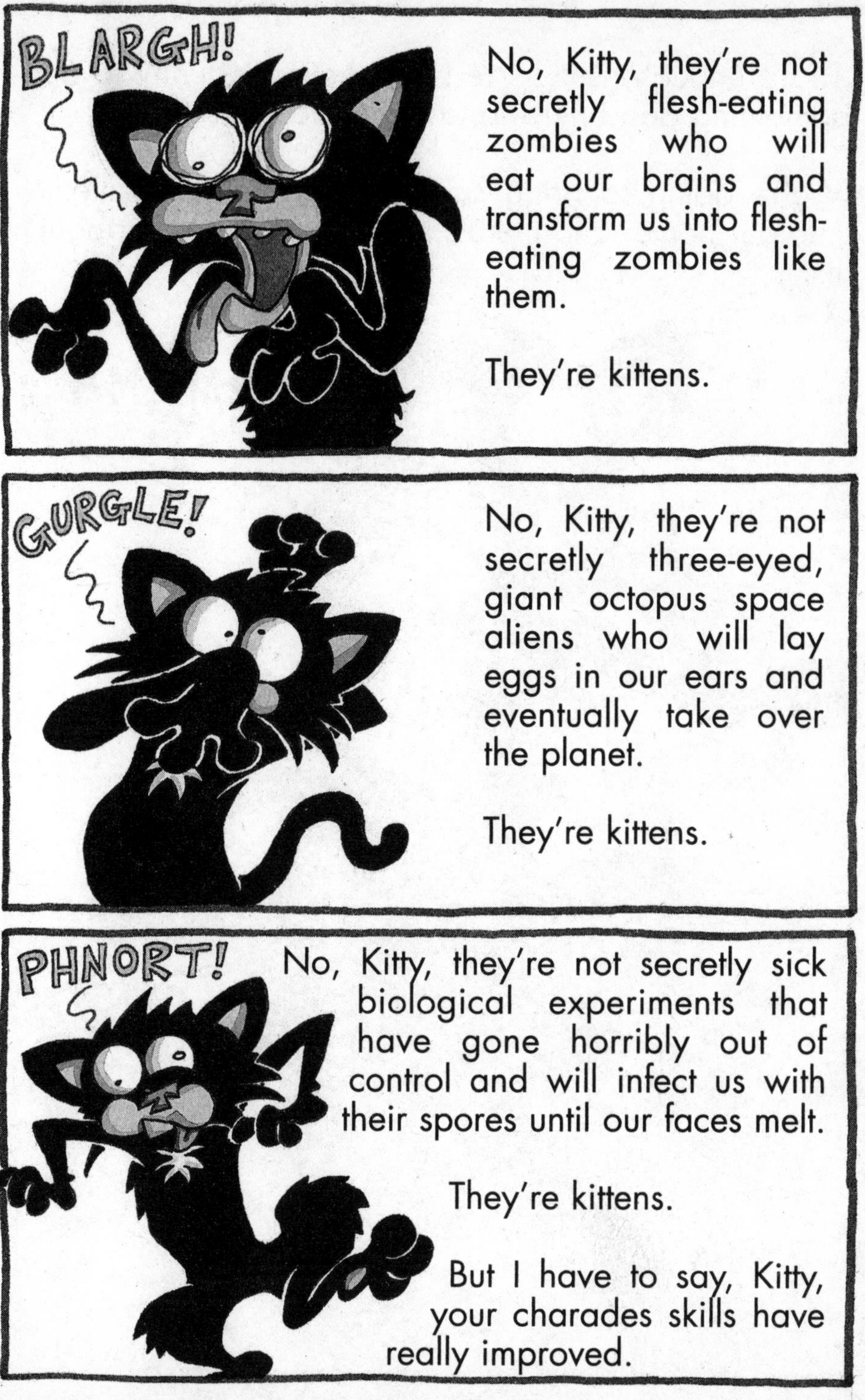
BLARGH!
No, Kitty, they're not secretly flesh-eating zombies who will eat our brains and transform us into flesh-eating zombies like them.
They're kittens.
GURGLE!
No, Kitty, they're not secretly three-eyed, giant octopus space aliens who will lay eggs in our ears and eventually take over the planet.
They're kittens.
PHNORT!
No, Kitty, they're not secretly sick biological experiments that have gone horribly out of control and will infect us with their spores until our faces melt.
They're kittens.
But I have to say, Kitty, your charades skills have really improved.

That's enough, Kitty! We have the opportunity to do something good here, and we're going to take it.

We're going to bring some sweet, innocent kittens into our home, and there's nothing you can do about it!

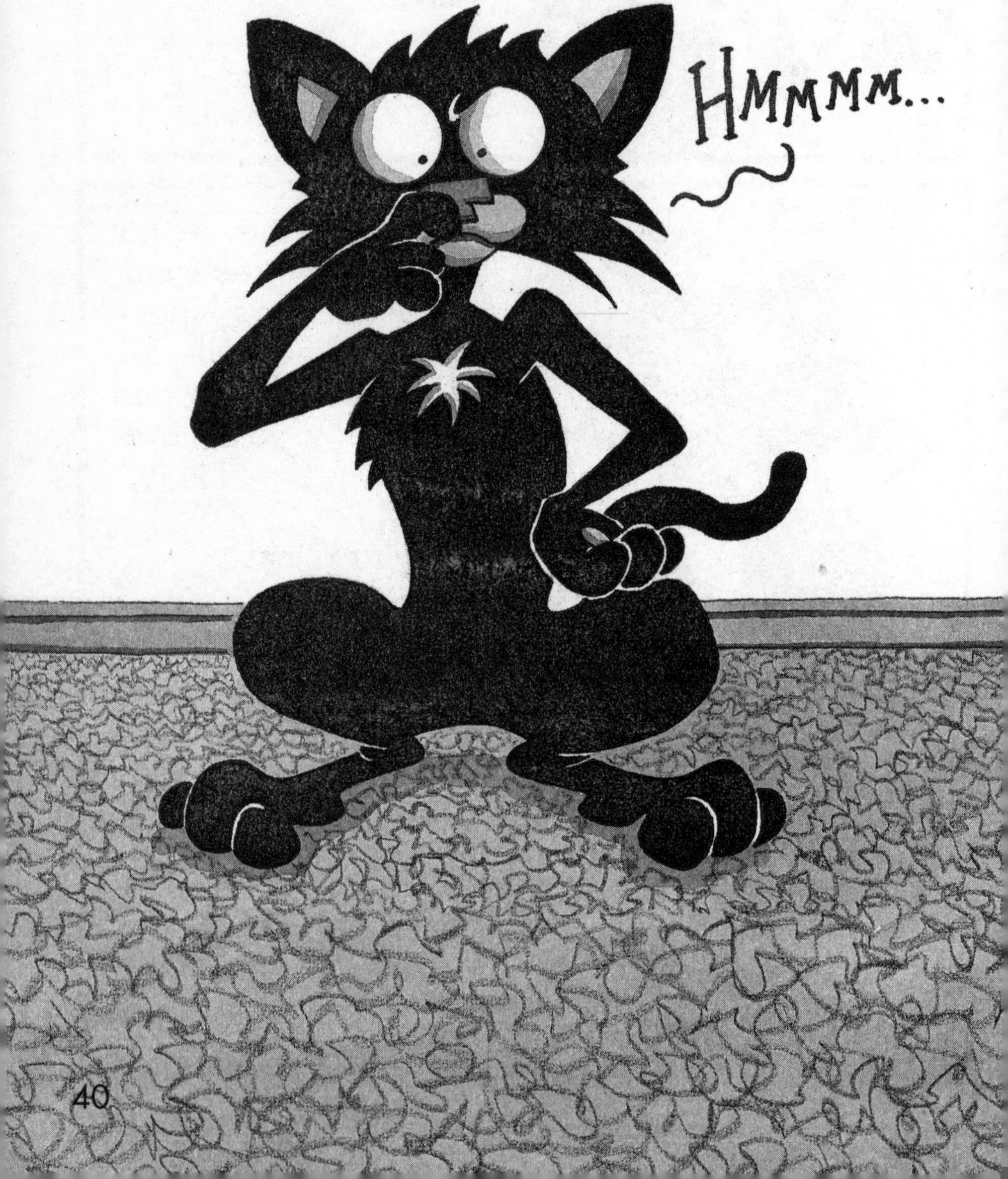
HMMMM...

Uh . . . Kitty. Why are you giving me that "I'm-really-annoyed-with-you-but-now-I-have-a-diabolical-plan-from-which-I-will-receive-cruel-pleasure-from-the-misery-of-others" face?

Kitty? Kitty?

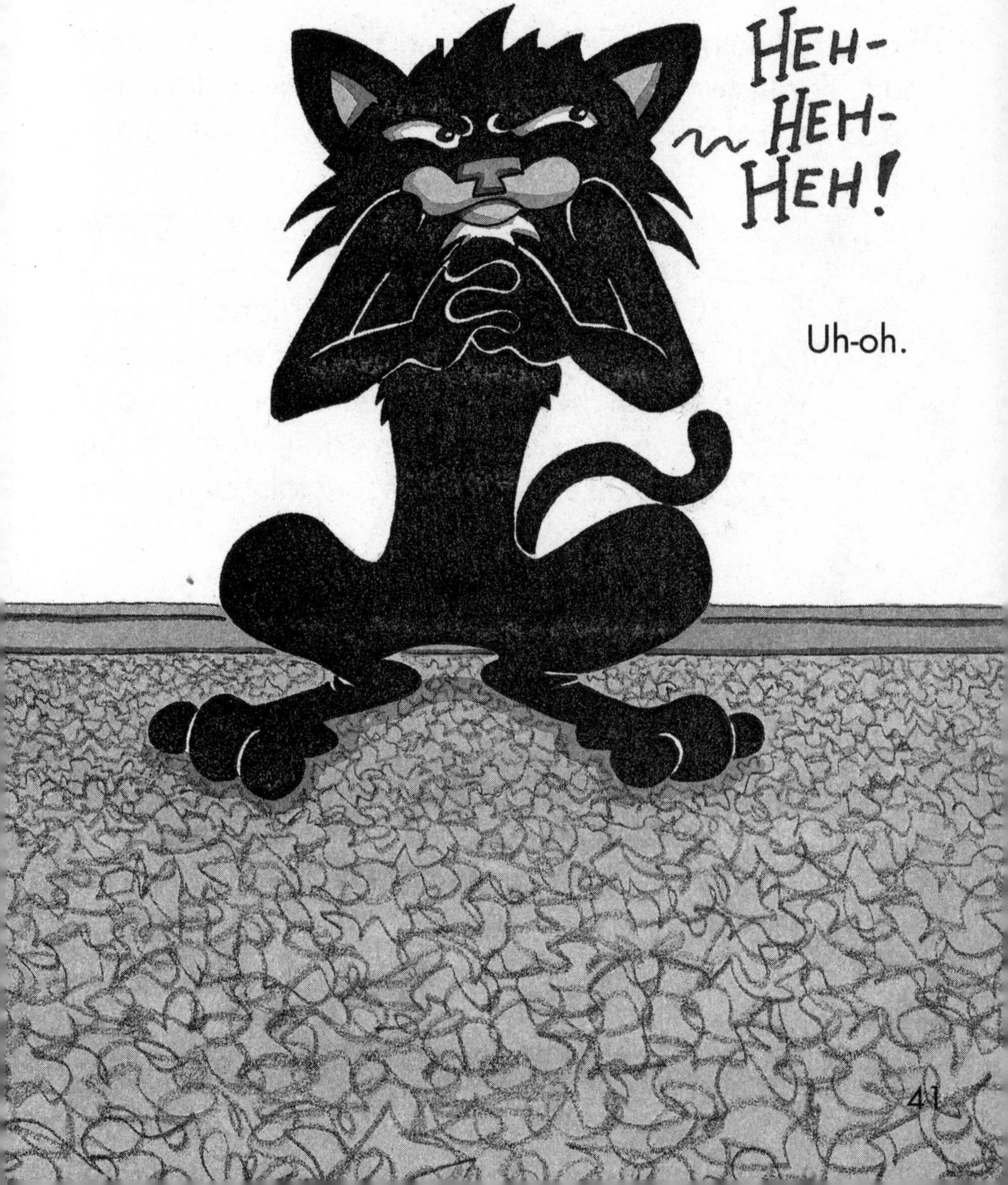
HEH-
HEH-
HEH!

Uh-oh.

UNCLE MURRAY'S FUN FACTS

WHY DO CATS NOT GET ALONG WITH OTHER CATS?

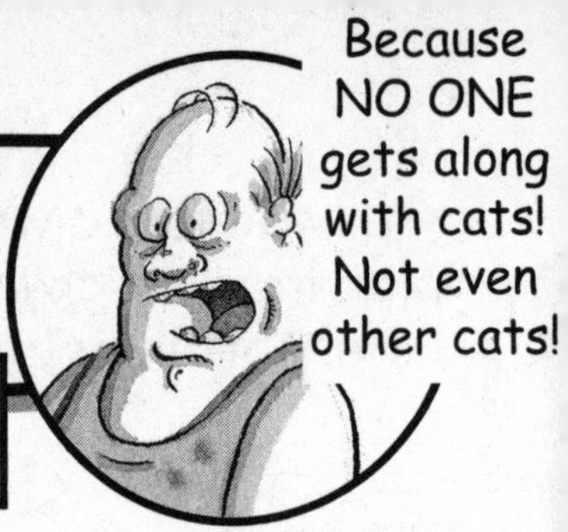
Because NO ONE gets along with cats! Not even other cats!

Some cats actually DO get along very well with other cats. For instance, many kittens who grow up together become cats who live very peacefully with each other.

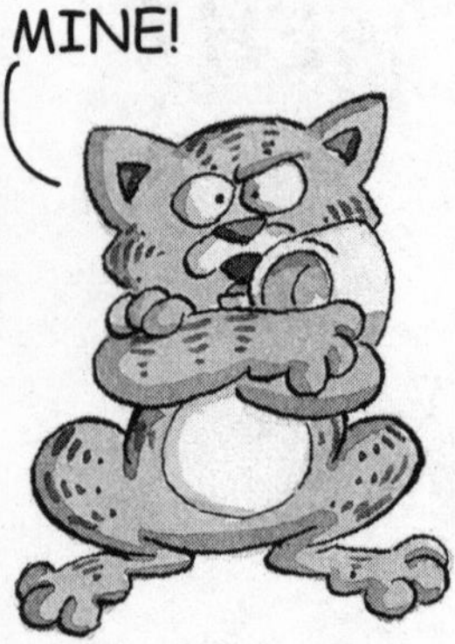
MINE!

What about cats who don't grow up with other cats?
Cats, by nature, are territorial, which means that they tend to be very possessive of their space, their belongings, and even their owners. In other words—cats don't like to share, especially with other cats.

What will happen if a new cat is brought into a home where there's already a cat?
The old cat is NOT going to share with the new cat. The old cat is not being selfish. In its mind, the old cat is being protective of all the things it believes it owns.

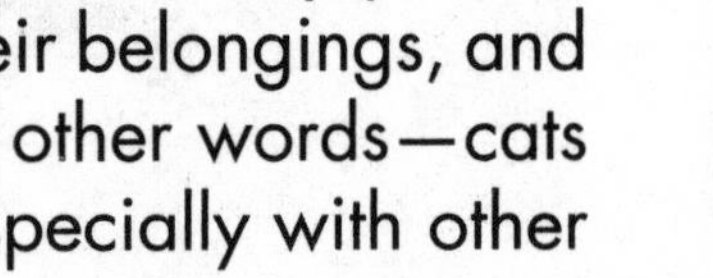
MINE!

What if the new cat wants to share?
If the old cat catches the new cat playing with one of its toys

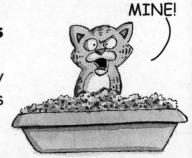

MINE!

or eating from its food bowl or even getting pets from their owner, the result could be some angry hissing, spitting, chasing, and even fighting.

What should an owner do if the cats are fighting?

The worst thing you can do is ignore the problem. DON'T ignore the problem! Even though cats will usually run away from each other before getting caught up in a heated battle, it's still possible for them to get hurt.

If you sense that a fight is about to begin, maybe because you see one cat is stalking another, the best thing to do is to break them up by loudly clapping your hands or splashing a little water on the cats.

What if one cat is starting more fights than the other?

MINE!

Try not to play favorites. "Punishing" one cat more than the other they will only make them both feel resentful. That will make YOU a part of the problem.

•CHAPTER THREE•

NEW ARRIVALS

Hello there, Strange Kitty. I didn't know you were a kitten rescue worker. It's so nice of you to escort the kittens here from the other neighborhood. How's the conflict going, S.K.?

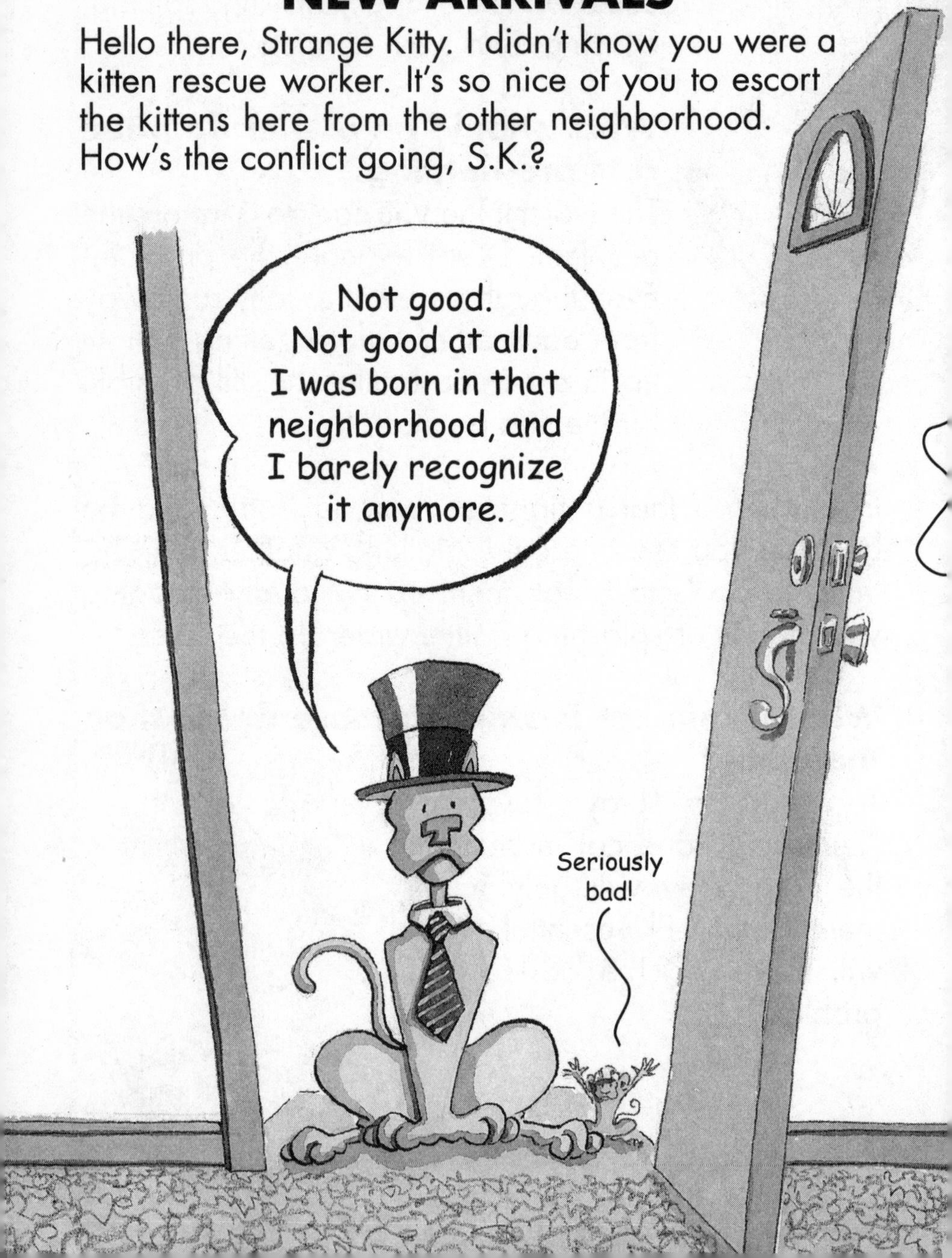
Not good. Not good at all. I was born in that neighborhood, and I barely recognize it anymore.
Seriously bad!

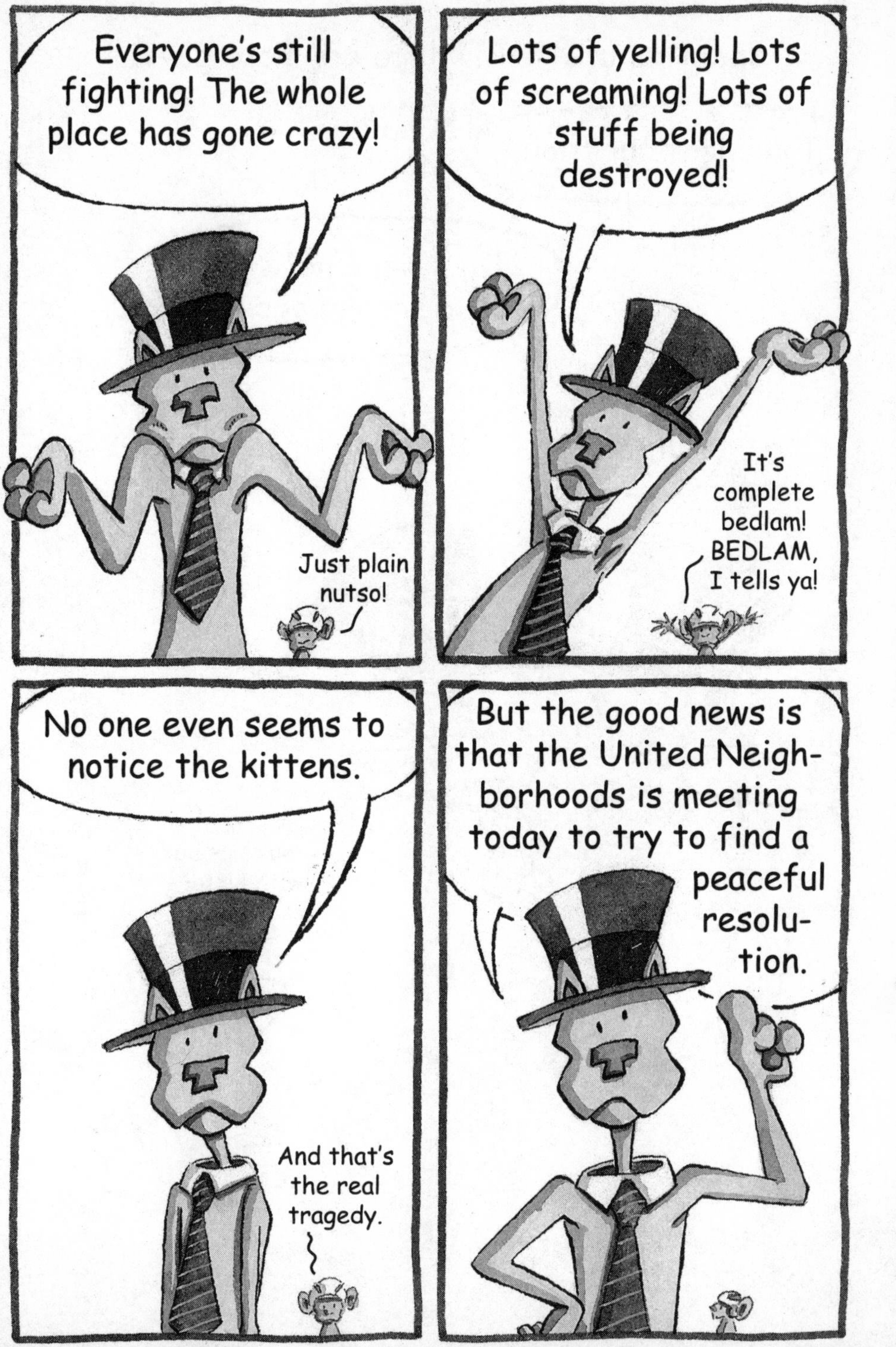
Everyone's still fighting! The whole place has gone crazy!
Just plain nutso!
Lots of yelling! Lots of screaming! Lots of stuff being destroyed!
It's complete bedlam! BEDLAM, I tells ya!
No one even seems to notice the kittens.
And that's the real tragedy.
But the good news is that the United Neigh-borhoods is meeting today to try to find a peaceful resolu-tion.

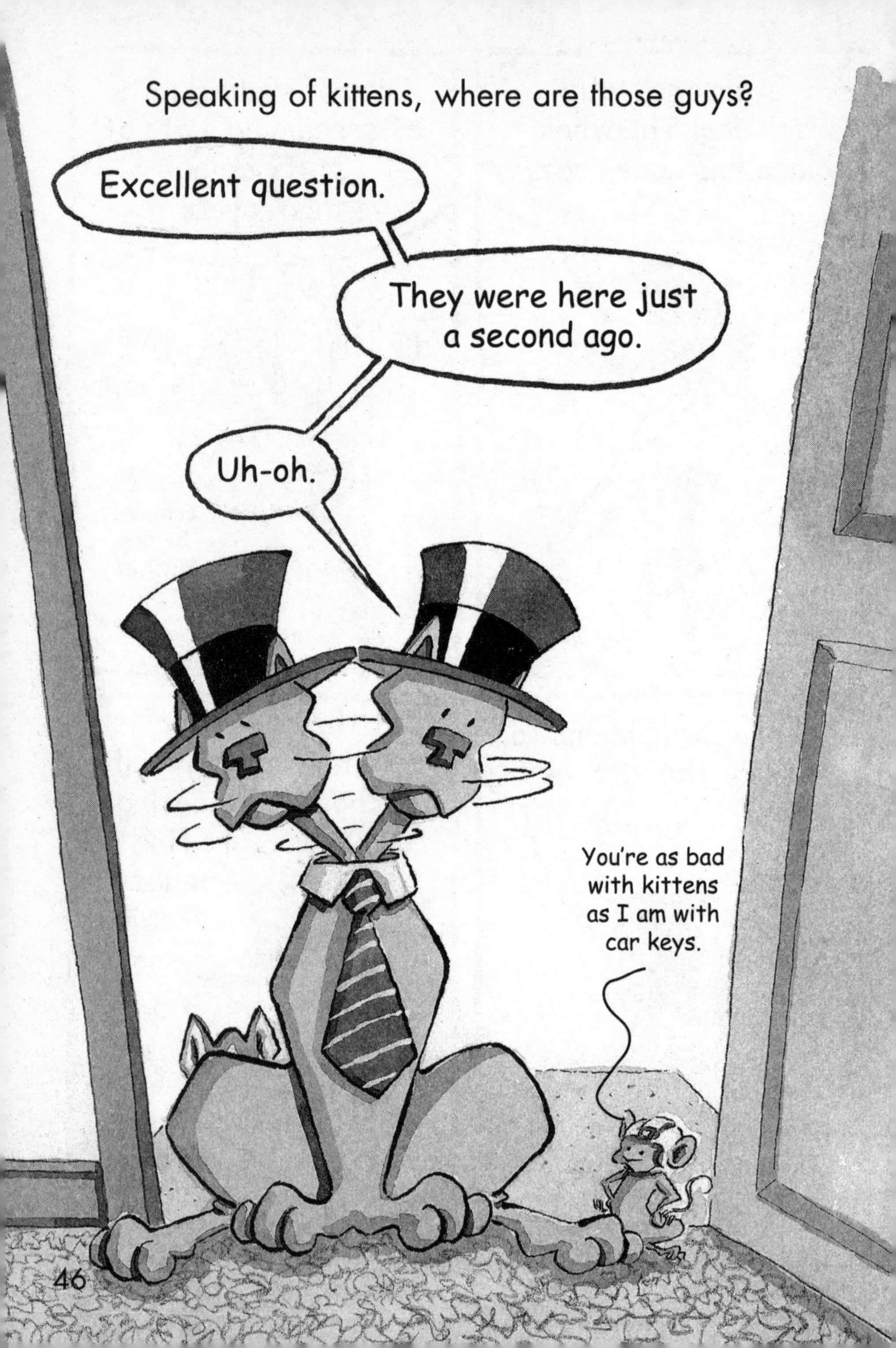
Speaking of kittens, where are those guys?
Excellent question.
They were here just a second ago.
Uh-oh.
You're as bad with kittens as I am with car keys.

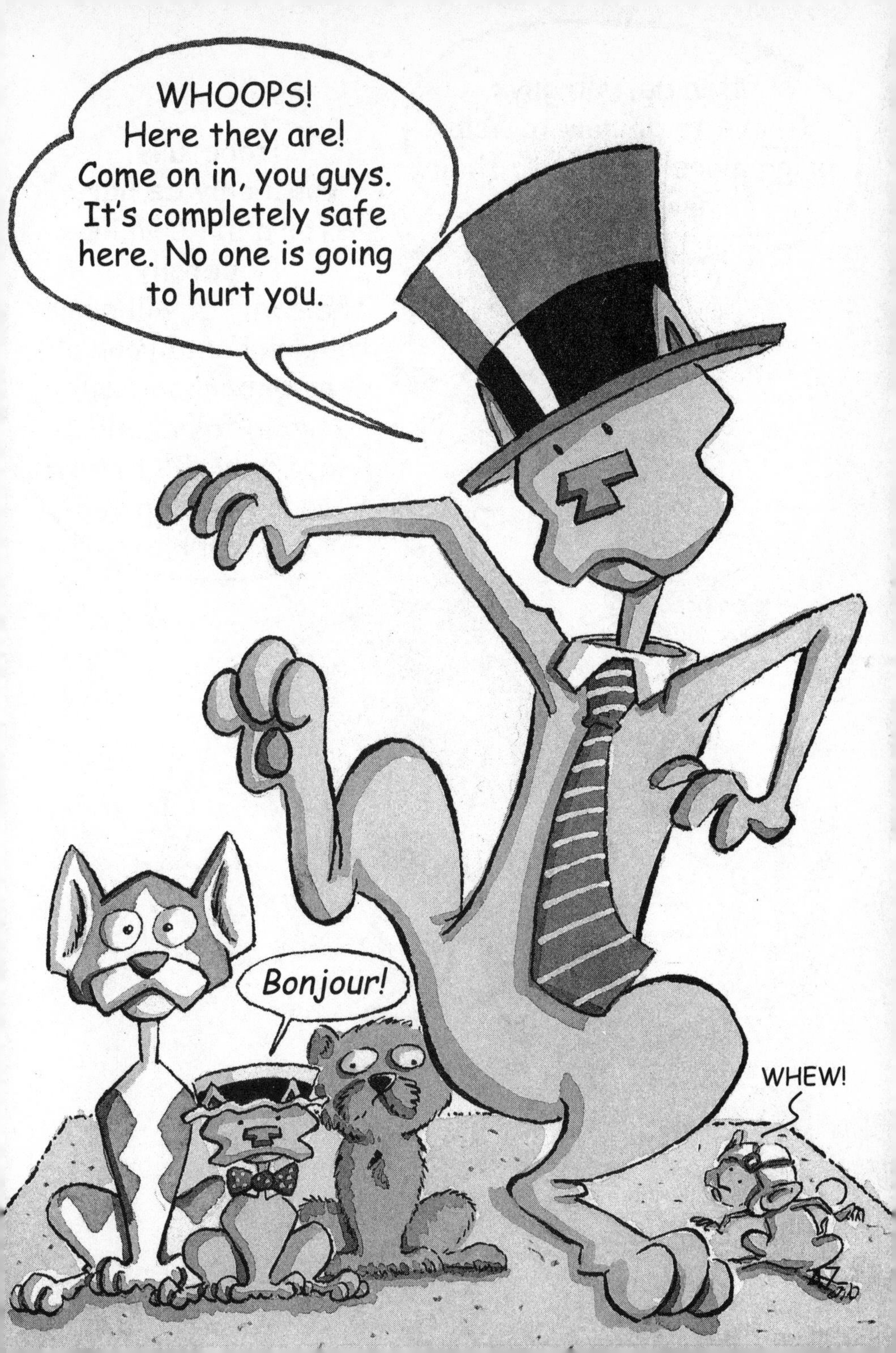
WHOOPS! Here they are! Come on in, you guys. It's completely safe here. No one is going to hurt you.
Bonjour!
WHEW!

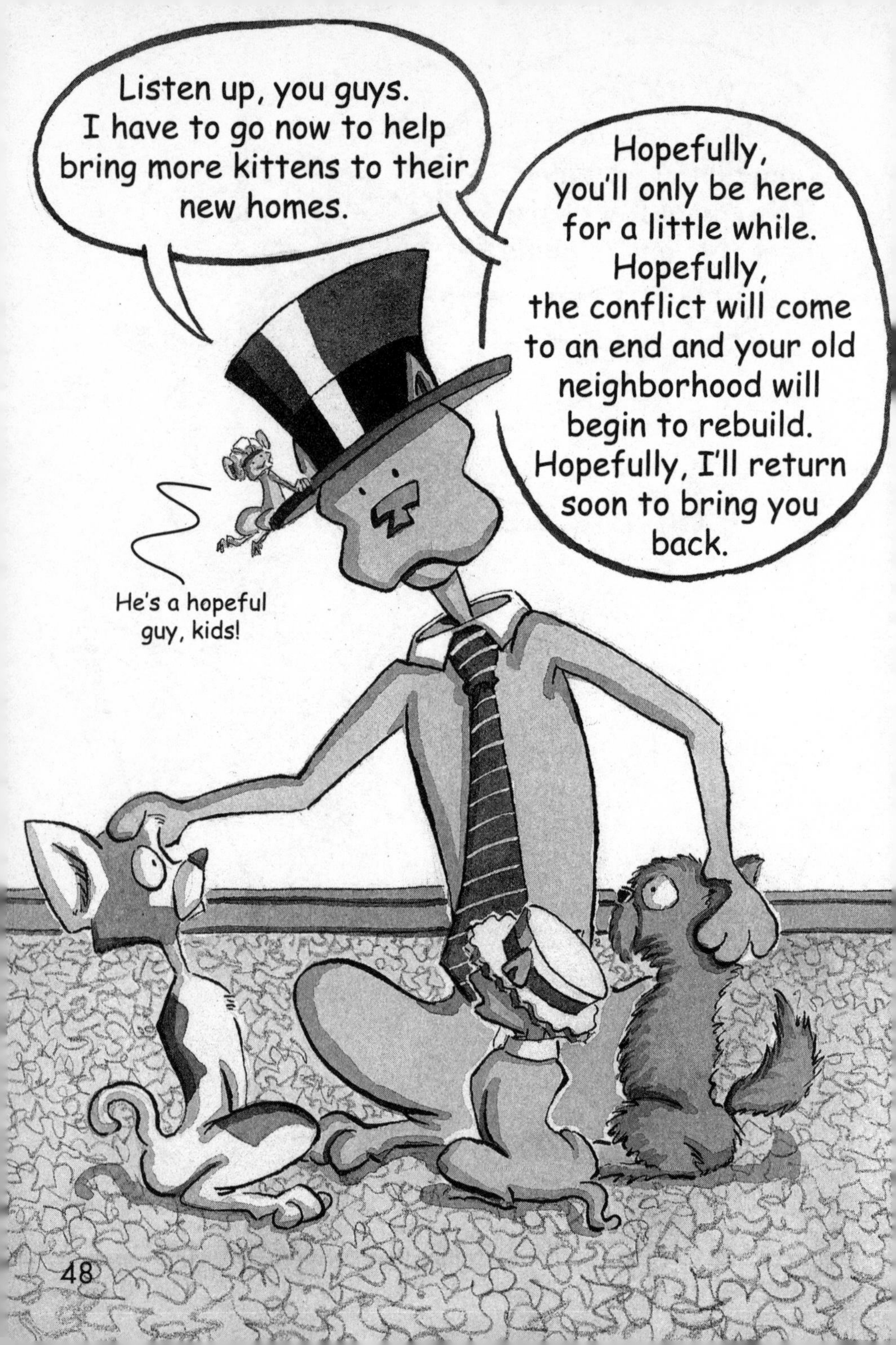
Listen up, you guys. I have to go now to help bring more kittens to their new homes.
Hopefully, you'll only be here for a little while. Hopefully, the conflict will come to an end and your old neighborhood will begin to rebuild. Hopefully, I'll return soon to bring you back.
He's a hopeful guy, kids!

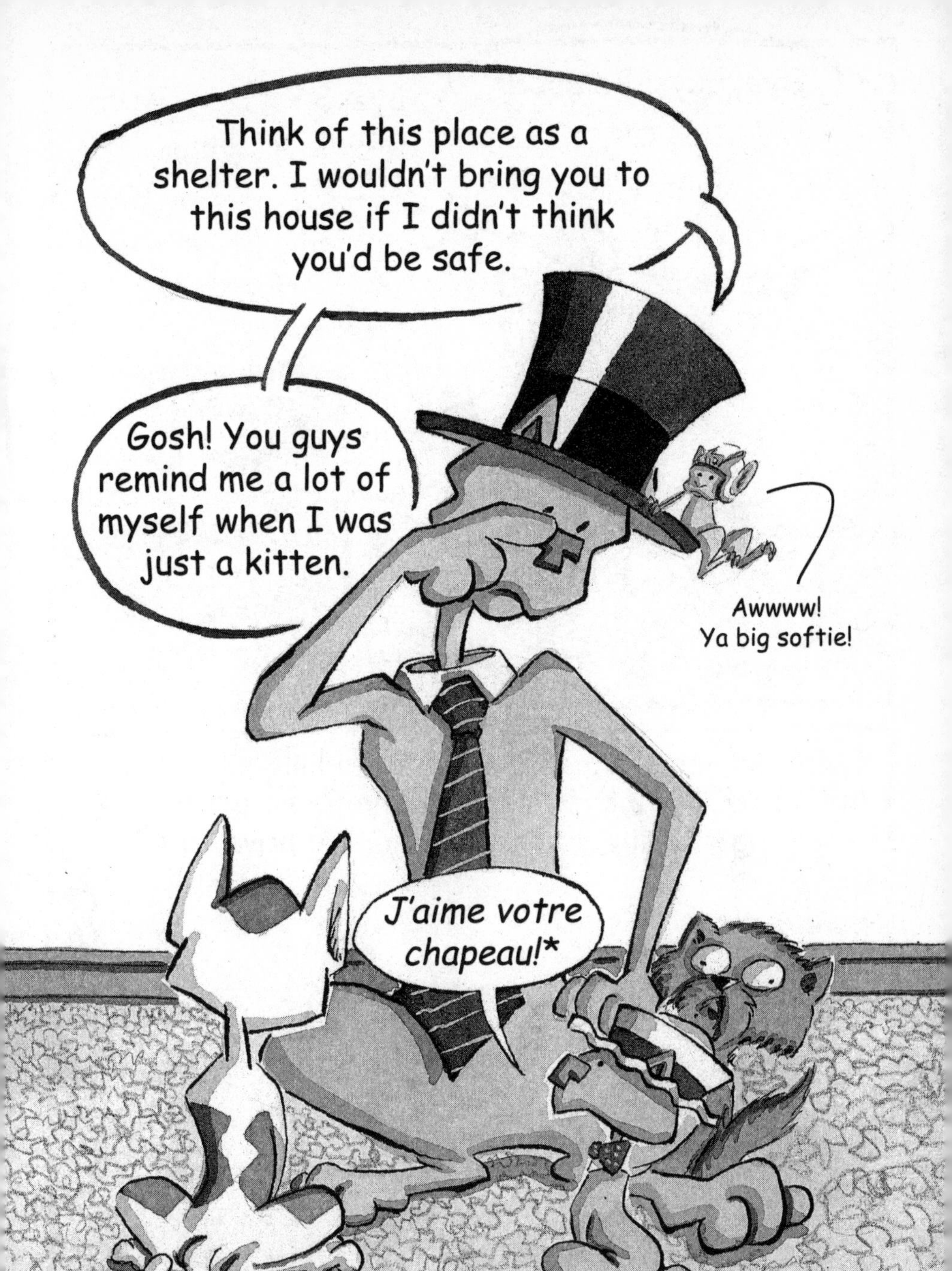
Think of this place as a shelter. I wouldn't bring you to this house if I didn't think you'd be safe.
Gosh! You guys remind me a lot of myself when I was just a kitten.
Awwww! Ya big softie!
*J'aime votre chapeau!**

* Look for a Glossary of this kitten's words translated into English at the end of this book.

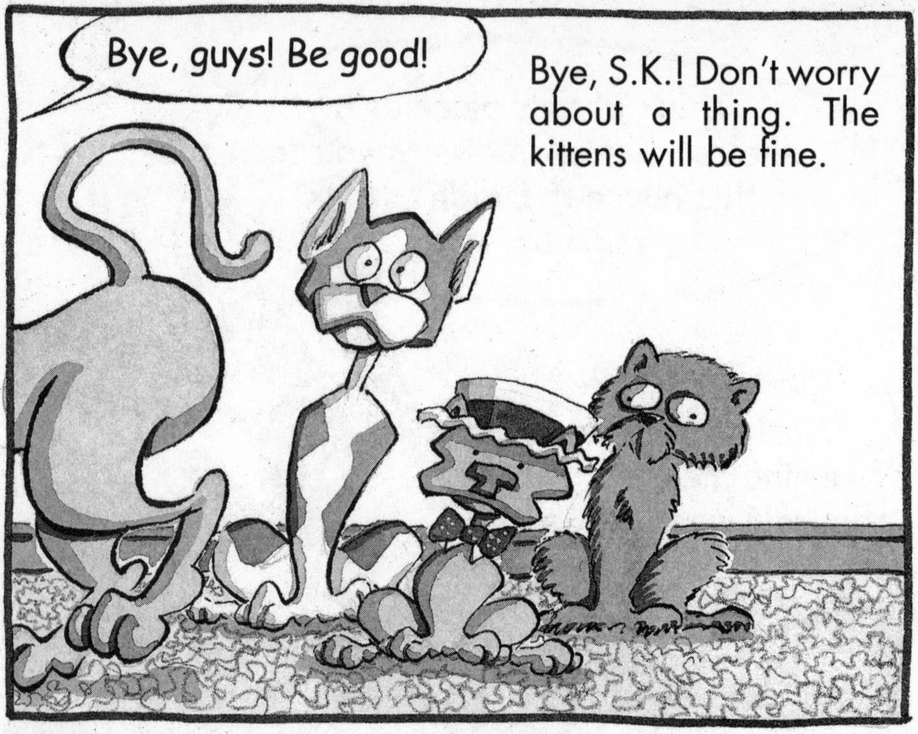
Bye, guys! Be good!
Bye, S.K.! Don't worry about a thing. The kittens will be fine.

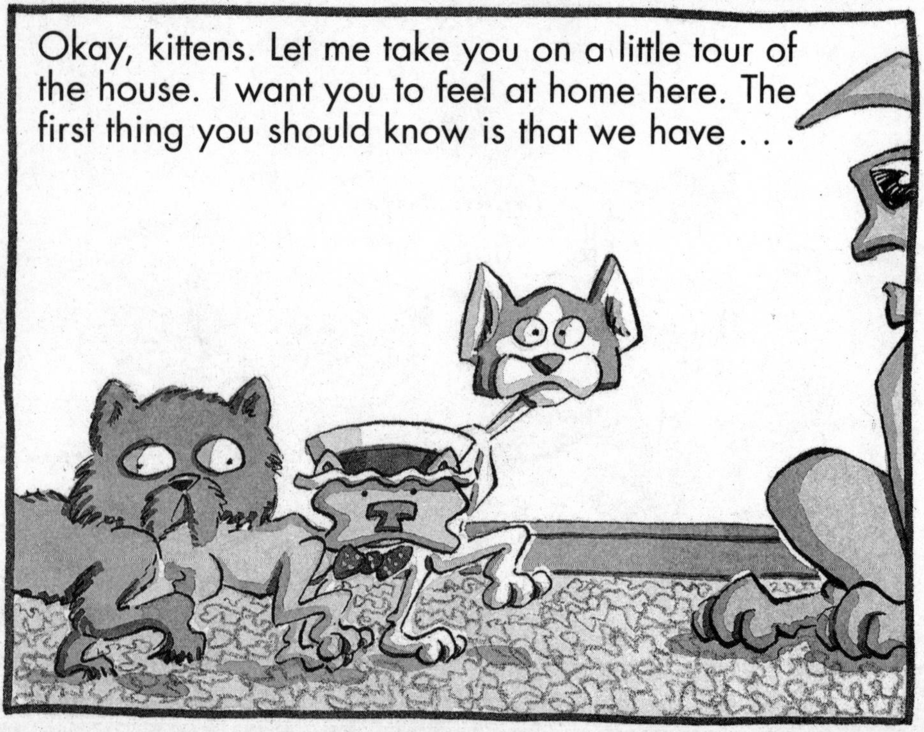
Okay, kittens. Let me take you on a little tour of the house. I want you to feel at home here. The first thing you should know is that we have . . .

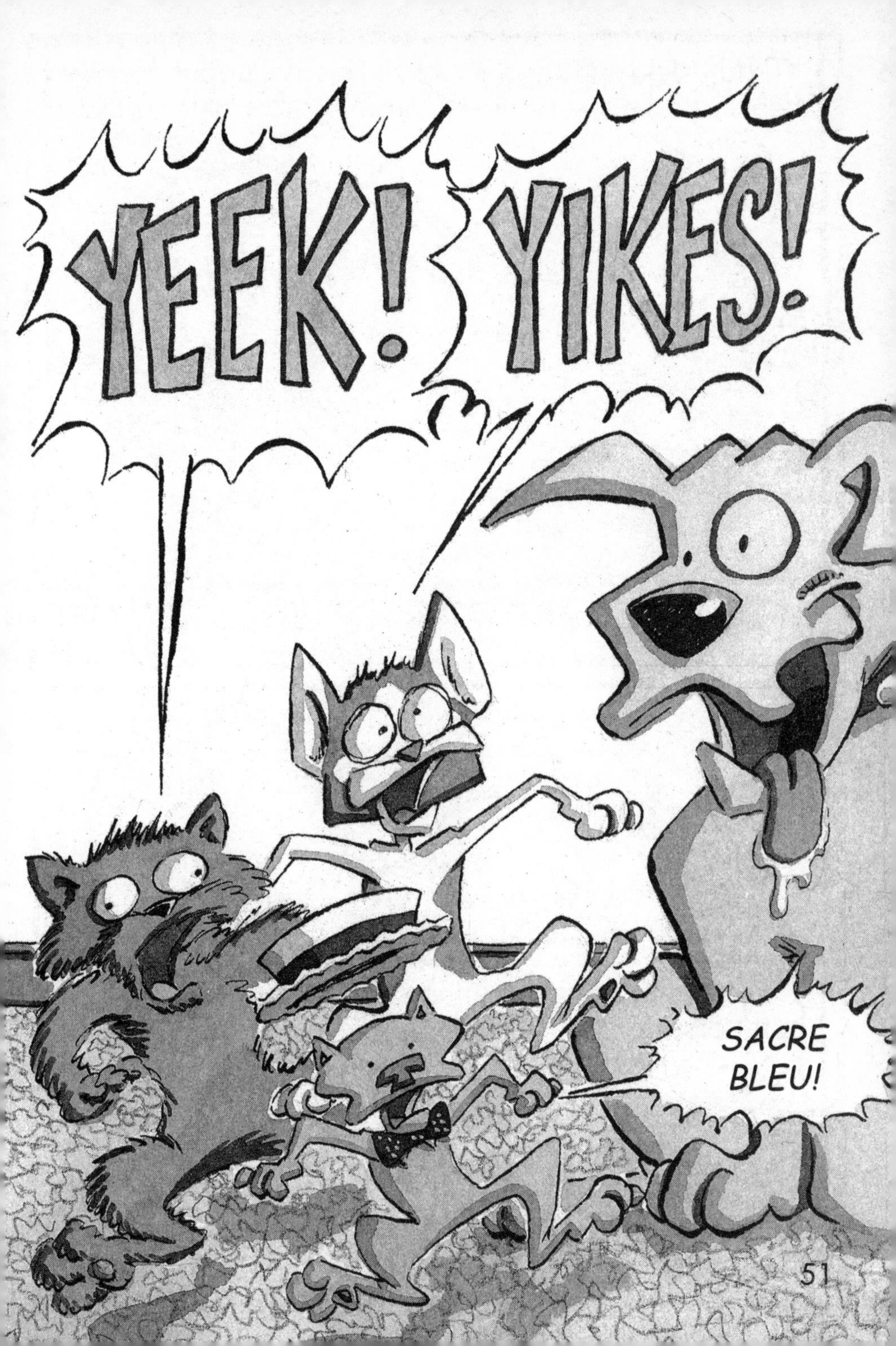
YEEK!
YIKES!
SACRE
BLEU!

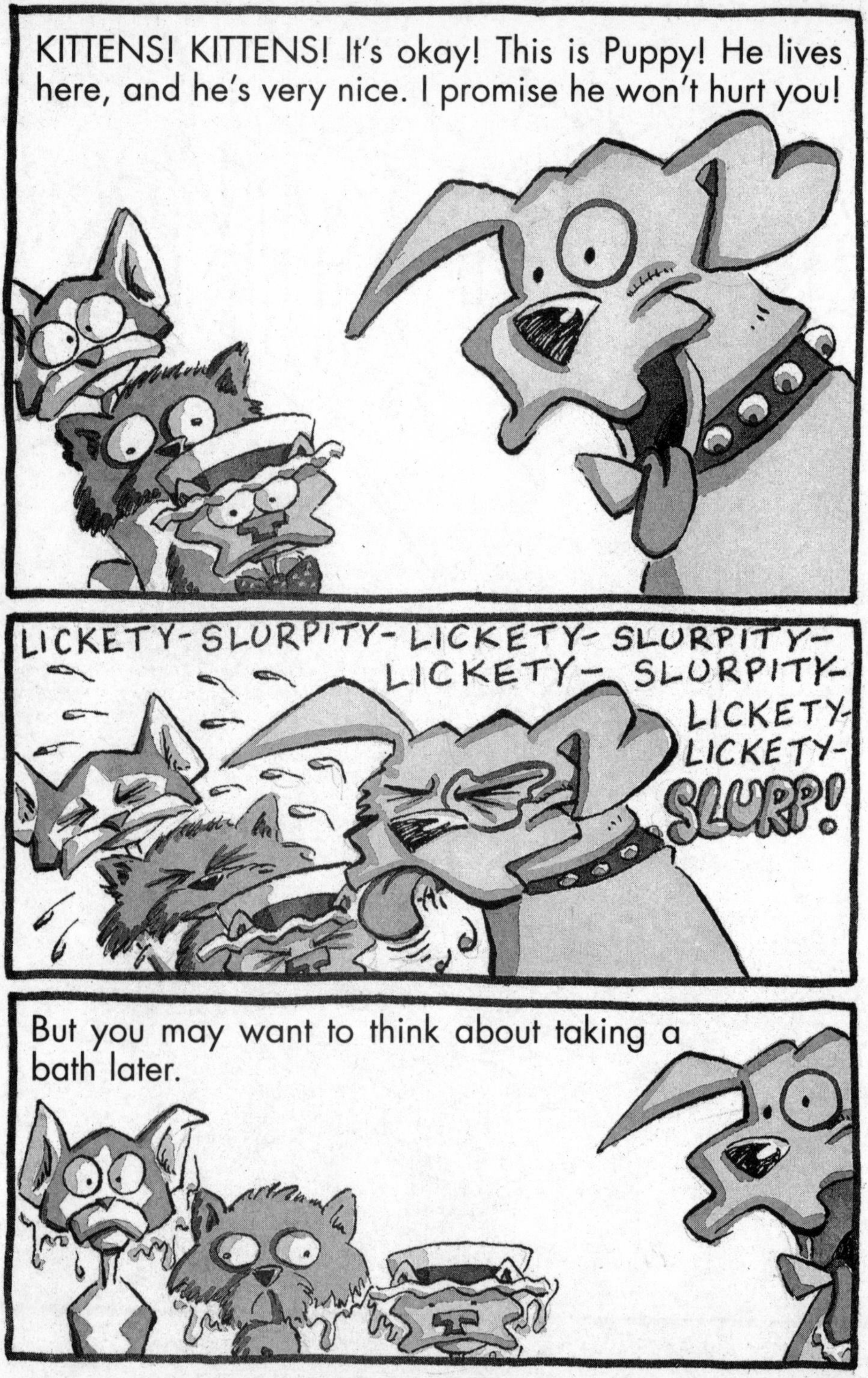
KITTENS! KITTENS! It's okay! This is Puppy! He lives here, and he's very nice. I promise he won't hurt you!
LICKETY-SLURPITY-LICKETY-SLURPITY-LICKETY-SLURPITY-LICKETY-LICKETY-SLURP!
But you may want to think about taking a bath later.

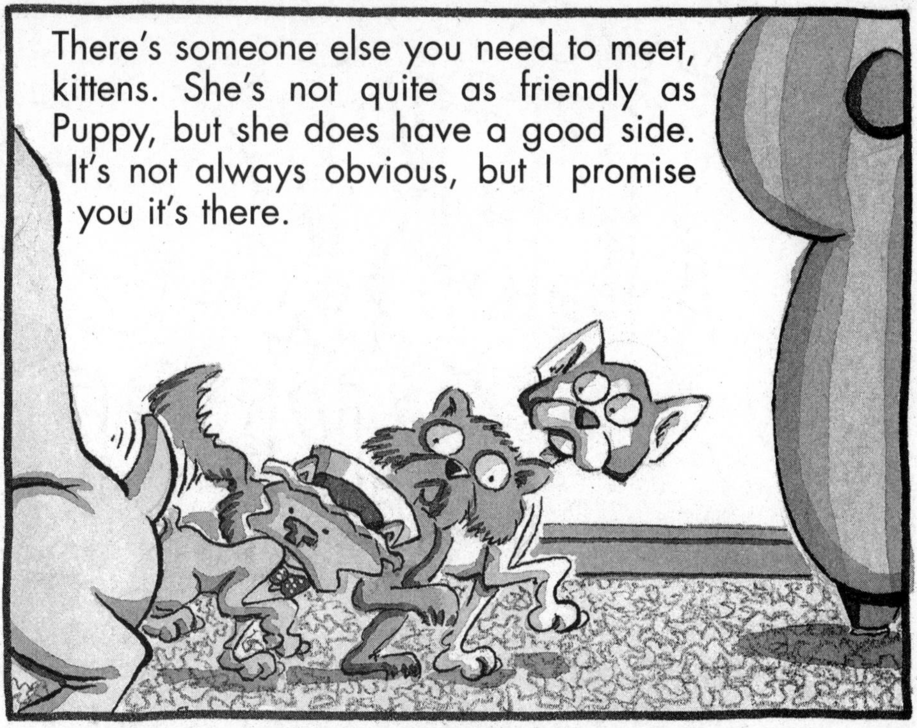
There's someone else you need to meet, kittens. She's not quite as friendly as Puppy, but she does have a good side. It's not always obvious, but I promise you it's there.

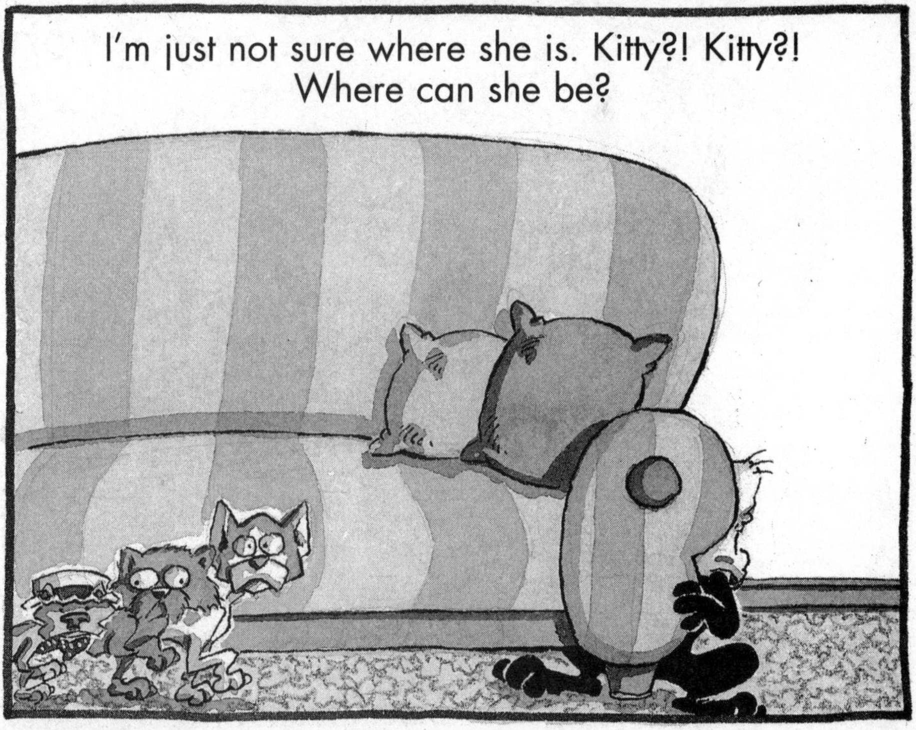
I'm just not sure where she is. Kitty?! Kitty?! Where can she be?

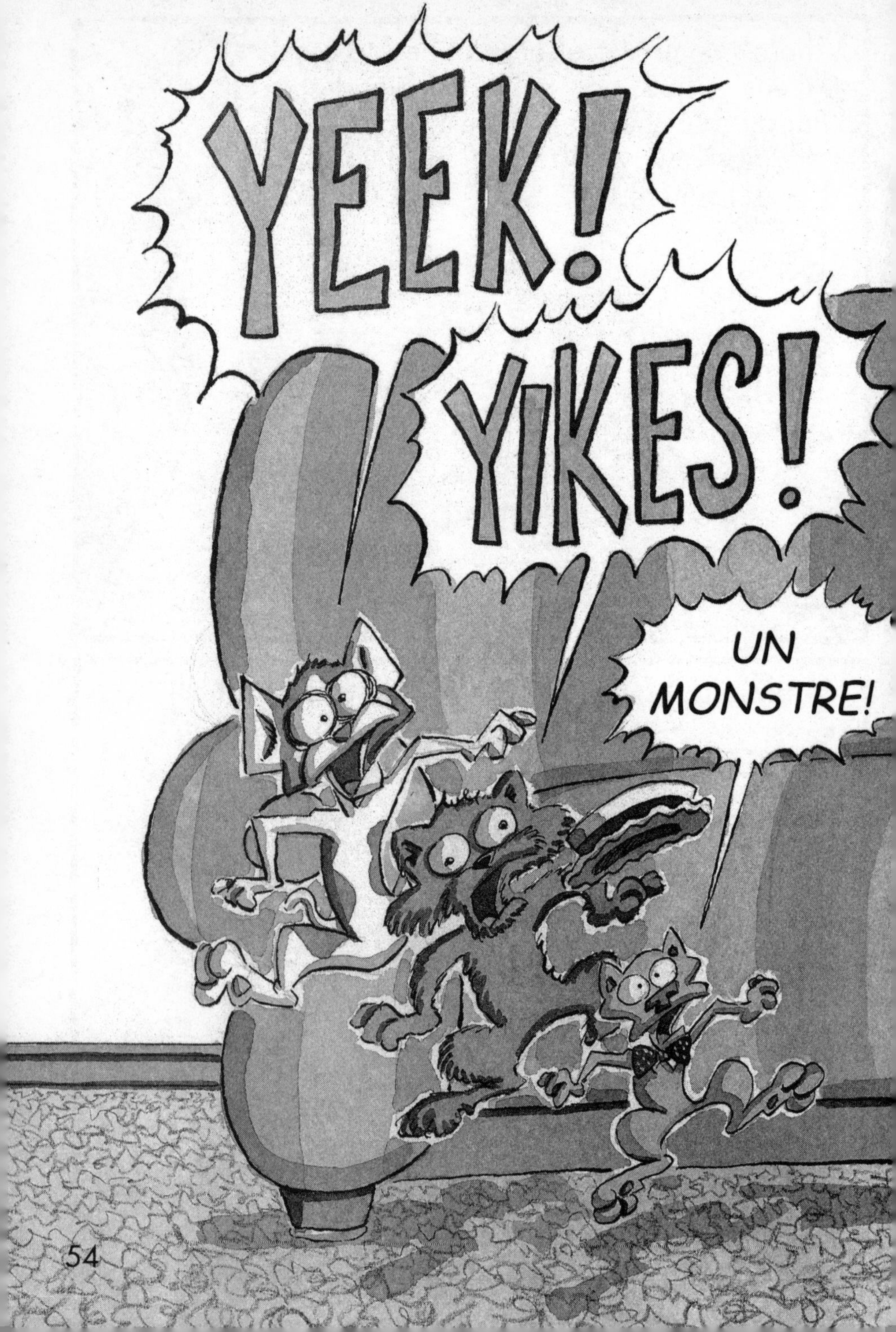
YEEK!
YIKES!
UN MONSTRE!

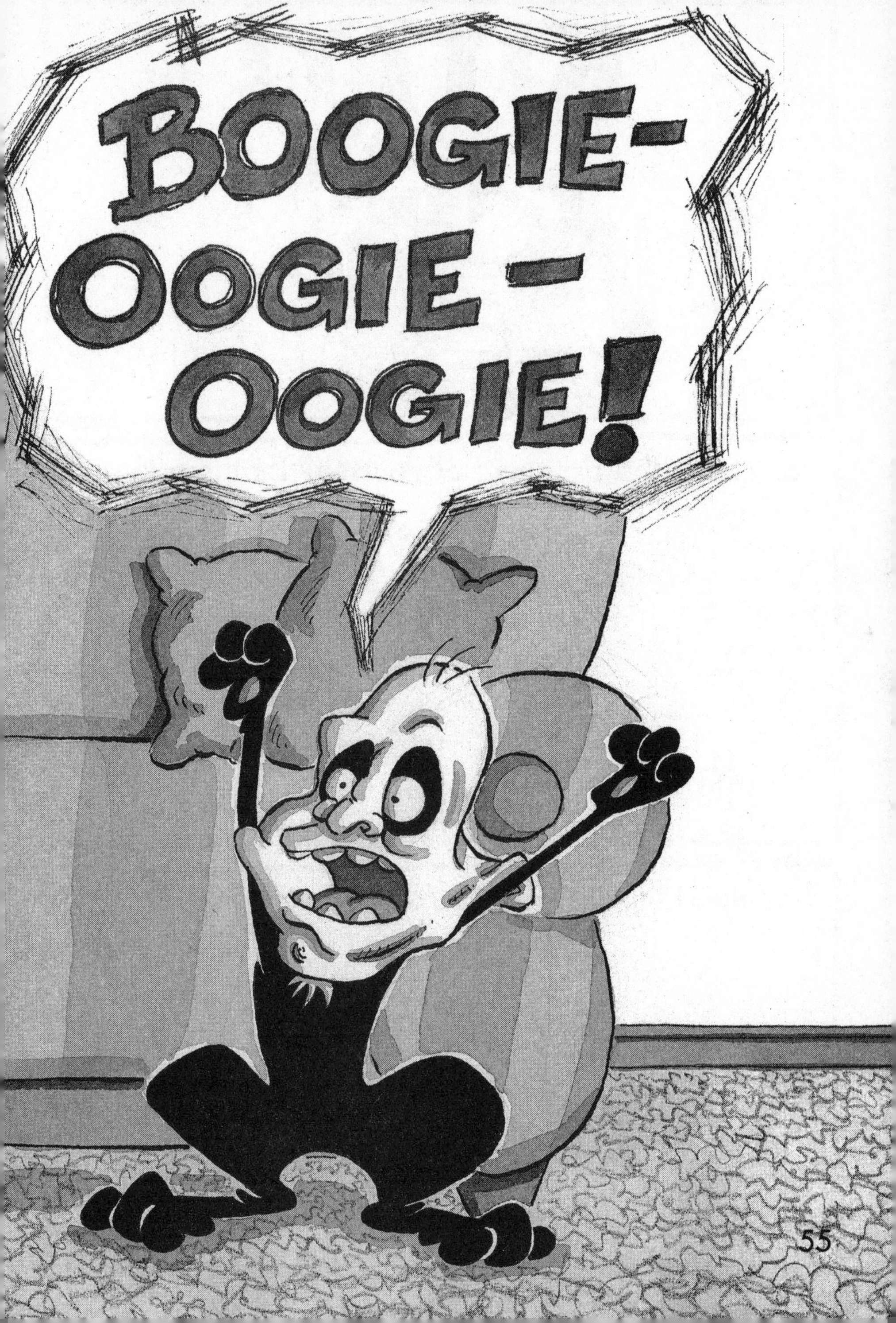
BOOGIE-
OOGIE-
OOGIE!

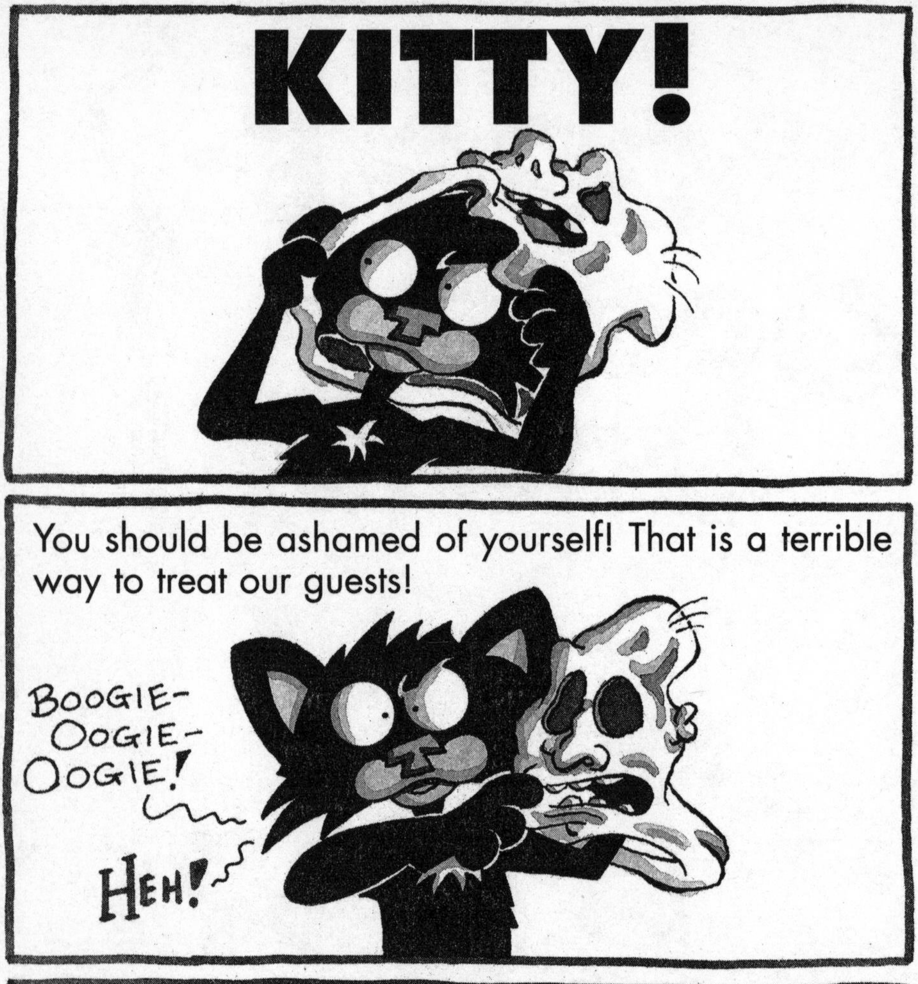
KITTY!
You should be ashamed of yourself! That is a terrible way to treat our guests!
BOOGIE-OOGIE-OOGIE!
HEH!
I demand that you apologize to them right NOW!

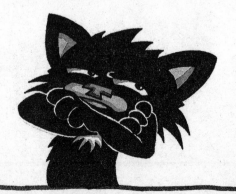

That is the worst apology I've ever seen.

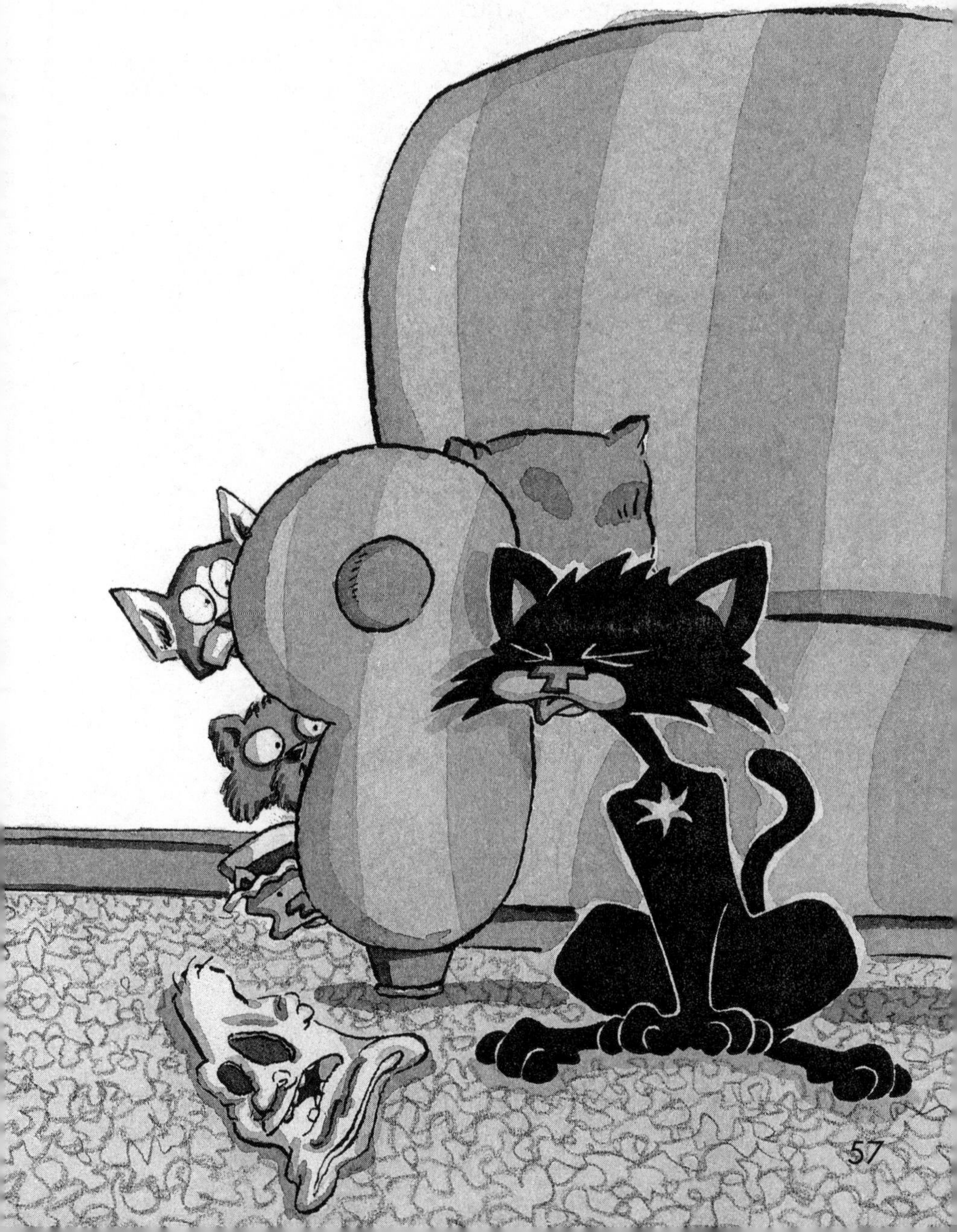

Kitty, you have so much, and they have so little. It's time you learned how to share. For instance, look at this massive pile of toys you have. You don't even play with most of them anymore. Why don't you let the kittens play with them?

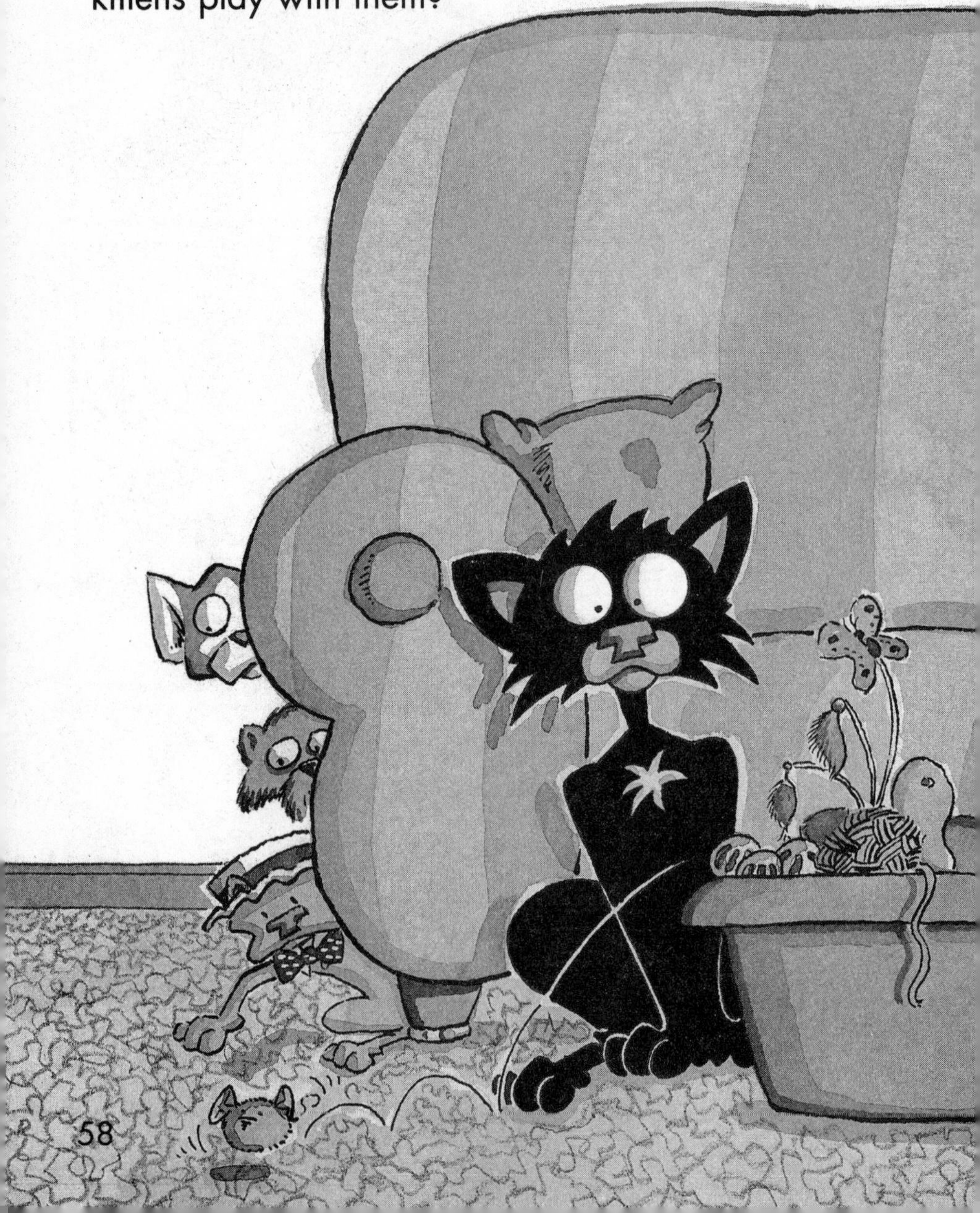

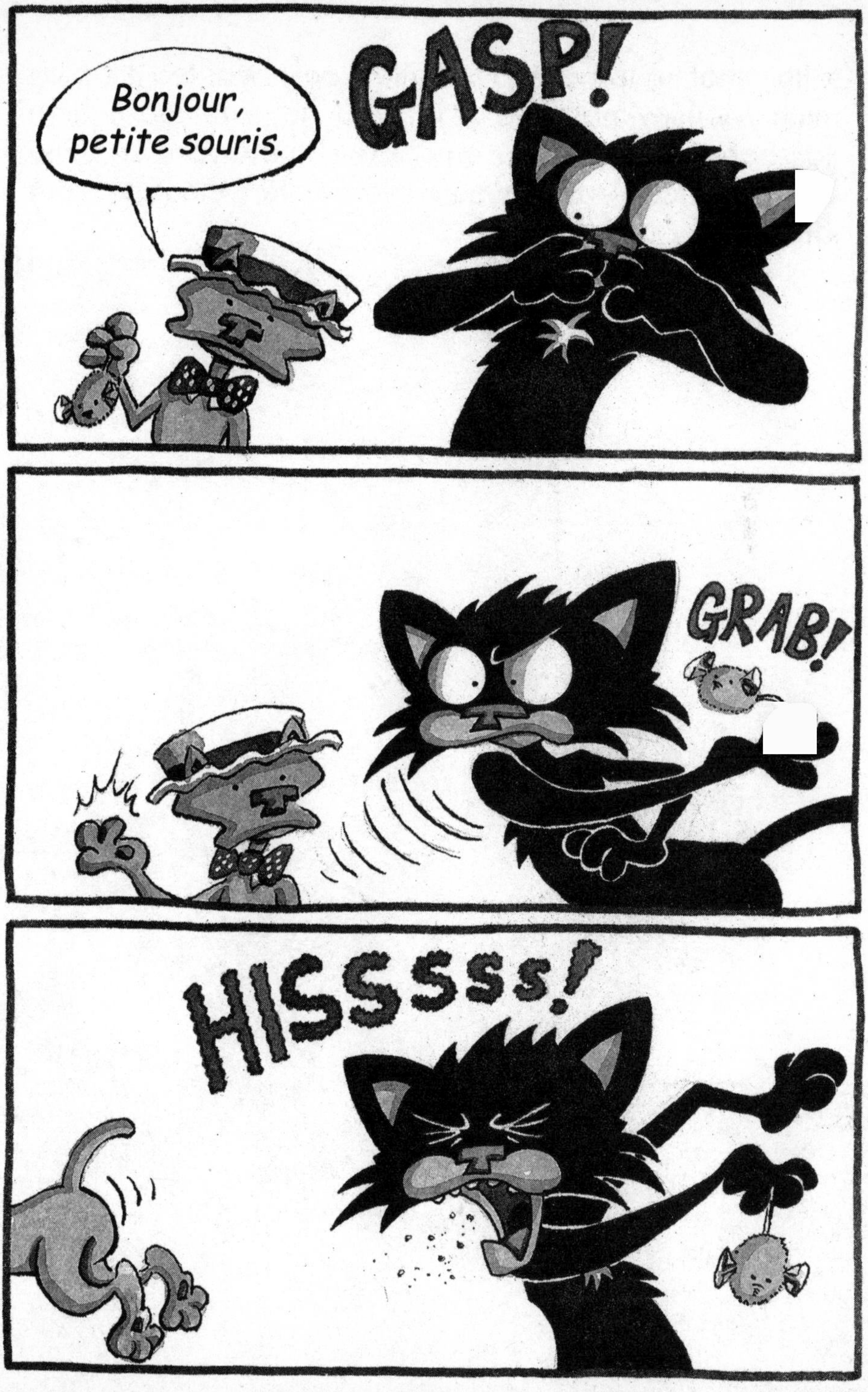
Bonjour,
petite souris.
GASP!
GRAB!
HISSSSS!

Kitty, that is terrible! The kitten only wanted to play with Mousey-mouse a little. You have to learn how to share. You have so much, and they have so little. For instance, you haven't even eaten most of your breakfast.

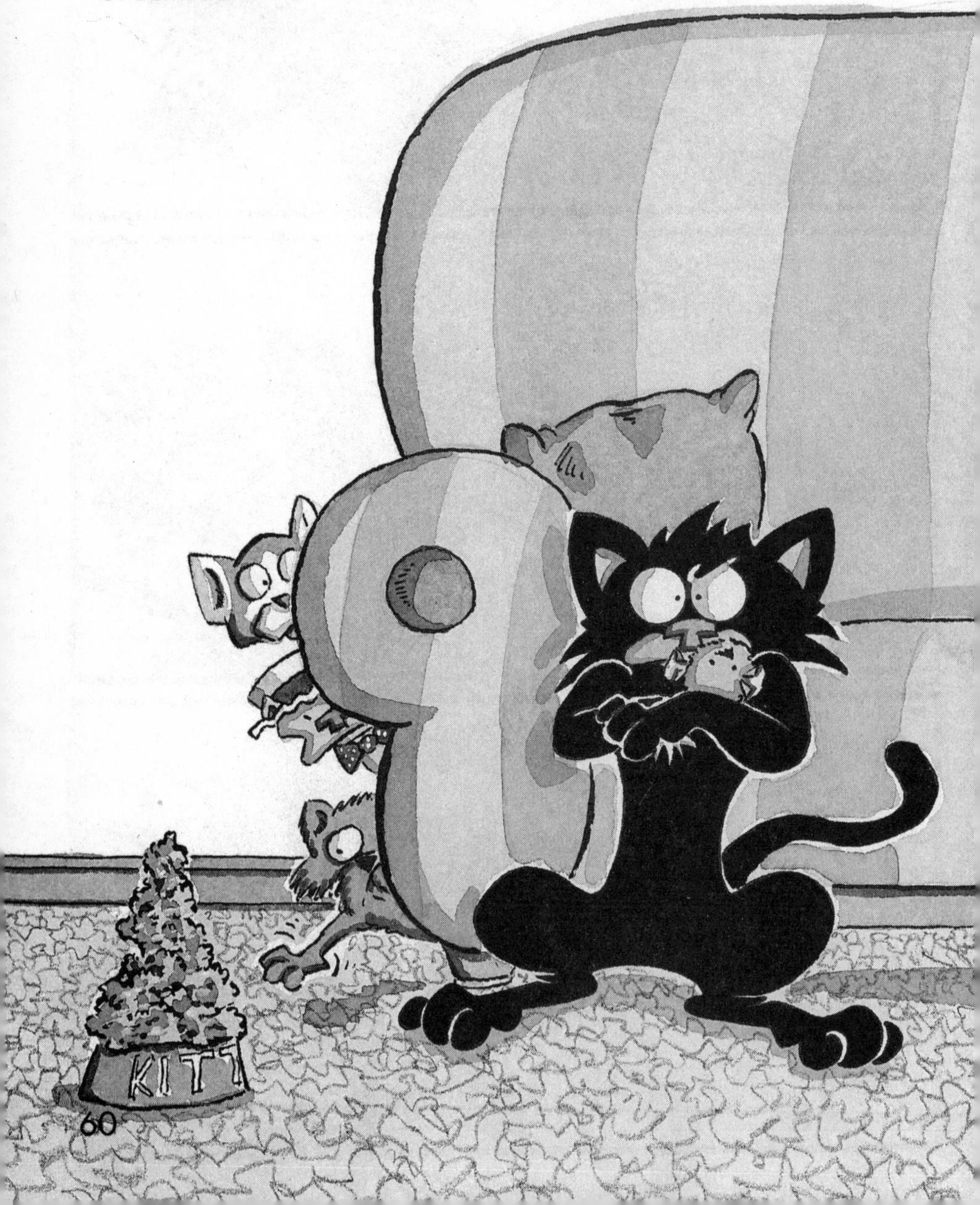
KITT

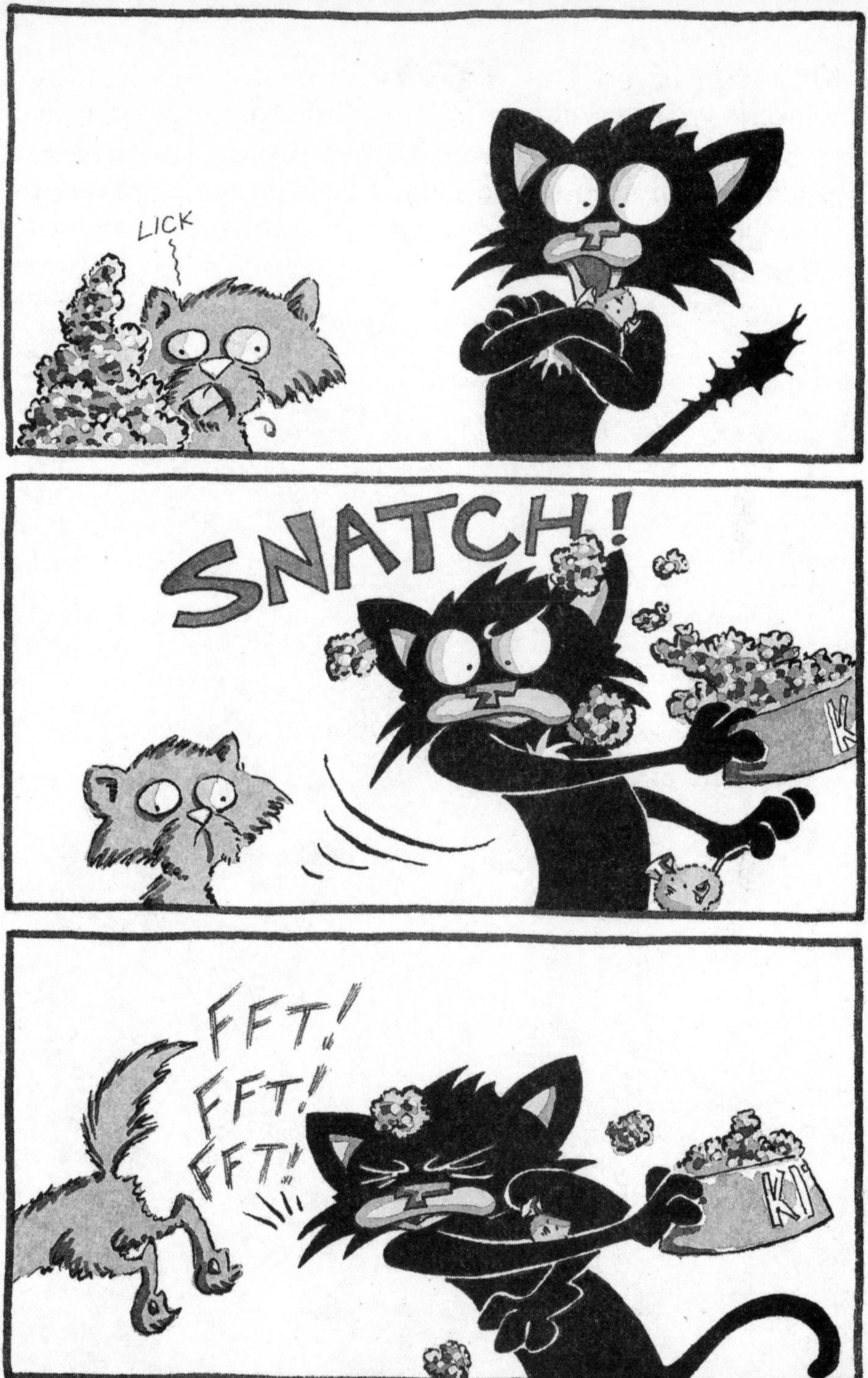
LICK
SNATCH!
FFT!
FFT!
FFT!

KITTY!

What is wrong with you?! The kitten only wanted a little to eat. You have to learn how to share. You have so much, and they have so little. For instance, last week I bought you a brand new cat tree. I haven't seen you climb on it even once.

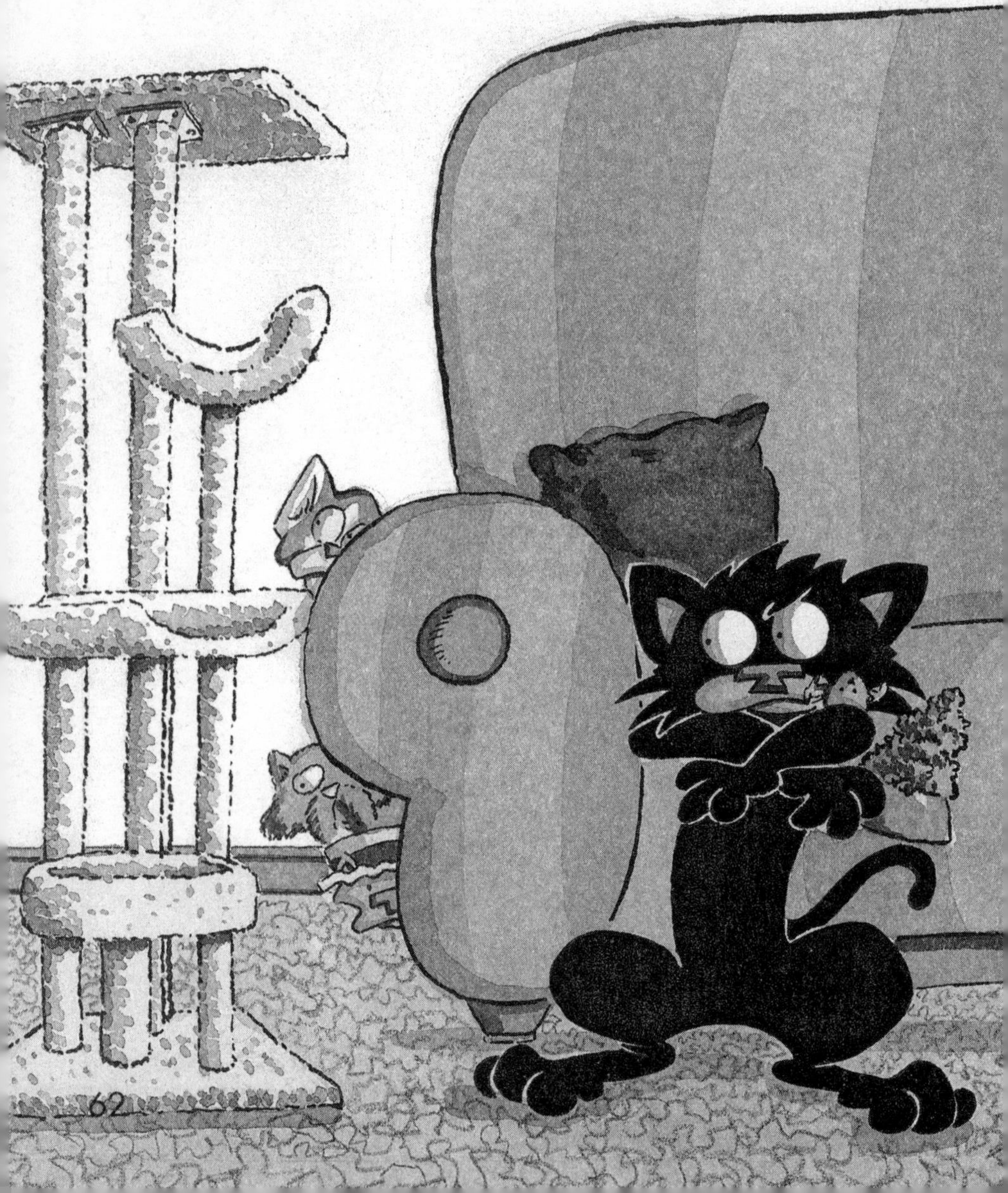

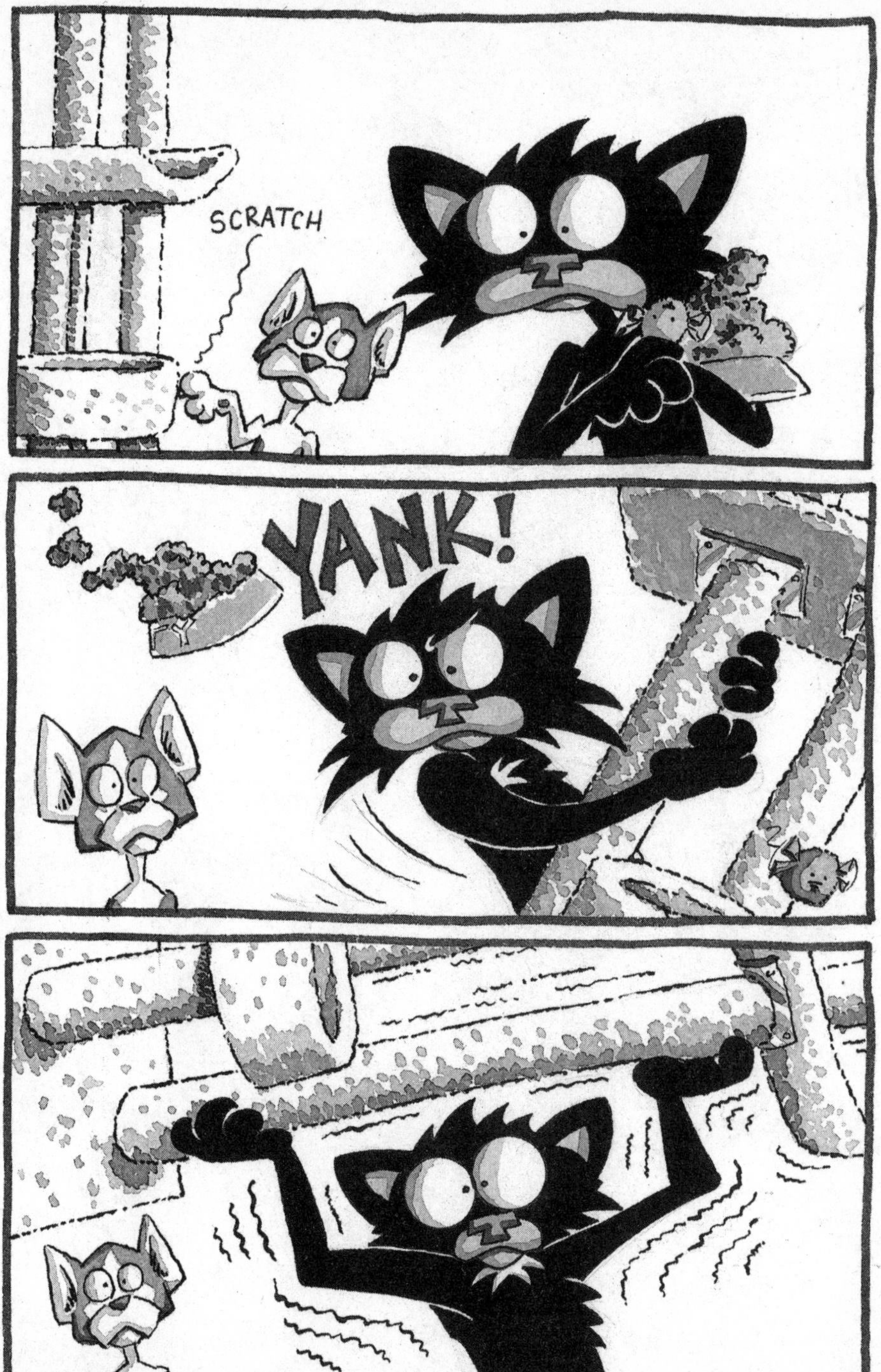
SCRATCH
YANK!

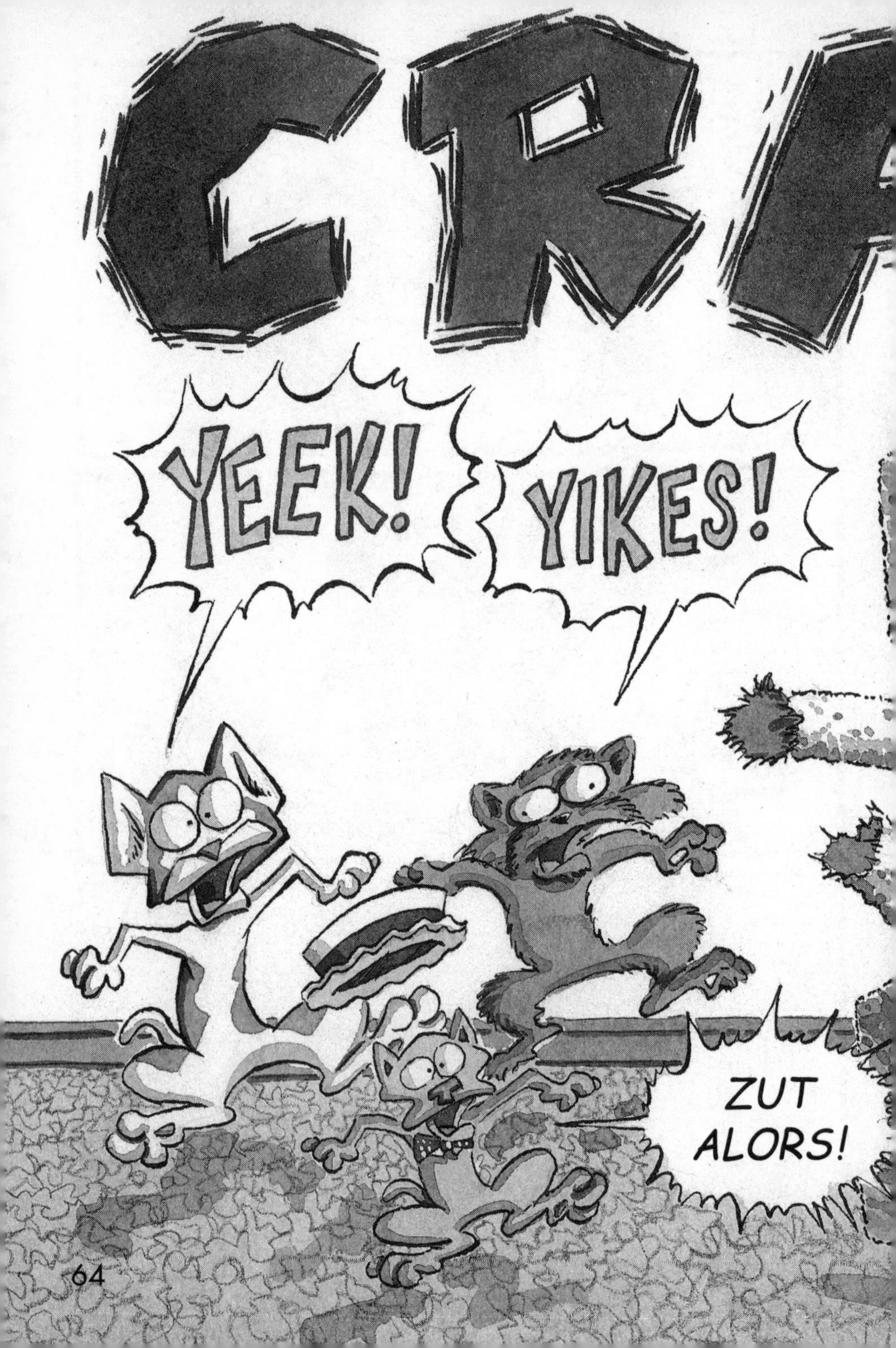
CRA
YEEK!
YIKES!
ZUT
ALORS!

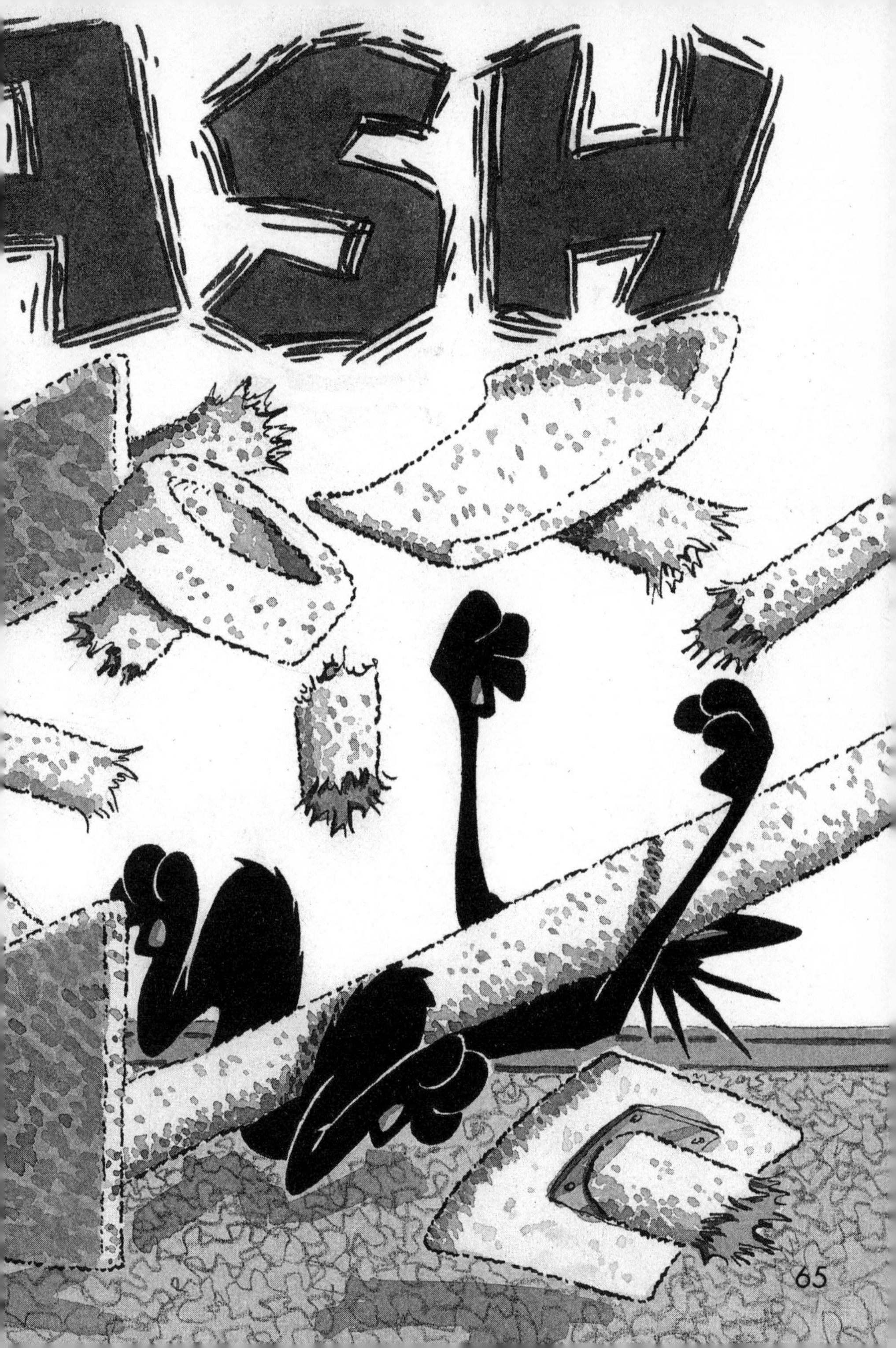
SH

KITTY!

Look at what you just did!

You destroyed your cat tree AND you scared the kittens. All this, just because you don't want to share.

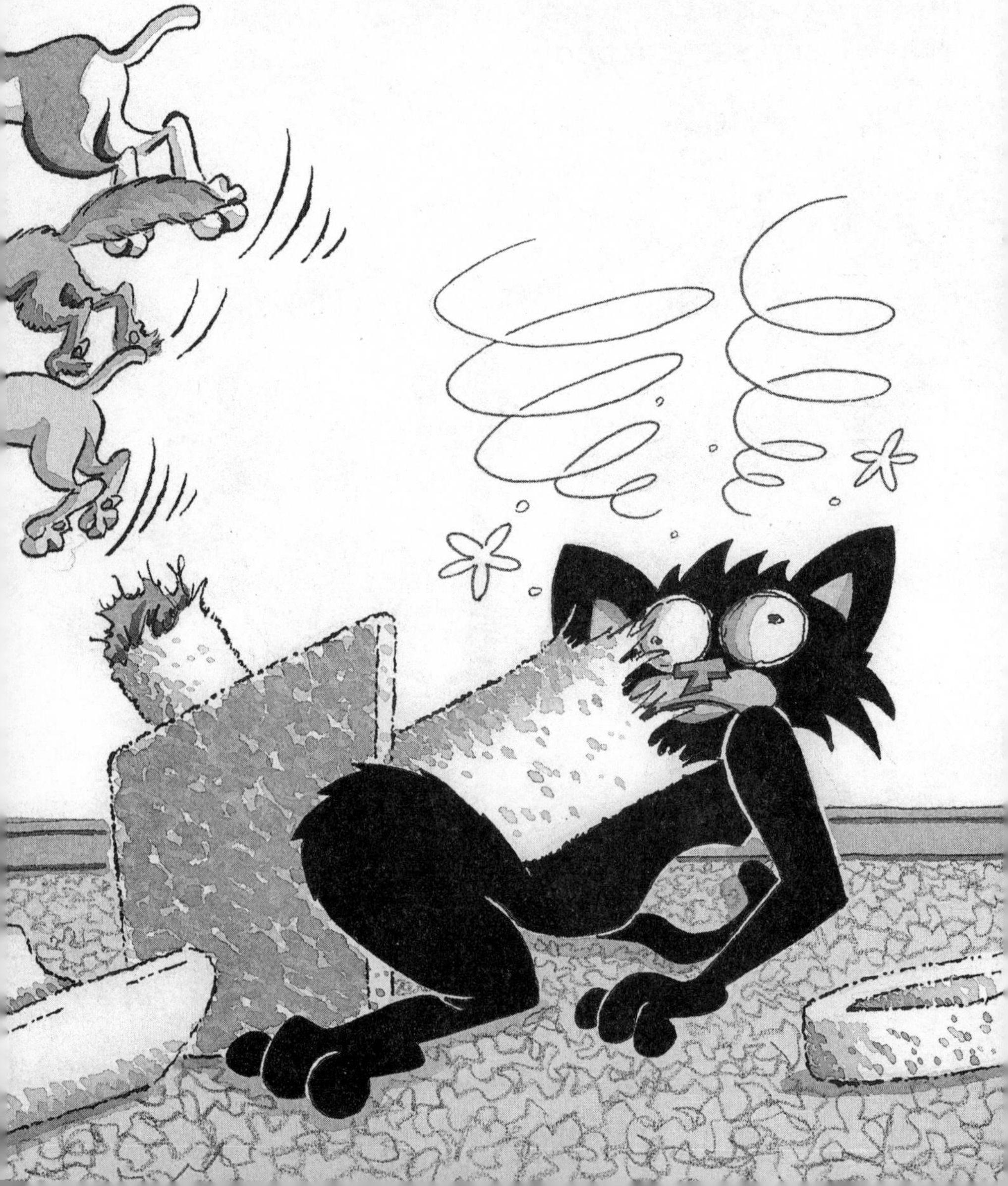

Kitty, I know sharing is not easy for you. It's not always easy for ANYONE. But you have to remember that these kittens come from a place of terrible conflict. Most of what they own was destroyed. Plus, loud noises can be especially frightening to them.

Now get up and help me find these kittens so we can make them feel safe again.

THREE HOURS LATER

Kitty, the kittens have been missing for hours and you still haven't lifted a claw to help me find them! I've looked everywhere. They're very good at hiding. Living in a neighborhood with so much conflict has taught them how to hide from danger very well.

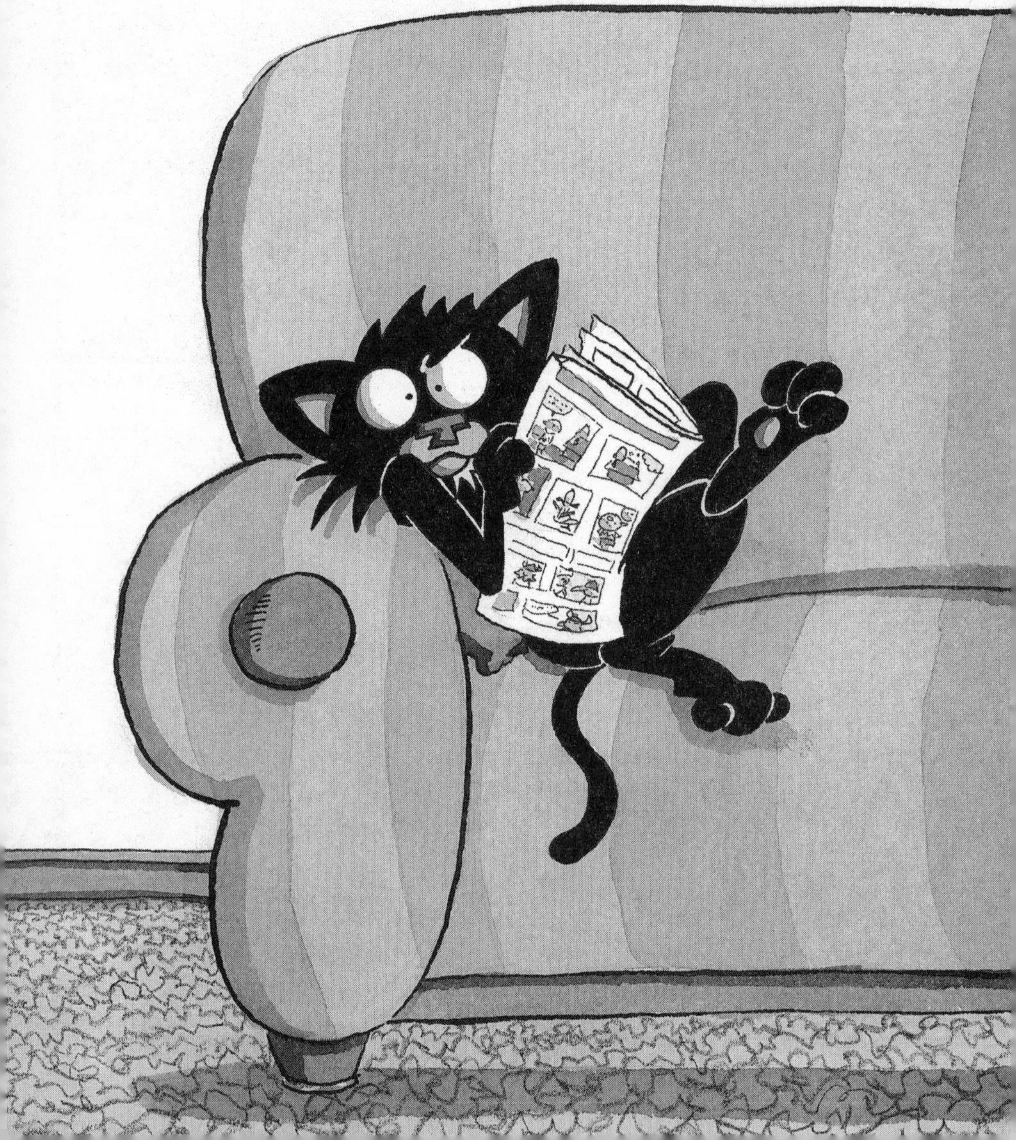

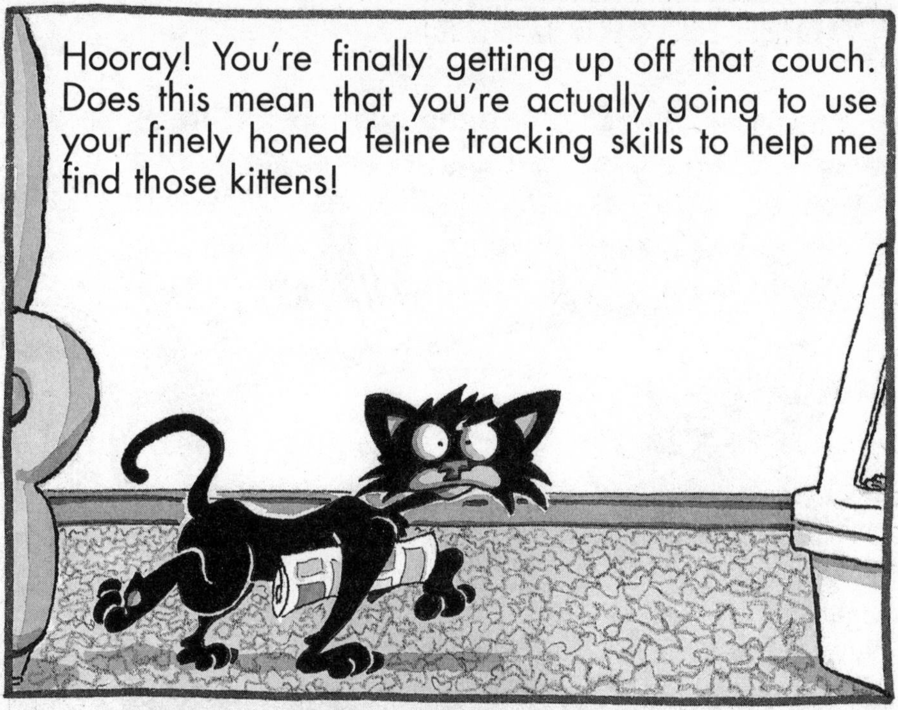
Hooray! You're finally getting up off that couch. Does this mean that you're actually going to use your finely honed feline tracking skills to help me find those kittens!

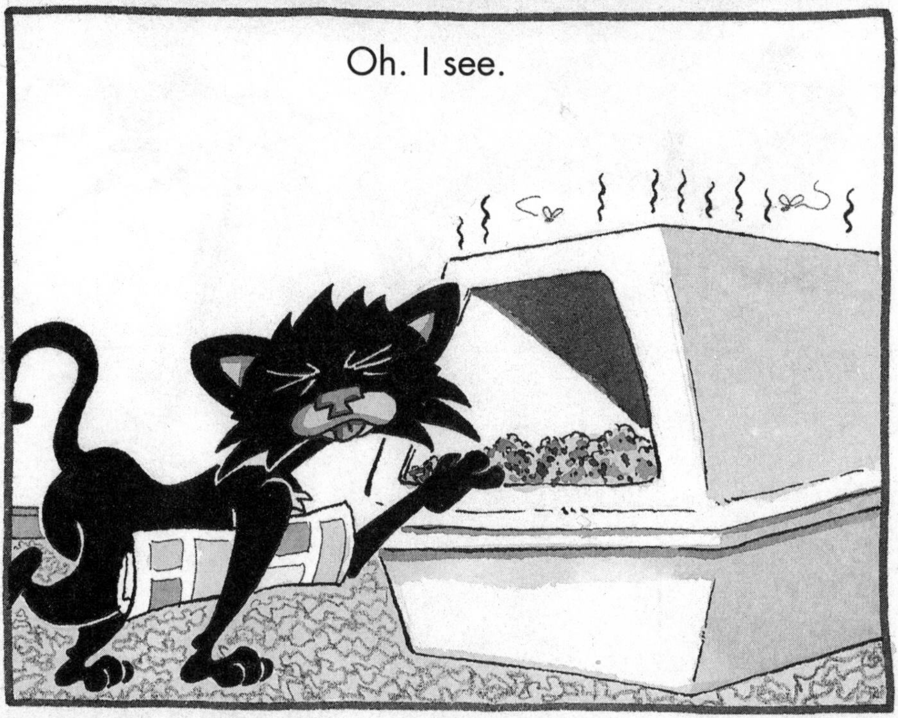
Oh. I see.

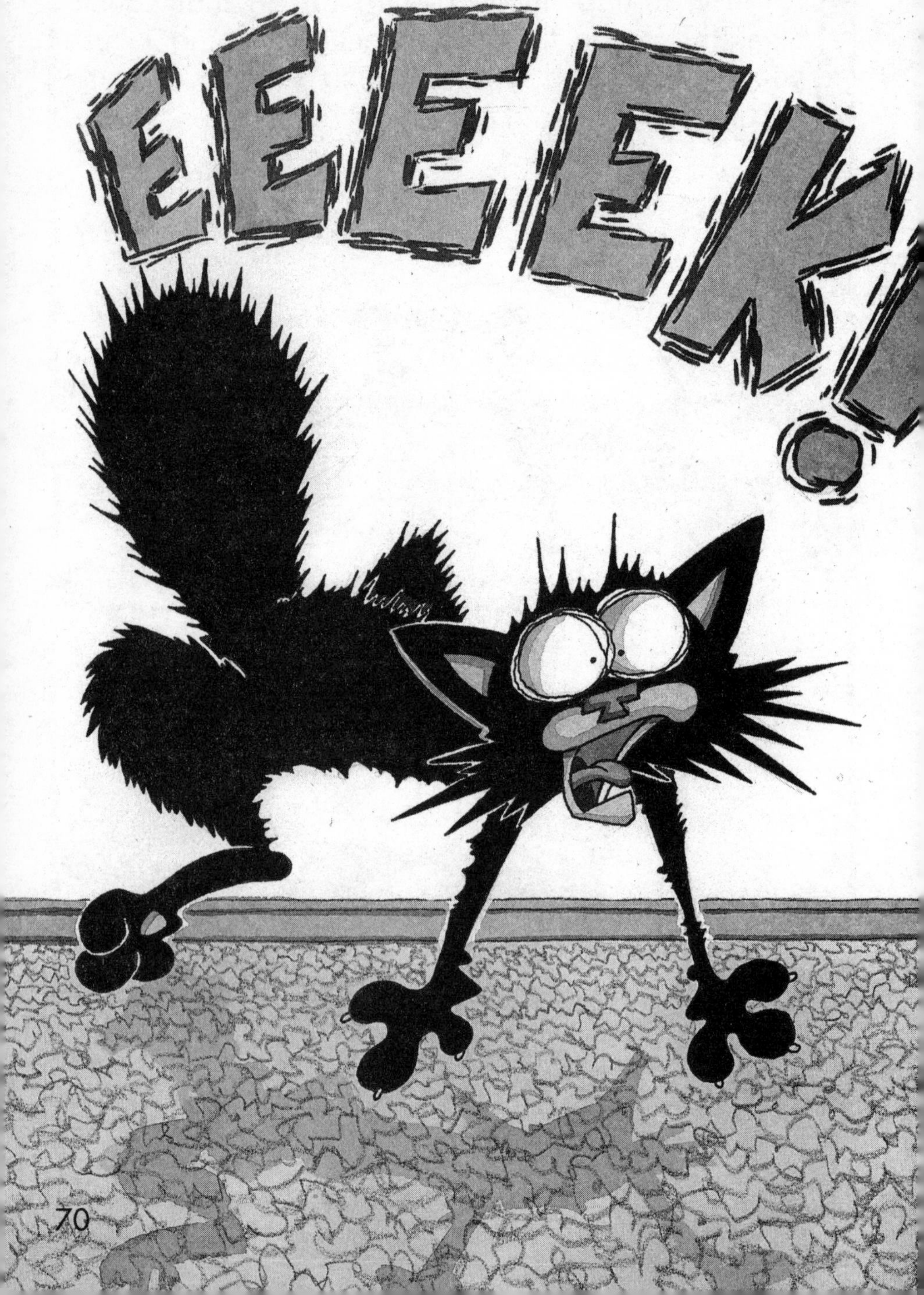
EEEEK!

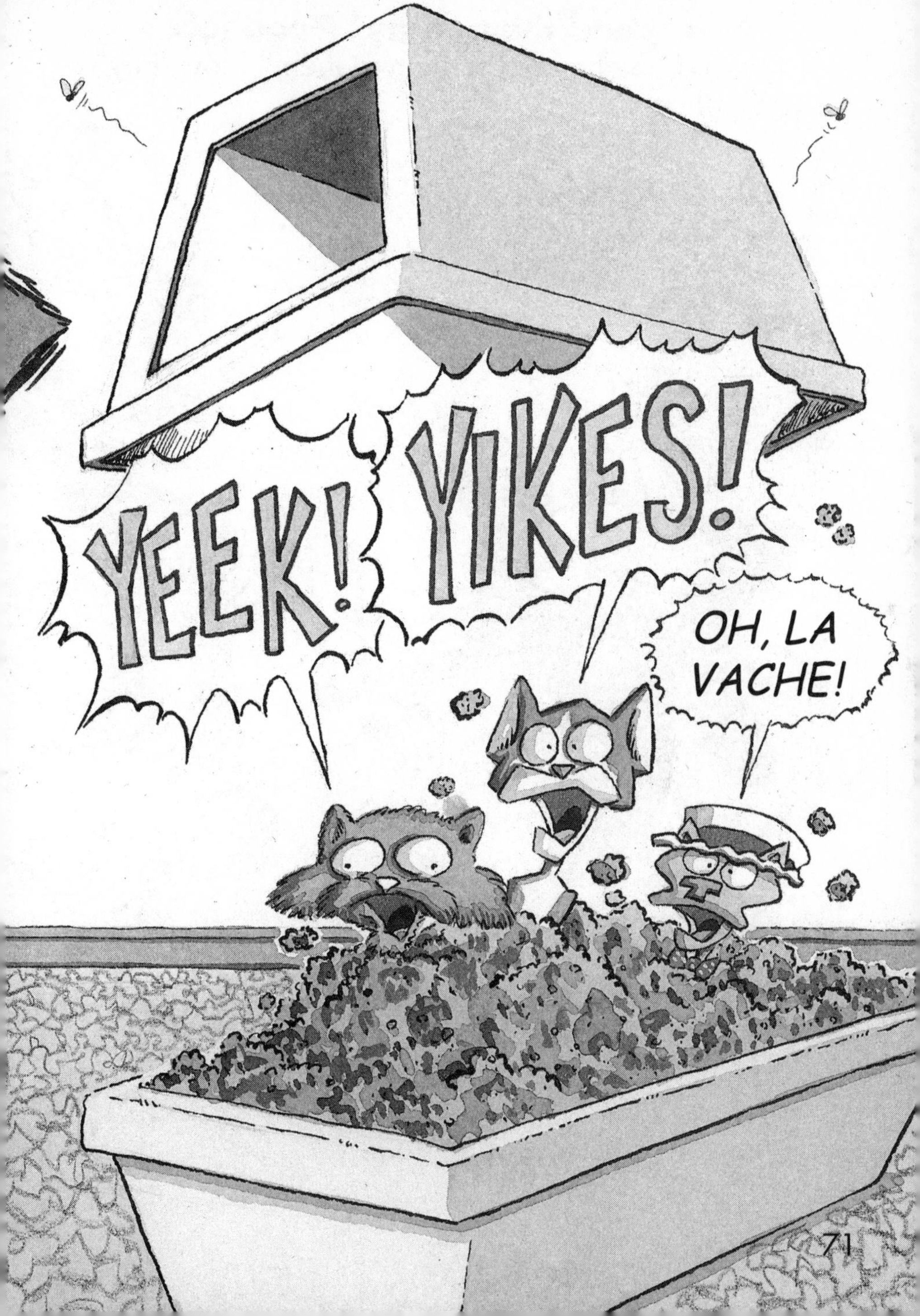
YEEK!
YIKES!
OH, LA VACHE!

You found them, Kitty! Good job!
But why did you have to scream at them? Now they've run off yet again.

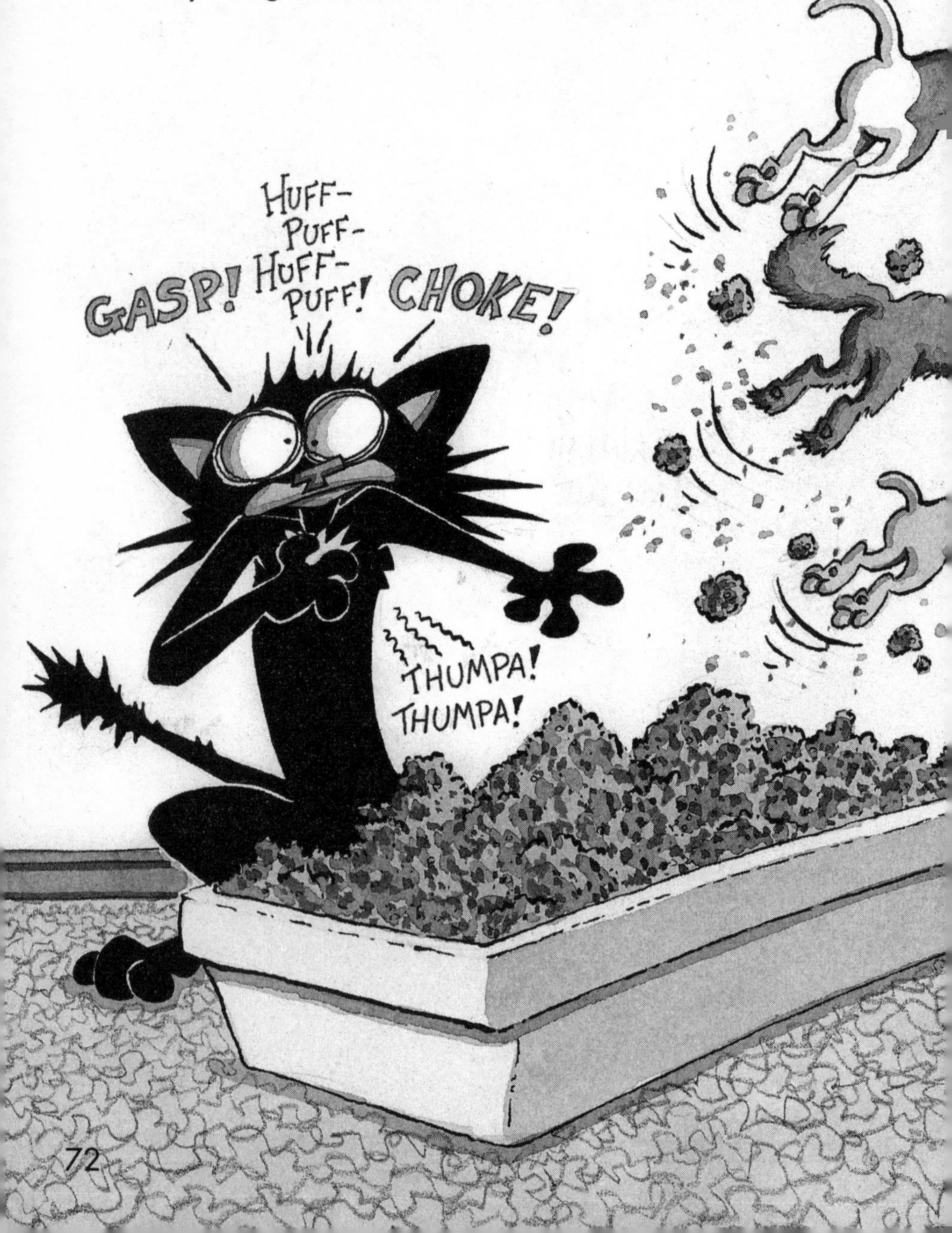
HUFF-
PUFF-
GASP!
HUFF-
PUFF!
CHOKE!
THUMPA!
THUMPA!

That does it! You've forced my hand, Kitty. I'm calling in good ol' **Uncle Murray**. He's the nicest guy we know, and he's going to show you the proper way to treat our guests.

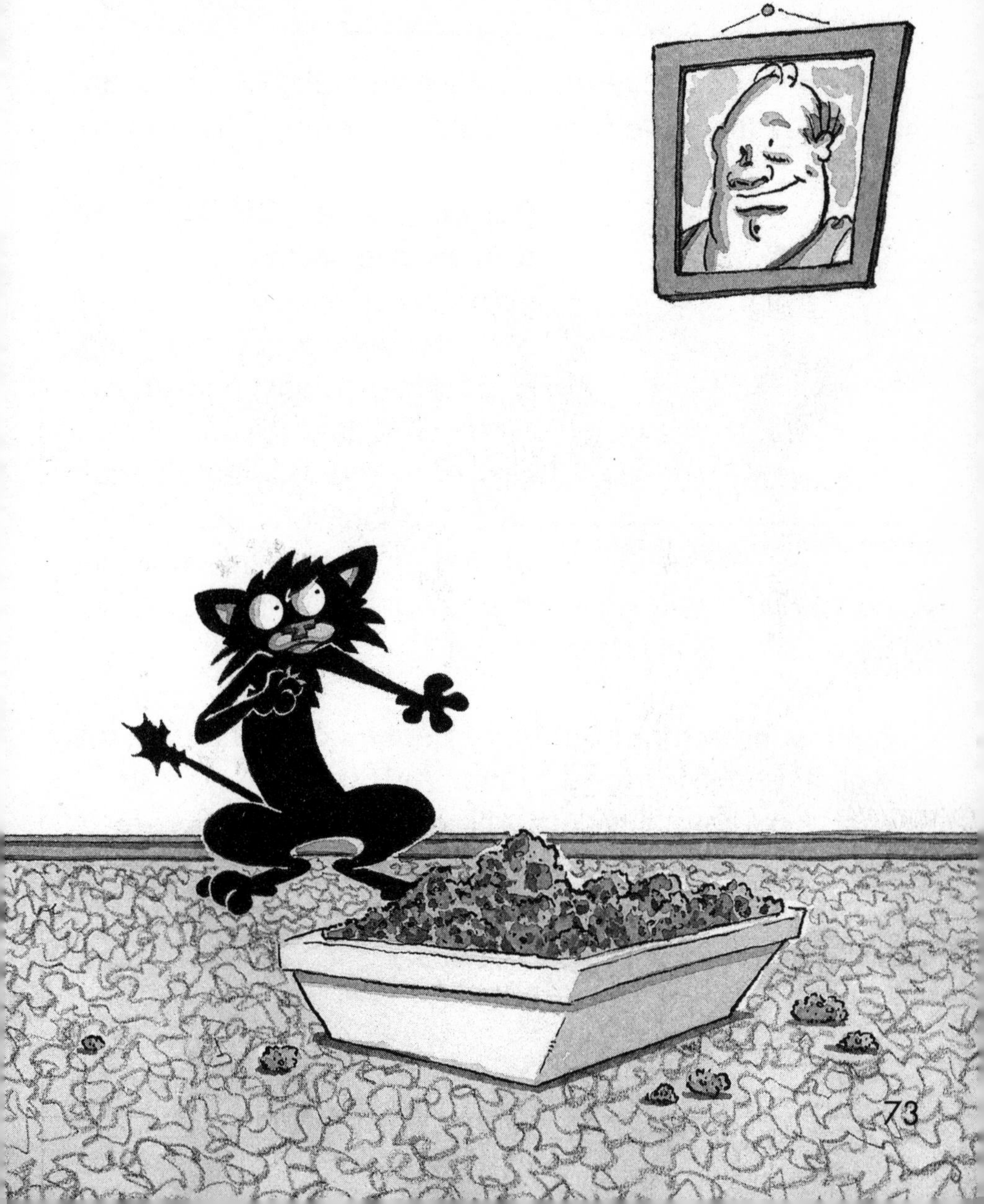

UNCLE MURRAY'S FUN FACTS

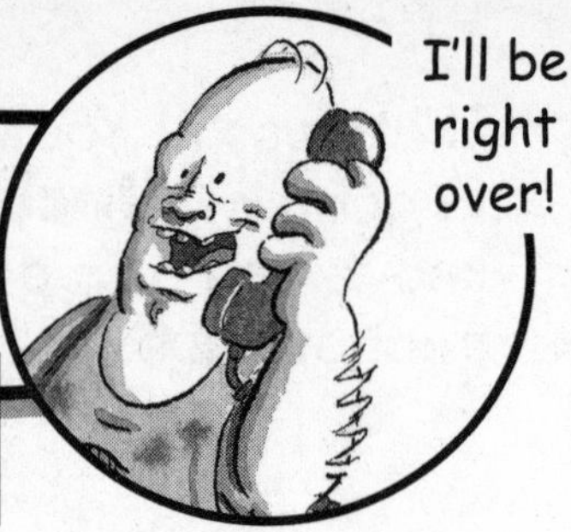
I'll be right over!

DO CATS EVER LIVE IN GROUPS?

Cats are typically independent animals, which means that they are quite comfortable living all by themselves.

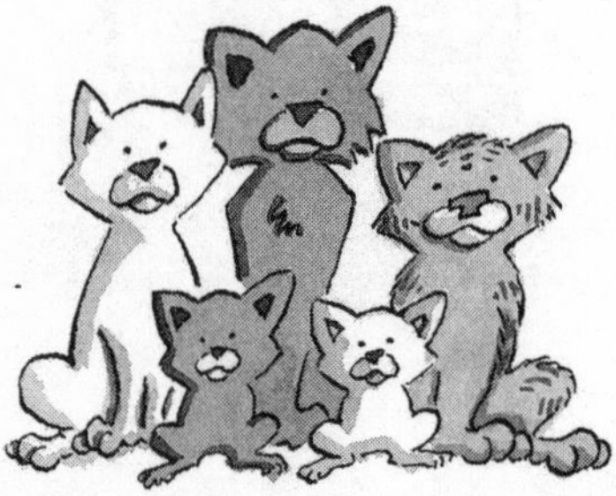

Female cats living in a group

Do cats ever CHOOSE to live in a group?
Sometimes, in the wild, a group of cats will gather together and form a colony, also known as a "clowder." Usually, these clowders are all female cats who collectively take care of their kittens. Interestingly, no one cat will be in charge. Unlike with dog packs, no one cat is the "alpha" cat.

But it's important to note that each cat in the clowder will still hunt for food alone. And if food is scarce, then the cats will become competitive with each other to protect their food and their kittens.

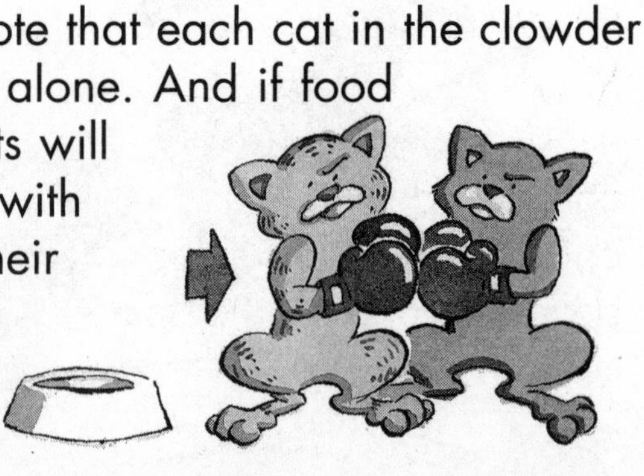

No Food ➡ Conflict!

Lots of Food ➡ **No Conflict**

On the other hand, if food is plentiful, perhaps because a human is feeding the entire clowder, then the need to be territorial and protective is removed and the whole clowder lives in relative peace and harmony.

What if one of the kittens in the clowder is a male?

If a kitten is male, he'll live among the female cats until he matures and becomes an adult cat. Then he'll move out to be on his own.

Then what?

Male cats tend to live by themselves. They might live NEAR a female clowder, but they don't live among them, and they don't like to live with other male cats. This is because male cats can be VERY territorial. In fact, the territory of a male cat can be as much as ten times larger than that of a clowder of females.

As far as wild cats are concerned, it's the male cats that have a harder time sharing than the females.

SCRATCH
SCRATCH

Male cat living by himself.

•CHAPTER FOUR•

GOOD OL' UNCLE MURRAY

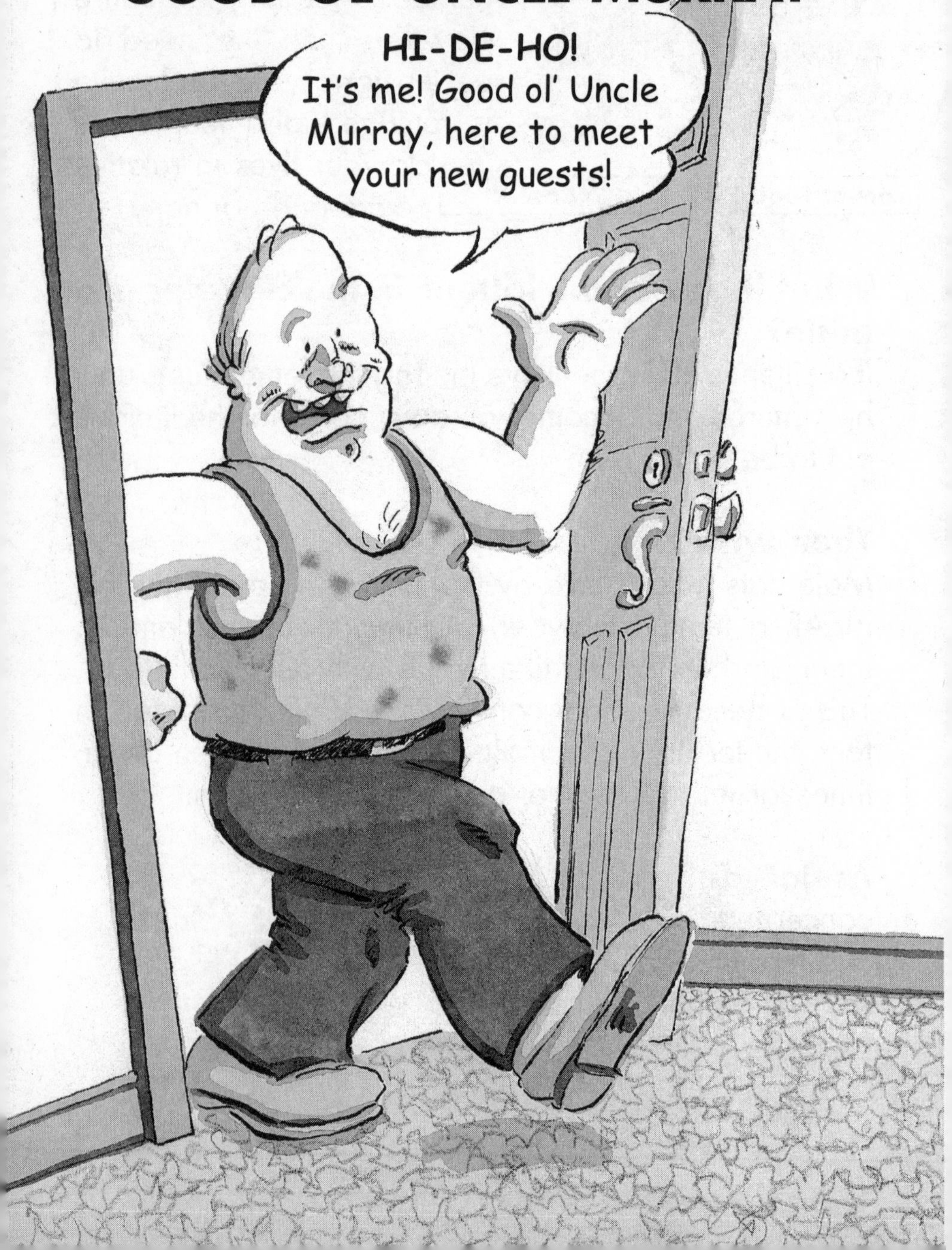
HI-DE-HO!
It's me! Good ol' Uncle Murray, here to meet your new guests!

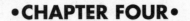

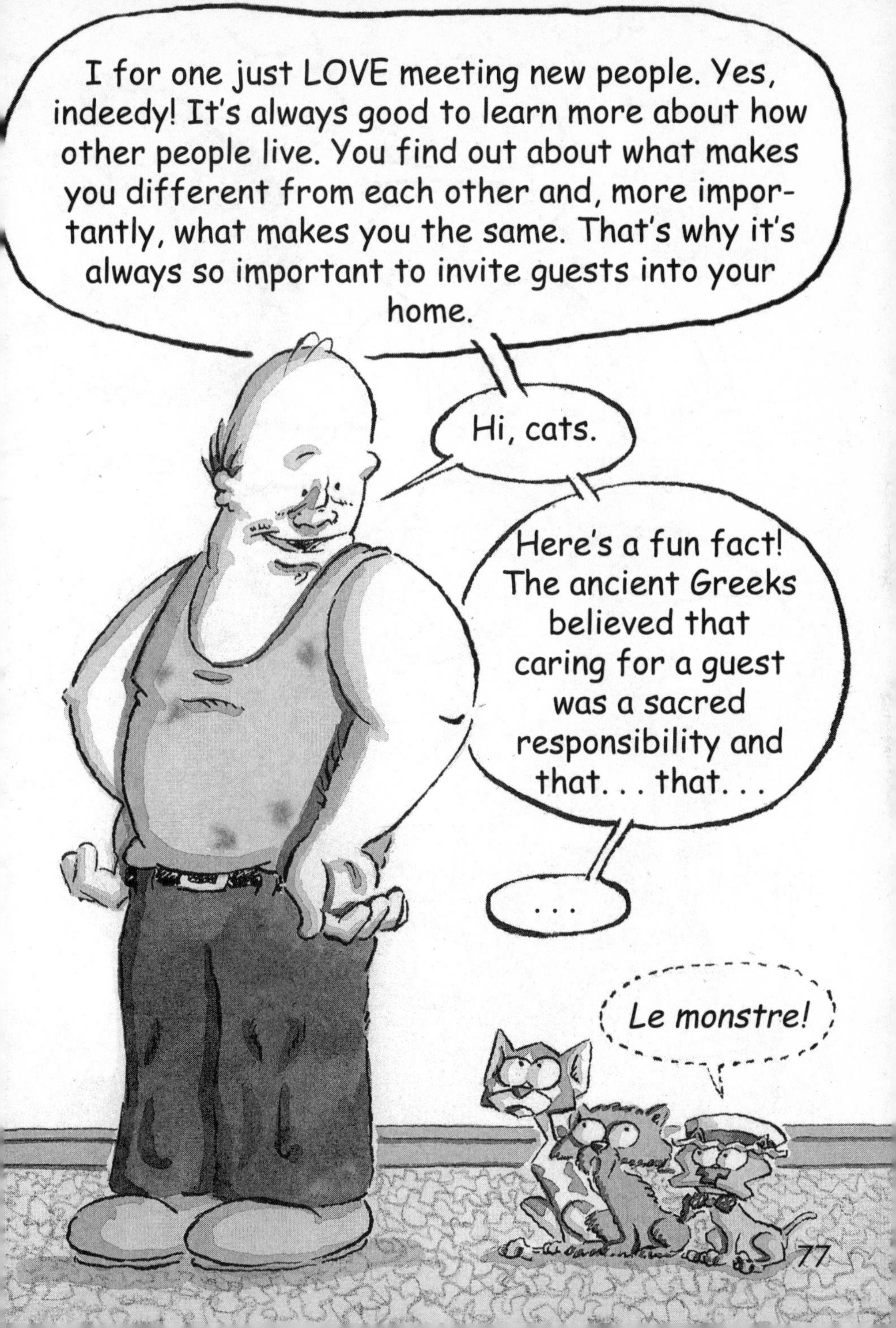
I for one just LOVE meeting new people. Yes, indeedy! It's always good to learn more about how other people live. You find out about what makes you different from each other and, more importantly, what makes you the same. That's why it's always so important to invite guests into your home.
Hi, cats.
Here's a fun fact! The ancient Greeks believed that caring for a guest was a sacred responsibility and that. . . that. . .
. . .
Le monstre!

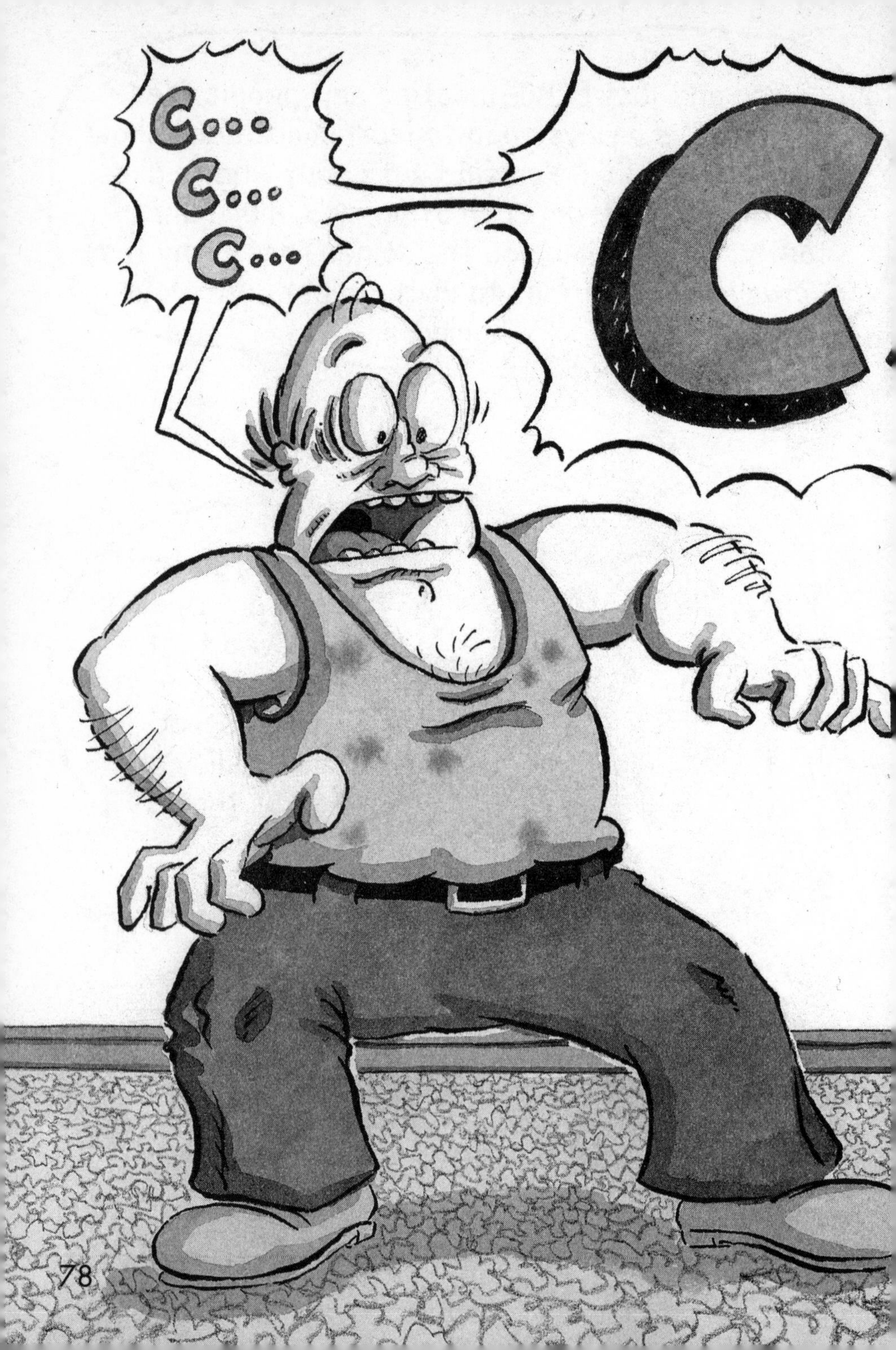
C... C... C...
C

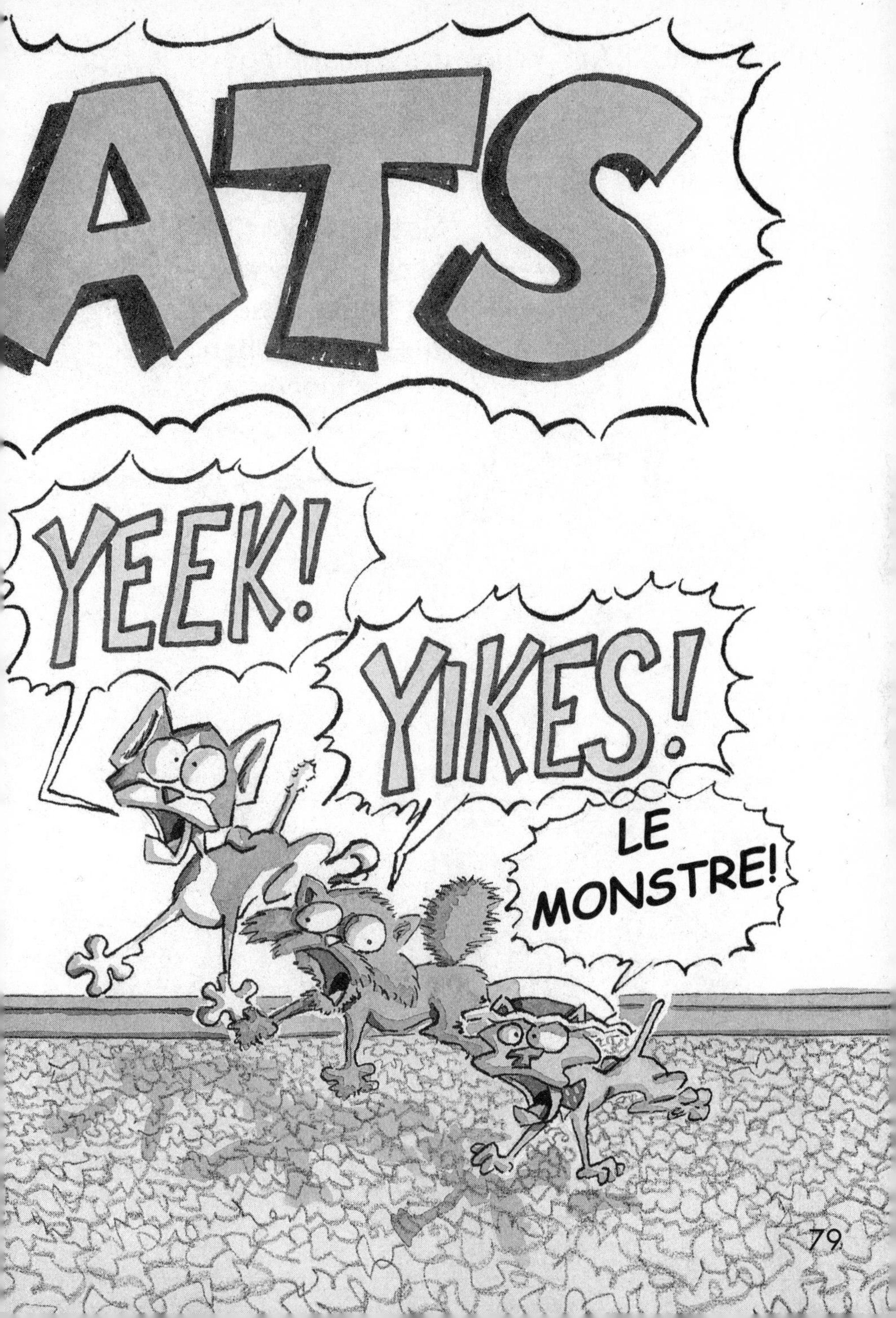
ATS
YEEK!
YIKES!
LE MONSTRE!

UNCLE MURRAY! What are you doing?! I just got those kittens to feel safe again, and then you started screaming!

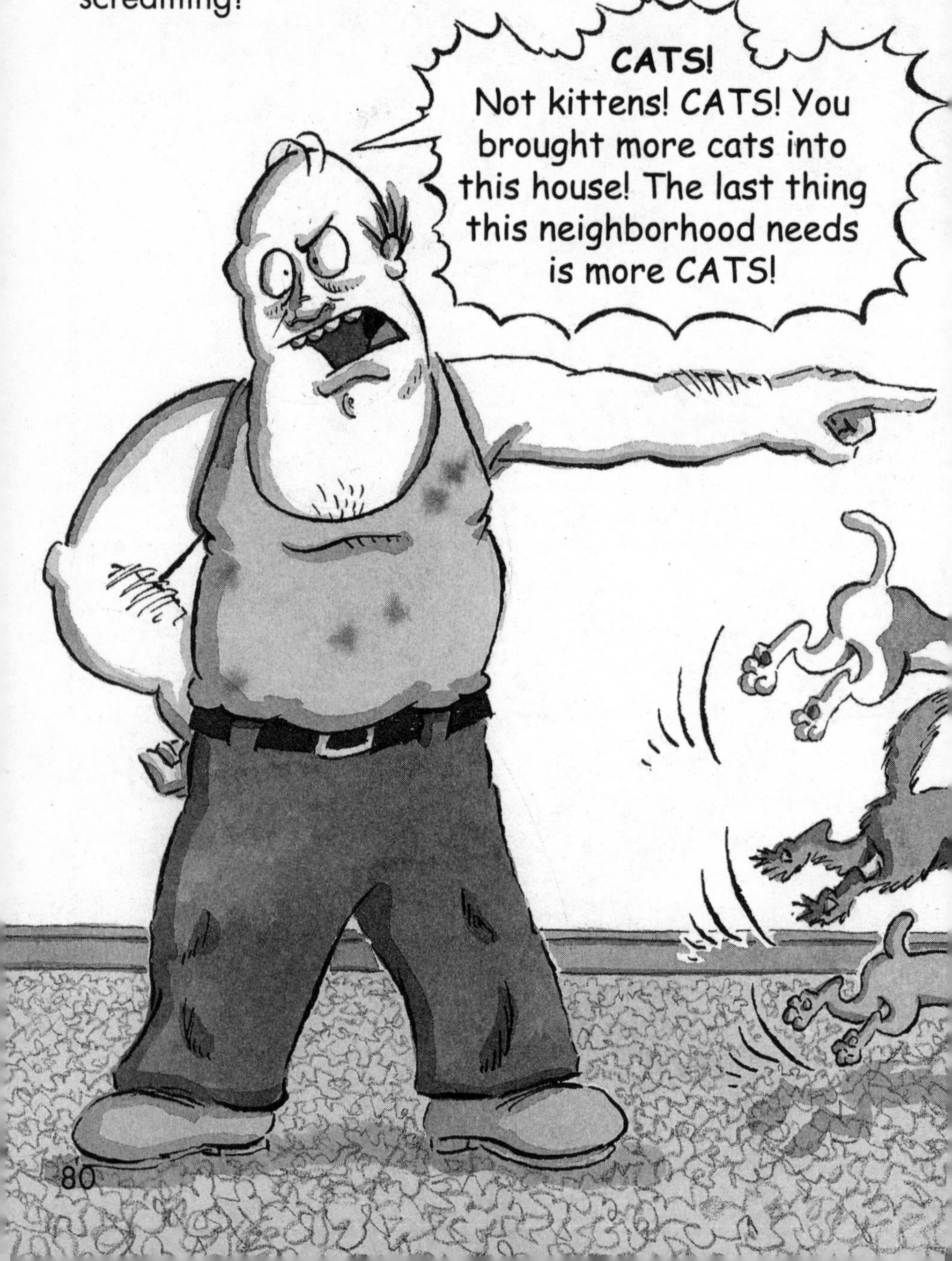
CATS!
Not kittens! CATS! You brought more cats into this house! The last thing this neighborhood needs is more CATS!

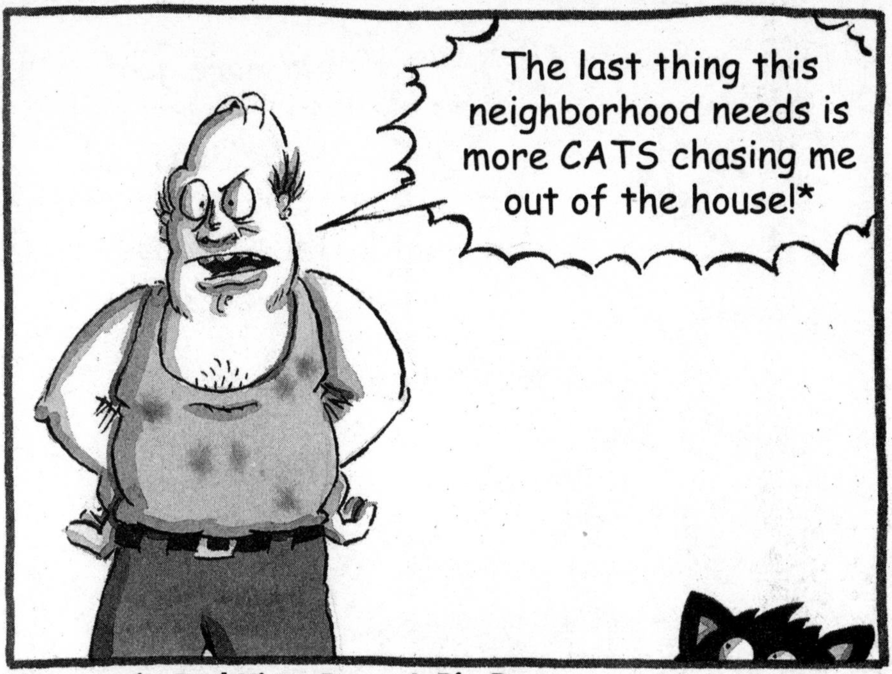
The last thing this neighborhood needs is more CATS chasing me out of the house!*

*As seen in ***Bad Kitty: Puppy's Big Day.***

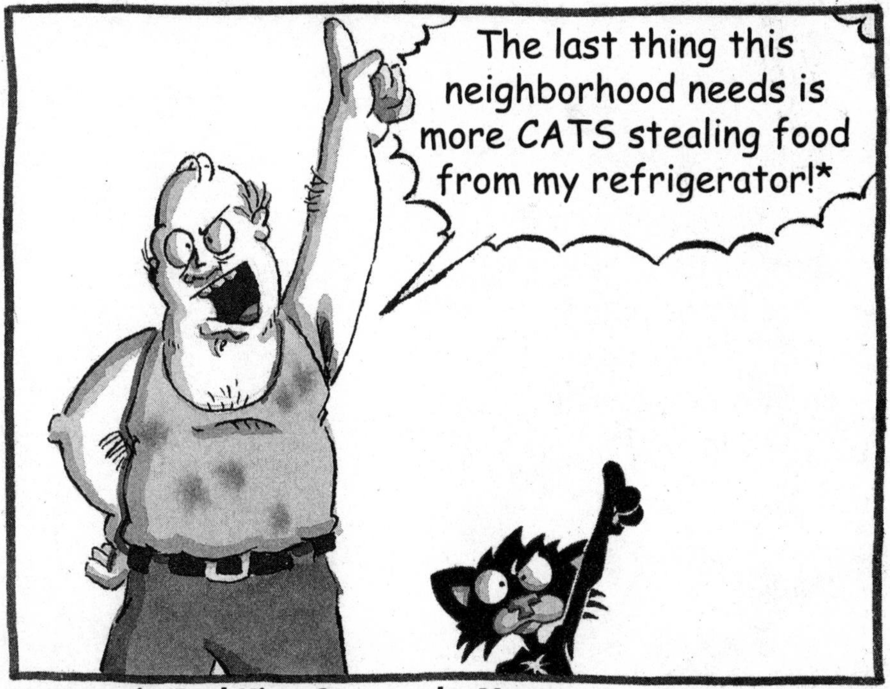
The last thing this neighborhood needs is more CATS stealing food from my refrigerator!*

*As seen in ***Bad Kitty Goes to the Vet.***

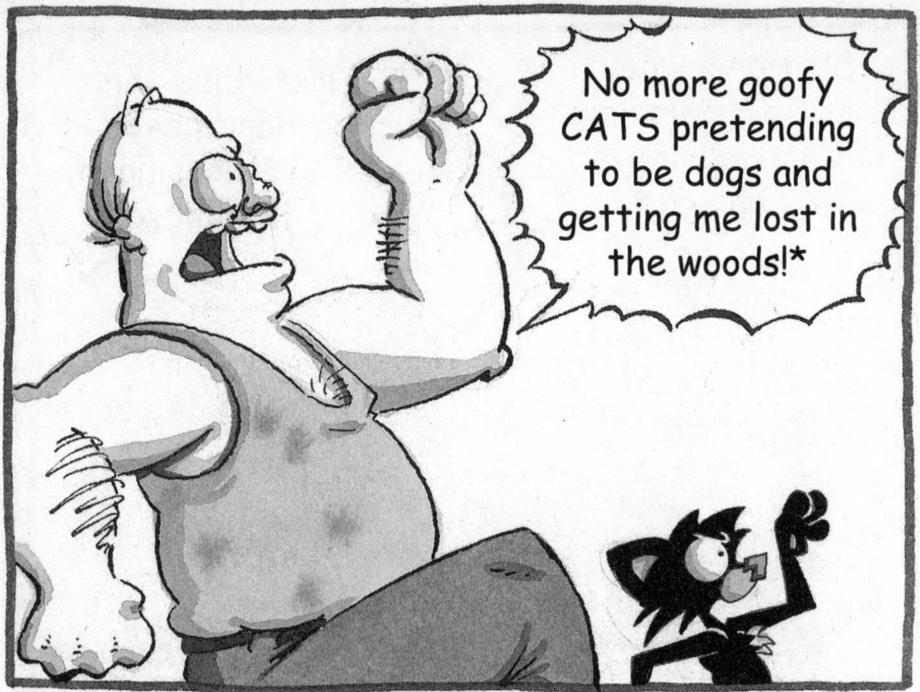
No more goofy CATS pretending to be dogs and getting me lost in the woods!*

*As seen in ***Bad Kitty: Camp Daze.***

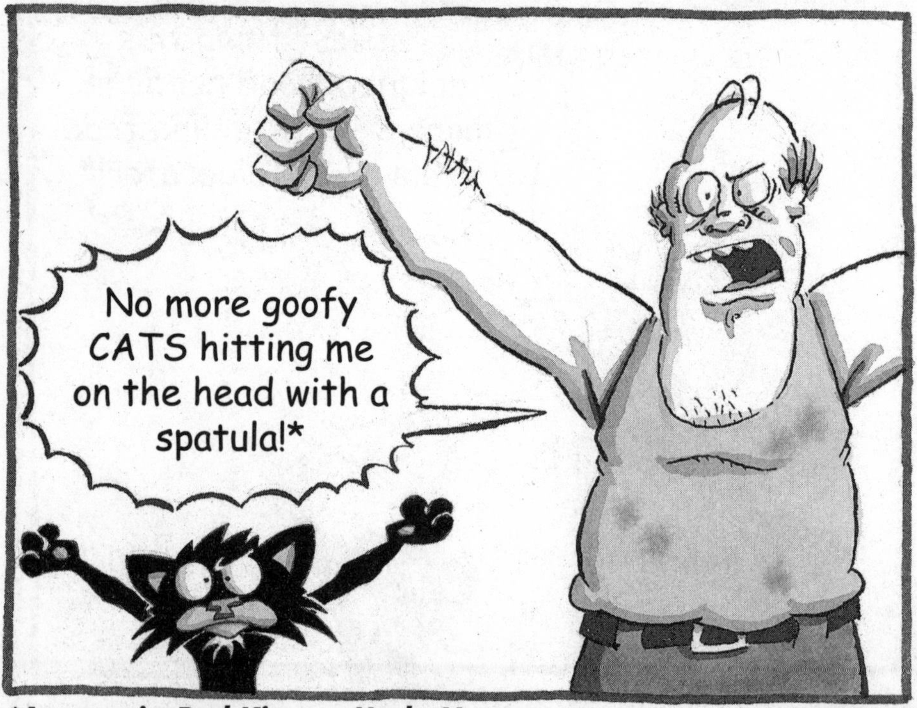
No more goofy CATS hitting me on the head with a spatula!*

*As seen in ***Bad Kitty vs Uncle Murray.***

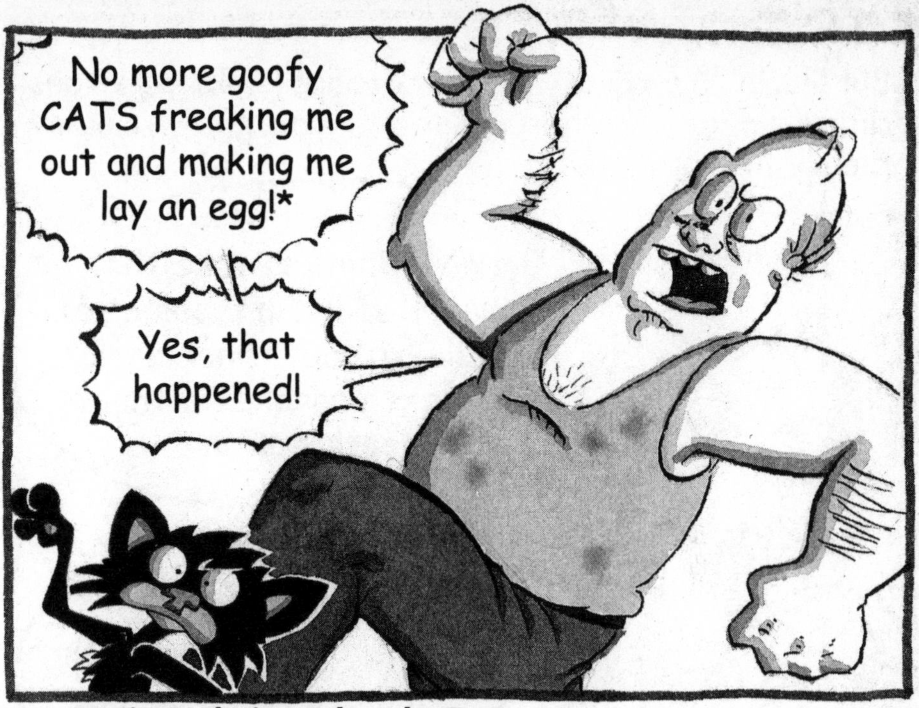
No more goofy CATS freaking me out and making me lay an egg!*
Yes, that happened!

*As seen in ***Bad Kitty Takes the Test.***

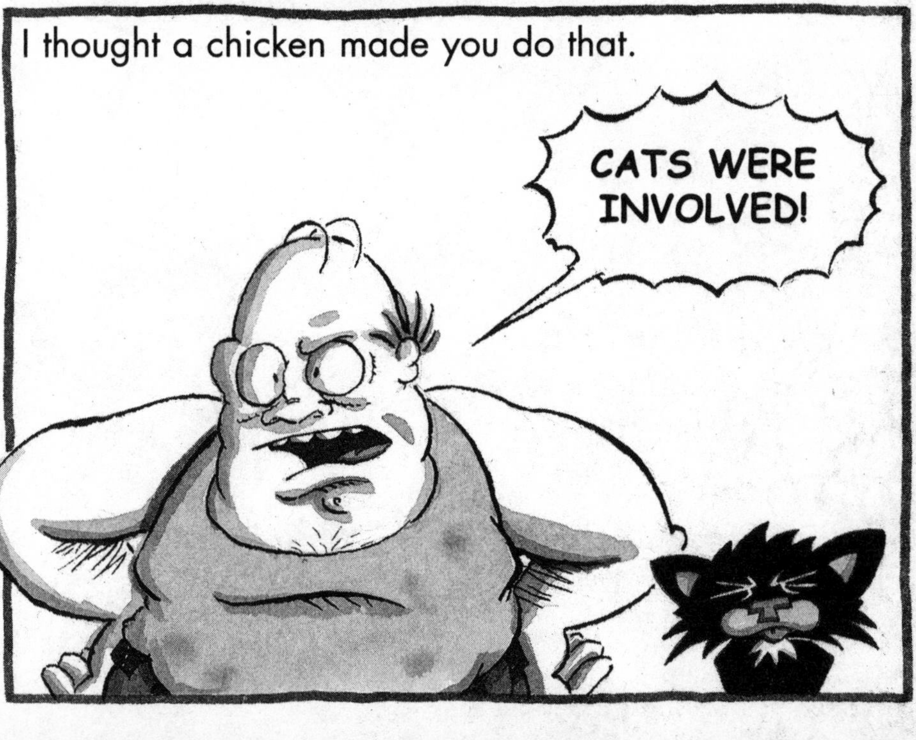
I thought a chicken made you do that.
CATS WERE INVOLVED!

But Uncle Murray, try to be reasonable. These kittens didn't do any of those things to you. They're completely innocent.

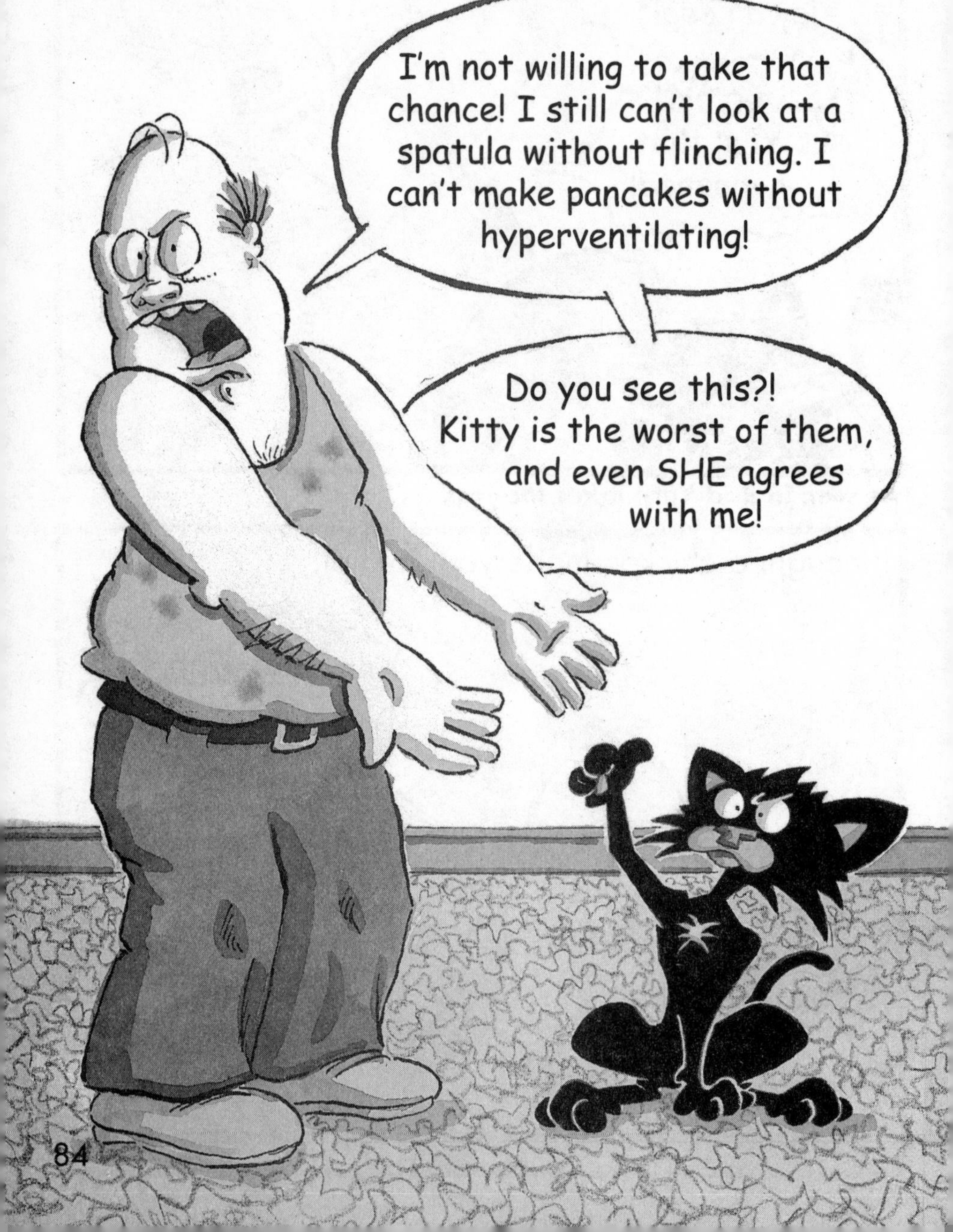
I'm not willing to take that chance! I still can't look at a spatula without flinching. I can't make pancakes without hyperventilating!
Do you see this?! Kitty is the worst of them, and even SHE agrees with me!

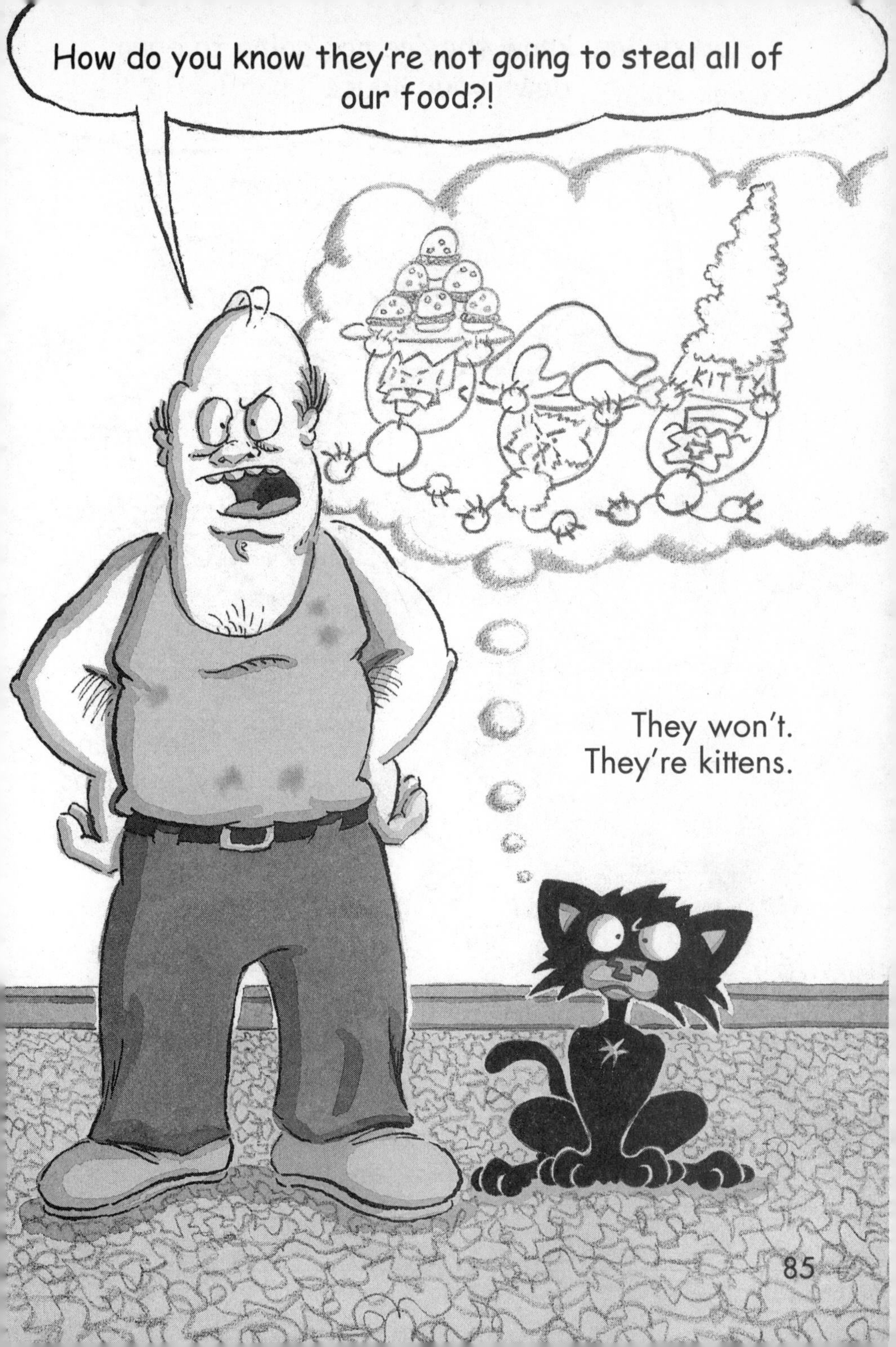
How do you know they're not going to steal all of our food?!
KITTY
They won't.
They're kittens.

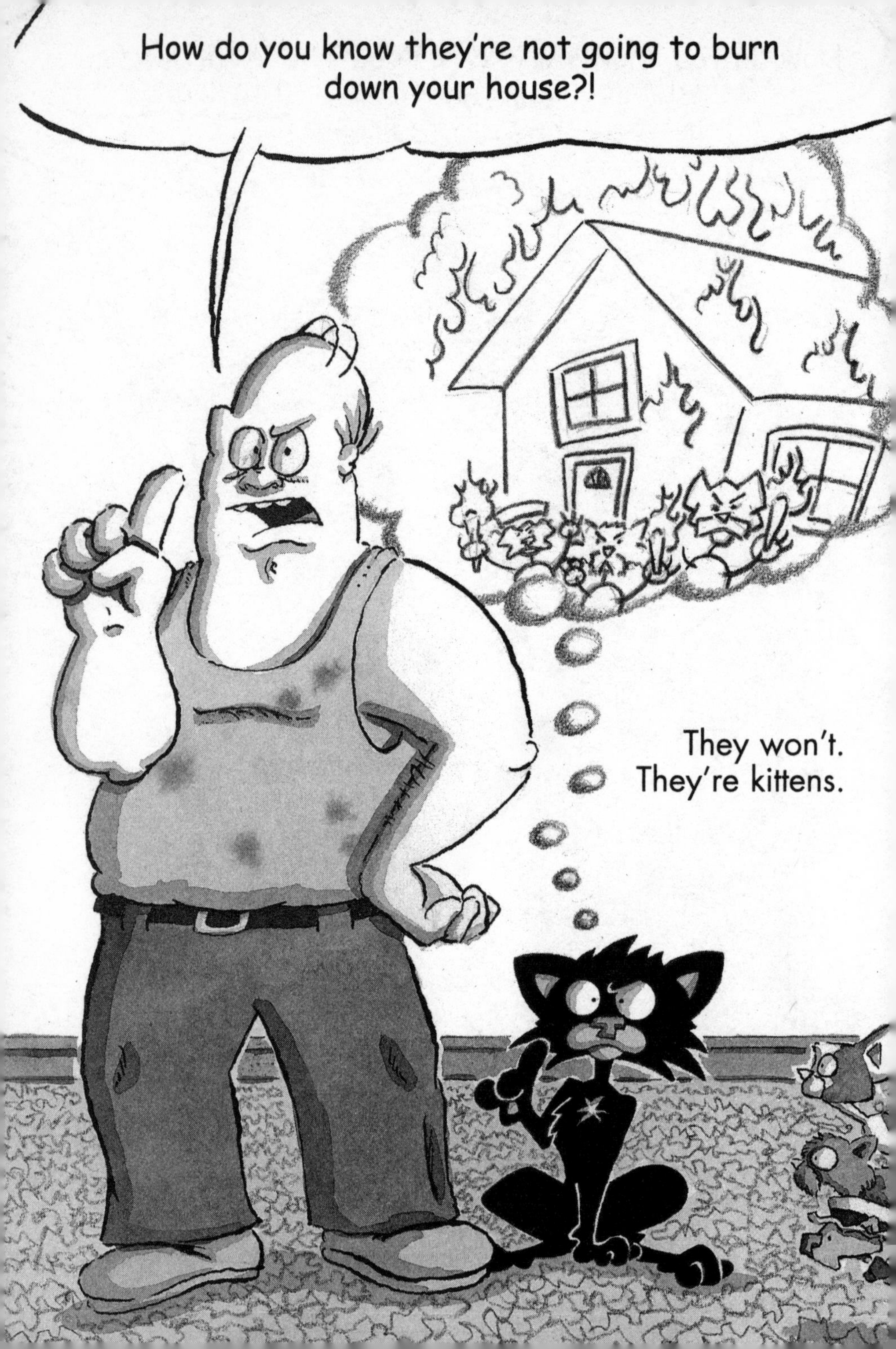
How do you know they're not going to burn down your house?!
They won't. They're kittens.

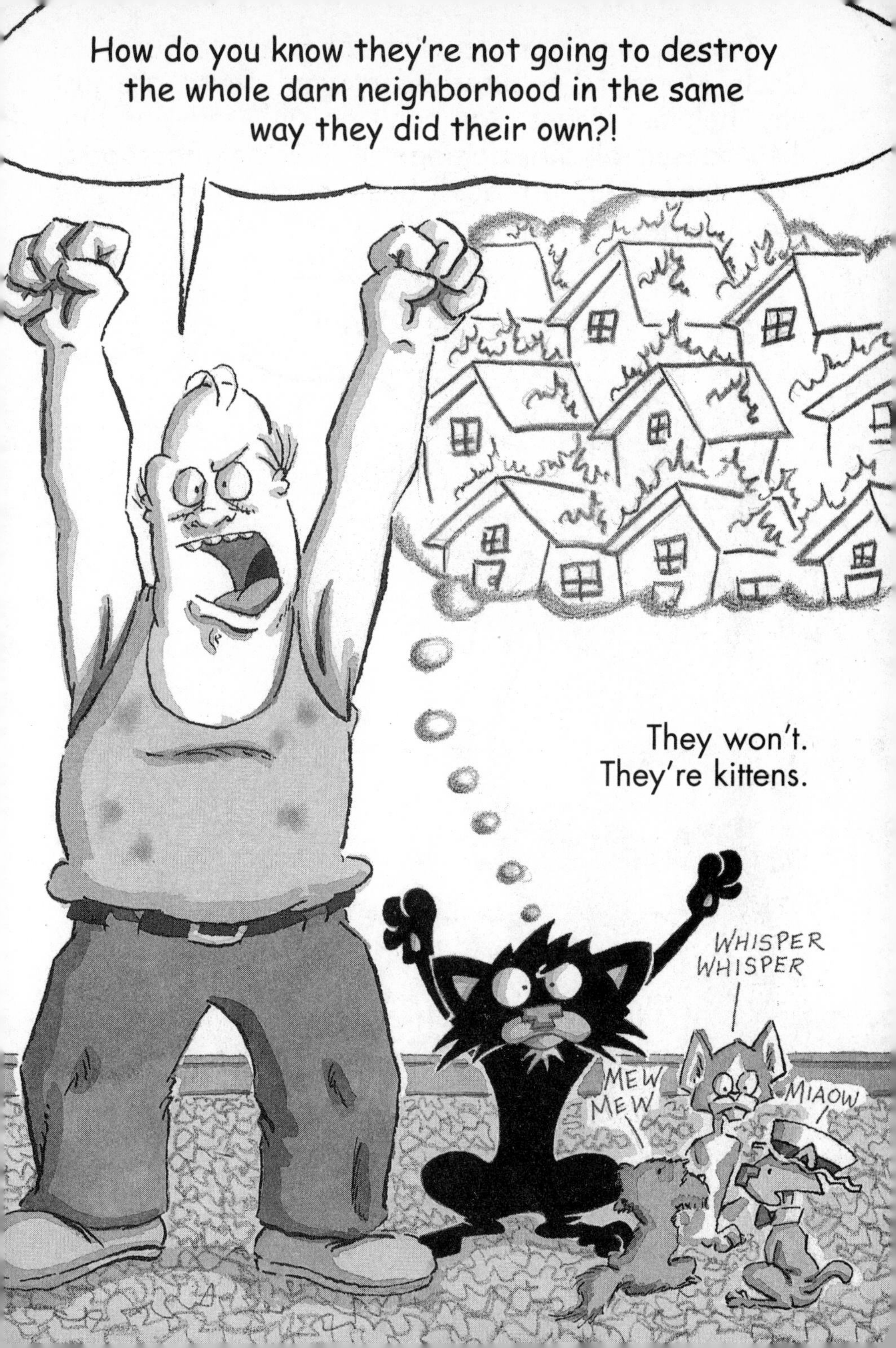
How do you know they're not going to destroy the whole darn neighborhood in the same way they did their own?!
They won't. They're kittens.
WHISPER WHISPER
MEW MEW
MIAOW

Uncle Murray! I'm surprised at you! These are just tiny, helpless kittens. You can't possibly imagine that they caused all that damage in their neighborhood. Everything you just described—that's what they're trying to escape from!

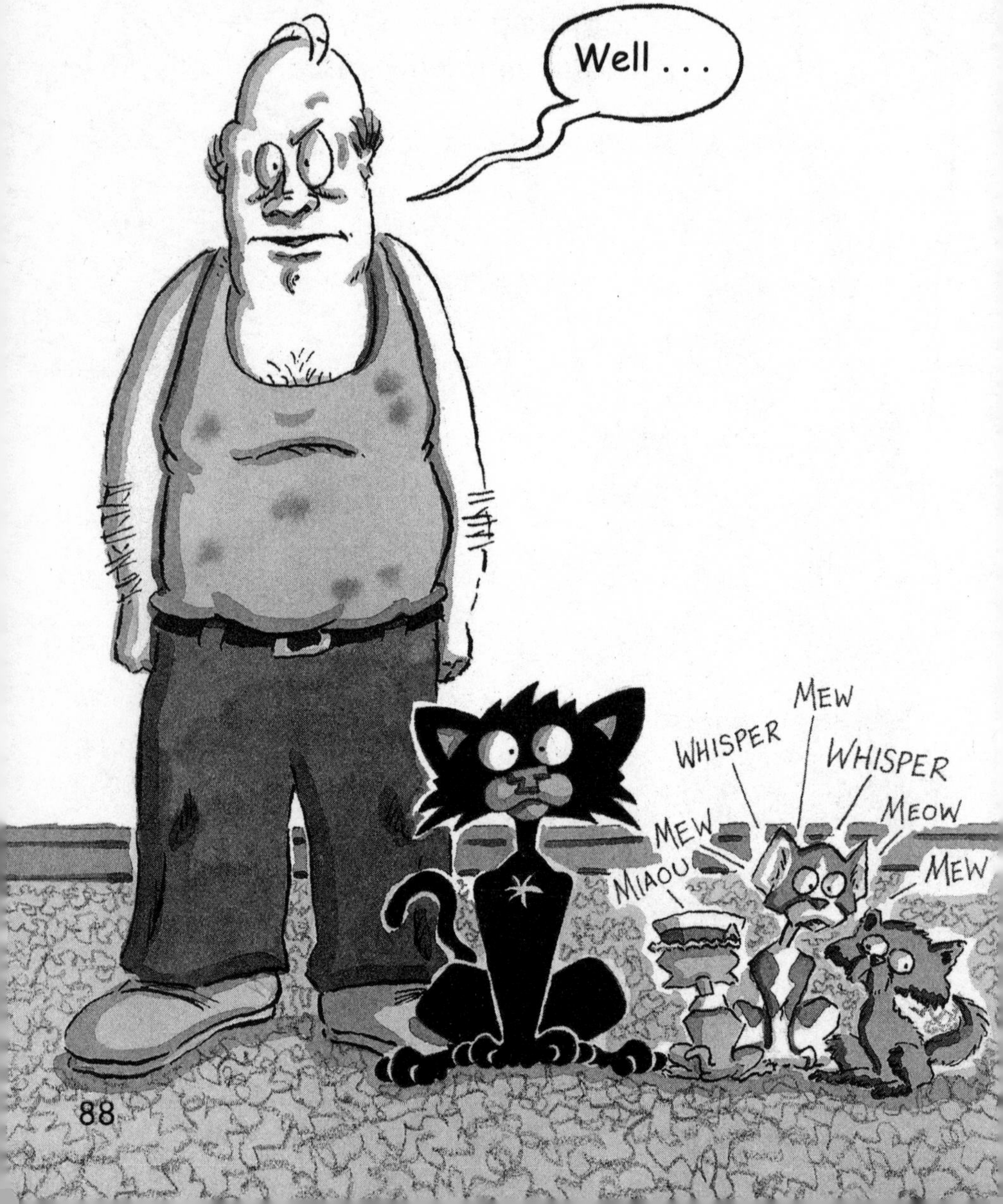
Well . . .
MEW
WHISPER
WHISPER
MEOW
MEW
MIAOU
MEW

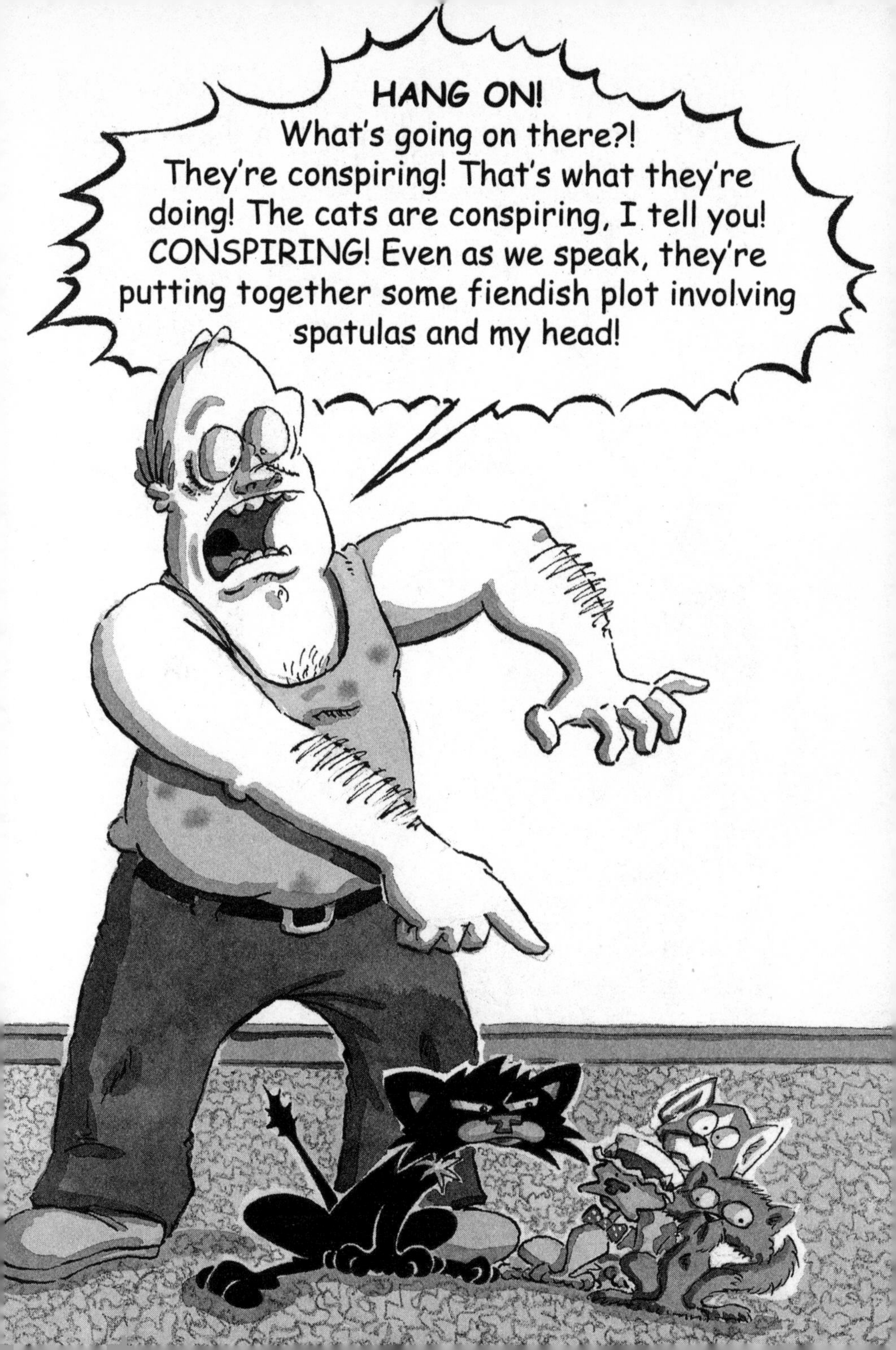
HANG ON!
What's going on there?!
They're conspiring! That's what they're doing! The cats are conspiring, I tell you! CONSPIRING! Even as we speak, they're putting together some fiendish plot involving spatulas and my head!

No, they're not! My goodness! I don't know why you're so afraid of these kittens when they've done nothing to harm you.

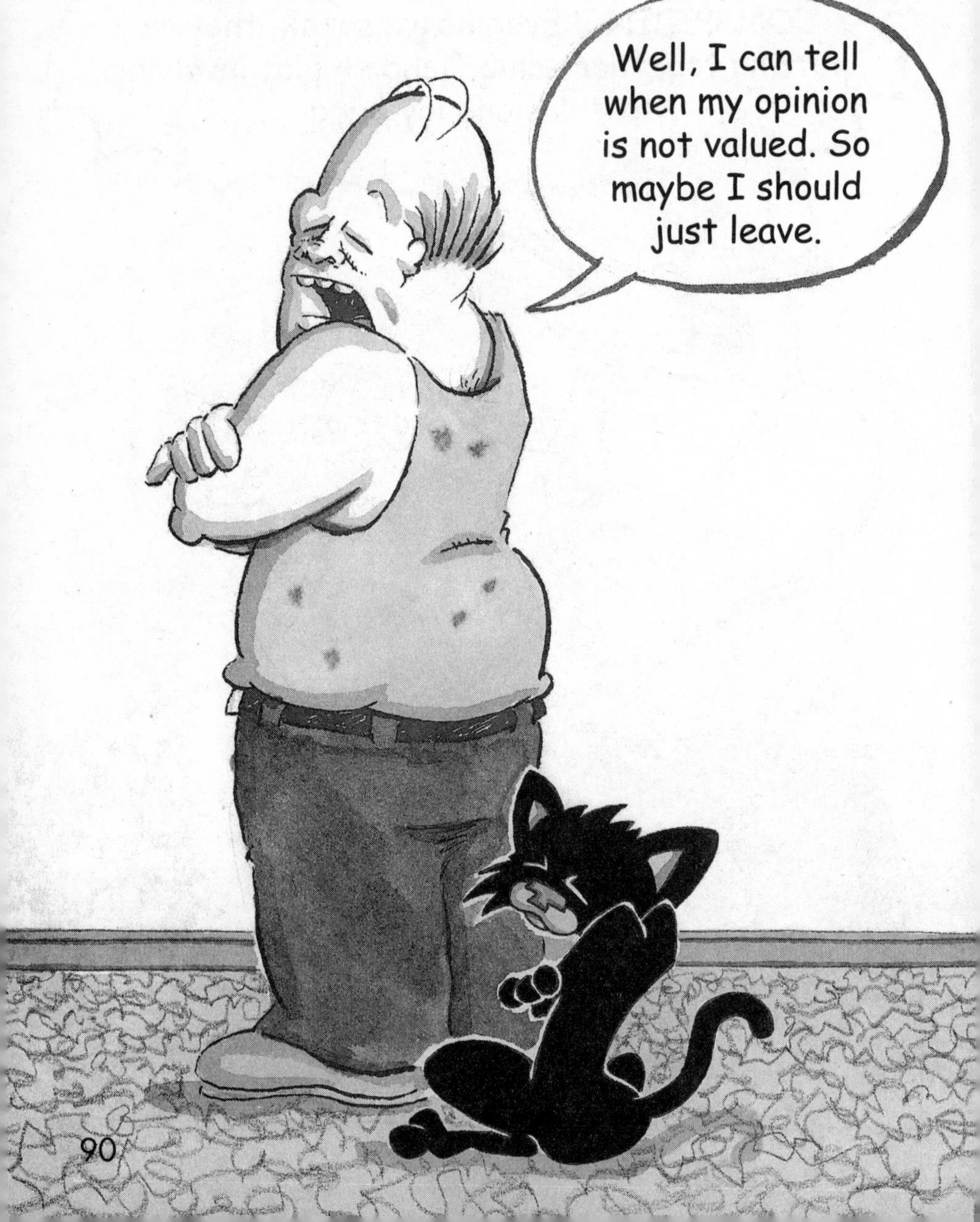
Well, I can tell when my opinion is not valued. So maybe I should just leave.

Oh, Uncle Murray. Don't be like that. You're a guest here as well. You can stay as long as you'd like.

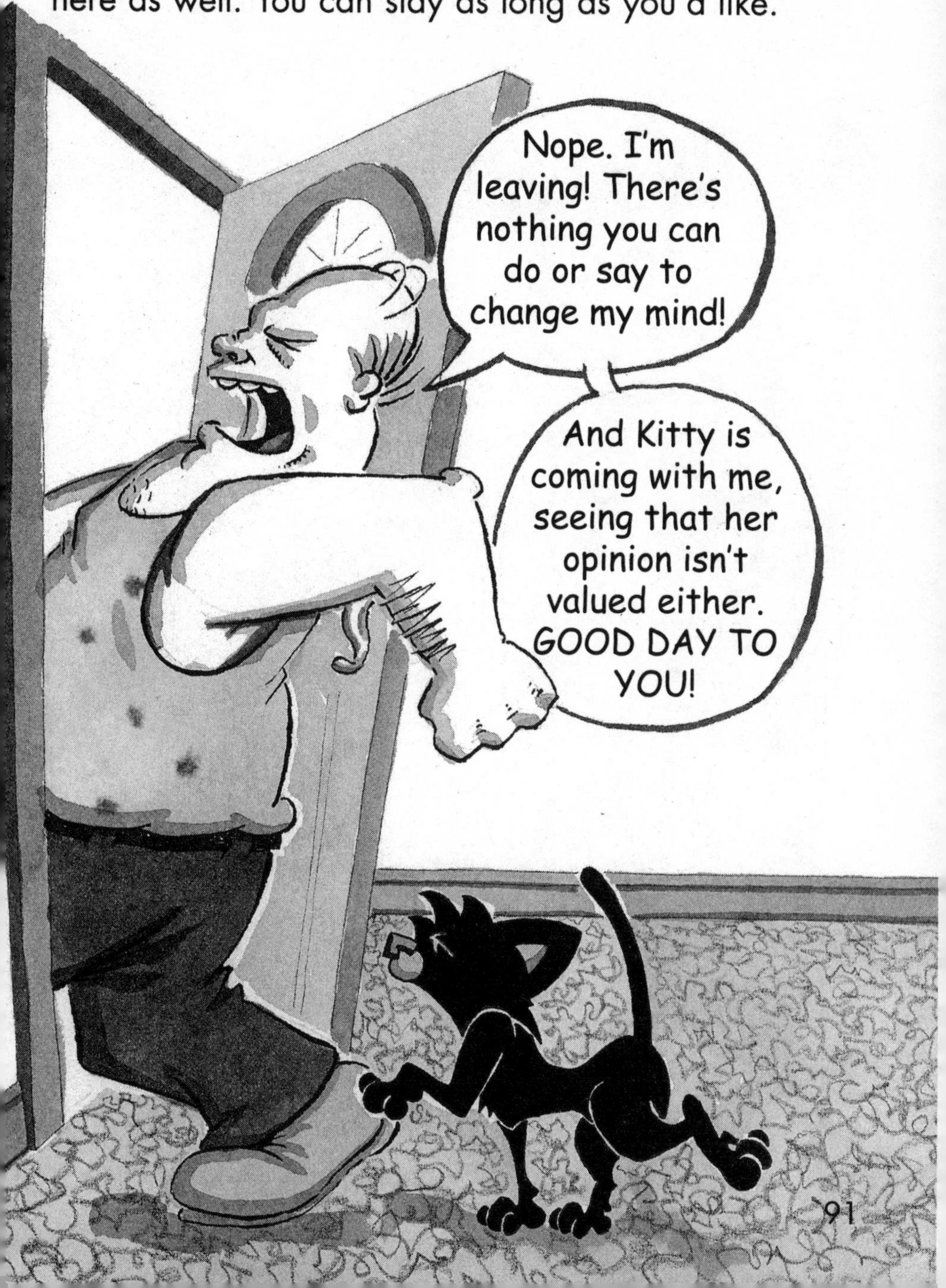
Nope. I'm leaving! There's nothing you can do or say to change my mind!
And Kitty is coming with me, seeing that her opinion isn't valued either. GOOD DAY TO YOU!

SIGH.

Uncle Murray really is a nice guy. But he can be very touchy.

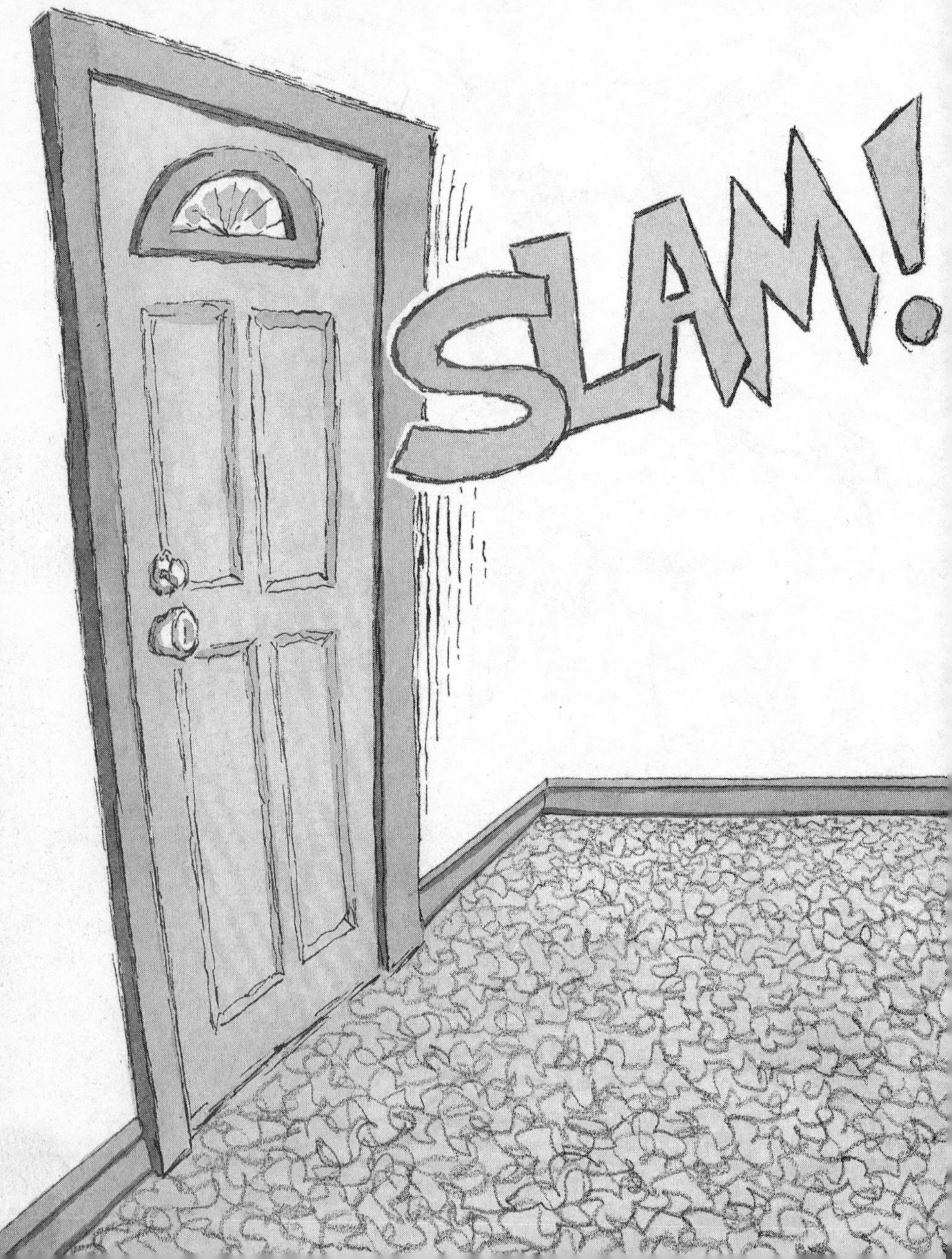
SLAM!

• CHAPTER FIVE •

KITTY AND MURRAY, TOGETHER AT LAST!

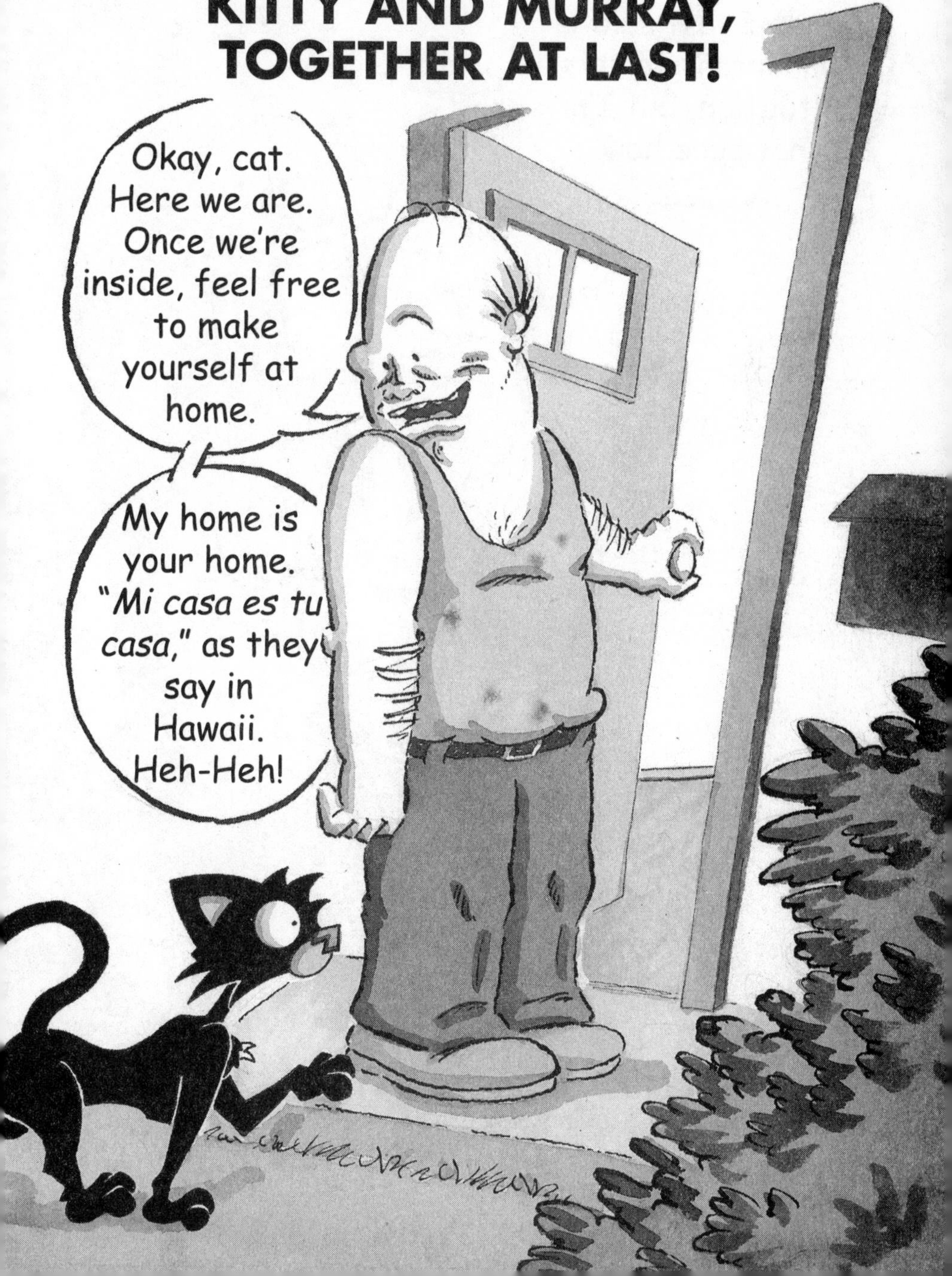
Okay, cat. Here we are. Once we're inside, feel free to make yourself at home.
My home is your home. "*Mi casa es tu casa*," as they say in Hawaii. Heh-Heh!

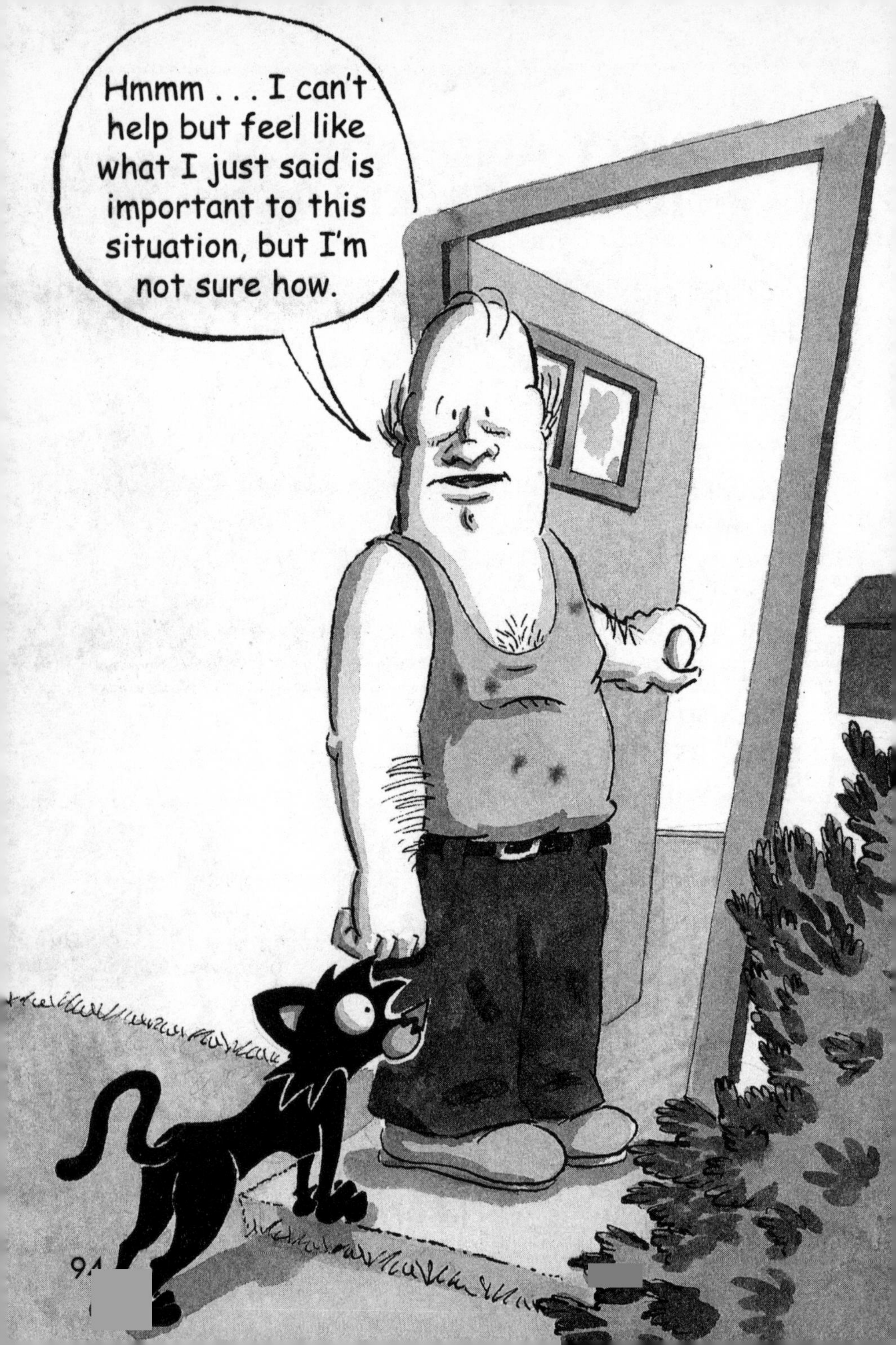
Hmmm . . . I can't help but feel like what I just said is important to this situation, but I'm not sure how.

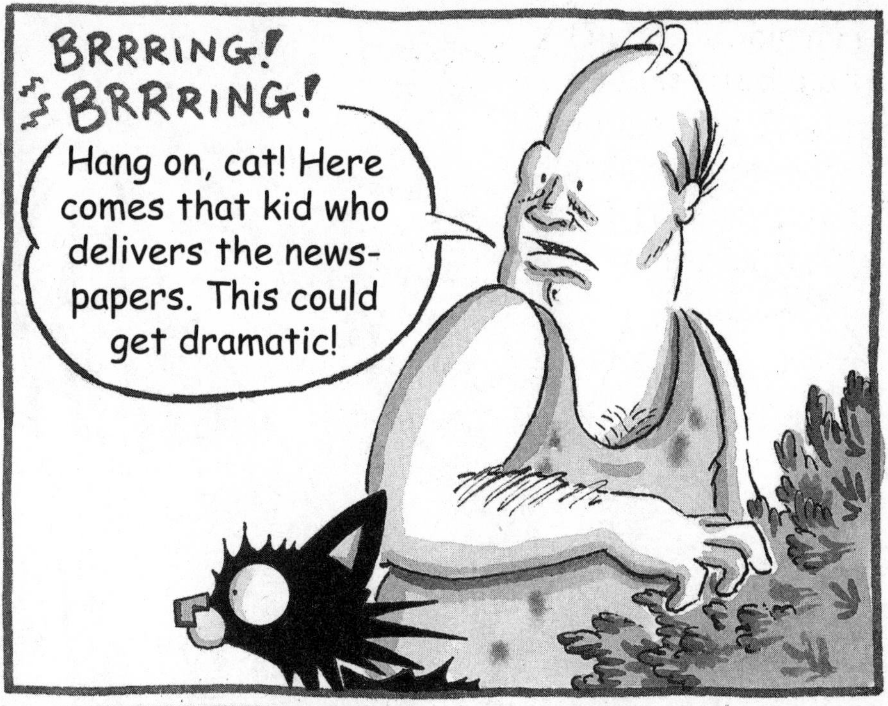
BRRRING!
BRRRING!
Hang on, cat! Here comes that kid who delivers the news- papers. This could get dramatic!

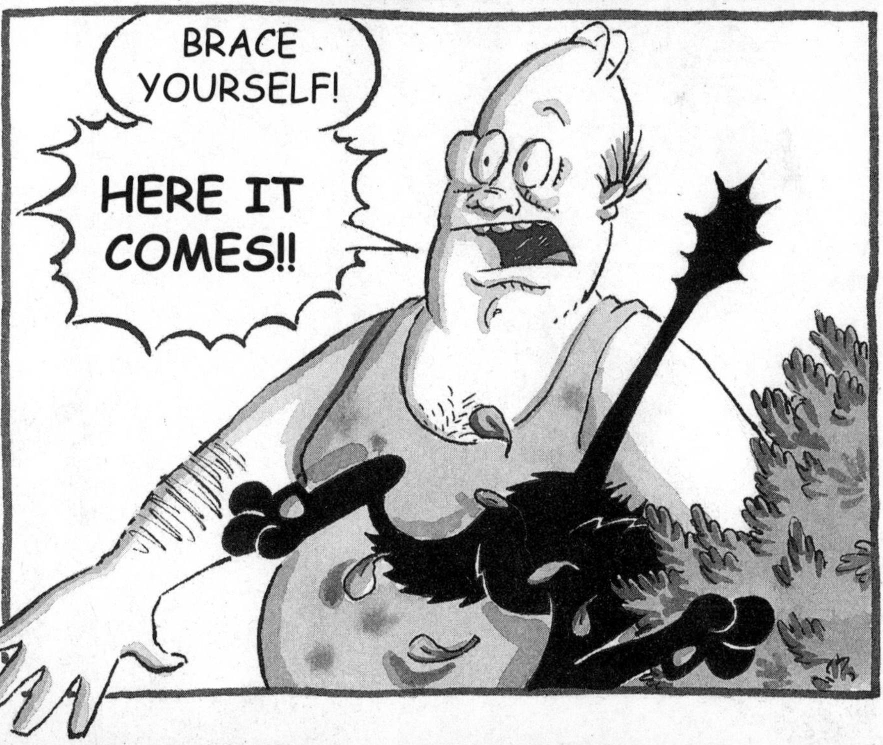
BRACE YOURSELF!
HERE IT COMES!!

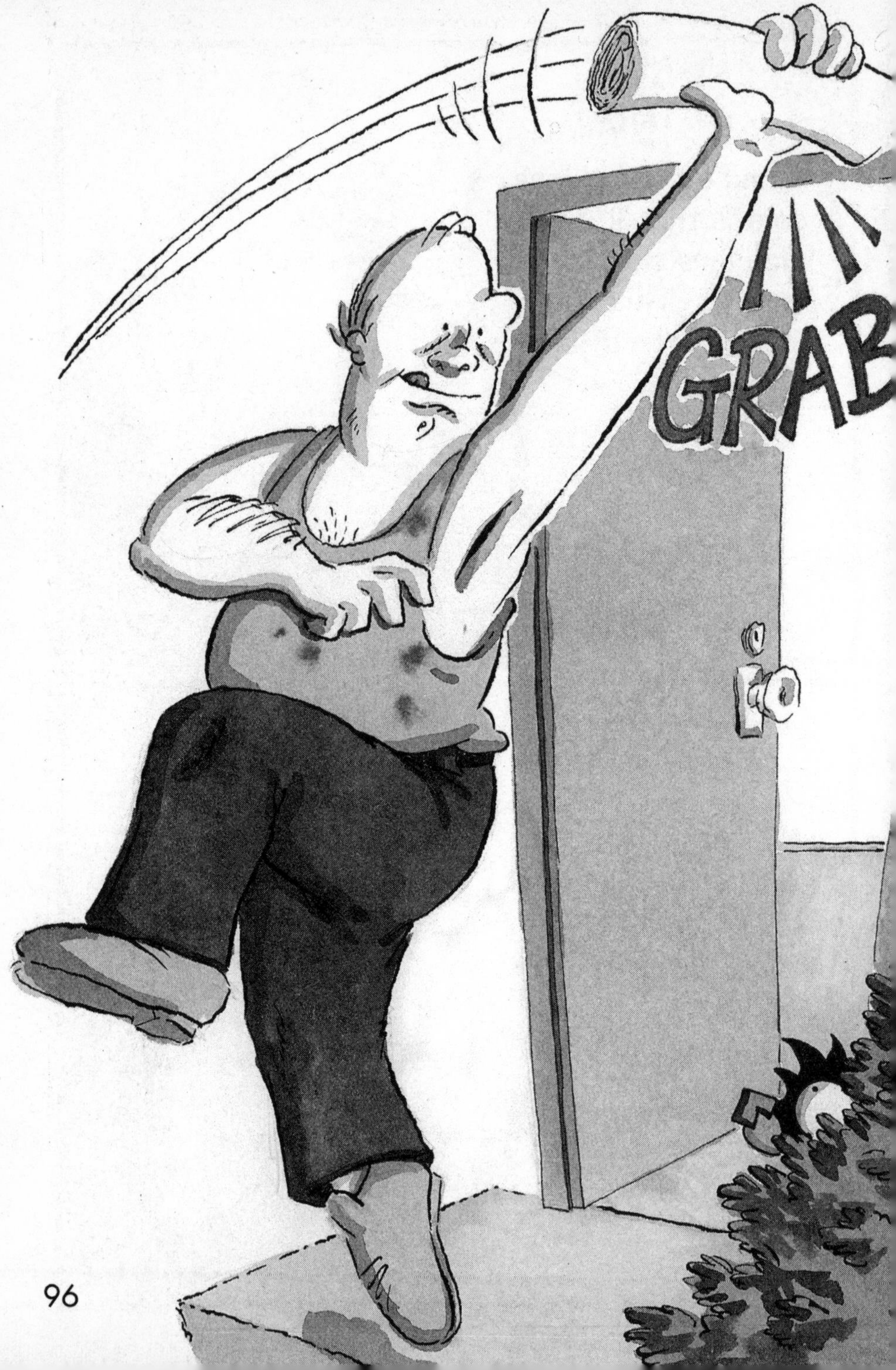
GRAB

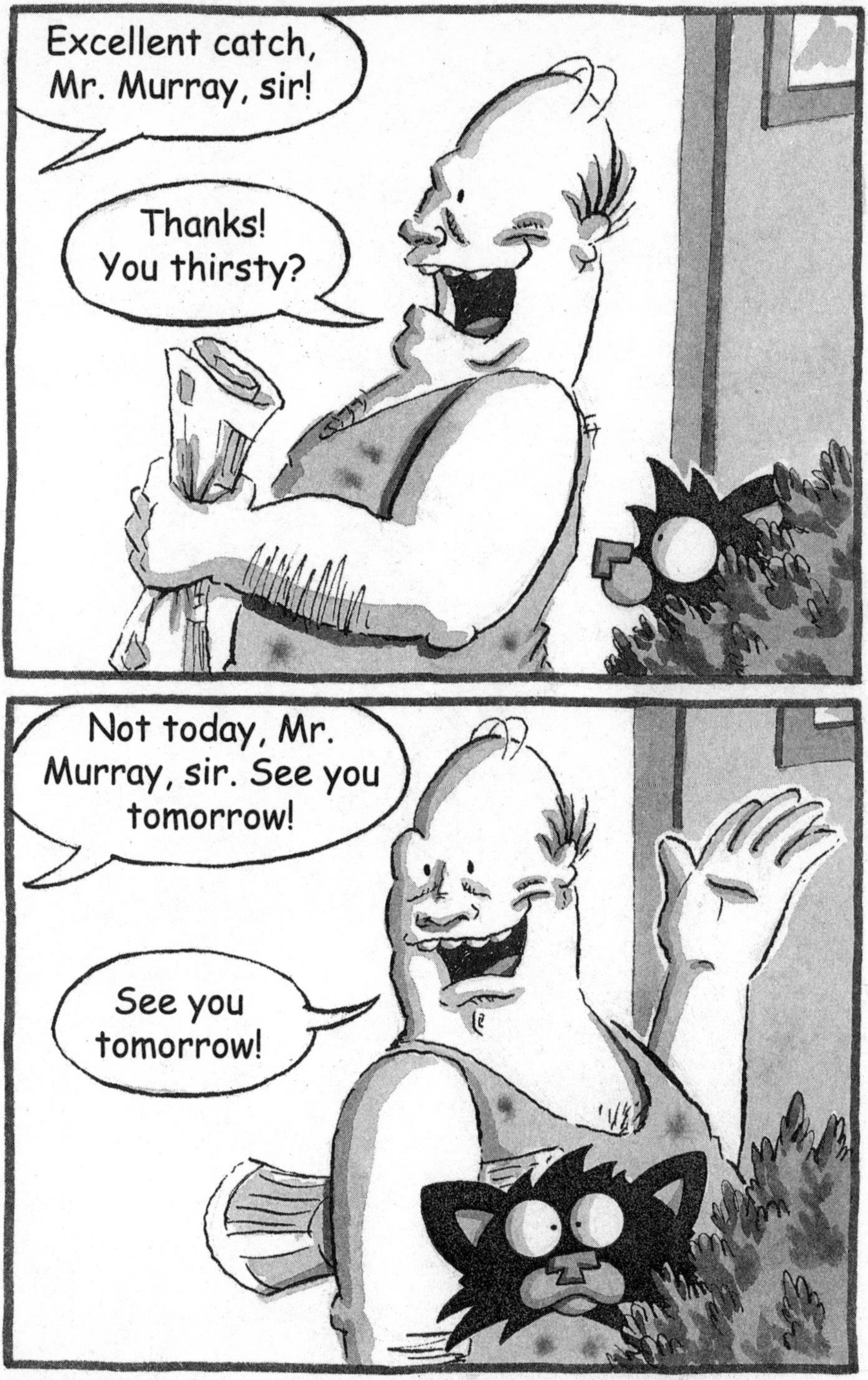
Excellent catch, Mr. Murray, sir!
Thanks! You thirsty?
Not today, Mr. Murray, sir. See you tomorrow!
See you tomorrow!

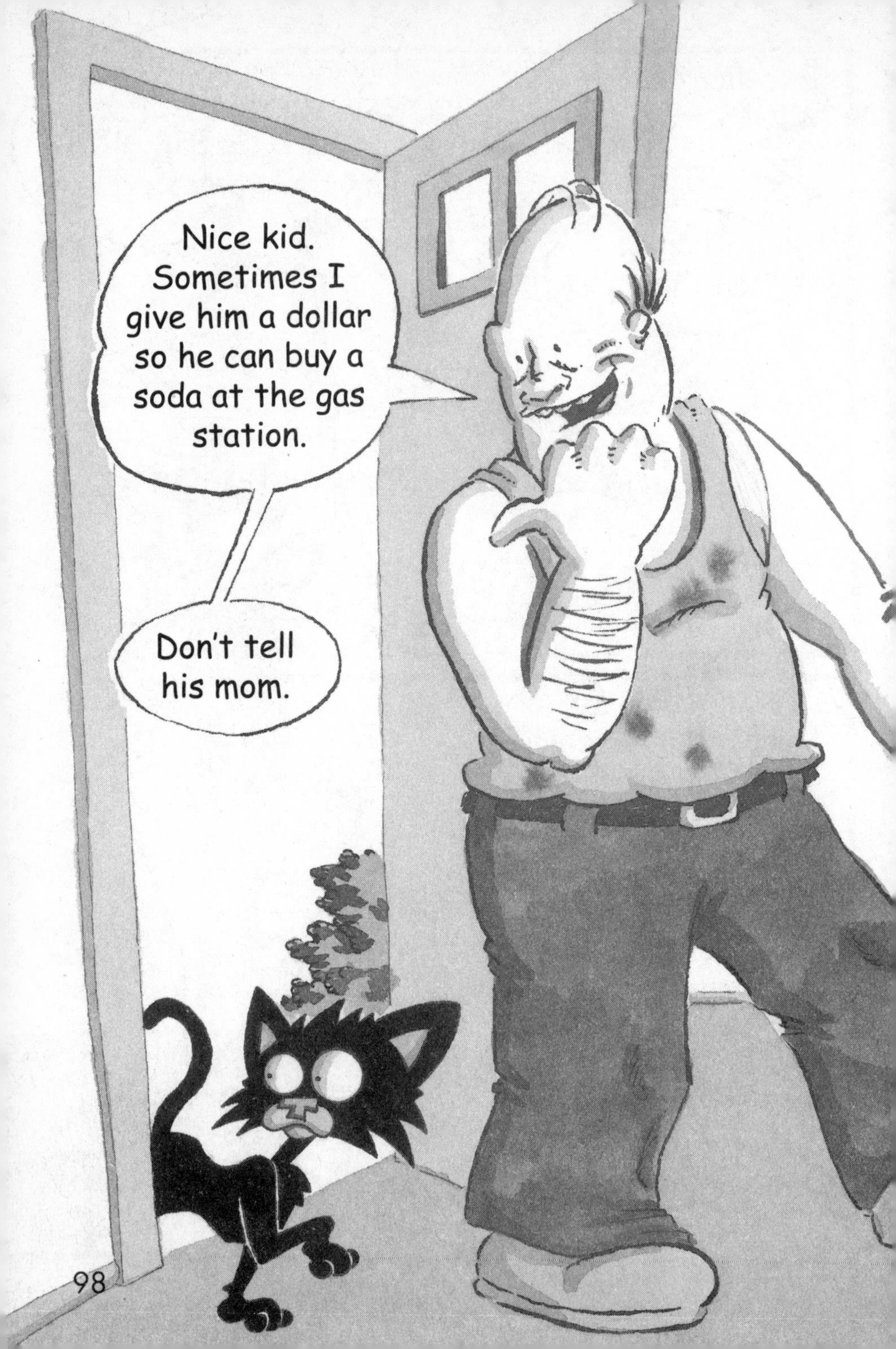
Nice kid. Sometimes I give him a dollar so he can buy a soda at the gas station.
Don't tell his mom.

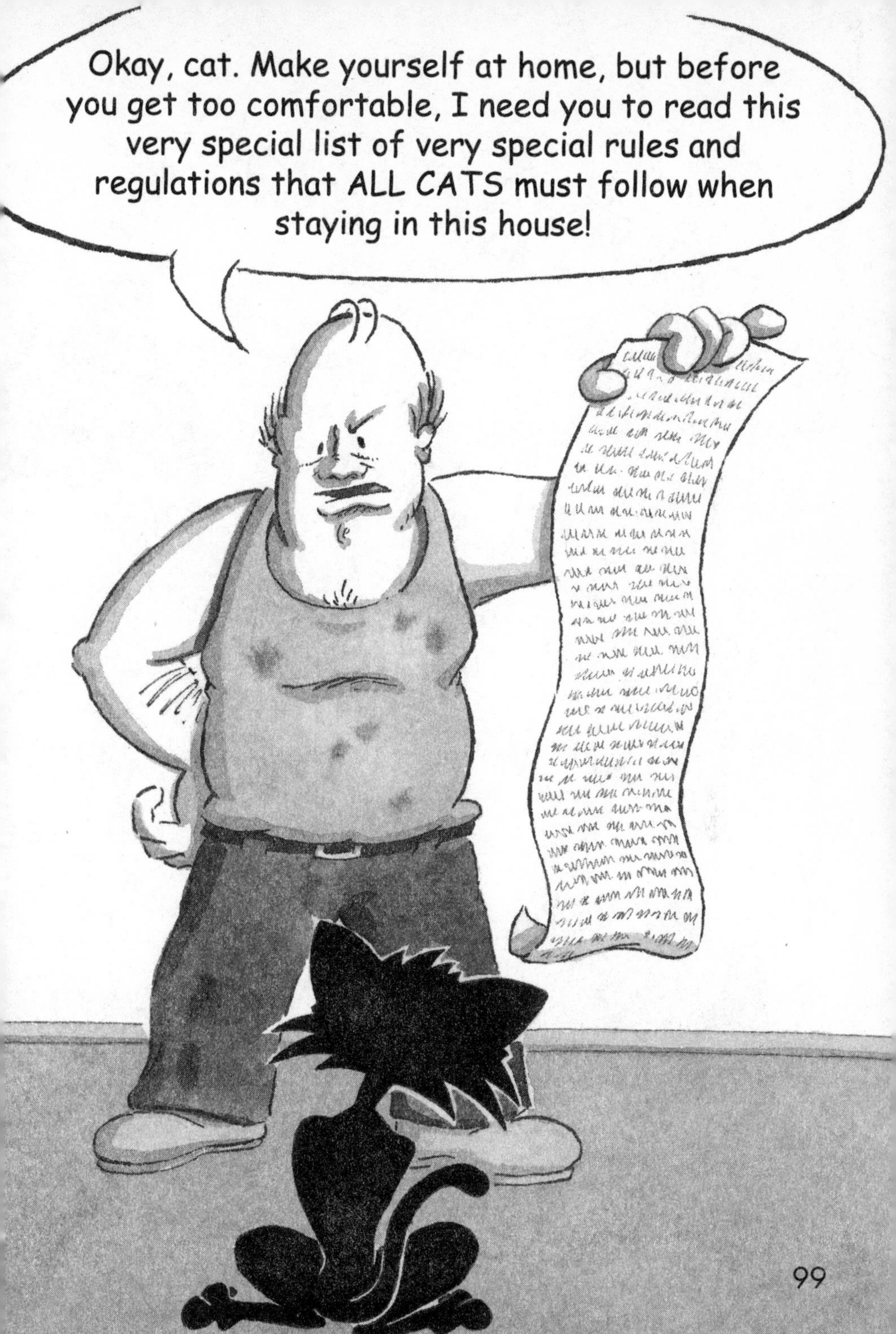
Okay, cat. Make yourself at home, but before you get too comfortable, I need you to read this very special list of very special rules and regulations that ALL CATS must follow when staying in this house!

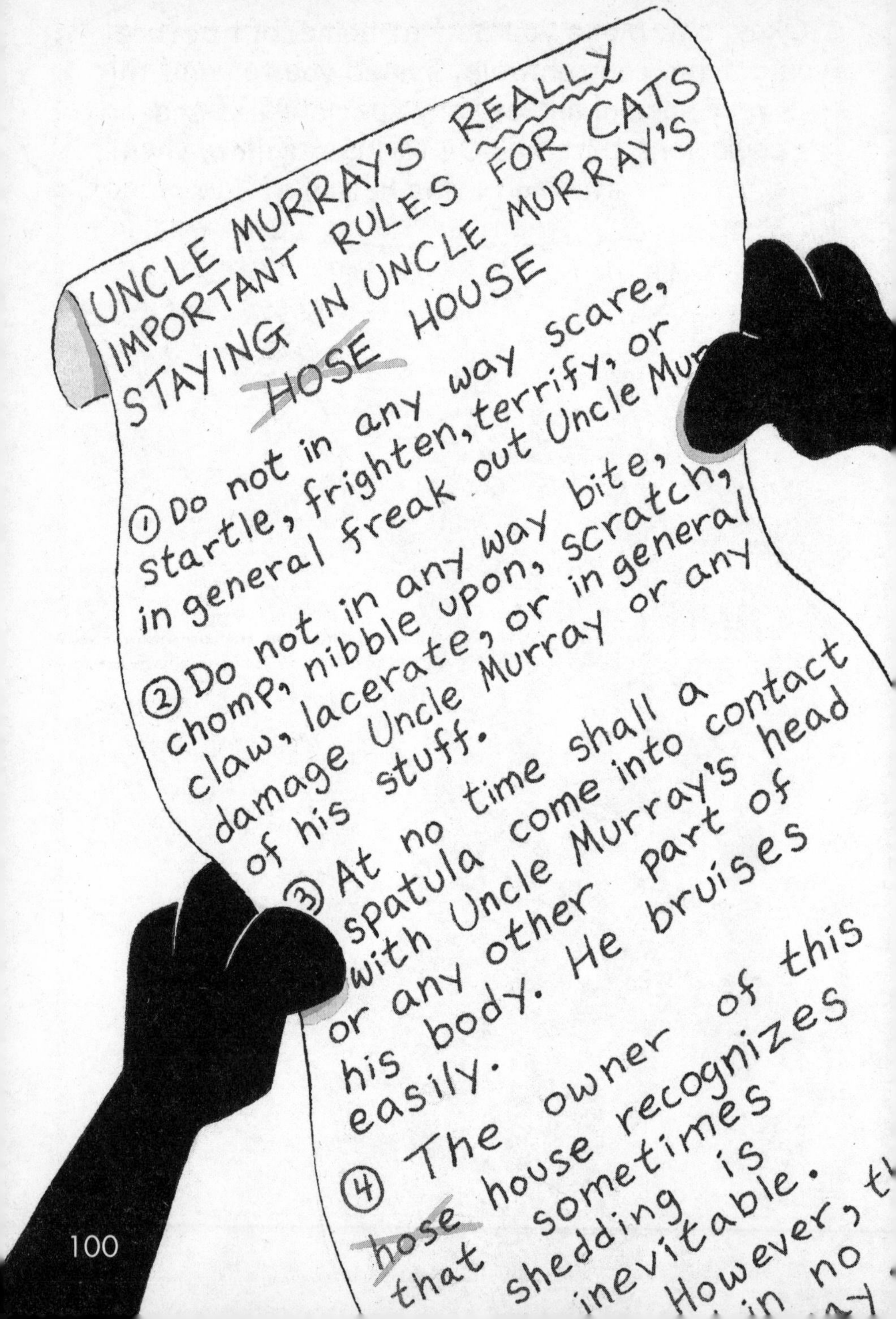
UNCLE MURRAY'S REALLY
IMPORTANT RULES FOR CATS
STAYING IN UNCLE MURRAY'S
~~HOSE~~ HOUSE
① Do not in any way scare,
startle, frighten, terrify, or
in general freak out Uncle Mu
② Do not in any way bite,
chomp, nibble upon, scratch,
claw, lacerate, or in general
damage Uncle Murray or any
of his stuff.
③ At no time shall a
spatula come into contact
with Uncle Murray's head
or any other part of
his body. He bruises
easily.
④ The owner of this
~~hose~~ house recognizes
that sometimes
shedding is
inevitable.
However, t
in no

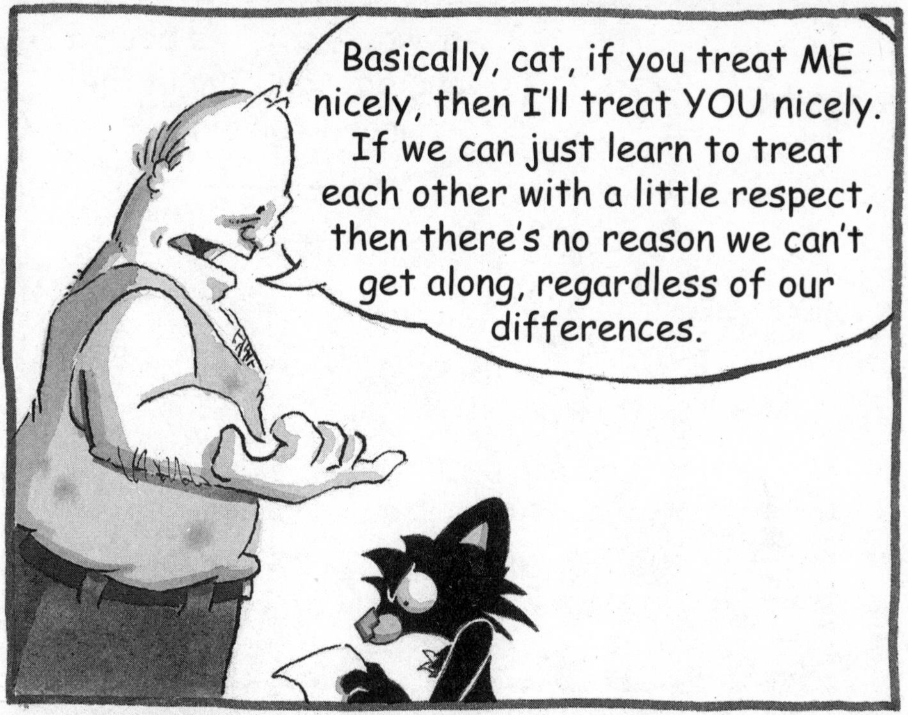
Basically, cat, if you treat ME nicely, then I'll treat YOU nicely. If we can just learn to treat each other with a little respect, then there's no reason we can't get along, regardless of our differences.

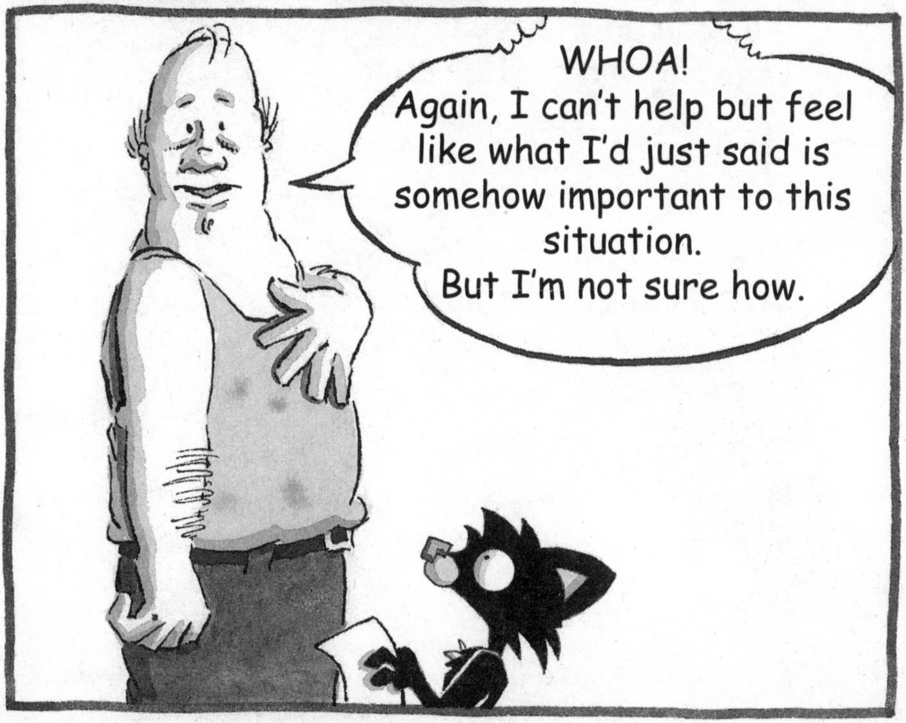
WHOA!
Again, I can't help but feel like what I'd just said is somehow important to this situation.
But I'm not sure how.

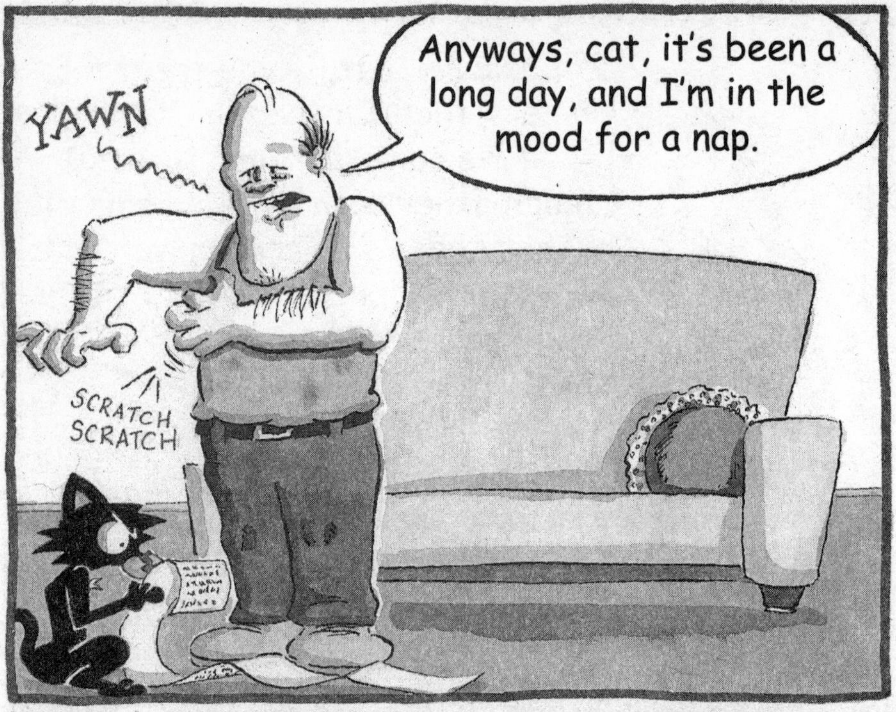
Anyways, cat, it's been a long day, and I'm in the mood for a nap.
YAWN
SCRATCH SCRATCH

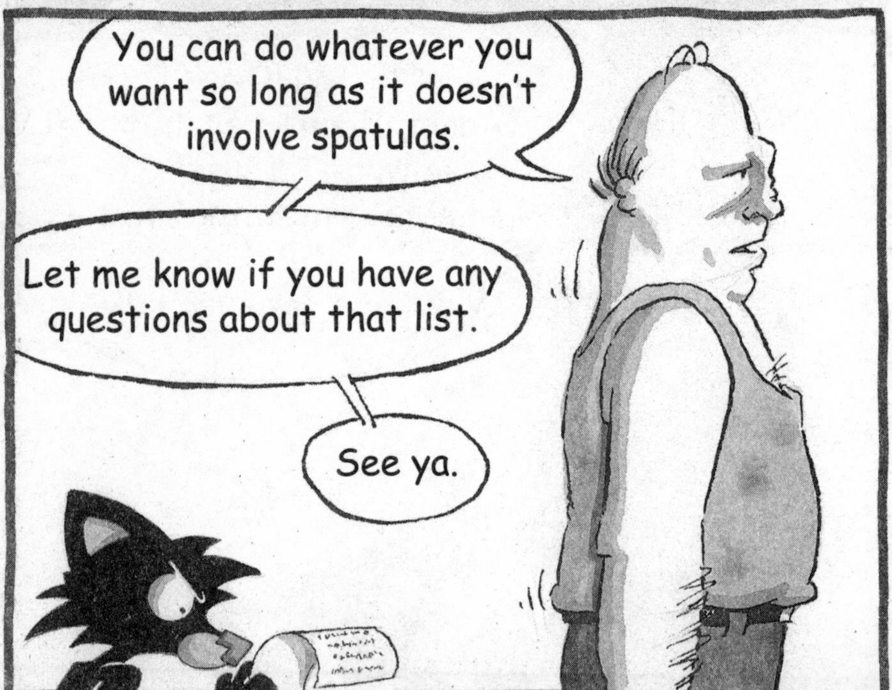
You can do whatever you want so long as it doesn't involve spatulas.
Let me know if you have any questions about that list.
See ya.

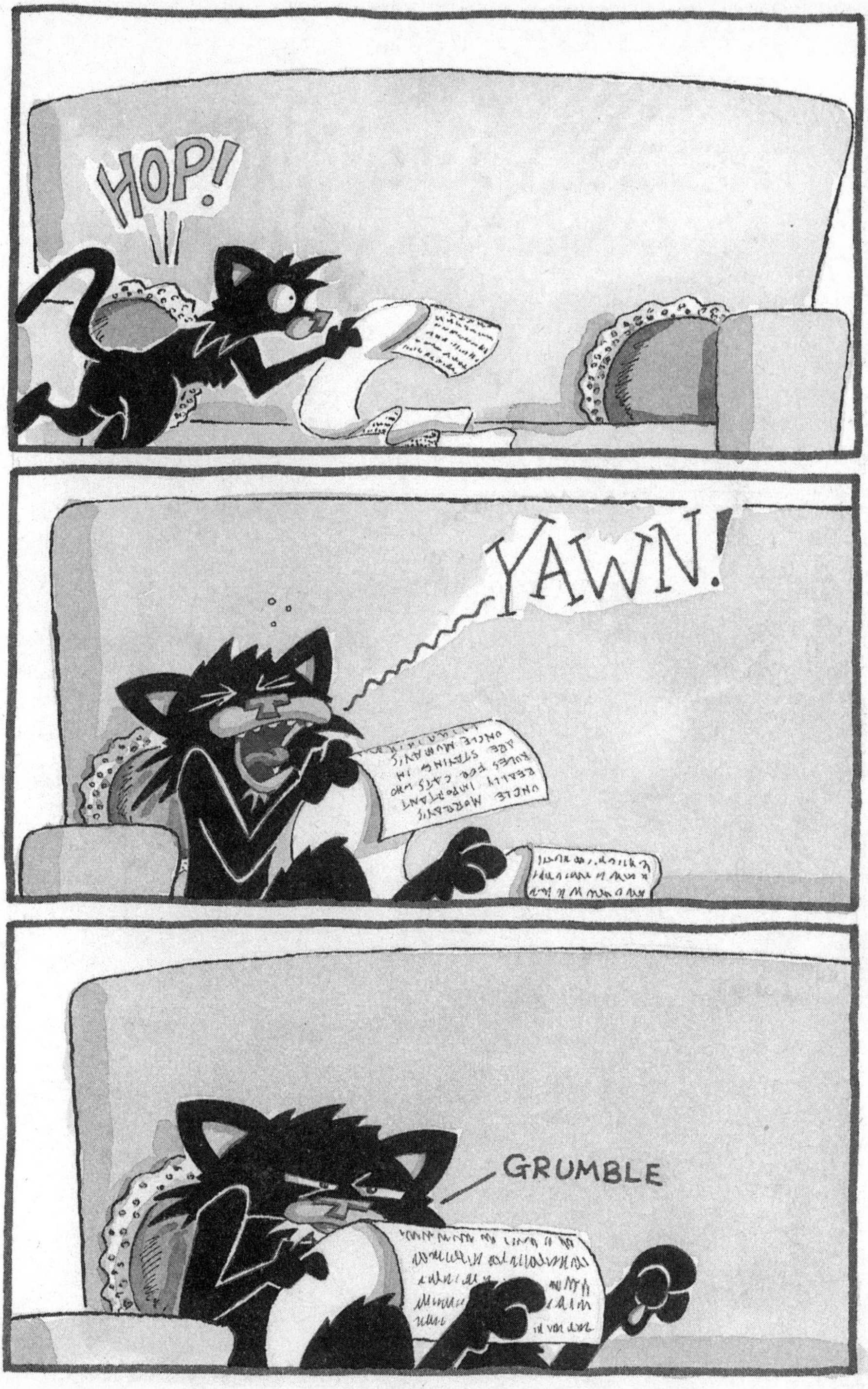
HOP!
YAWN!
UNCLE MURRAY'S
REALLY IMPORTANT
RULES FOR CATS WHO
ARE STAYING IN
UNCLE MURRAY'S
GRUMBLE

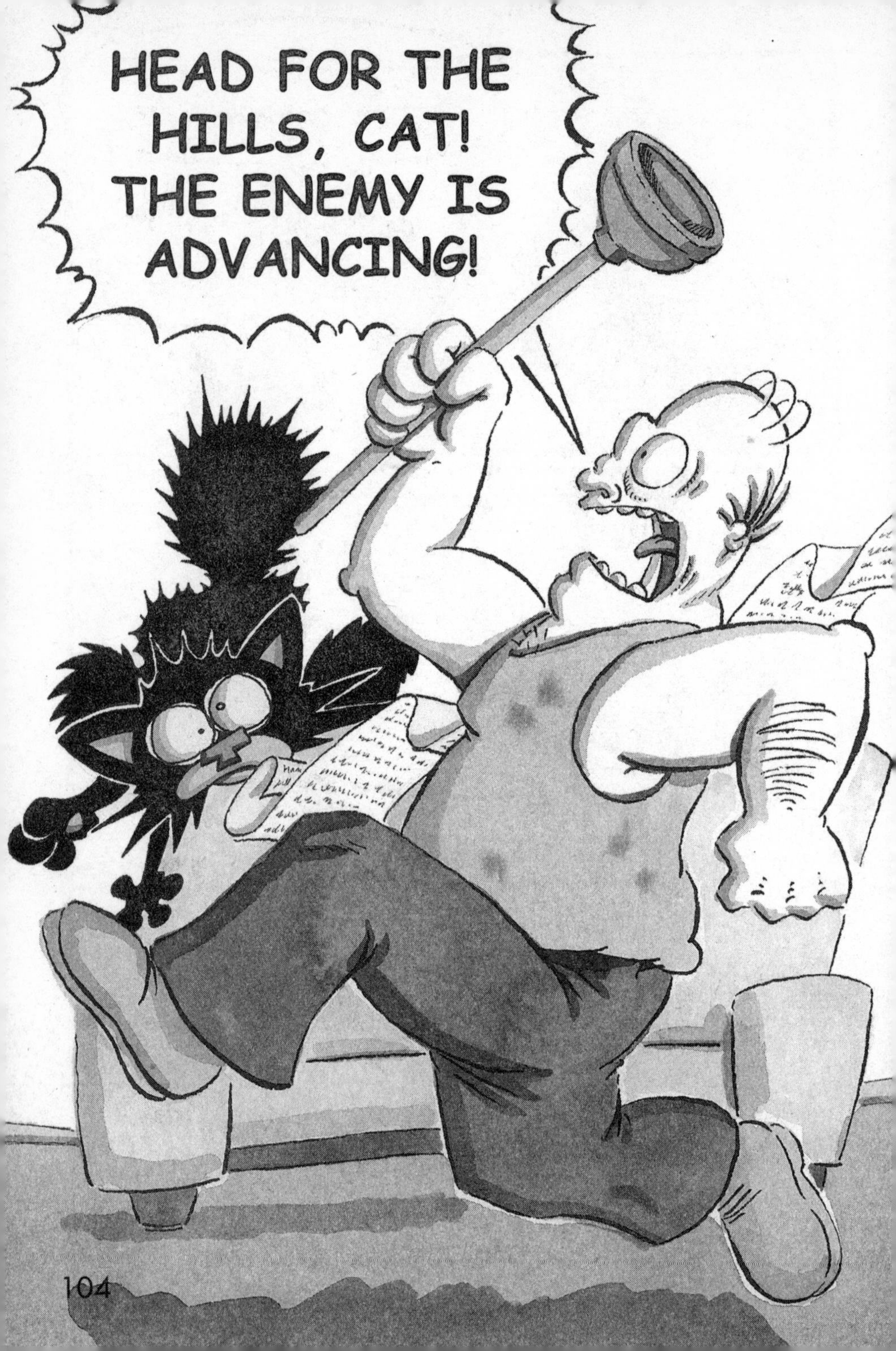
HEAD FOR THE HILLS, CAT! THE ENEMY IS ADVANCING!

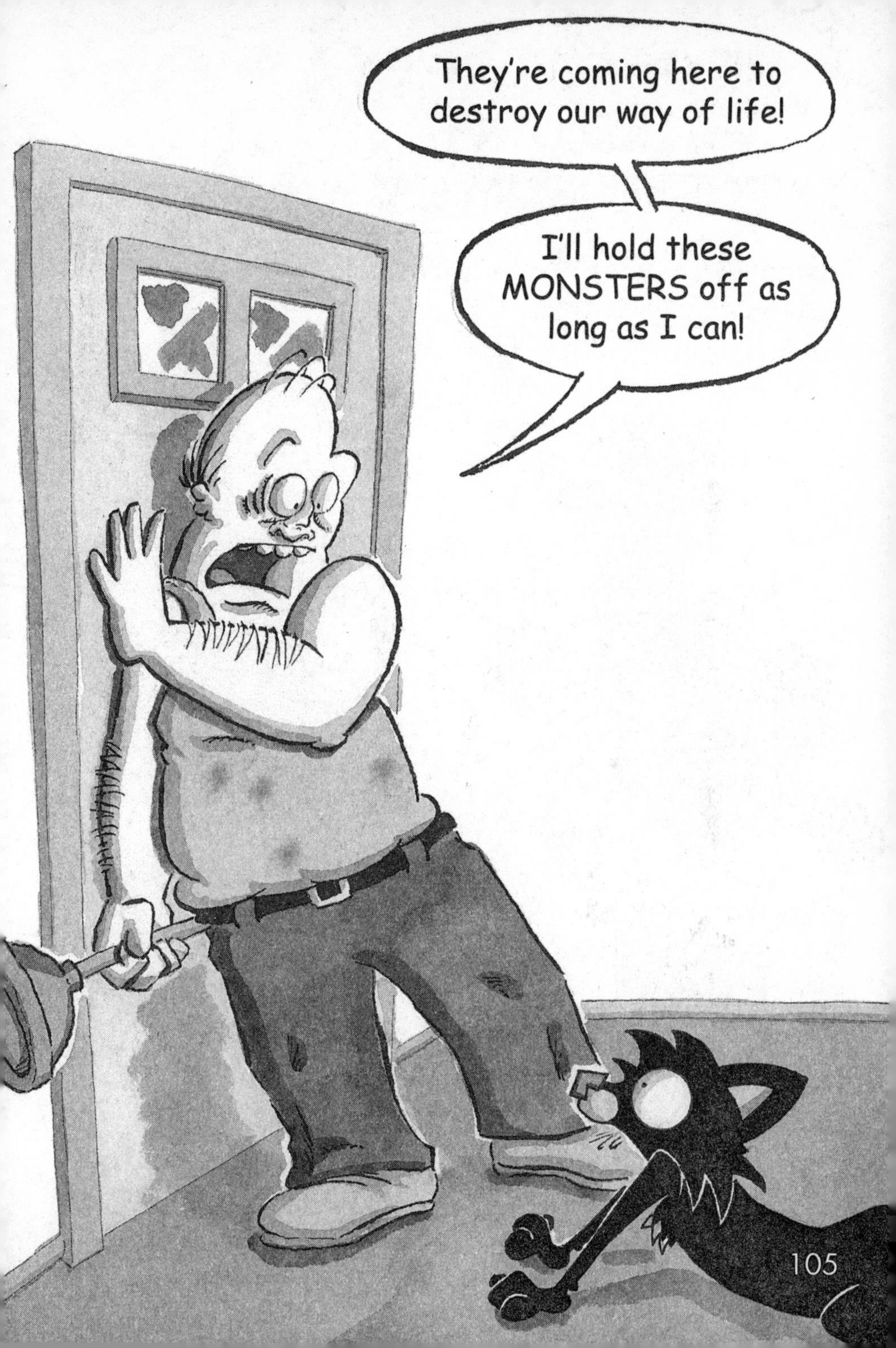
They're coming here to destroy our way of life!
I'll hold these MONSTERS off as long as I can!

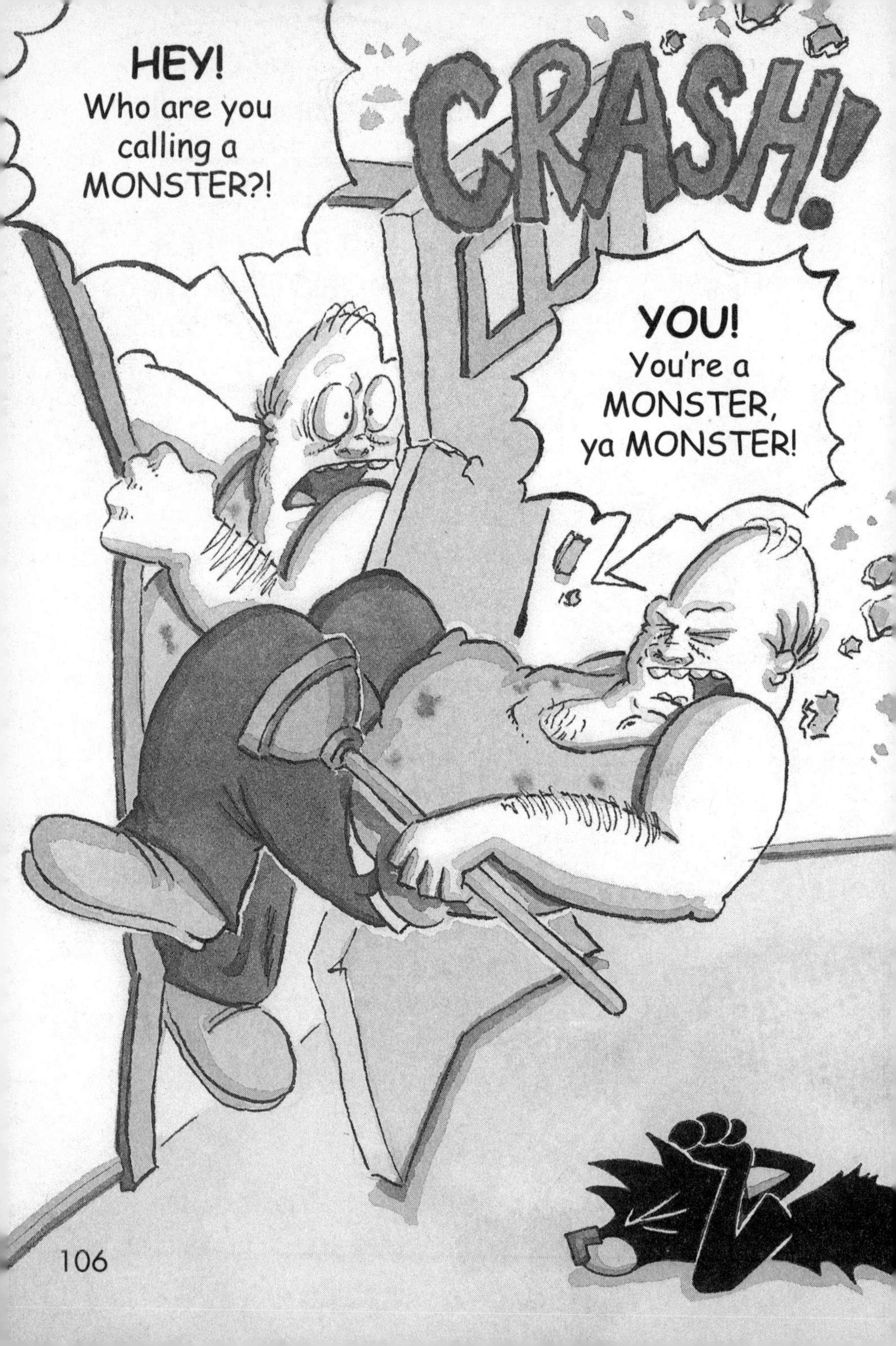
HEY! Who are you calling a MONSTER?!
CRASH!
YOU! You're a MONSTER, ya MONSTER!

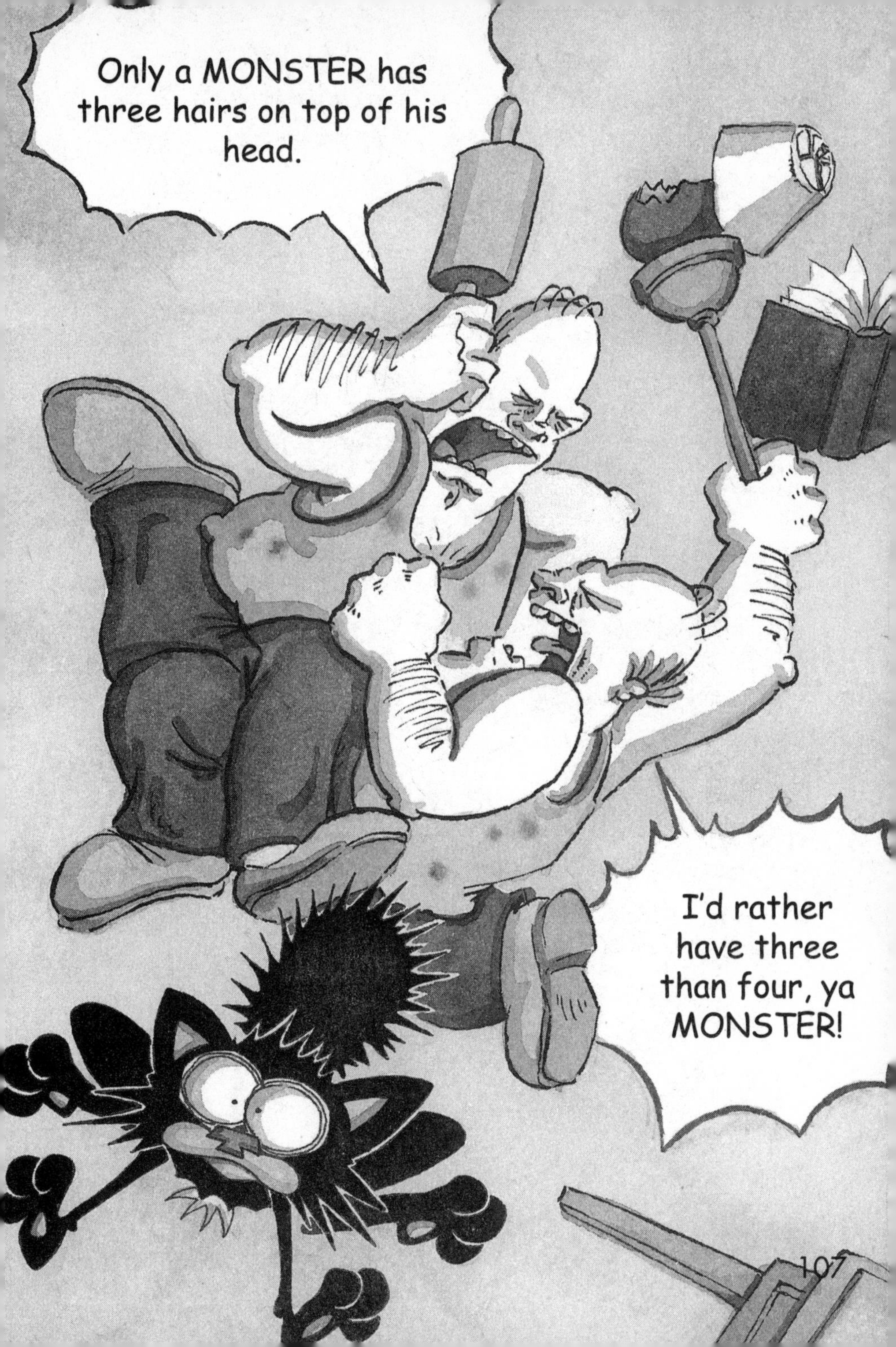
Only a MONSTER has three hairs on top of his head.
I'd rather have three than four, ya MONSTER!

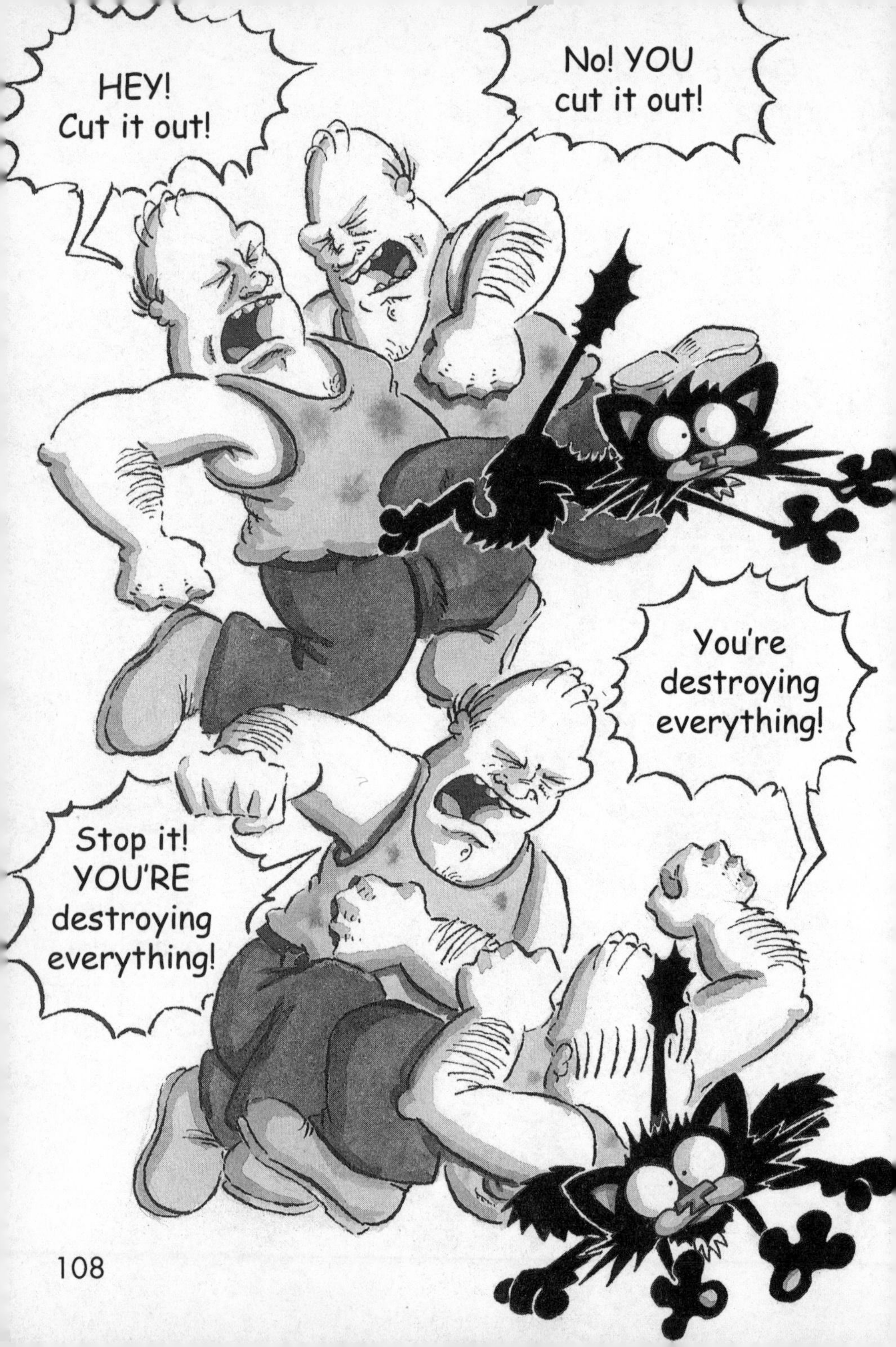
HEY! Cut it out!
No! YOU cut it out!
You're destroying everything!
Stop it! YOU'RE destroying everything!

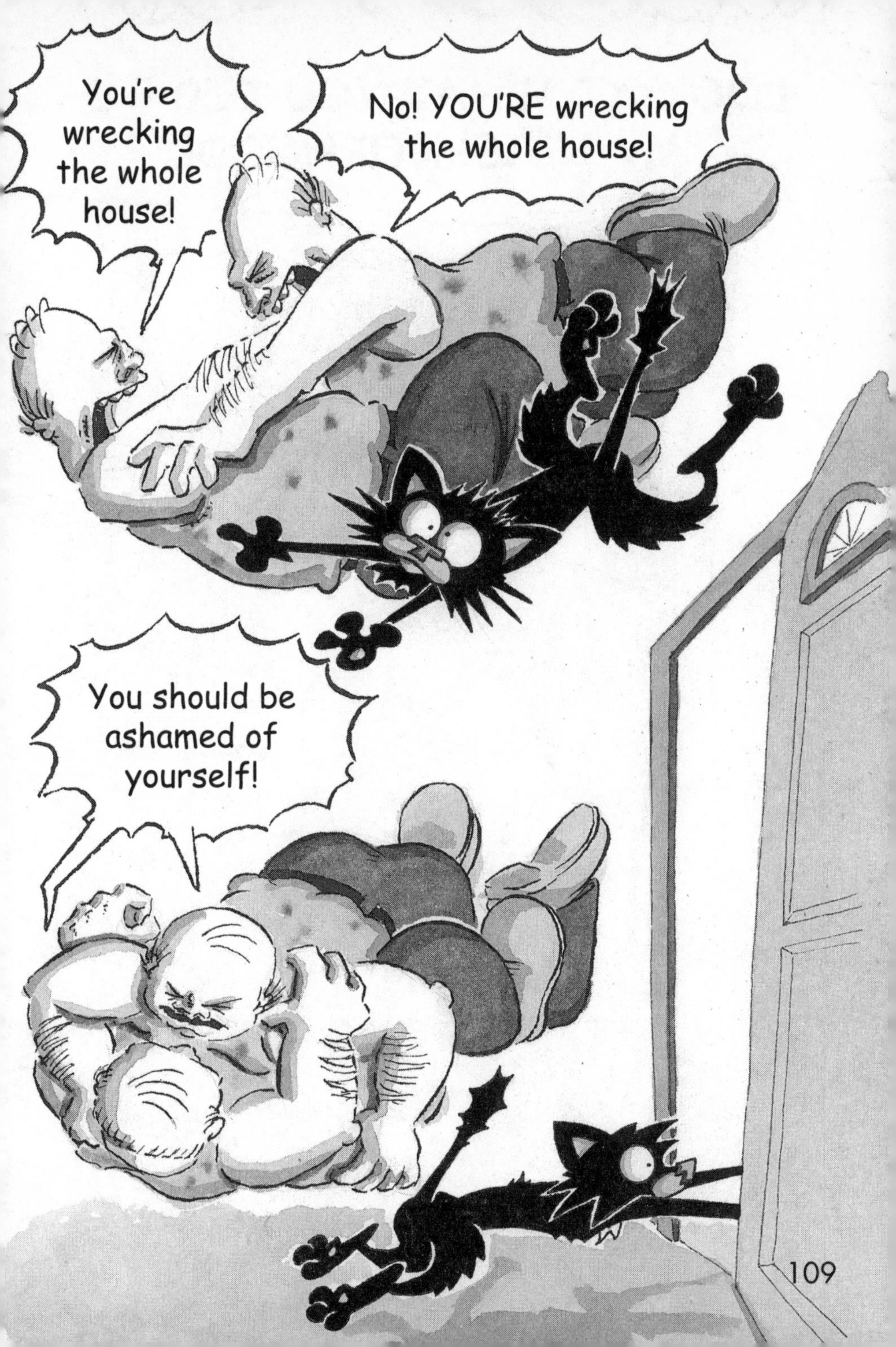
You're wrecking the whole house!
No! YOU'RE wrecking the whole house!
You should be ashamed of yourself!

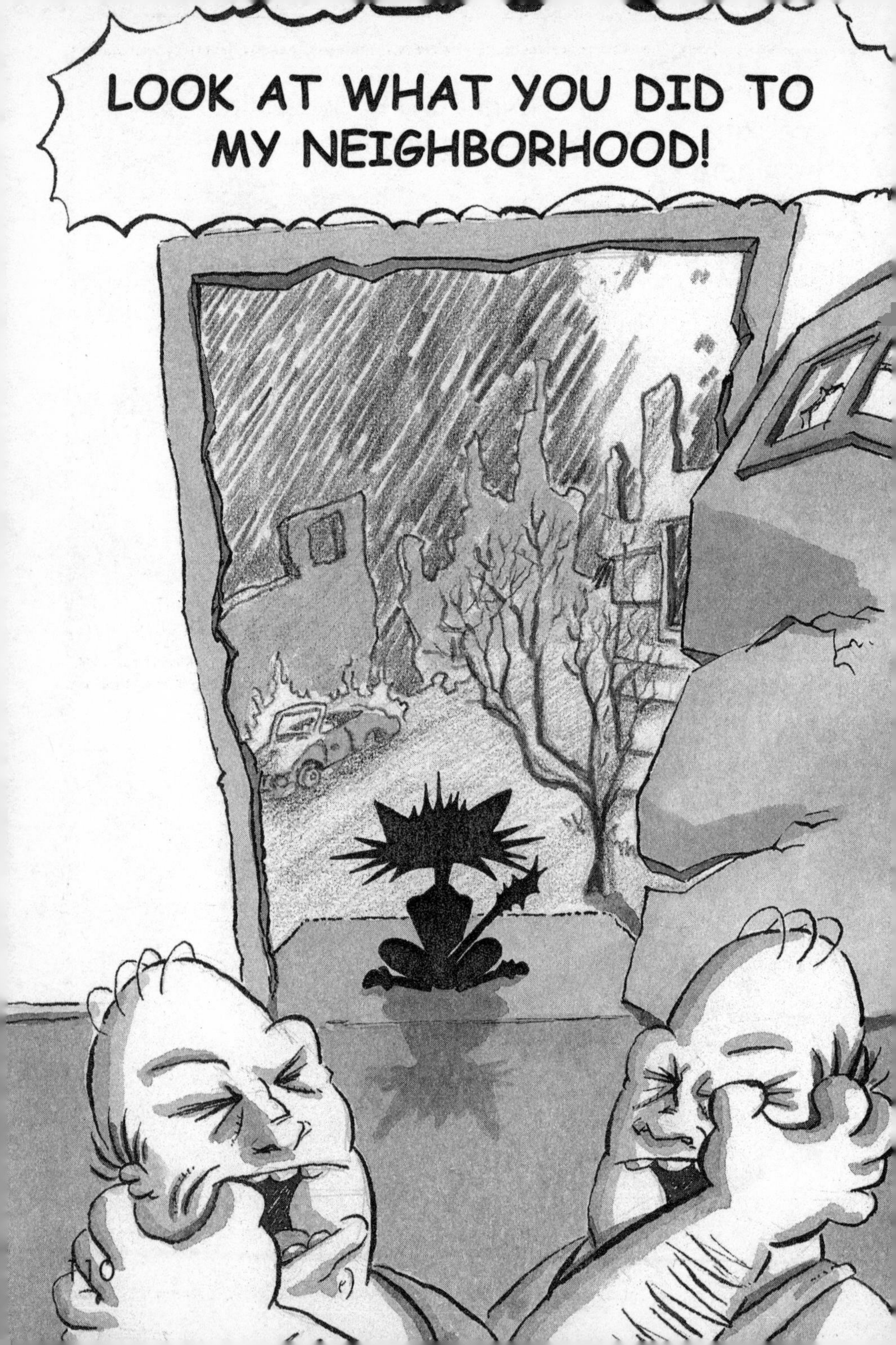
LOOK AT WHAT YOU DID TO MY NEIGHBORHOOD!

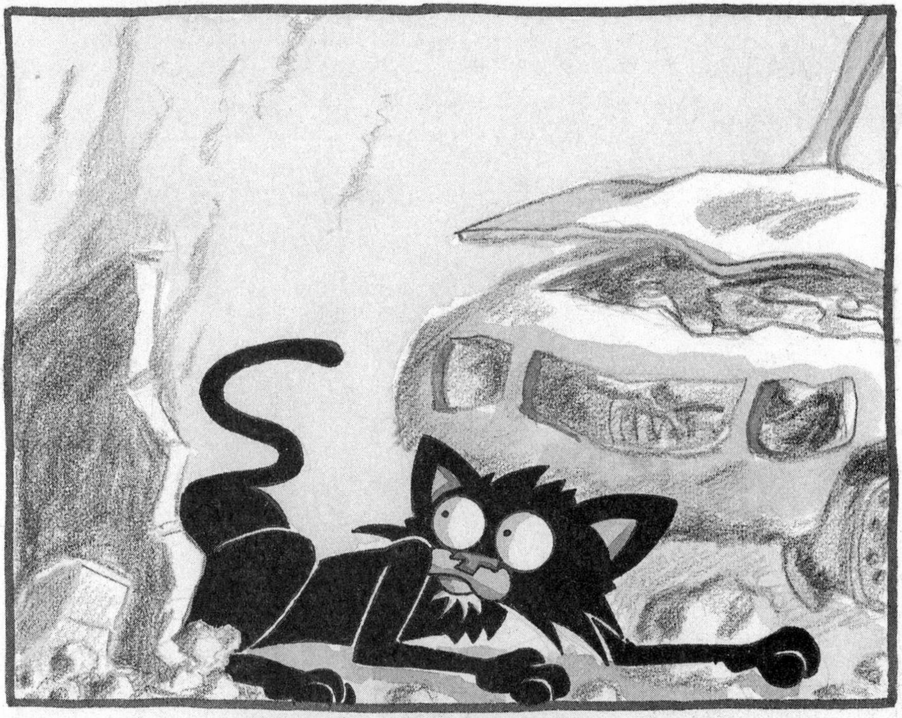
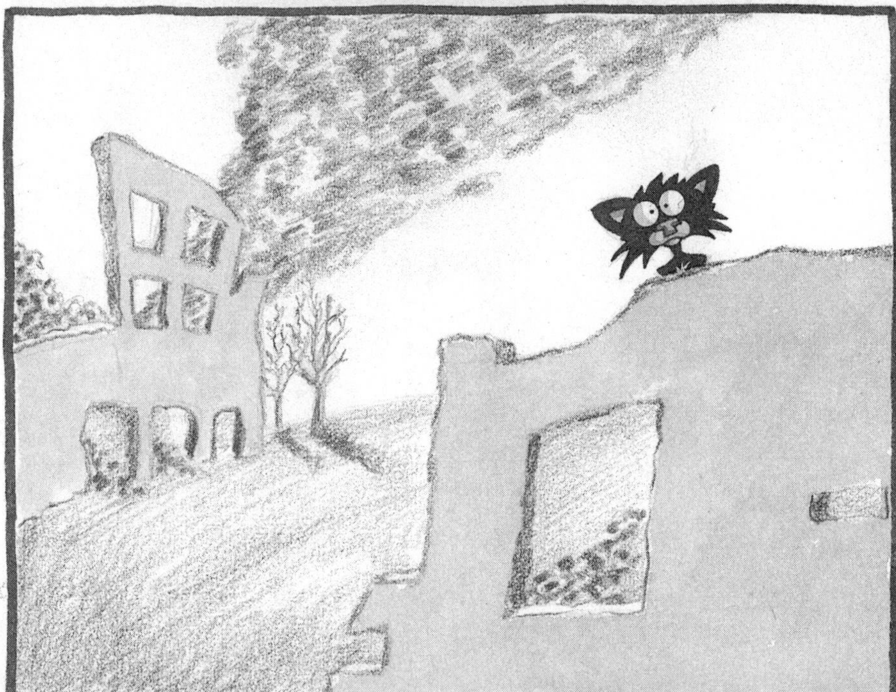

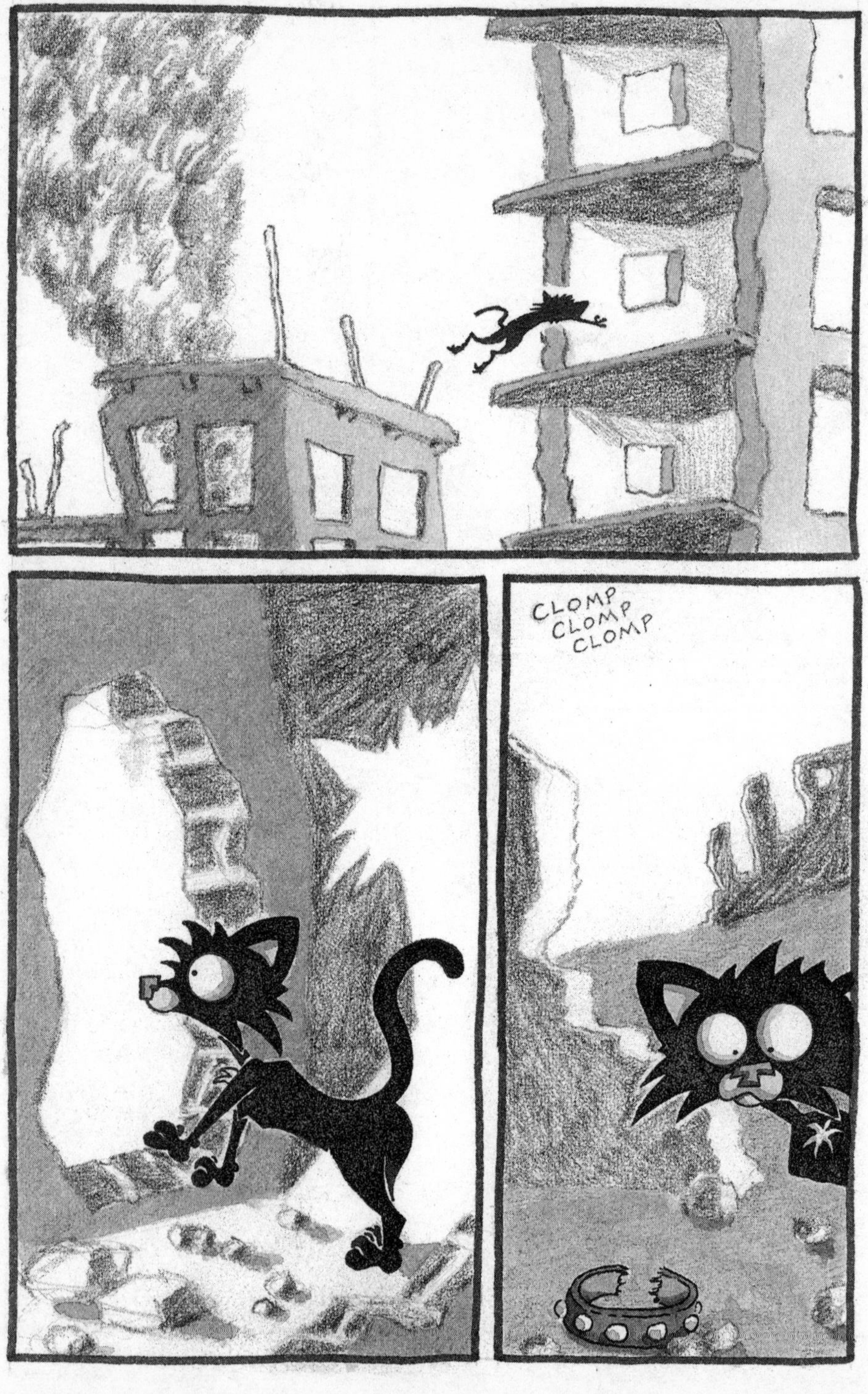
CLOMP
CLOMP
CLOMP

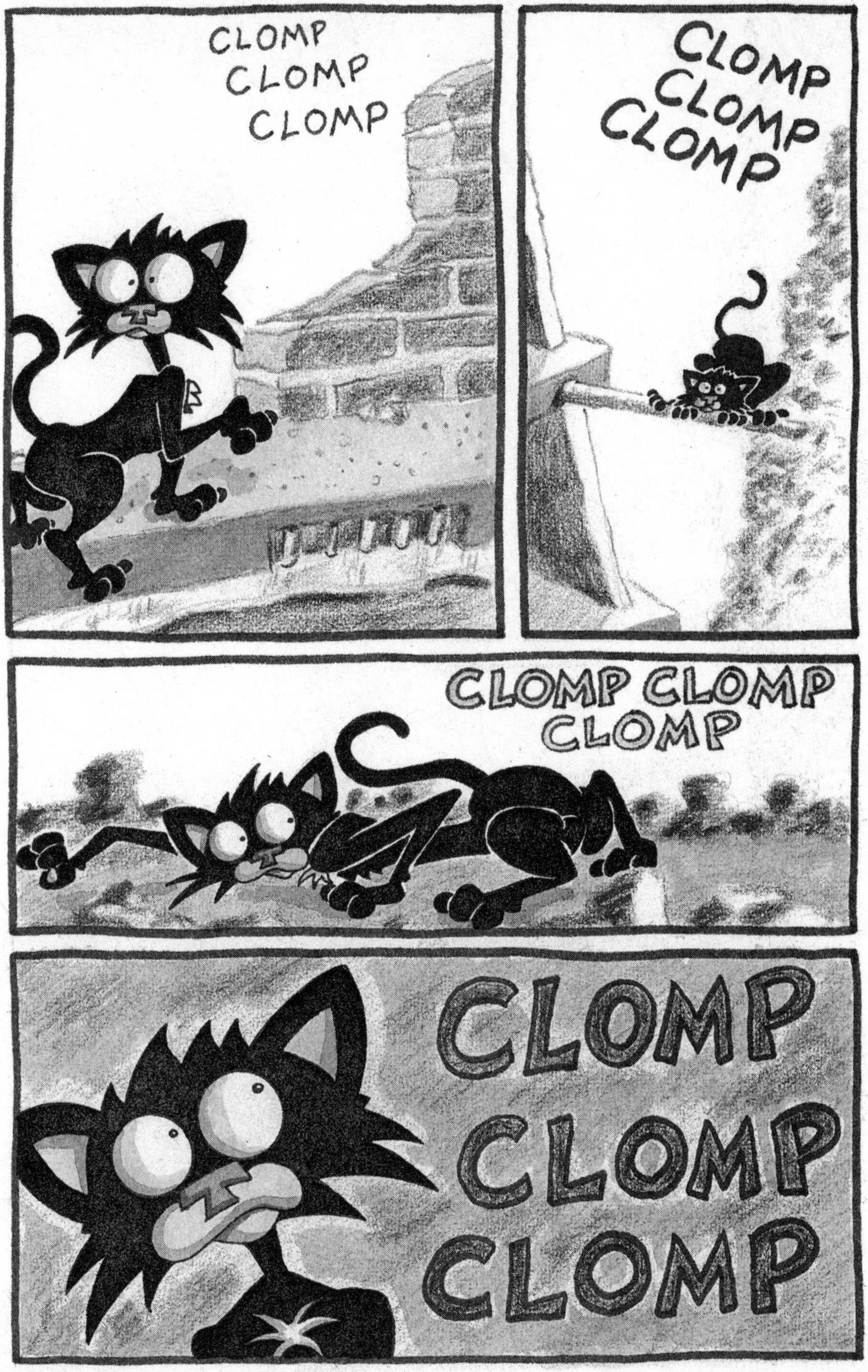
CLOMP
CLOMP
CLOMP
CLOMP
CLOMP
CLOMP
CLOMP CLOMP
CLOMP
CLOMP
CLOMP
CLOMP

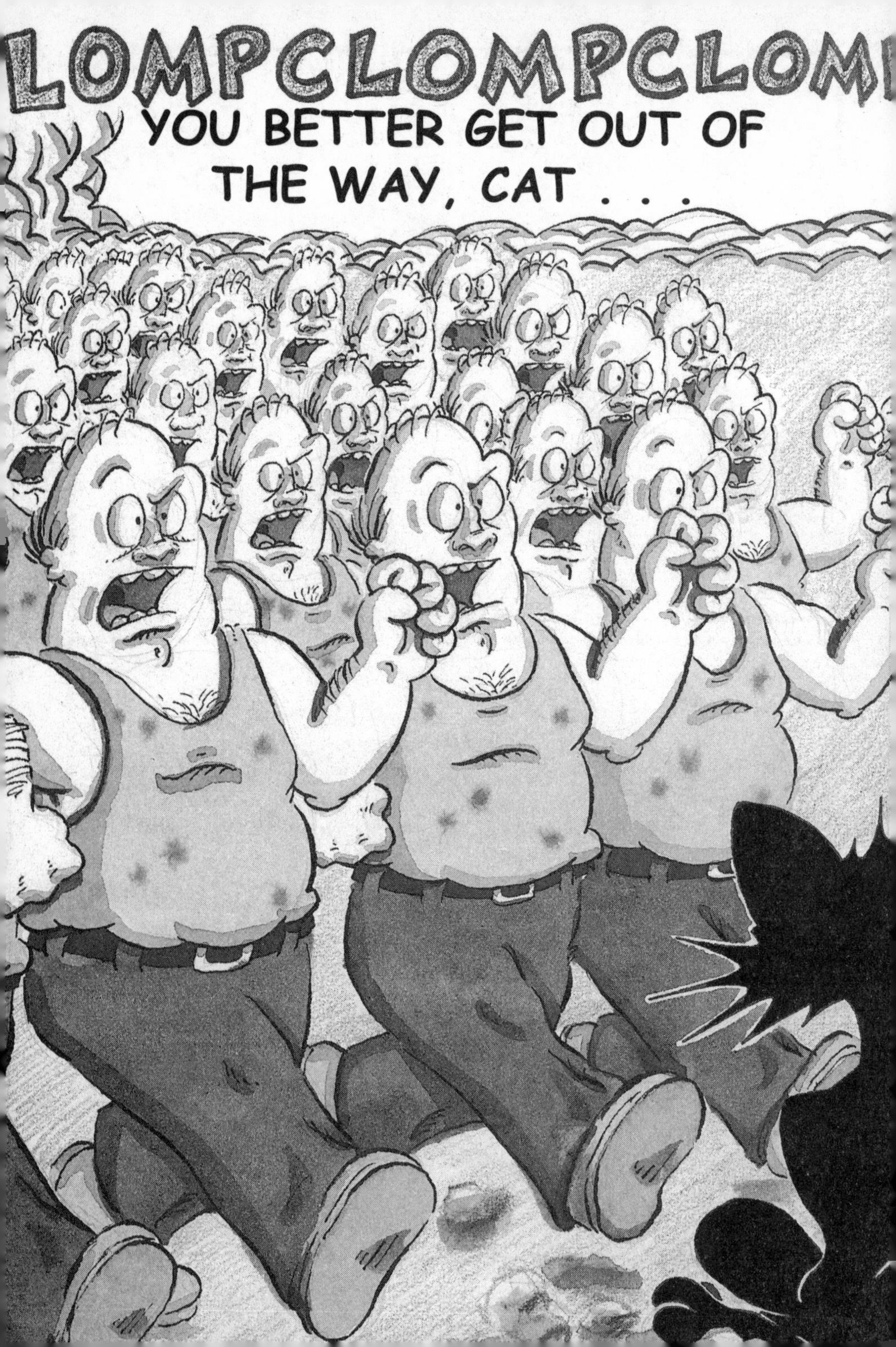
LOMPCLOMPCLOMP
YOU BETTER GET OUT OF THE WAY, CAT . . .

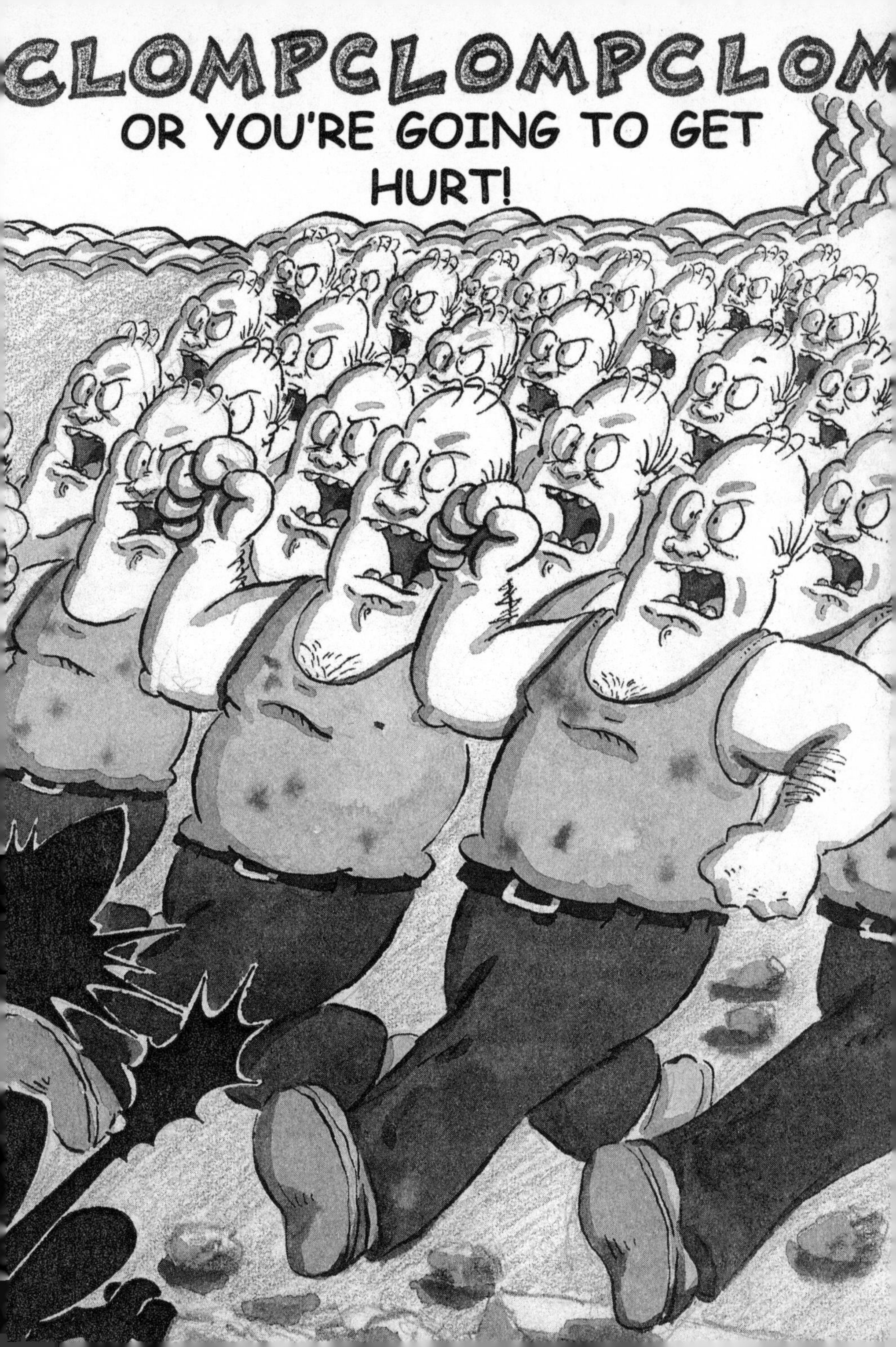
CLOMPCLOMPCLOM
OR YOU'RE GOING TO GET HURT!

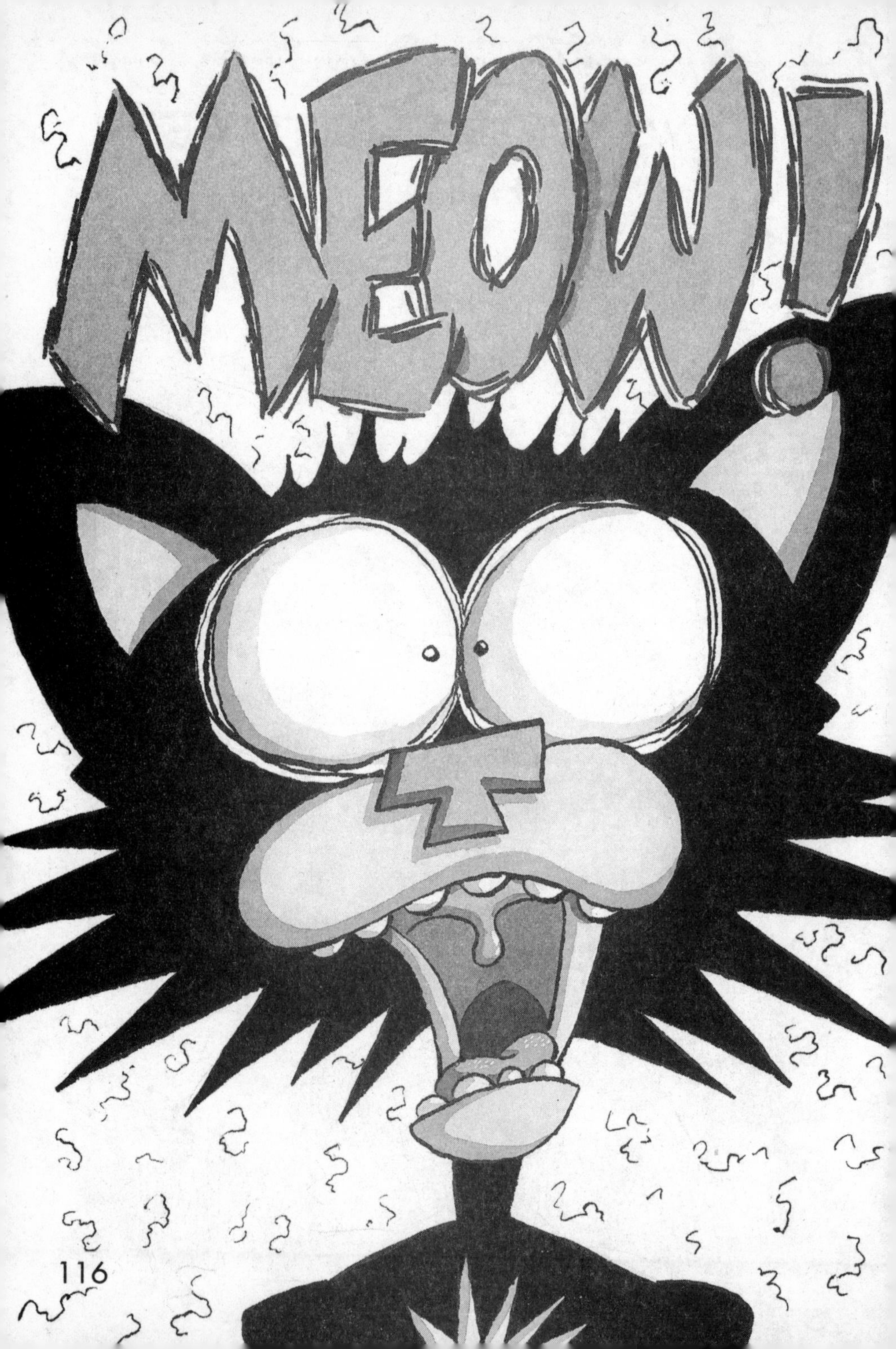
MEOW!!

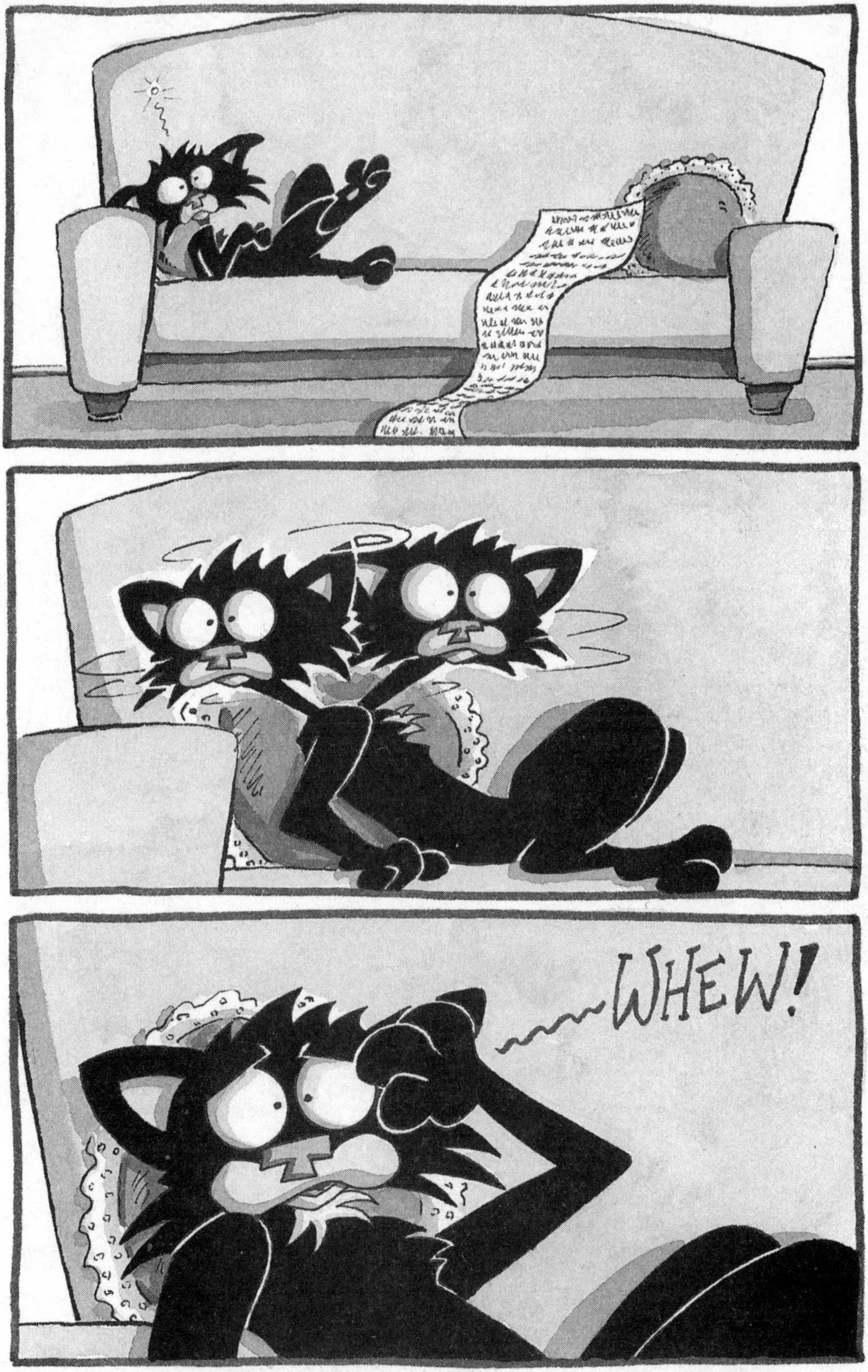
WHEW!

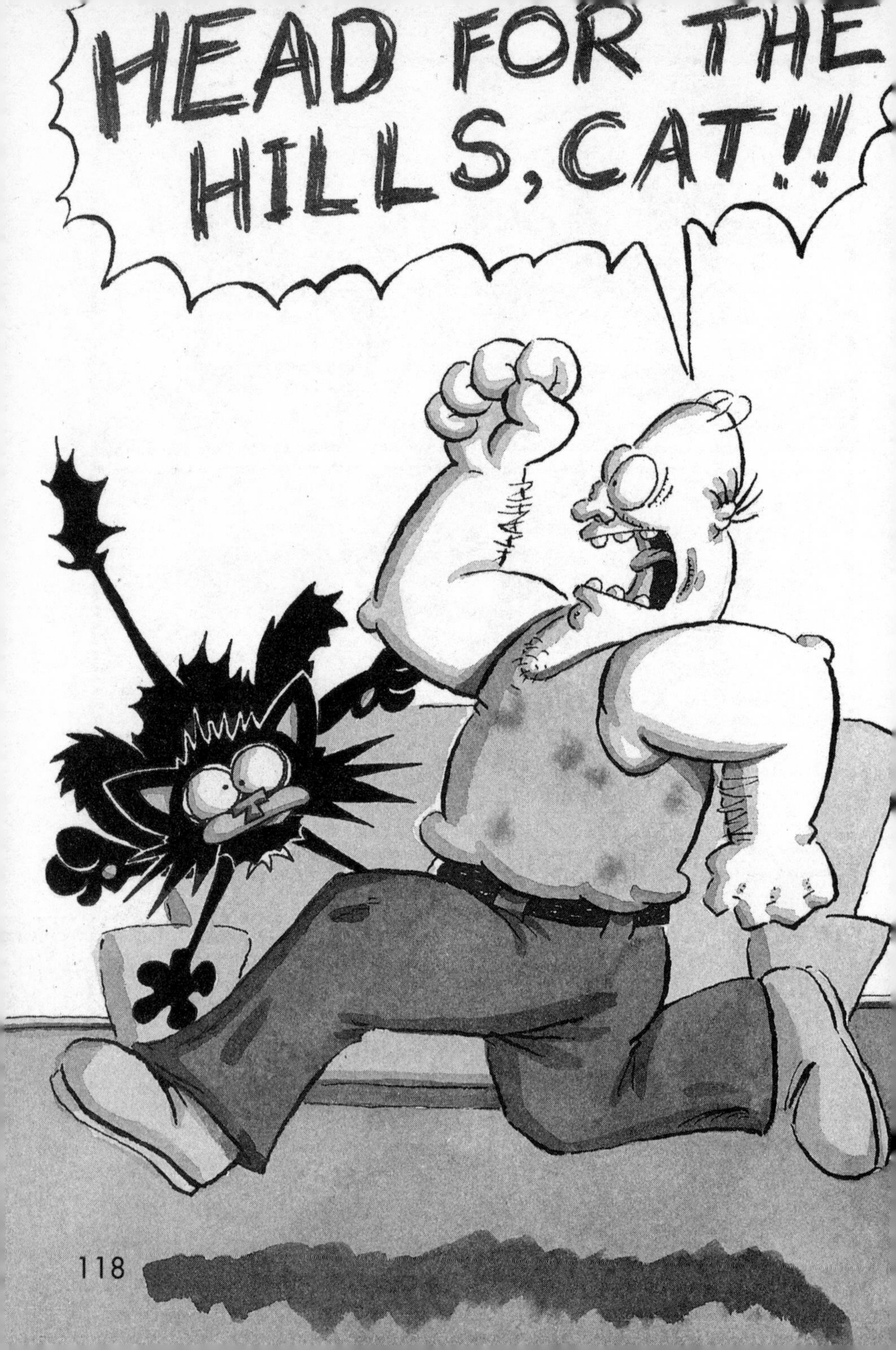
HEAD FOR THE HILLS, CAT!!

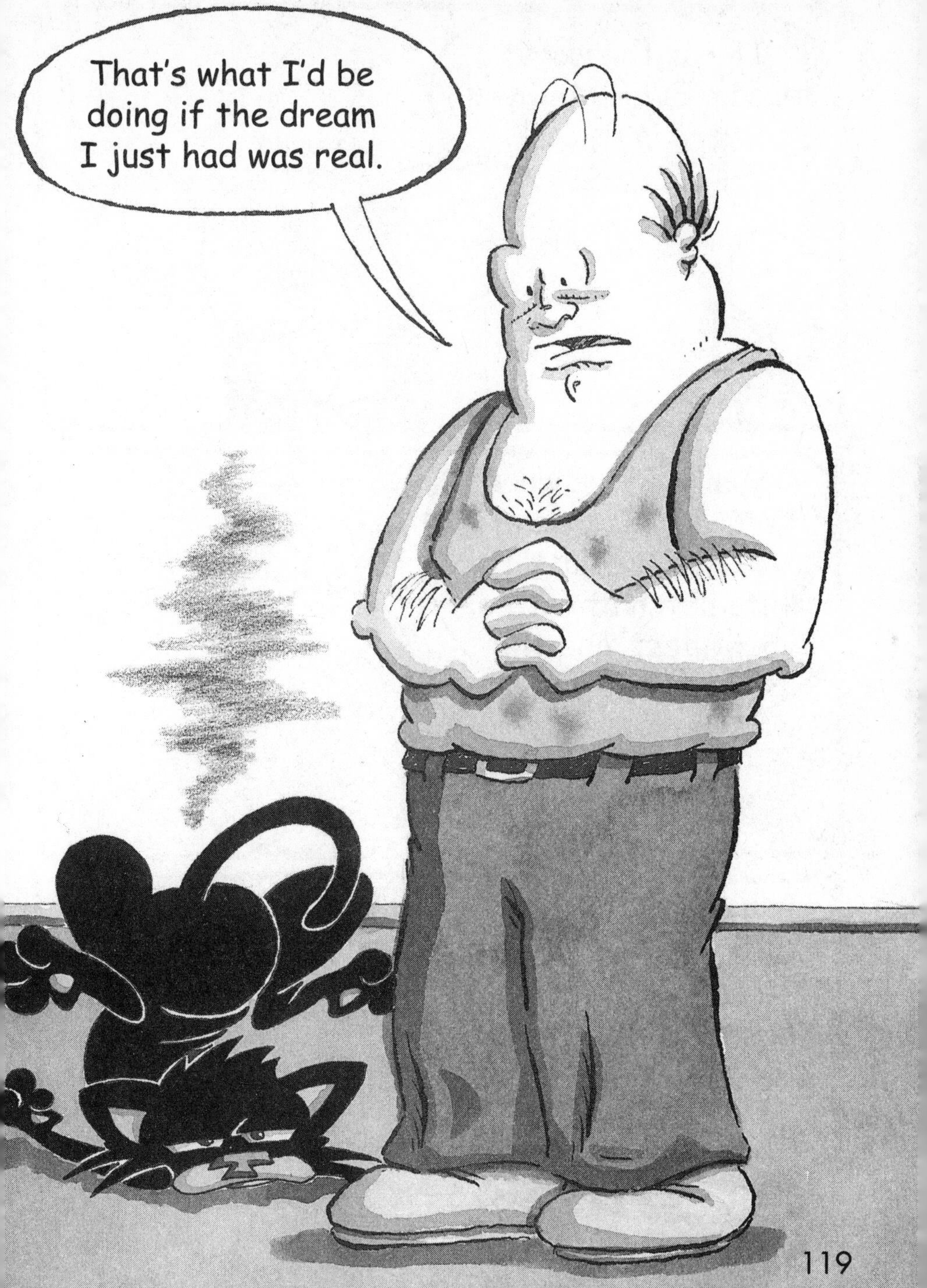
That's what I'd be doing if the dream I just had was real.

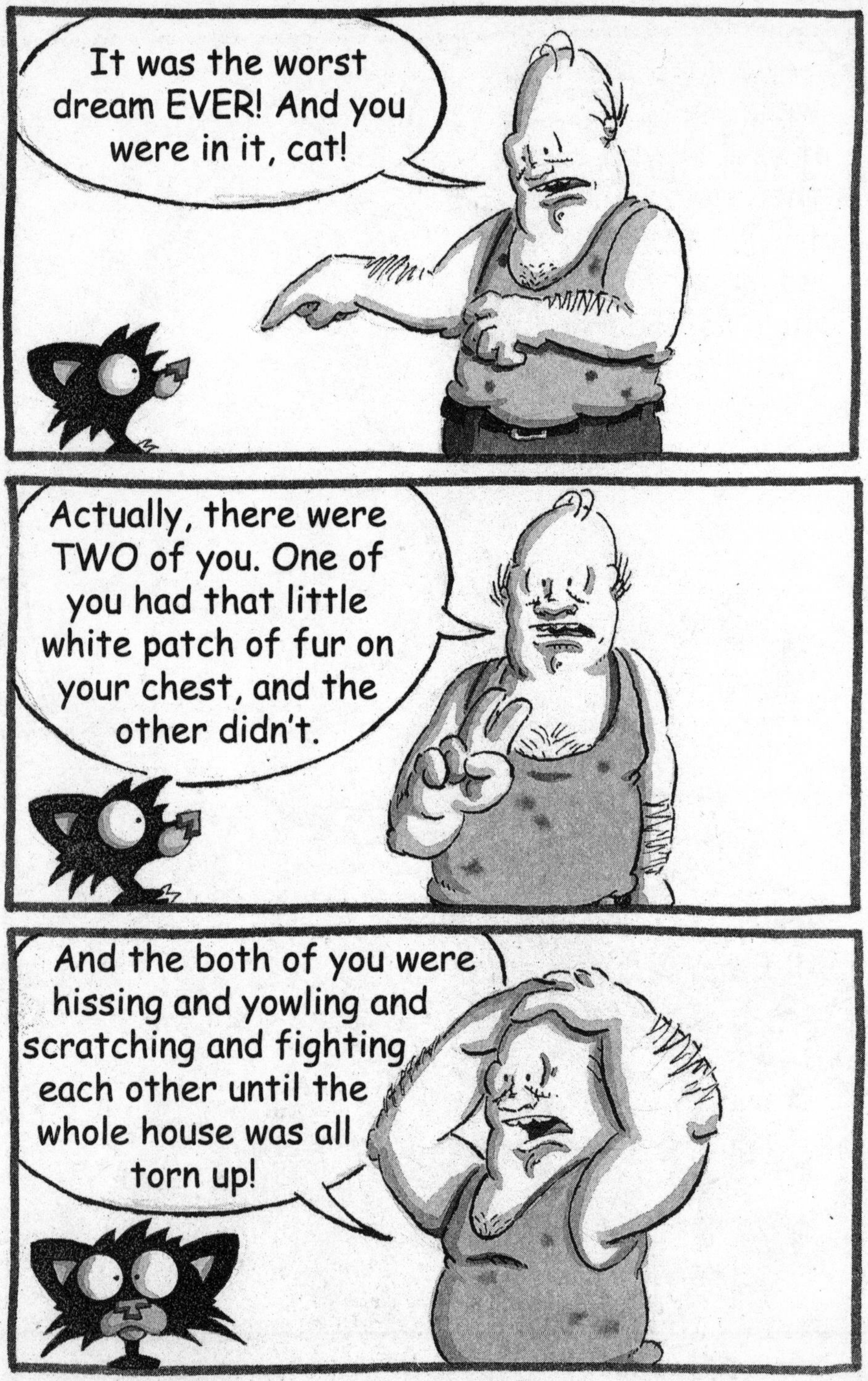
It was the worst dream EVER! And you were in it, cat!
Actually, there were TWO of you. One of you had that little white patch of fur on your chest, and the other didn't.
And the both of you were hissing and yowling and scratching and fighting each other until the whole house was all torn up!

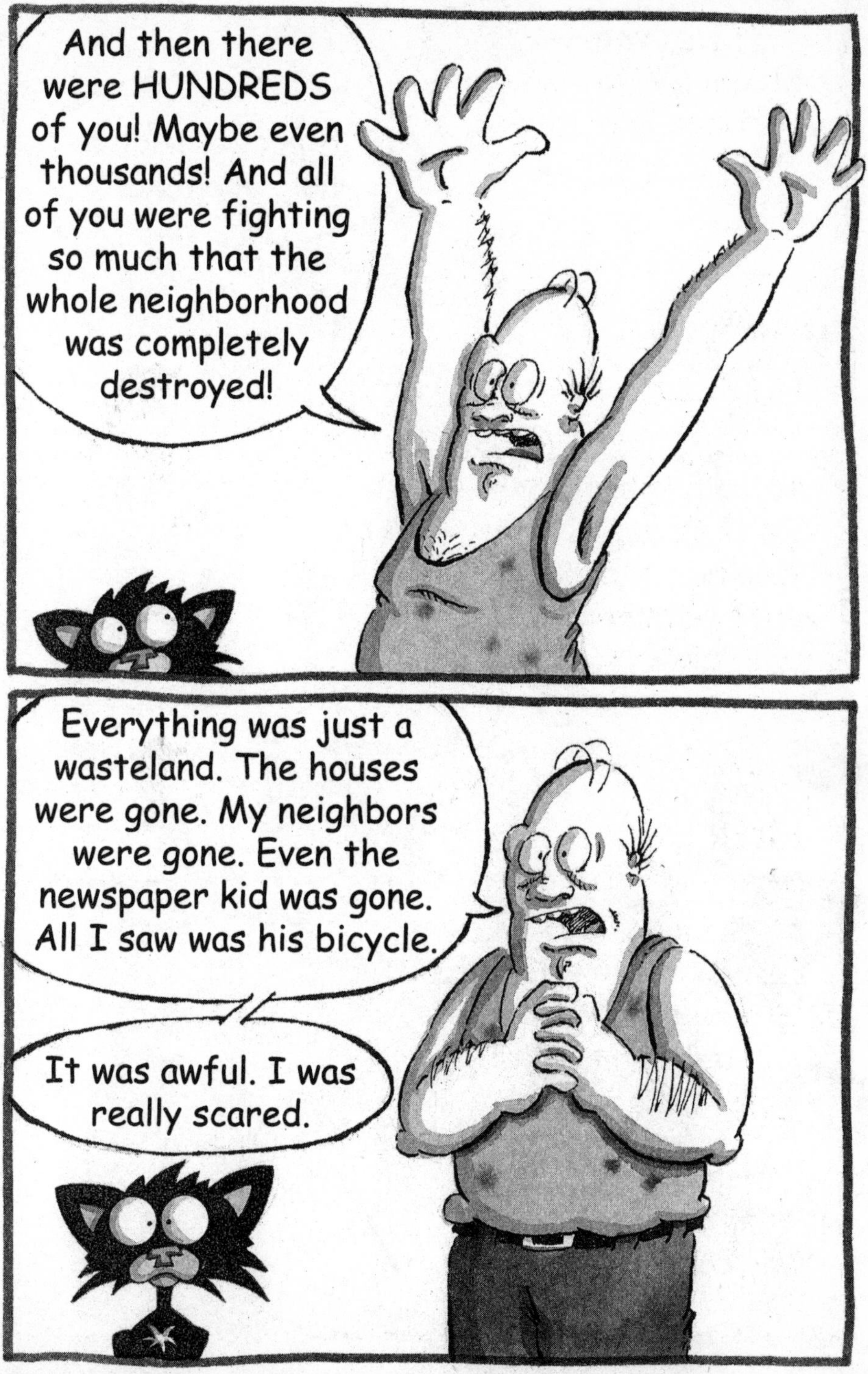
And then there were HUNDREDS of you! Maybe even thousands! And all of you were fighting so much that the whole neighborhood was completely destroyed!
Everything was just a wasteland. The houses were gone. My neighbors were gone. Even the newspaper kid was gone. All I saw was his bicycle.
It was awful. I was really scared.

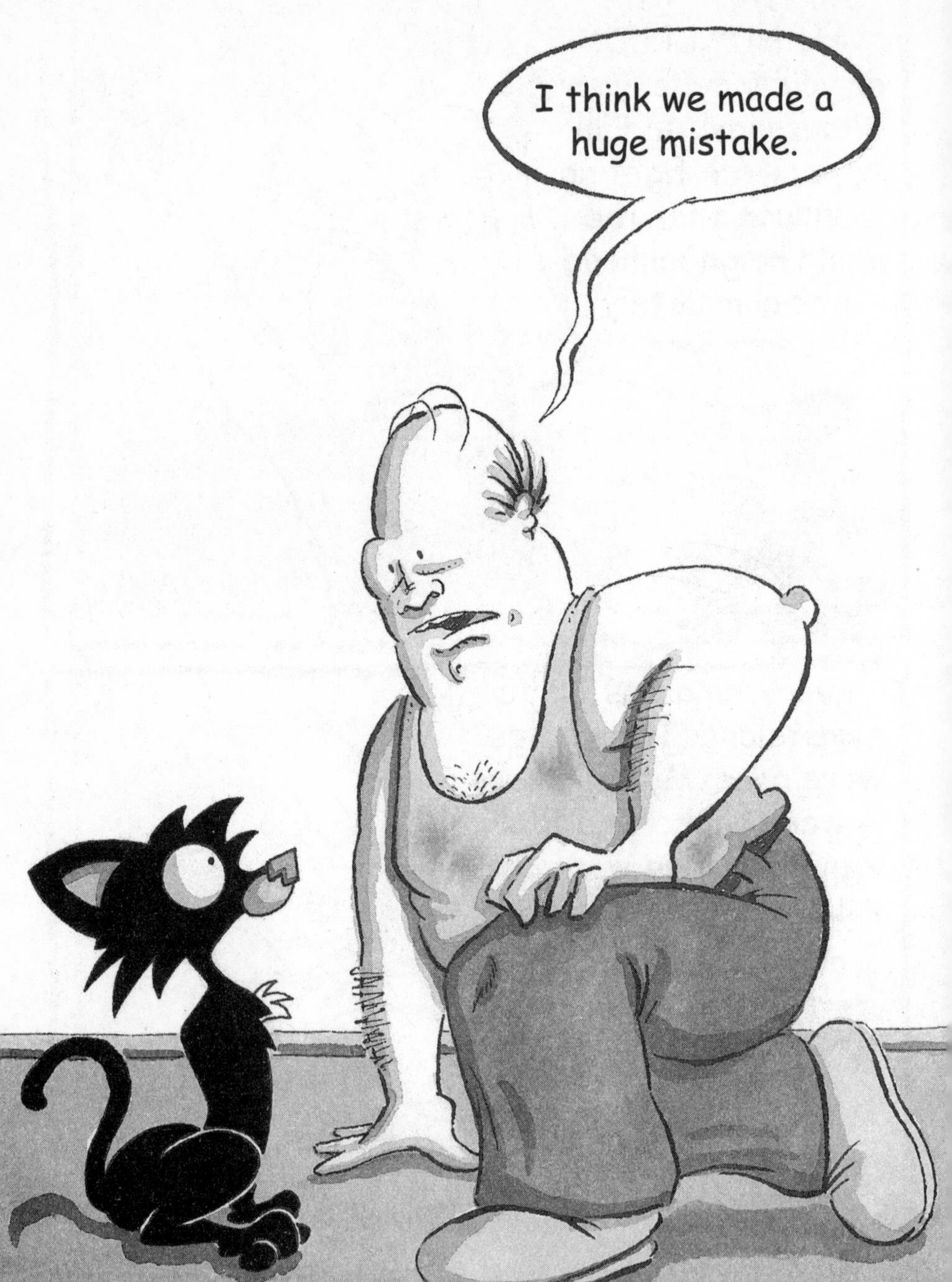
I think we made a huge mistake.

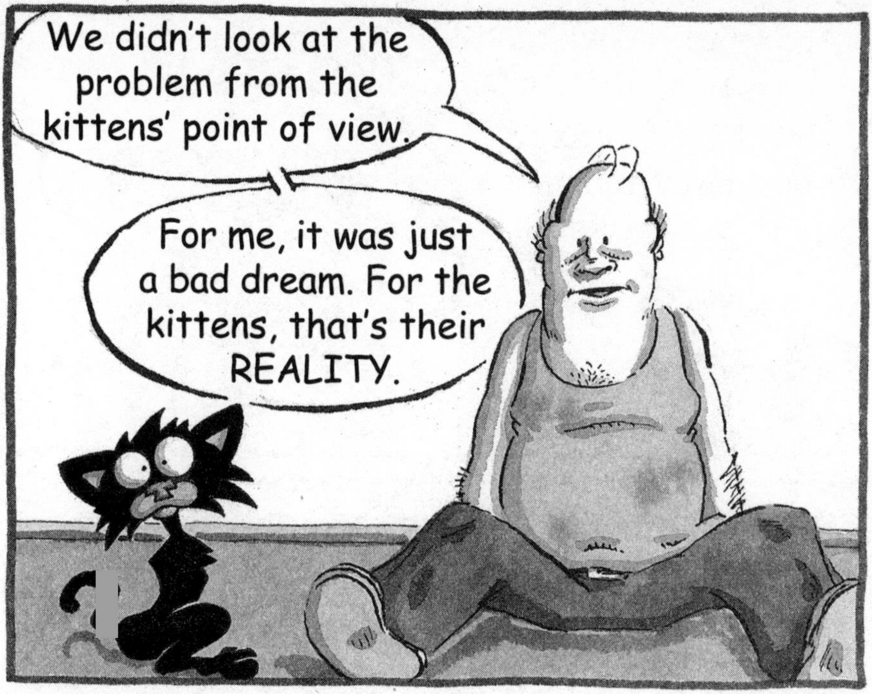

We didn't look at the problem from the kittens' point of view.
For me, it was just a bad dream. For the kittens, that's their REALITY.

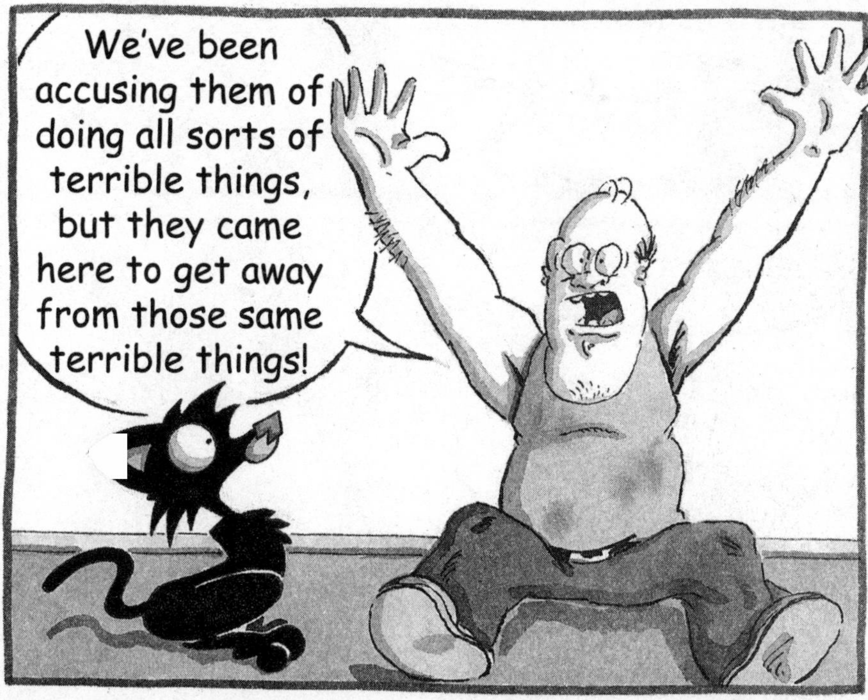

We've been accusing them of doing all sorts of terrible things, but they came here to get away from those same terrible things!

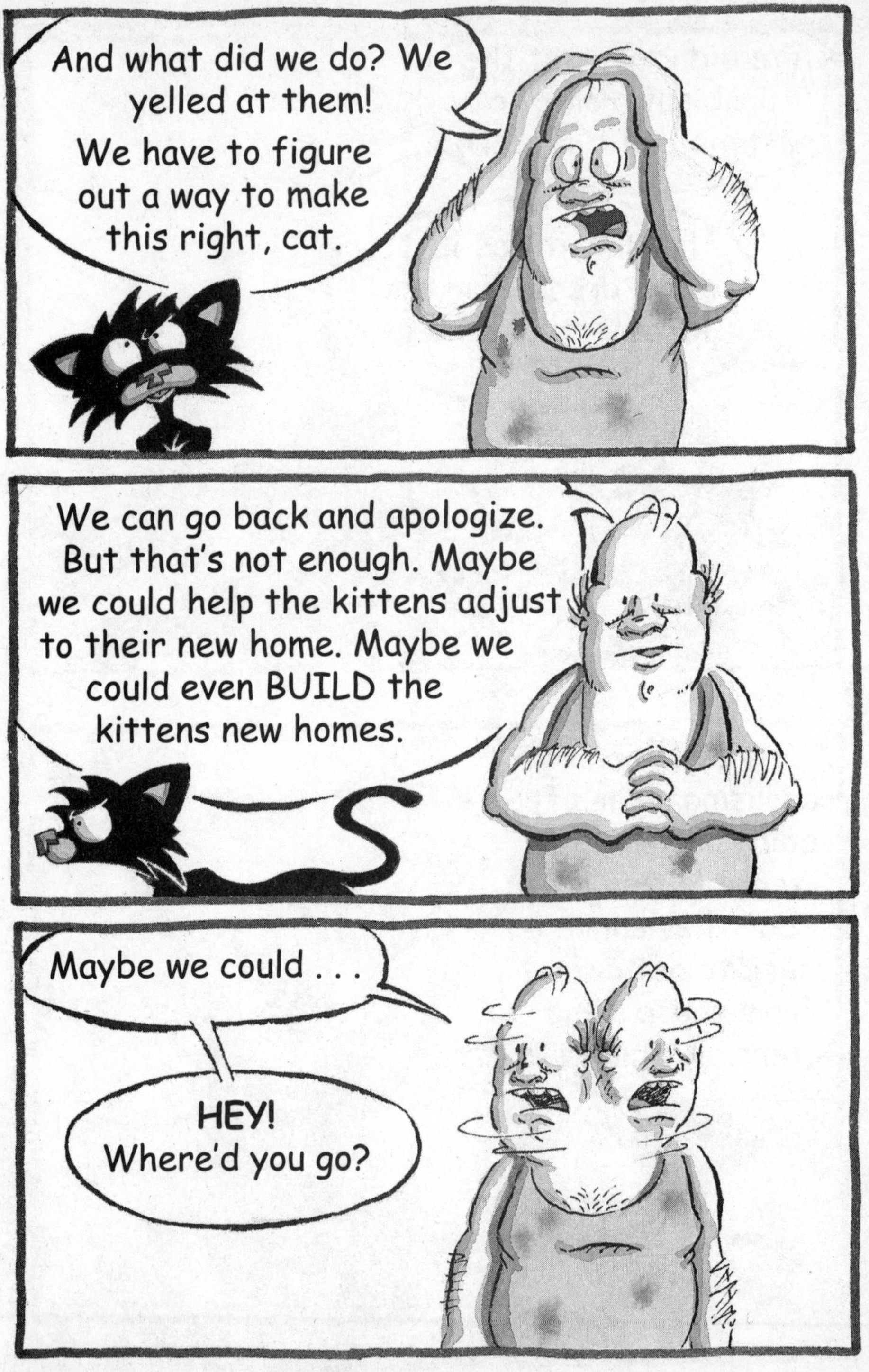

And what did we do? We yelled at them!
We have to figure out a way to make this right, cat.
We can go back and apologize. But that's not enough. Maybe we could help the kittens adjust to their new home. Maybe we could even BUILD the kittens new homes.
Maybe we could . . .
HEY!
Where'd you go?

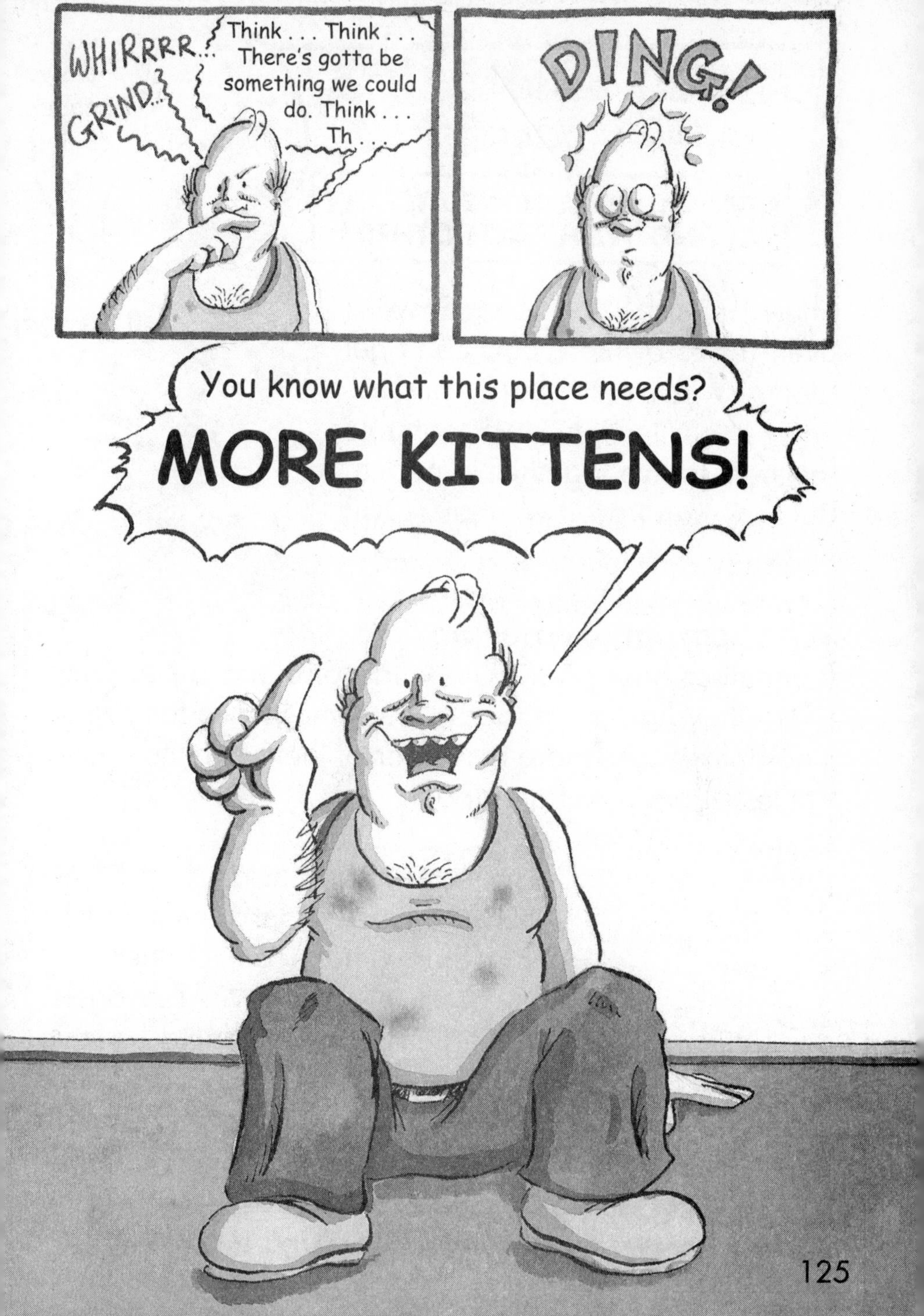
WHIRRRR...
GRIND...
Think . . . Think . . . There's gotta be something we could do. Think . . . Th . . .
DING!
You know what this place needs?
MORE KITTENS!

UNCLE MURRAY'S FUN FACTS

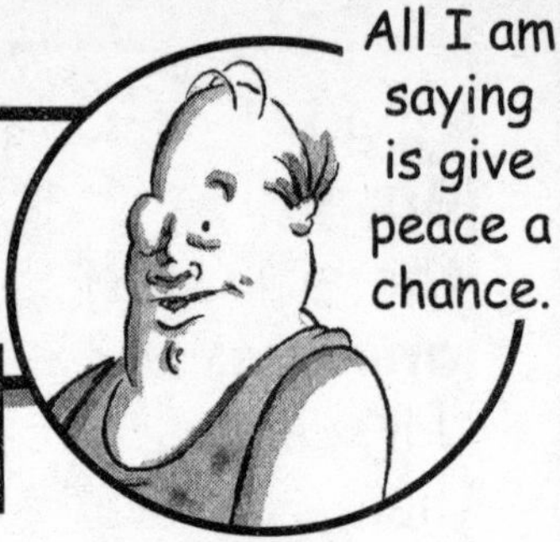
All I am saying is give peace a chance.

CAN CATS BE TRAINED TO GET ALONG WITH EACH OTHER?

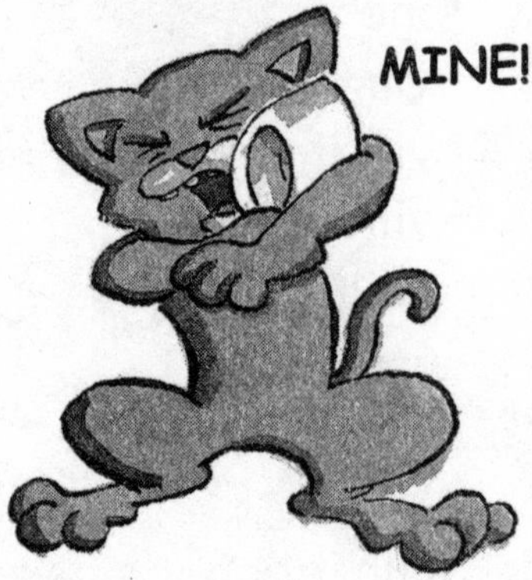
MINE!

Short answer: Yes. Long answer: Even if two or more cats can't get along, will never share, and always seem to fight, it IS possible for them to live together in peace. But they can't do it without YOUR help.

What can an owner do?

Remember how cats in the wild got along better when when they had more food? The same is true for cats inside houses. The more resources of their own they have, the less there is to fight about.

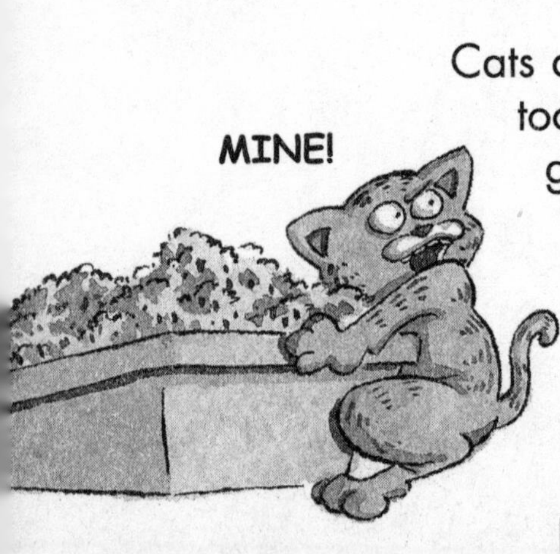
MINE!

Cats are territorial inside their home, too. So if you want them to live together without conflict, then they need to have fewer reasons to fight. Each cat should have its own food bowl, and it might be important to keep those bowls far away from each other. The same is true for water dishes, litter boxes, and even YOU.

But what if there is only one owner?

If it's difficult or chaotic to play with your cats together, then play with them separately. Play with one cat in one room and the other cat in another room. Or find someone who can play with one cat while you play with the other. Over time, you might be able to play with both cats in the same room, but it might take a while.

How long?

Honestly, your cats may never really learn to share with each other and play with each other the way you'd like. But if you make sure they all have enough resources at their disposal, then you can reduce the conflict a lot.

You'll never be able to force your cats to be best friends, but you can help them learn how to live in peace together. They're just like people that way.

•CHAPTER SIX•

HOME AGAIN

Well, well, well . . . look who's back. Welcome home, Kitty. Uncle Murray called and told me how much you both regretted your behavior. Do you have anything you want to say to me and the kittens?

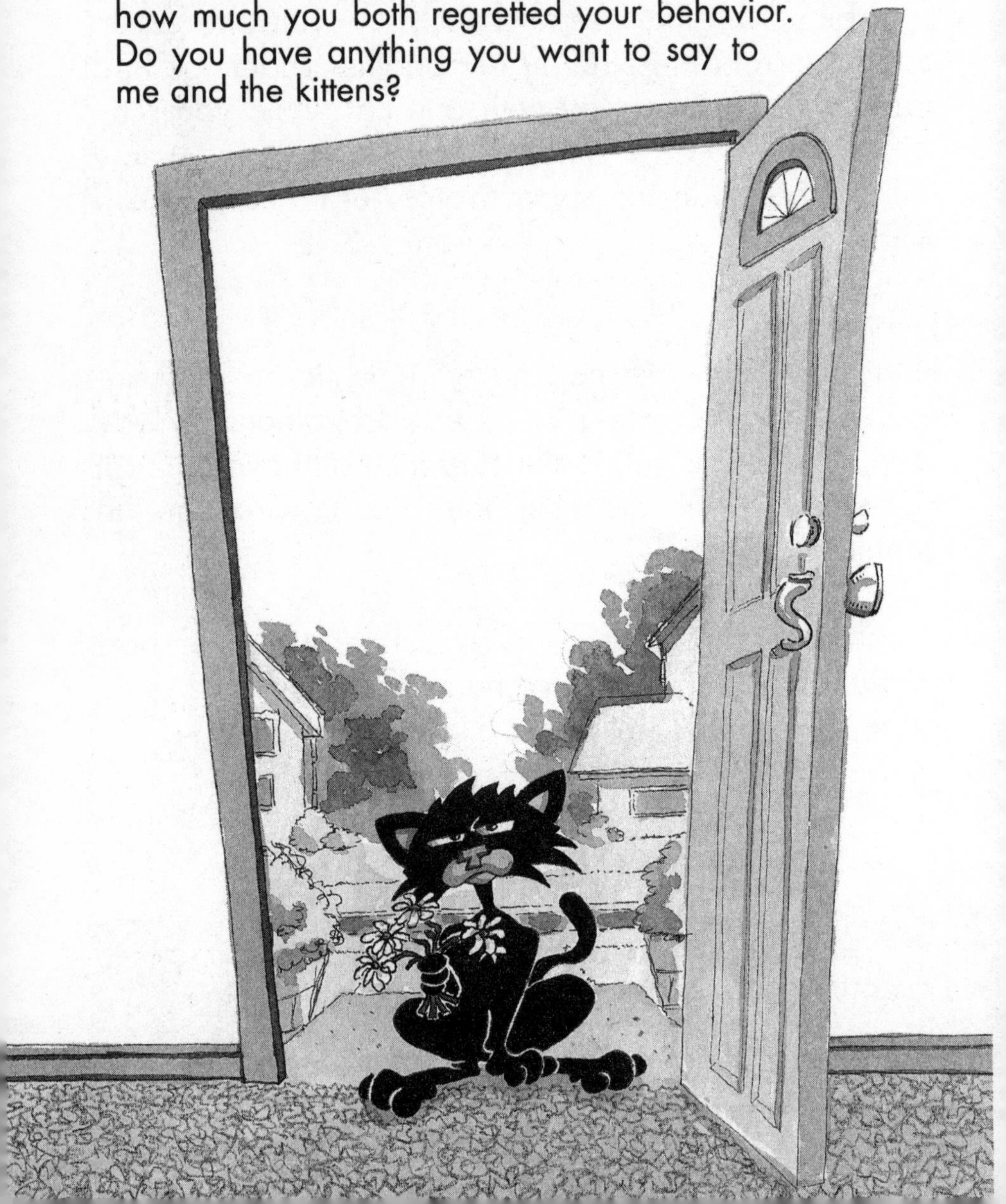

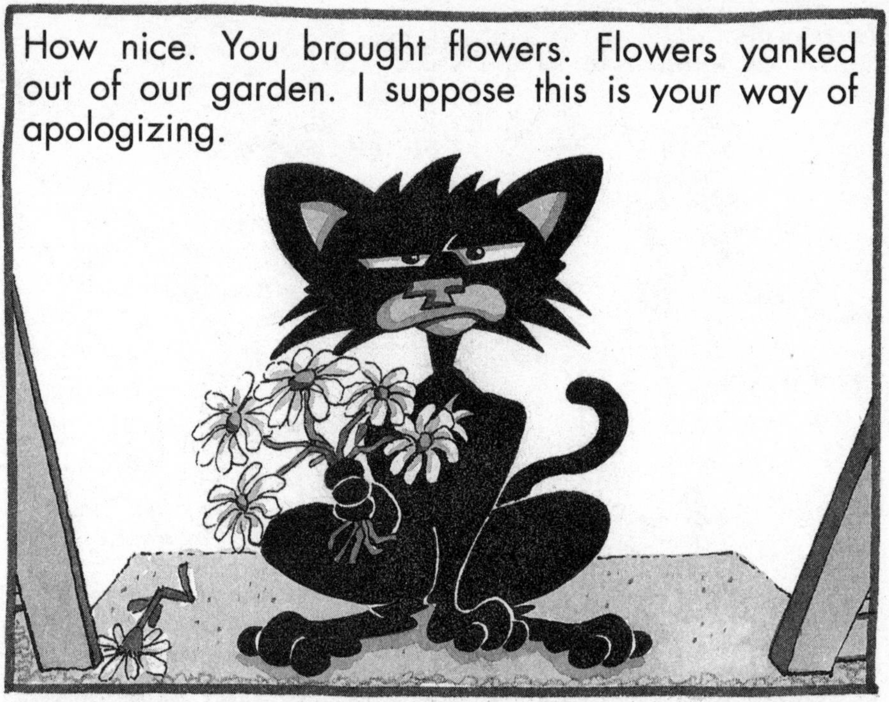
How nice. You brought flowers. Flowers yanked out of our garden. I suppose this is your way of apologizing.

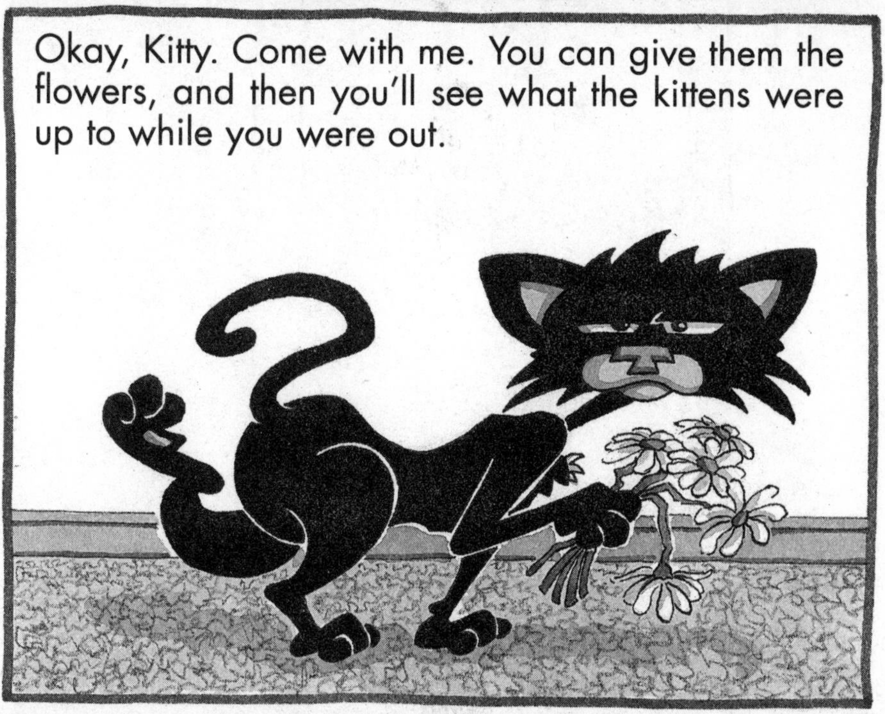
Okay, Kitty. Come with me. You can give them the flowers, and then you'll see what the kittens were up to while you were out.

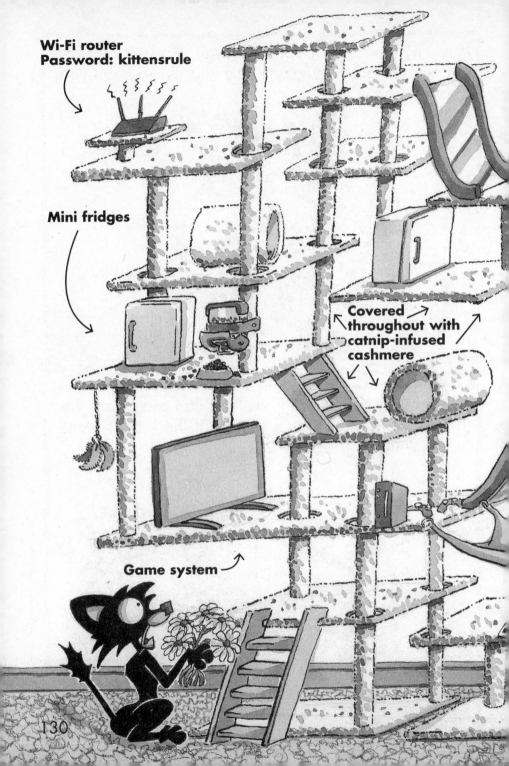

Wi-Fi router
Password: kittensrule

Mini fridges

Covered throughout with catnip-infused cashmere

Game system

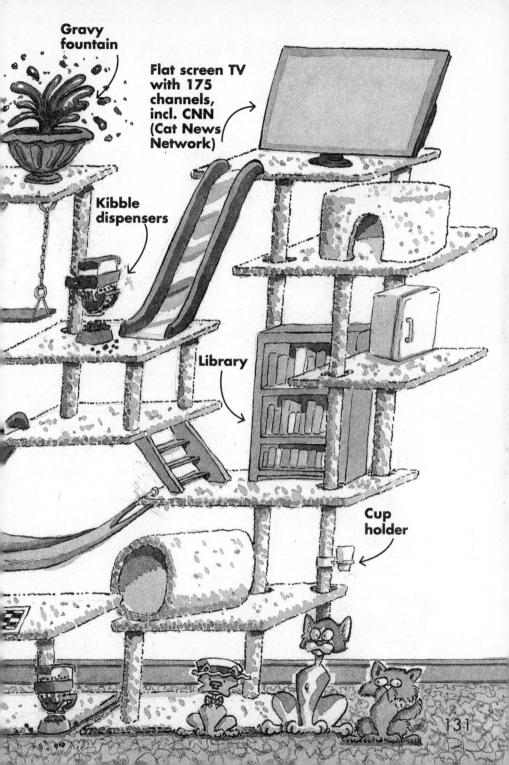

Gravy fountain

Flat screen TV with 175 channels, incl. CNN (Cat News Network)

Kibble dispensers

Library

Cup holder

131

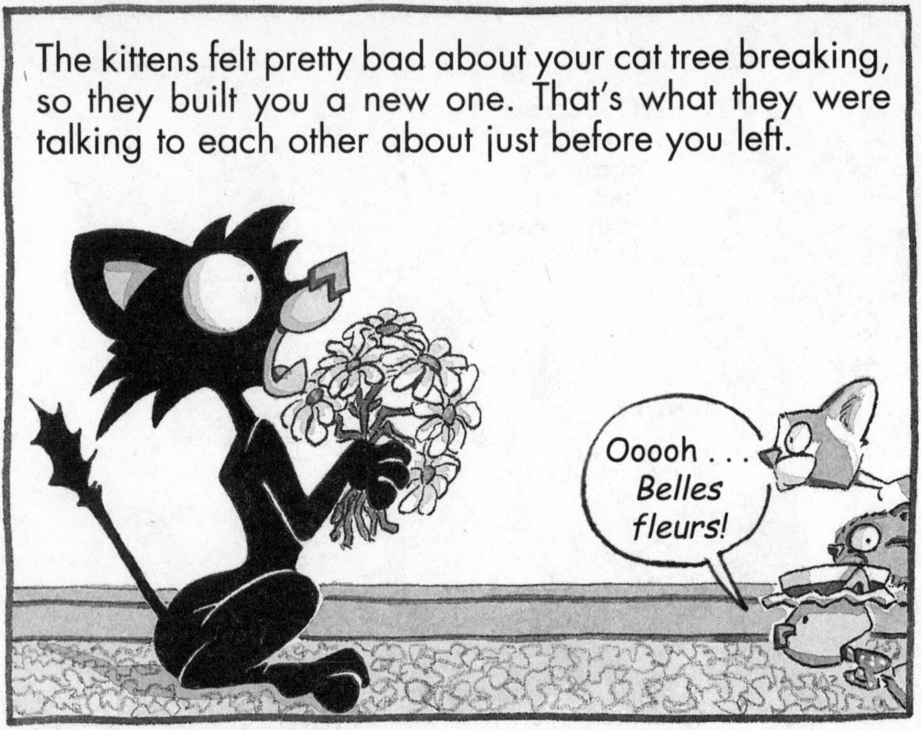
The kittens felt pretty bad about your cat tree breaking, so they built you a new one. That's what they were talking to each other about just before you left.
Ooooh . . . *Belles fleurs!*

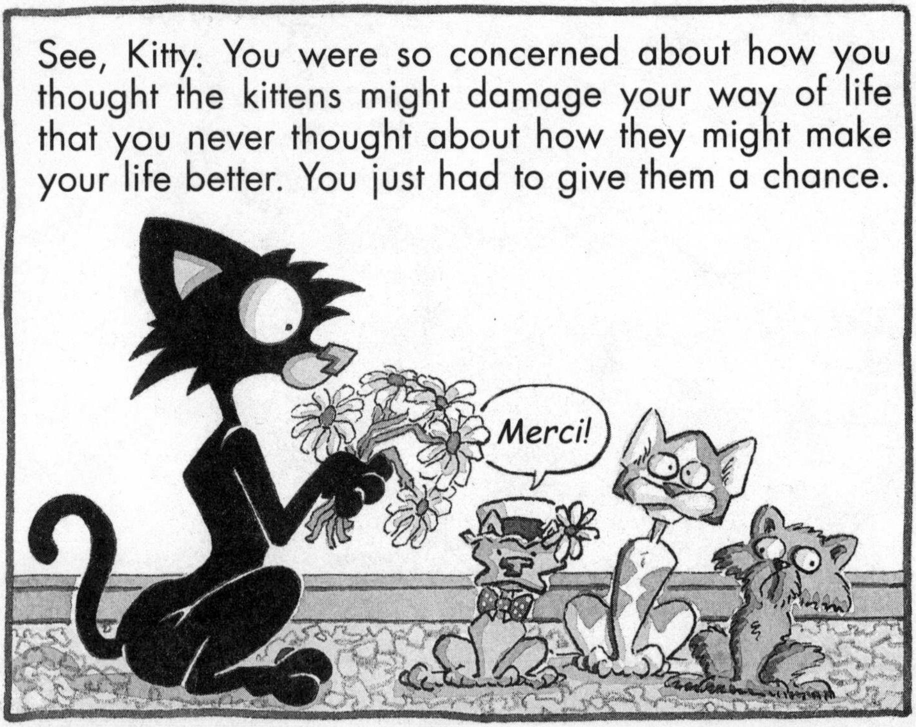
See, Kitty. You were so concerned about how you thought the kittens might damage your way of life that you never thought about how they might make your life better. You just had to give them a chance.
Merci!

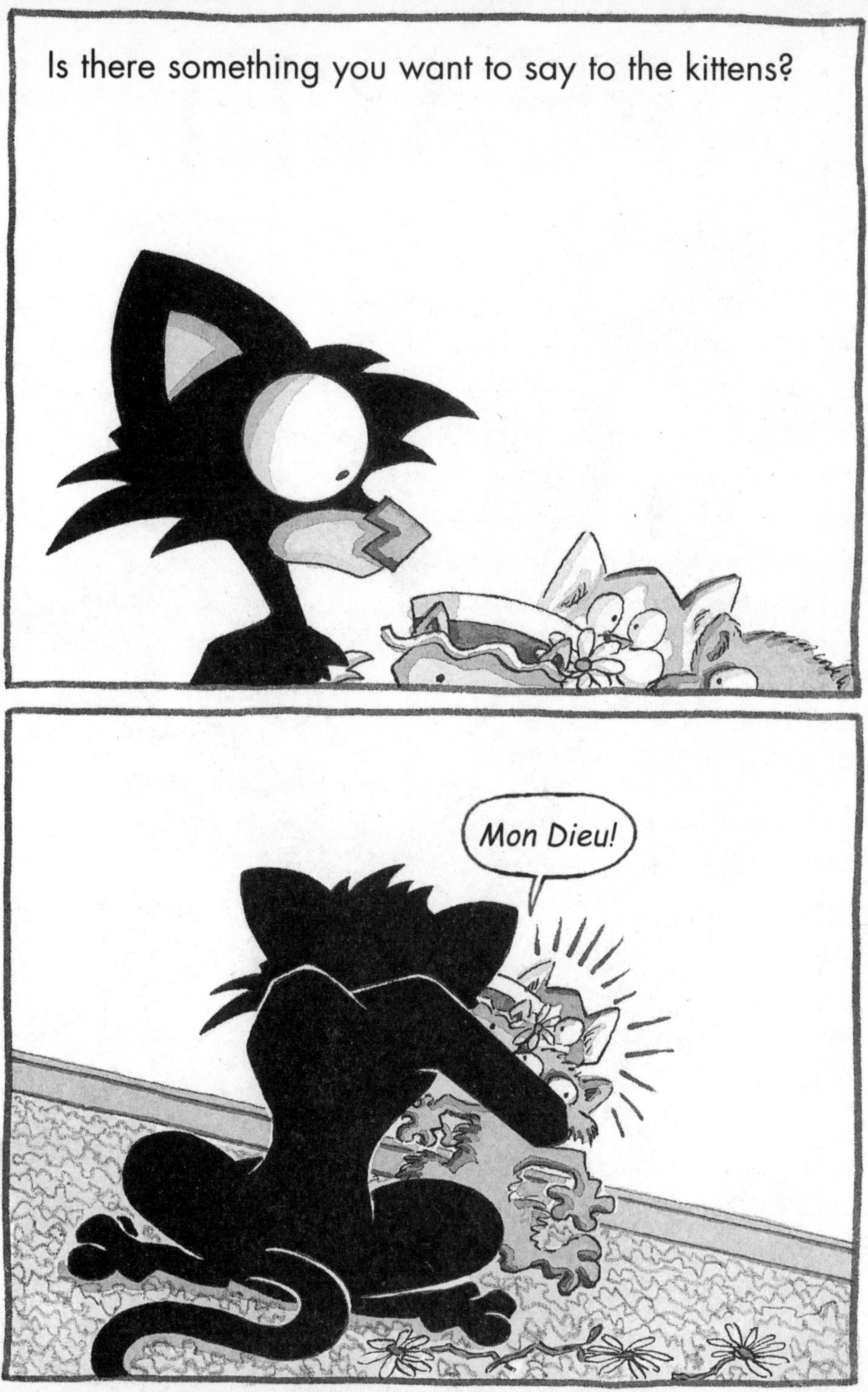
Is there something you want to say to the kittens?
Mon Dieu!

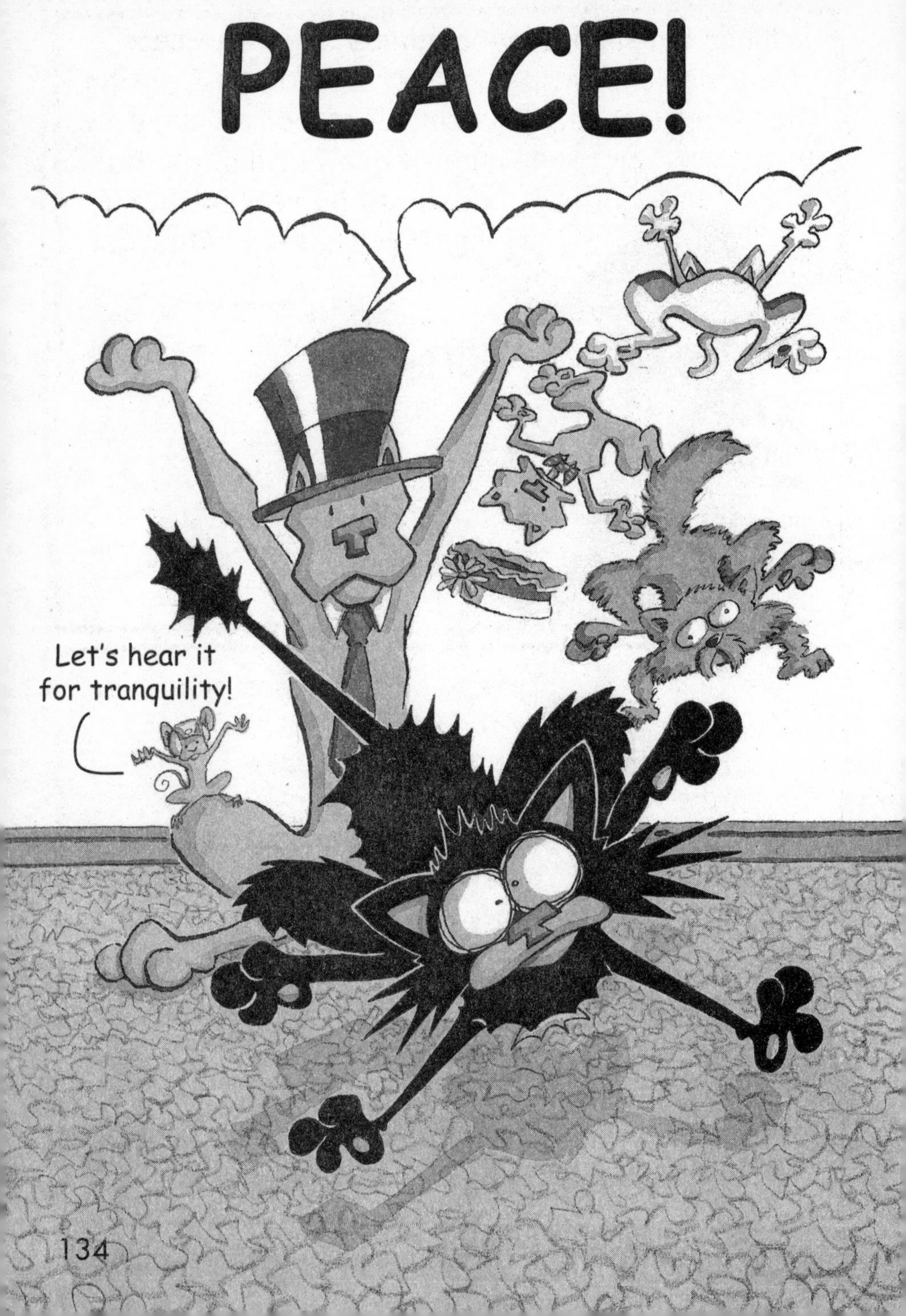
PEACE!
Let's hear it for tranquility!

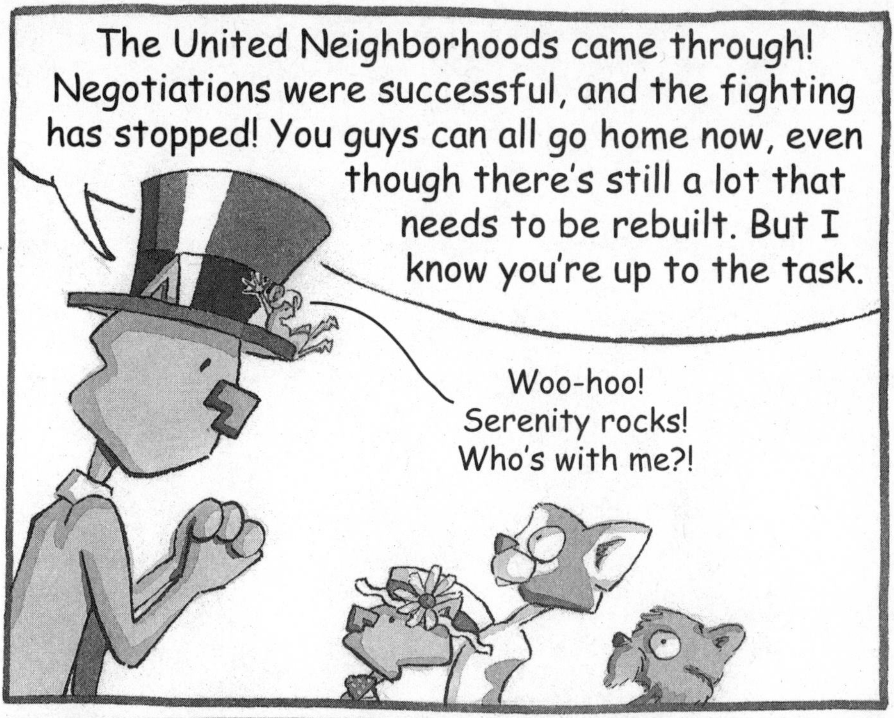
The United Neighborhoods came through! Negotiations were successful, and the fighting has stopped! You guys can all go home now, even though there's still a lot that needs to be rebuilt. But I know you're up to the task.
Woo-hoo! Serenity rocks! Who's with me?!

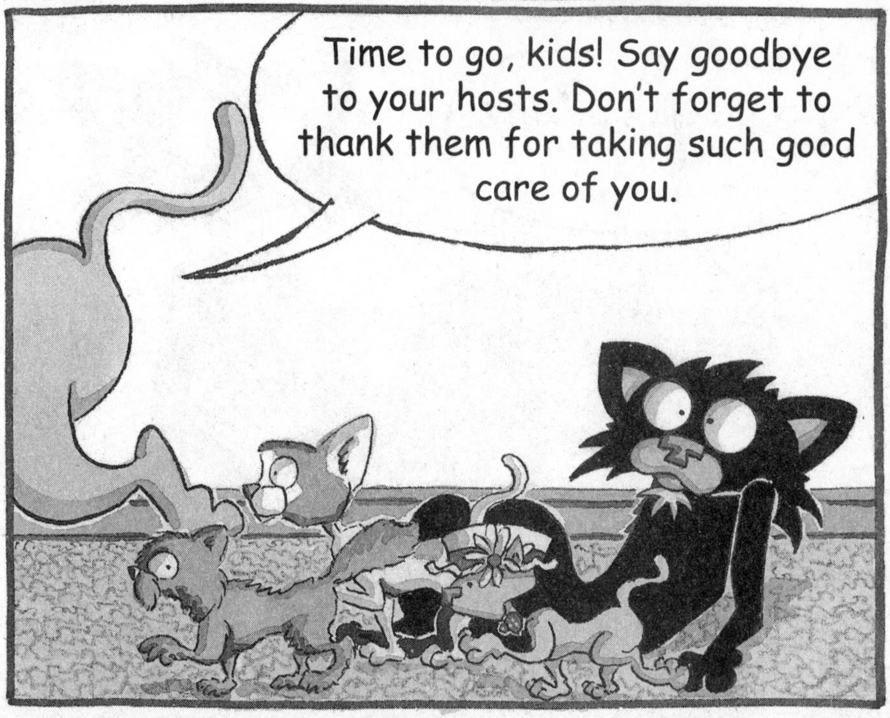
Time to go, kids! Say goodbye to your hosts. Don't forget to thank them for taking such good care of you.

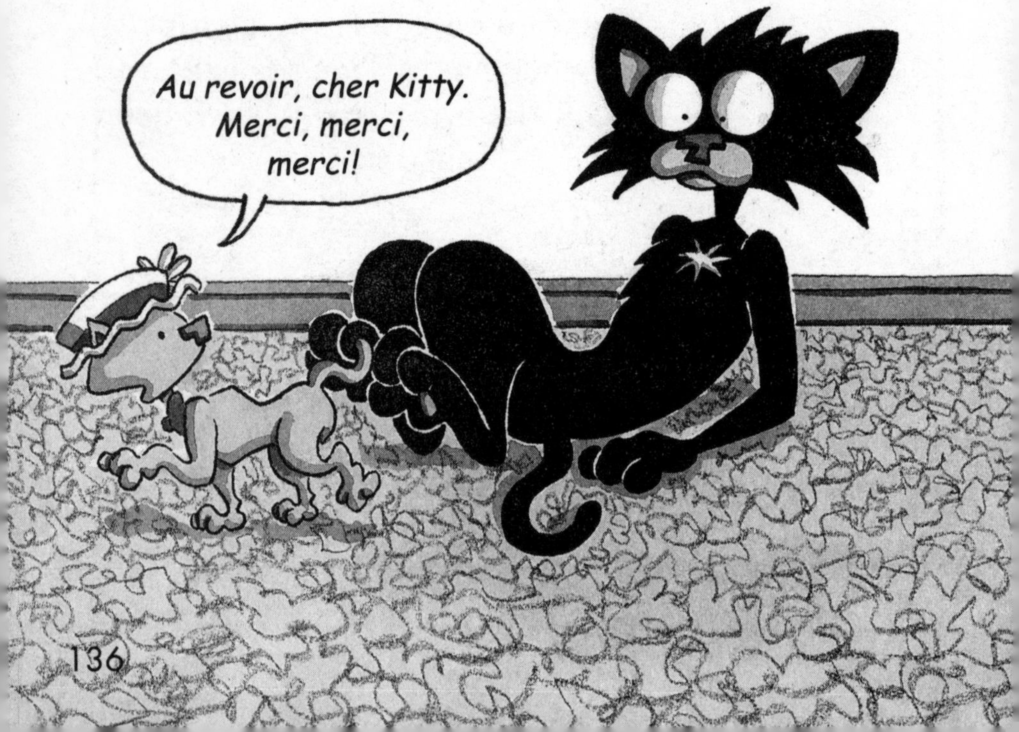
Au revoir, cher Kitty. Merci, merci, merci!

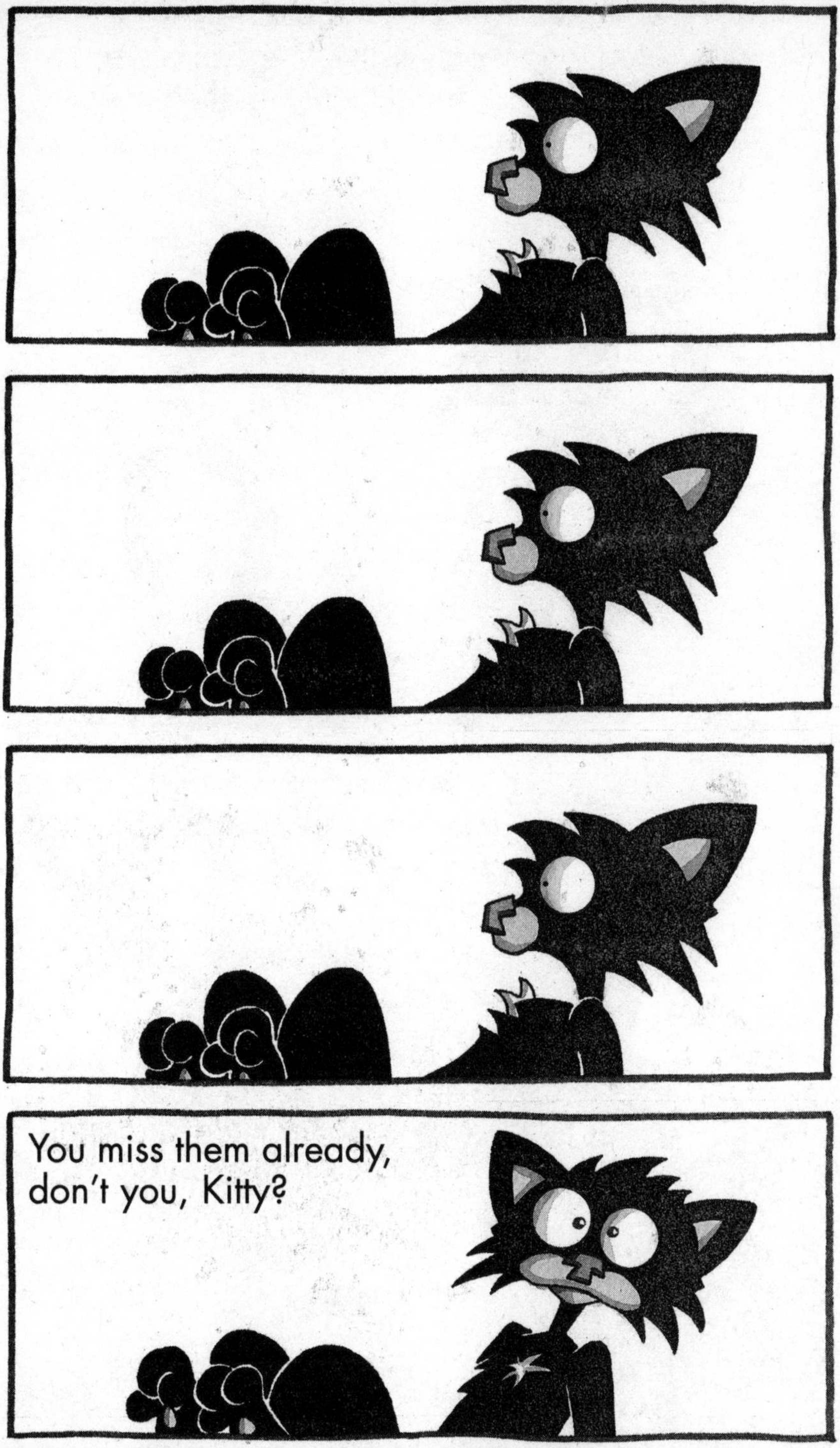
You miss them already,
don't you, Kitty?

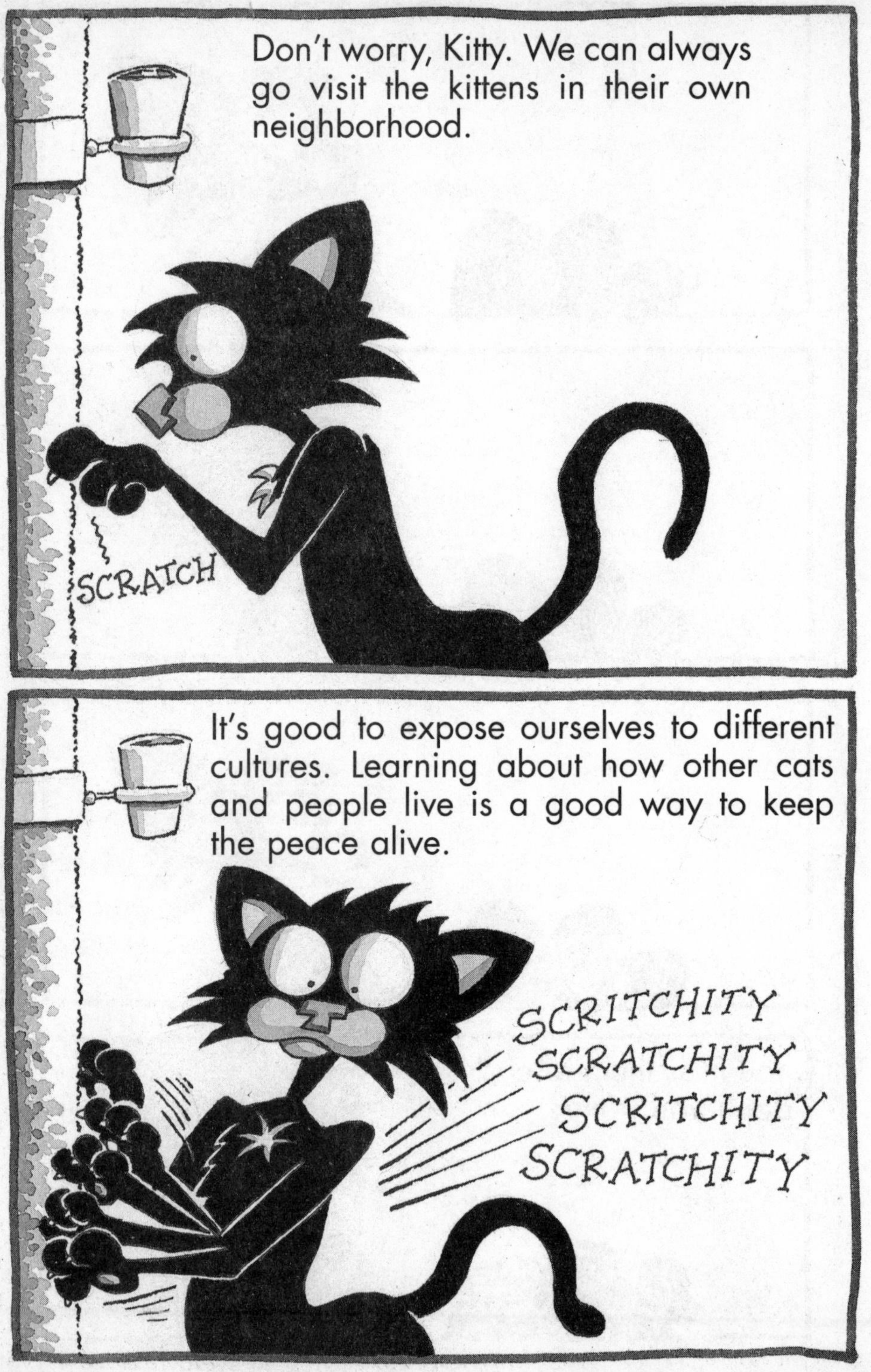
Don't worry, Kitty. We can always go visit the kittens in their own neighborhood.
SCRATCH
It's good to expose ourselves to different cultures. Learning about how other cats and people live is a good way to keep the peace alive.
SCRITCHITY
SCRATCHITY
SCRITCHITY
SCRATCHITY

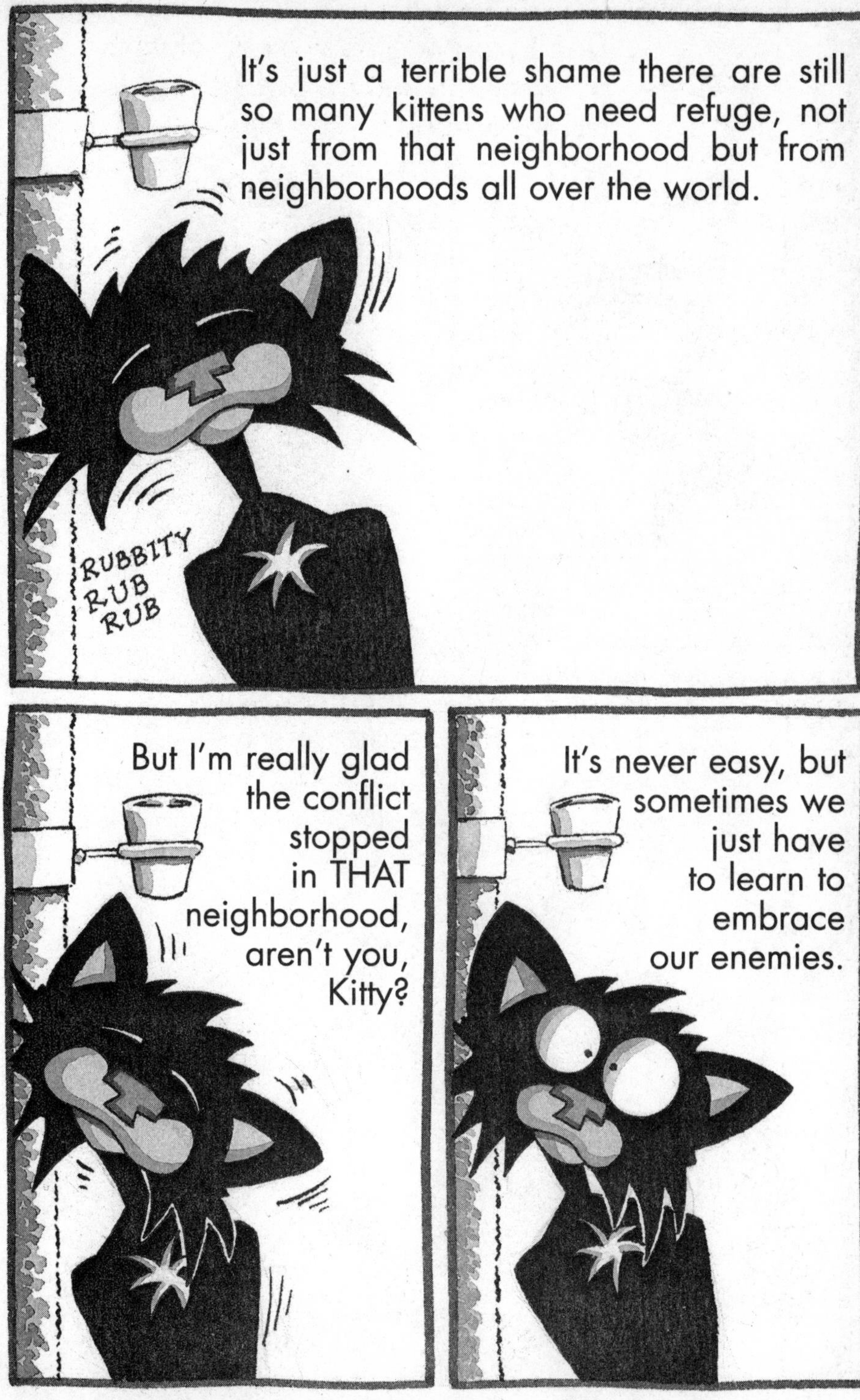
It's just a terrible shame there are still so many kittens who need refuge, not just from that neighborhood but from neighborhoods all over the world.
RUBBITY RUB RUB
But I'm really glad the conflict stopped in THAT neighborhood, aren't you, Kitty?
It's never easy, but sometimes we just have to learn to embrace our enemies.

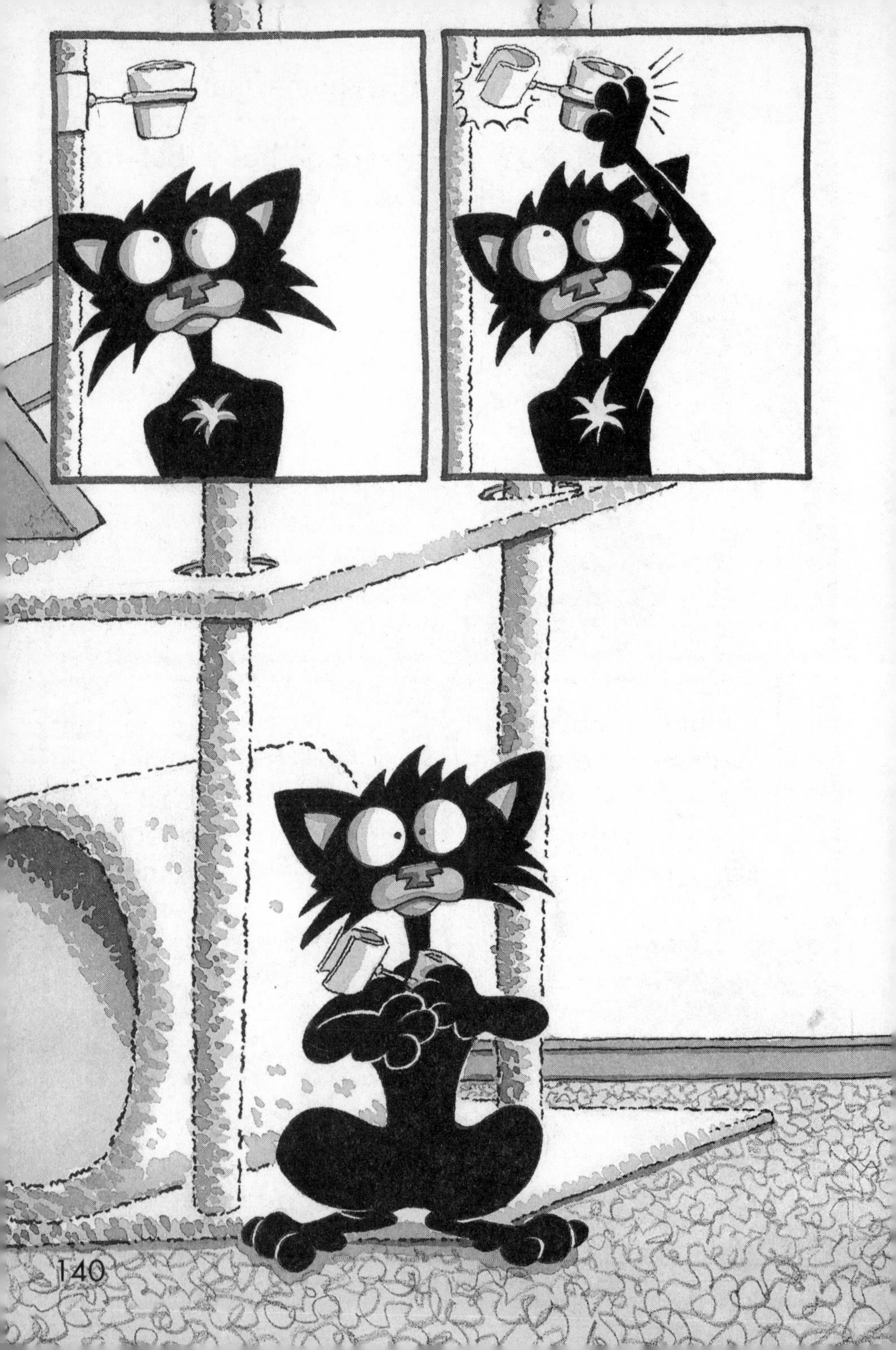

•CHAPTER SEVEN•

IT'S NEVER EASY

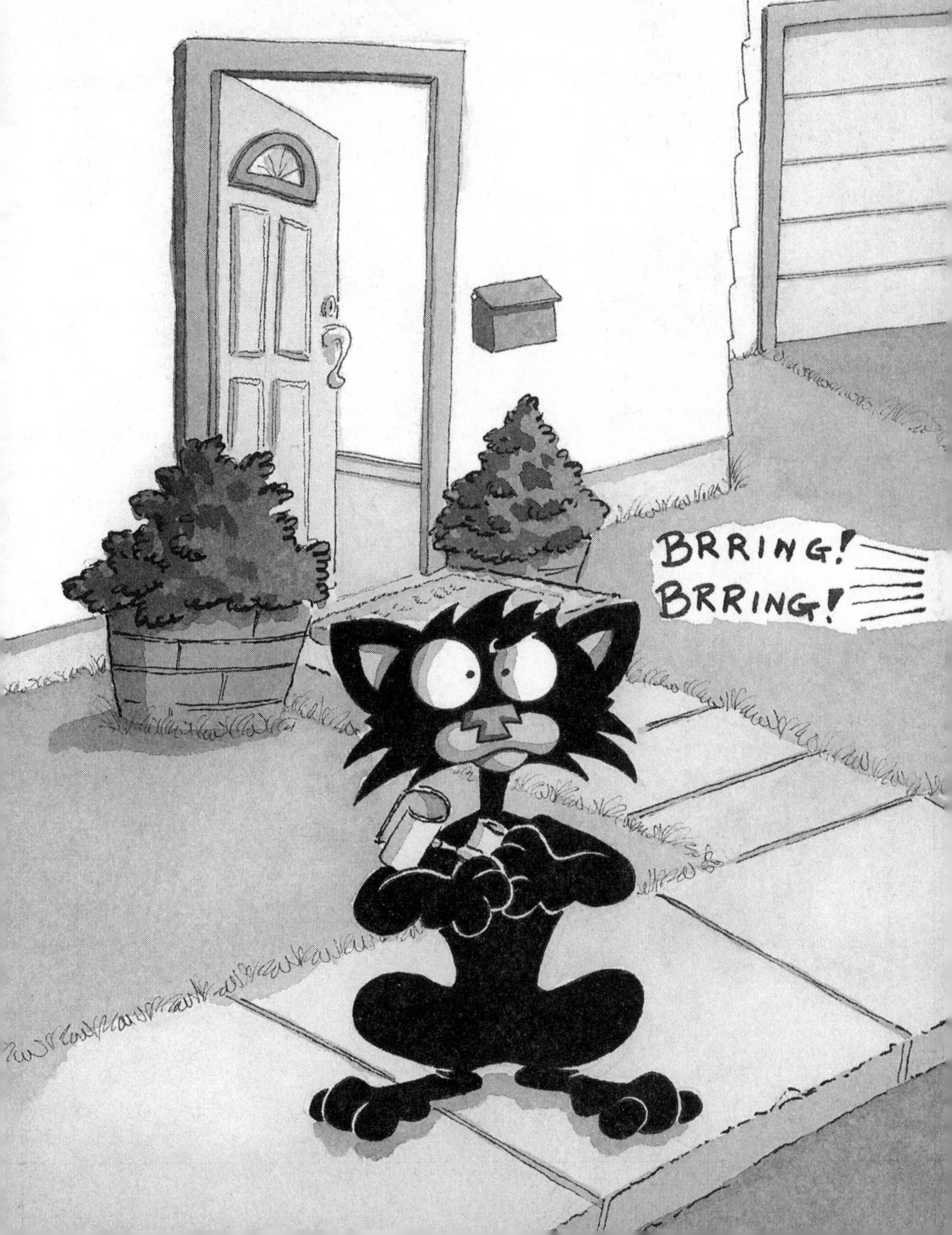
BRRING!
BRRING!

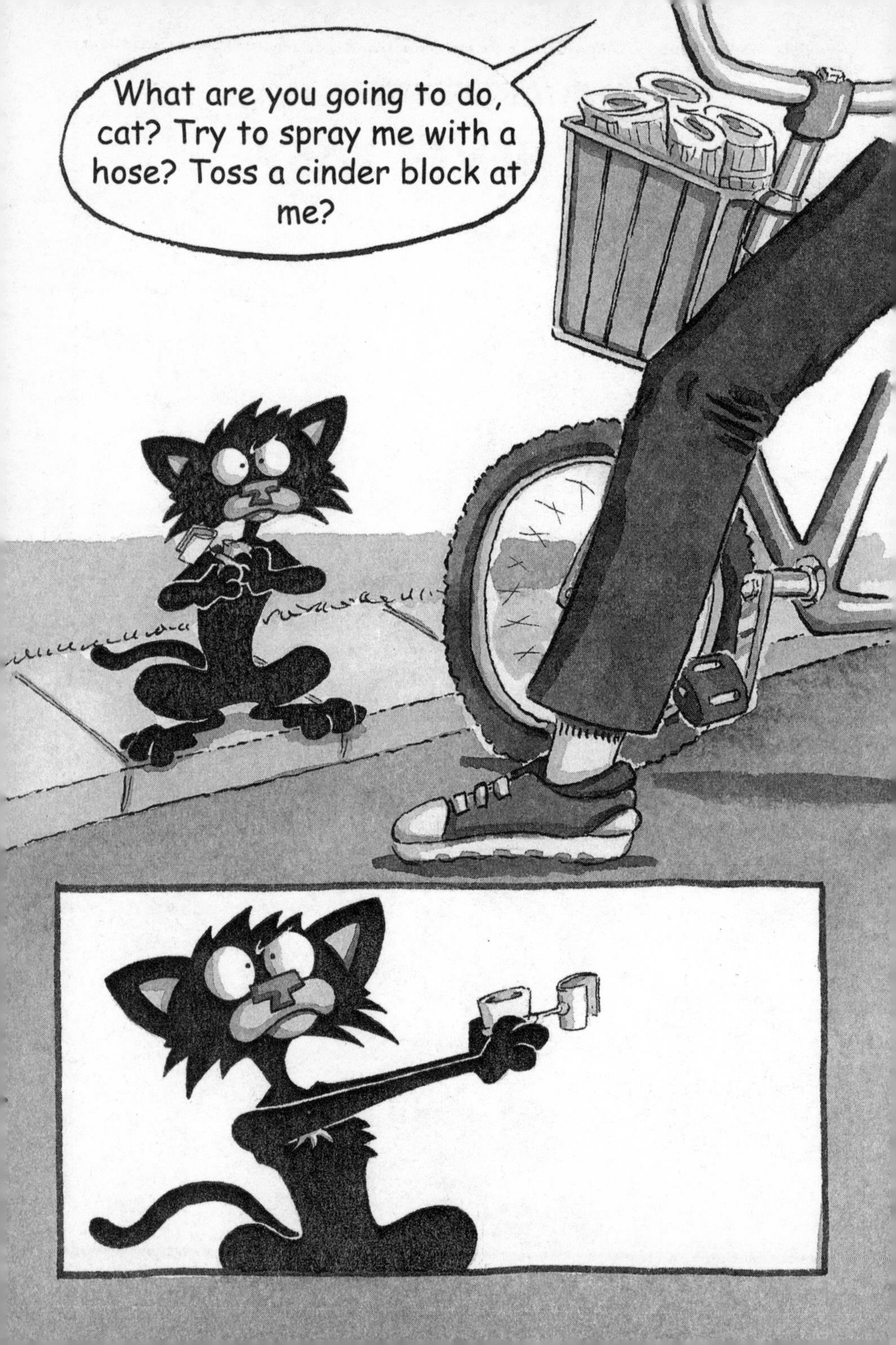
What are you going to do, cat? Try to spray me with a hose? Toss a cinder block at me?

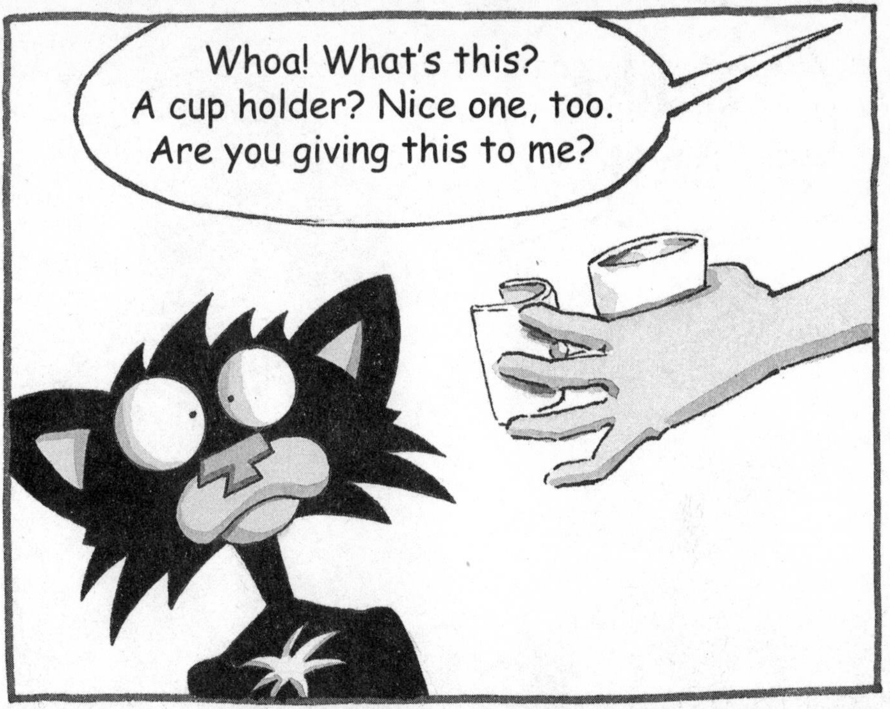
Whoa! What's this? A cup holder? Nice one, too. Are you giving this to me?

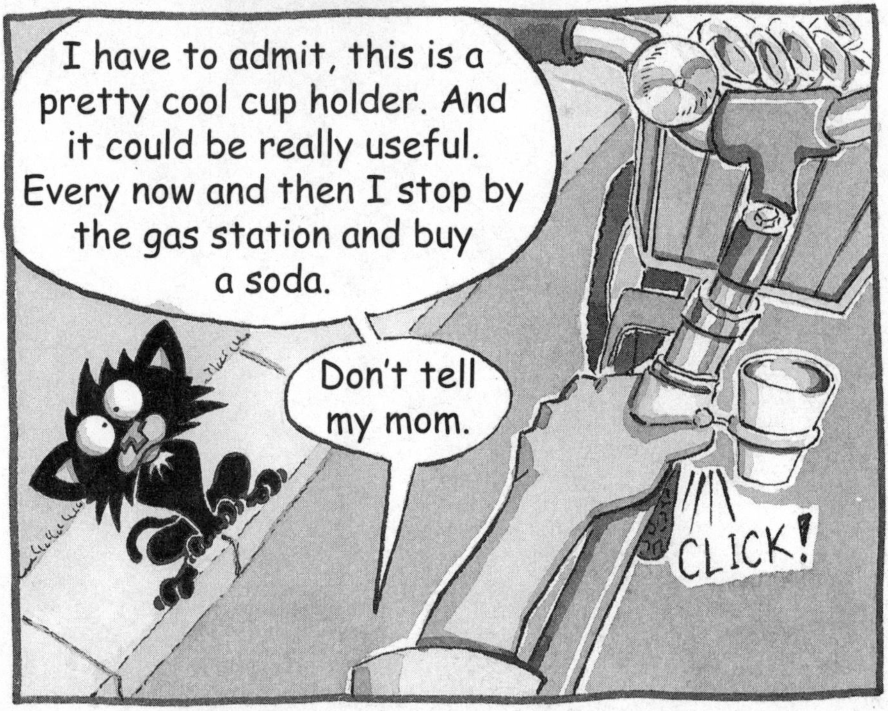
I have to admit, this is a pretty cool cup holder. And it could be really useful. Every now and then I stop by the gas station and buy a soda.
Don't tell my mom.
CLICK!

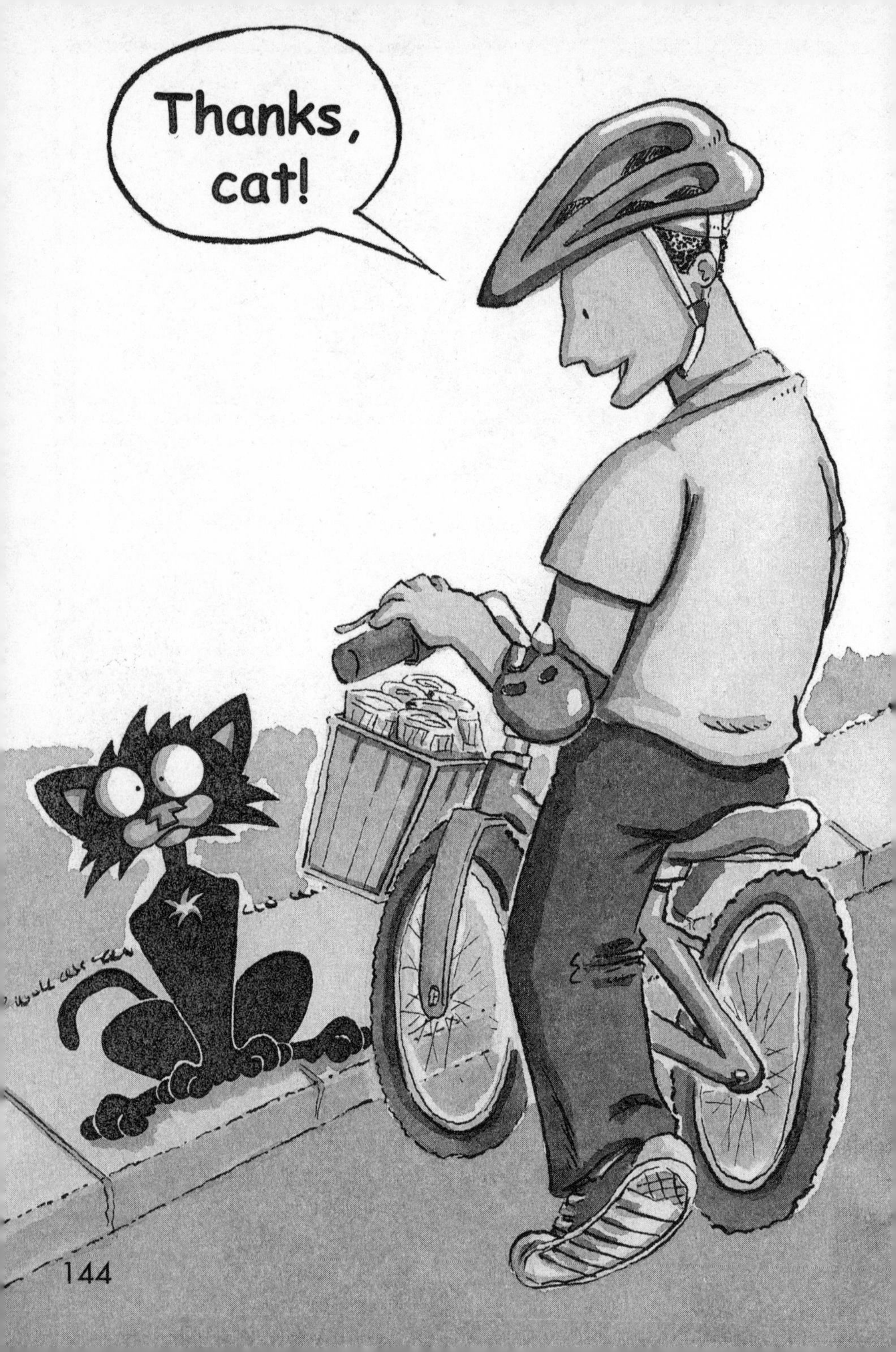
Thanks, cat!

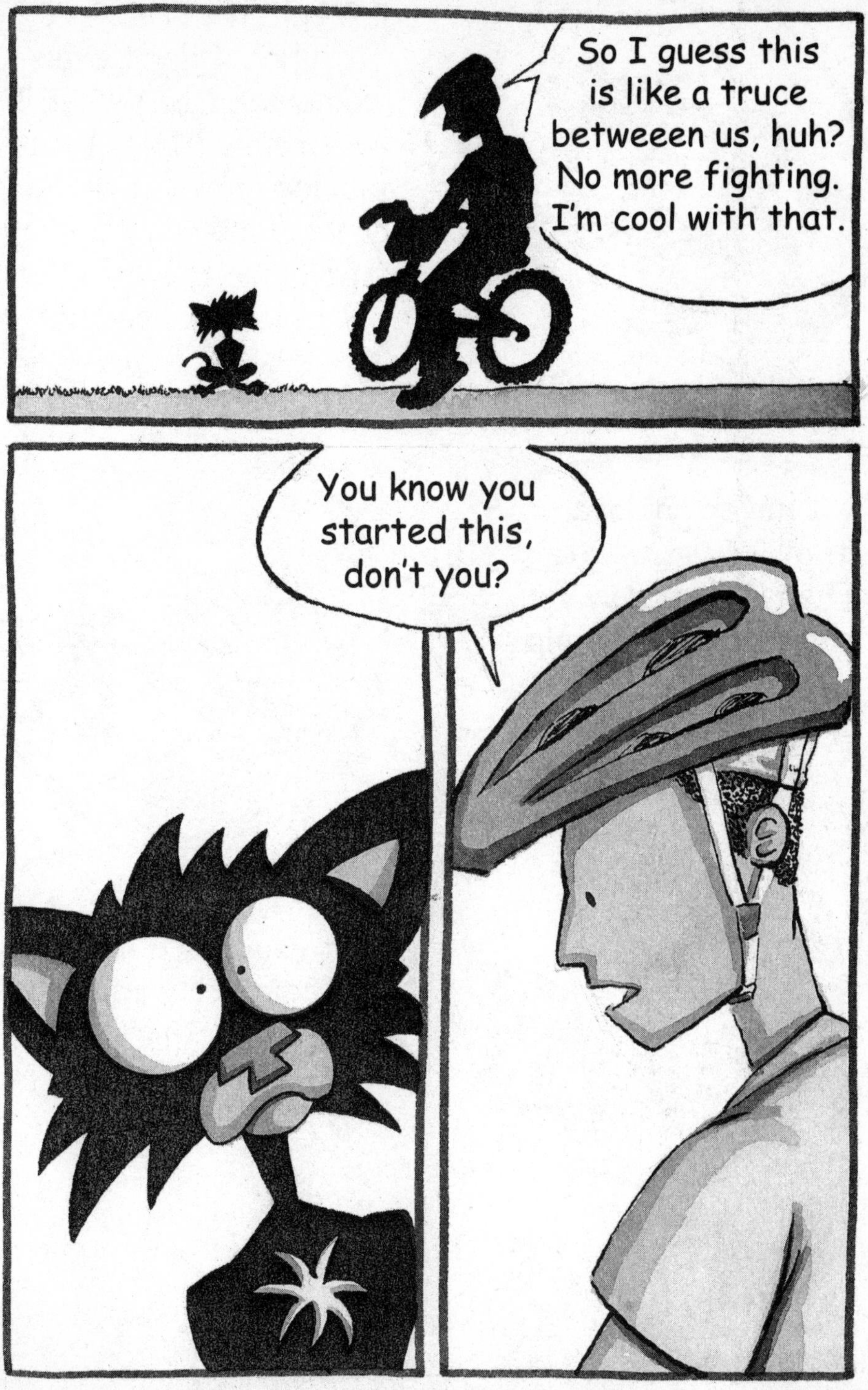
So I guess this is like a truce betweeen us, huh? No more fighting. I'm cool with that.
You know you started this, don't you?

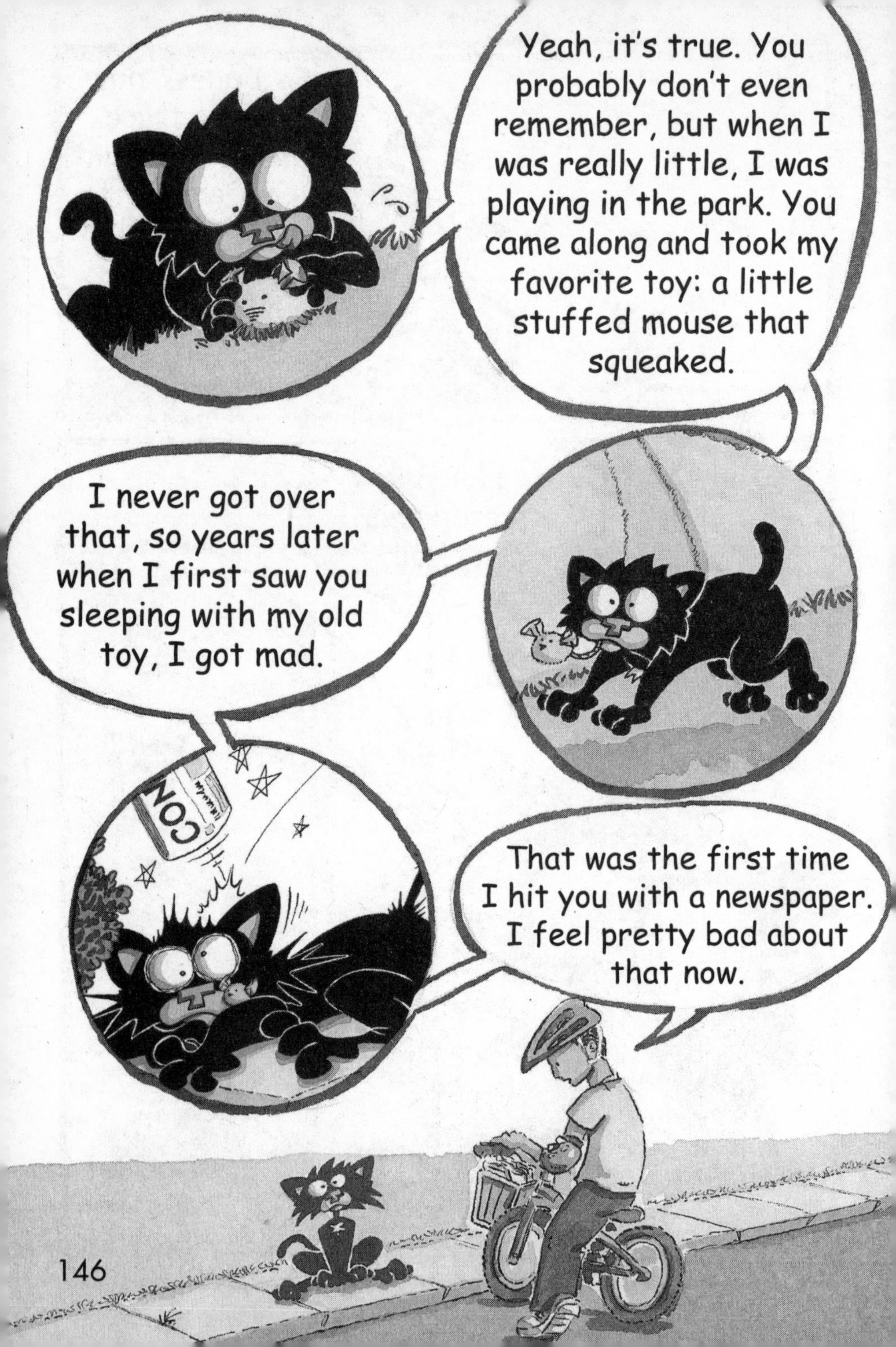
Yeah, it's true. You probably don't even remember, but when I was really little, I was playing in the park. You came along and took my favorite toy: a little stuffed mouse that squeaked.
I never got over that, so years later when I first saw you sleeping with my old toy, I got mad.
CON
That was the first time I hit you with a newspaper. I feel pretty bad about that now.

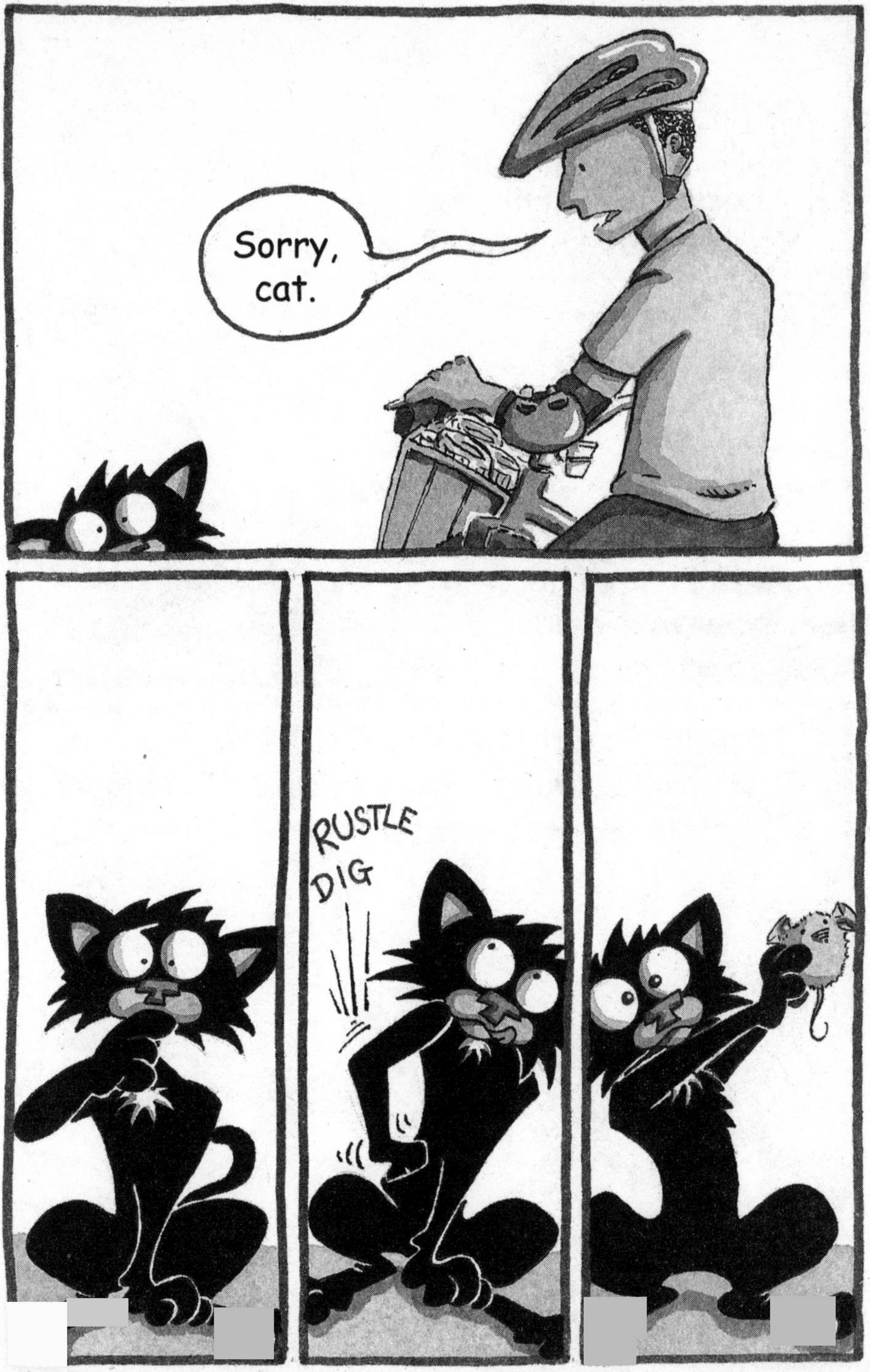

Sorry, cat.
RUSTLE
DIG

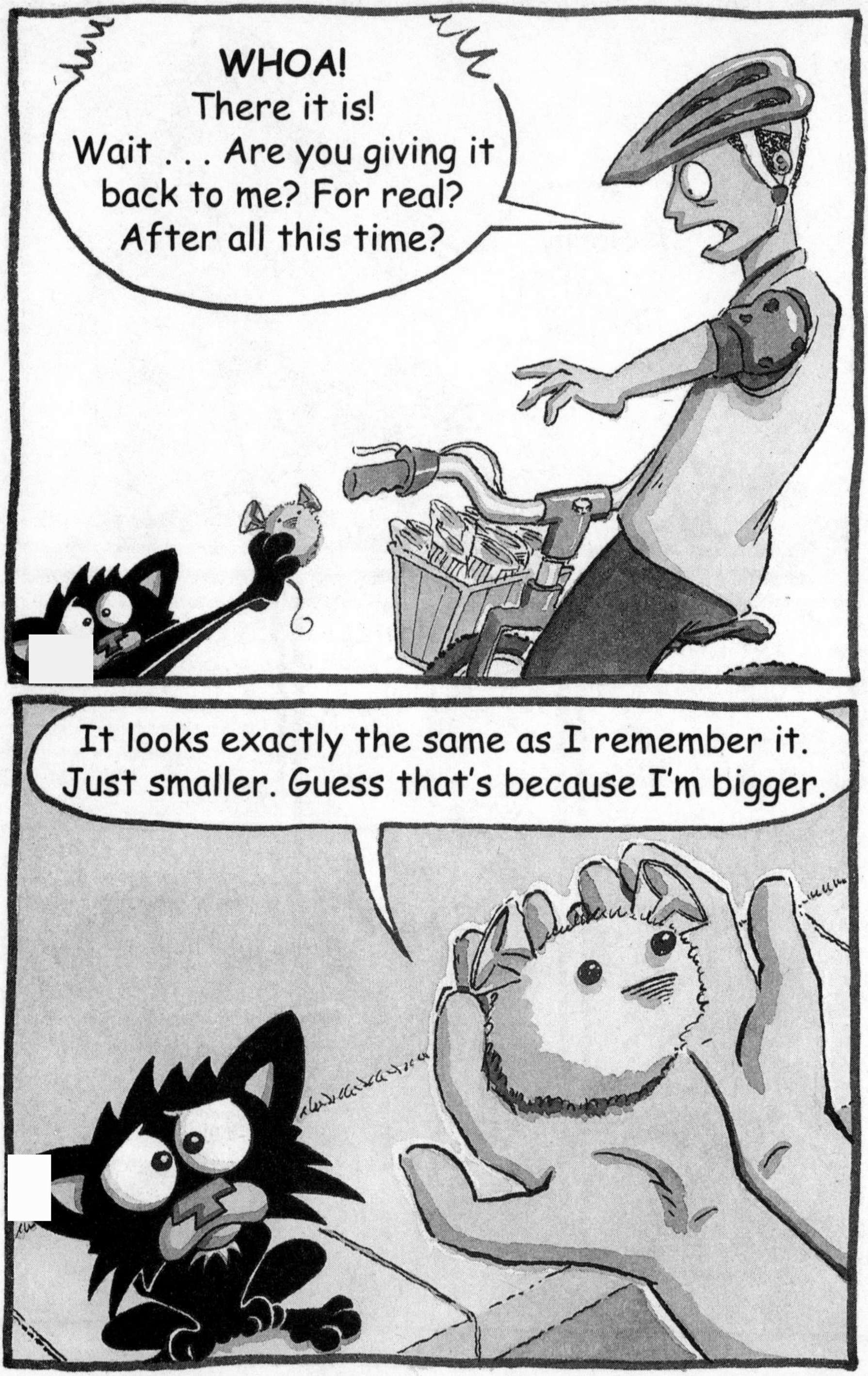
WHOA! There it is! Wait . . . Are you giving it back to me? For real? After all this time?
It looks exactly the same as I remember it. Just smaller. Guess that's because I'm bigger.

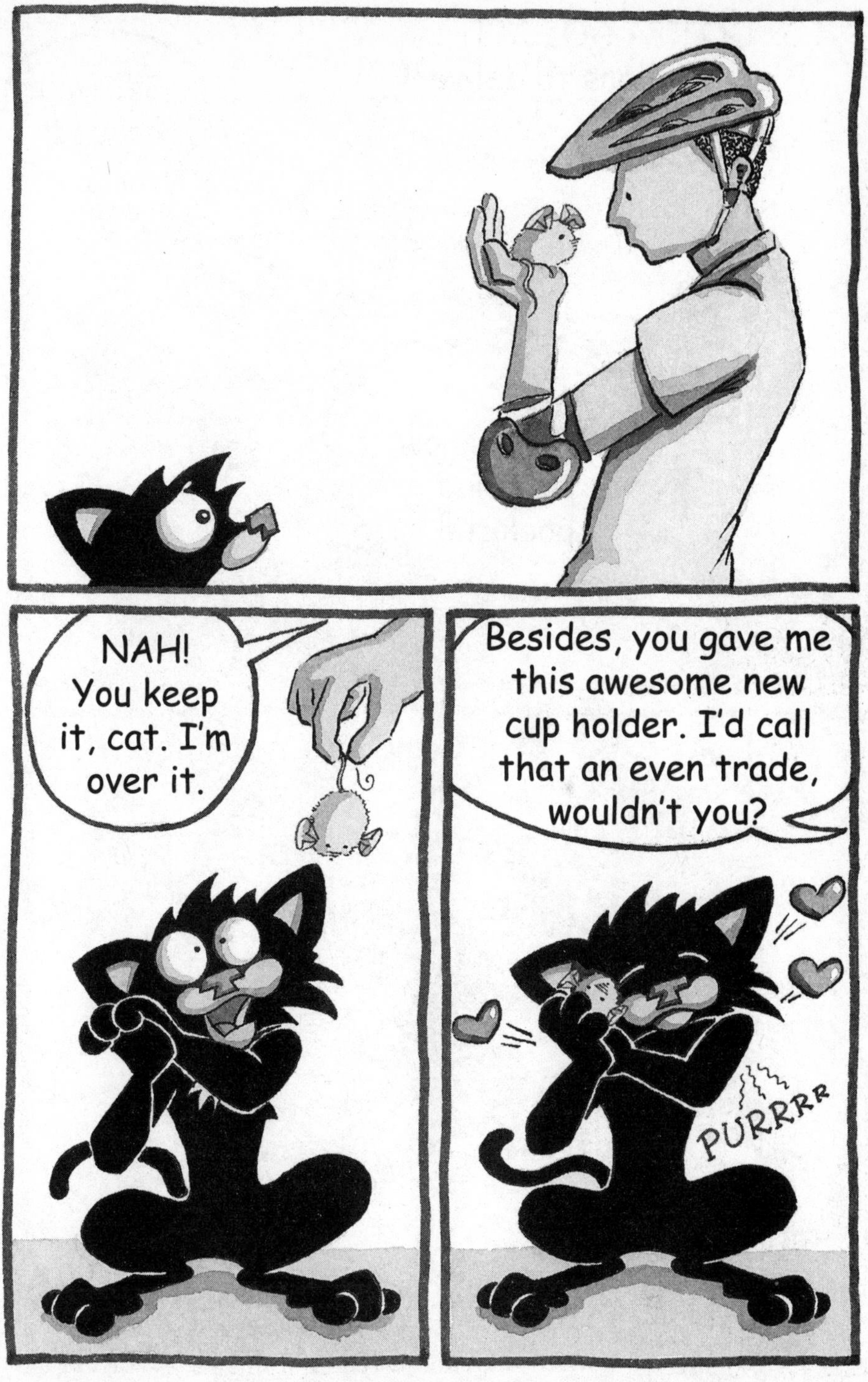
NAH! You keep it, cat. I'm over it.
Besides, you gave me this awesome new cup holder. I'd call that an even trade, wouldn't you?
PURRRR

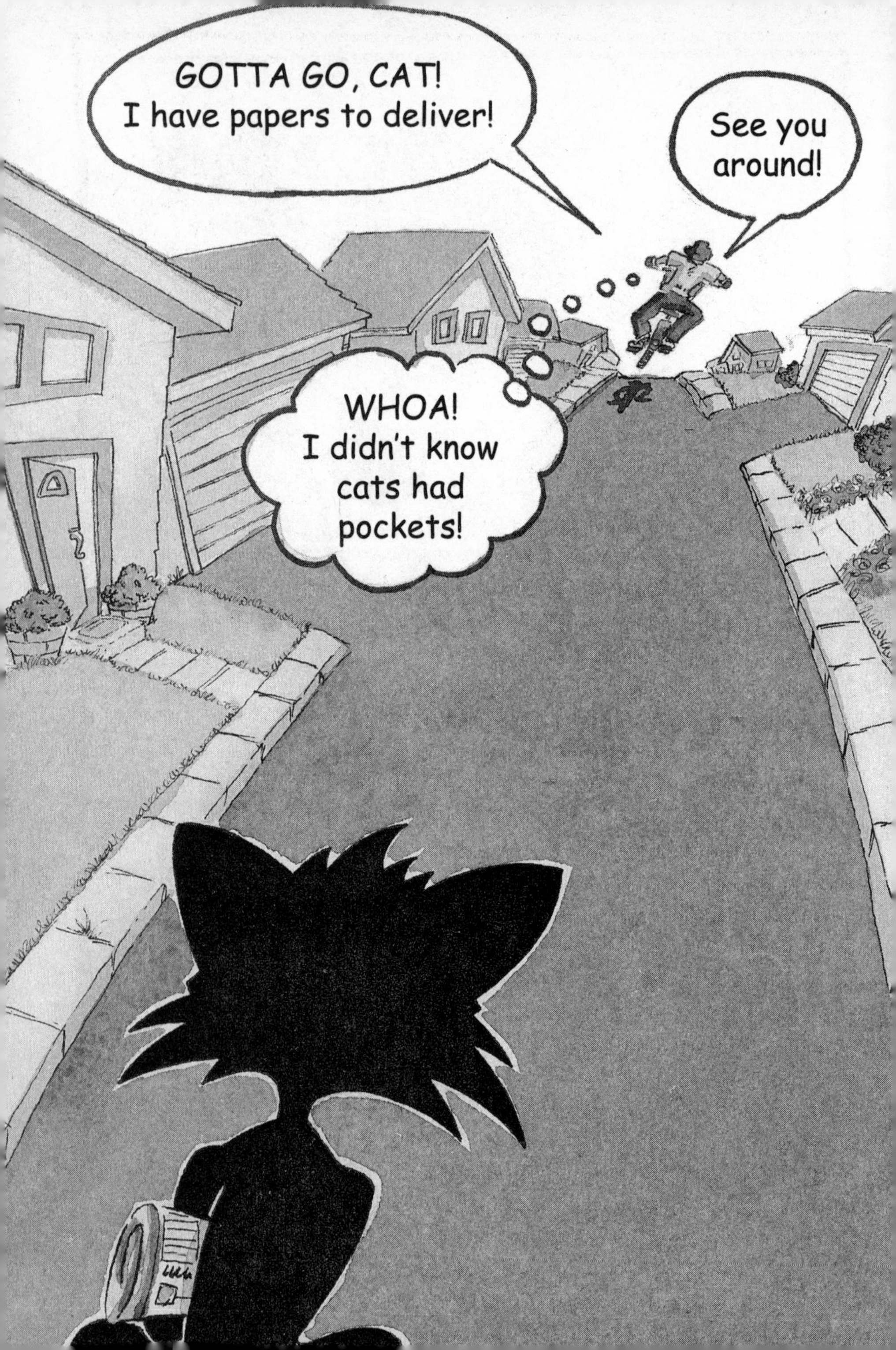
GOTTA GO, CAT!
I have papers to deliver!
See you around!
WHOA! I didn't know cats had pockets!

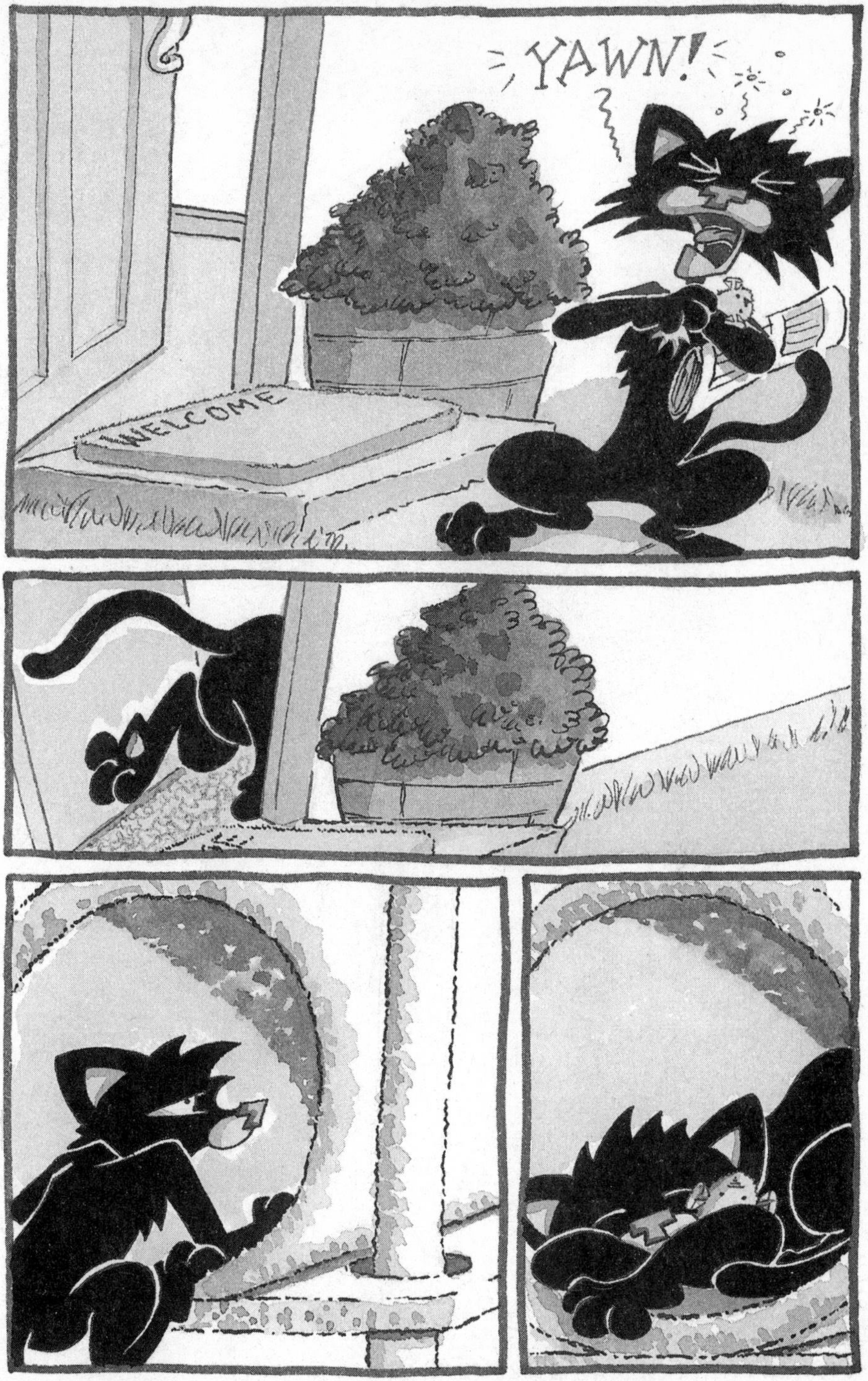
YAWN!
WELCOME

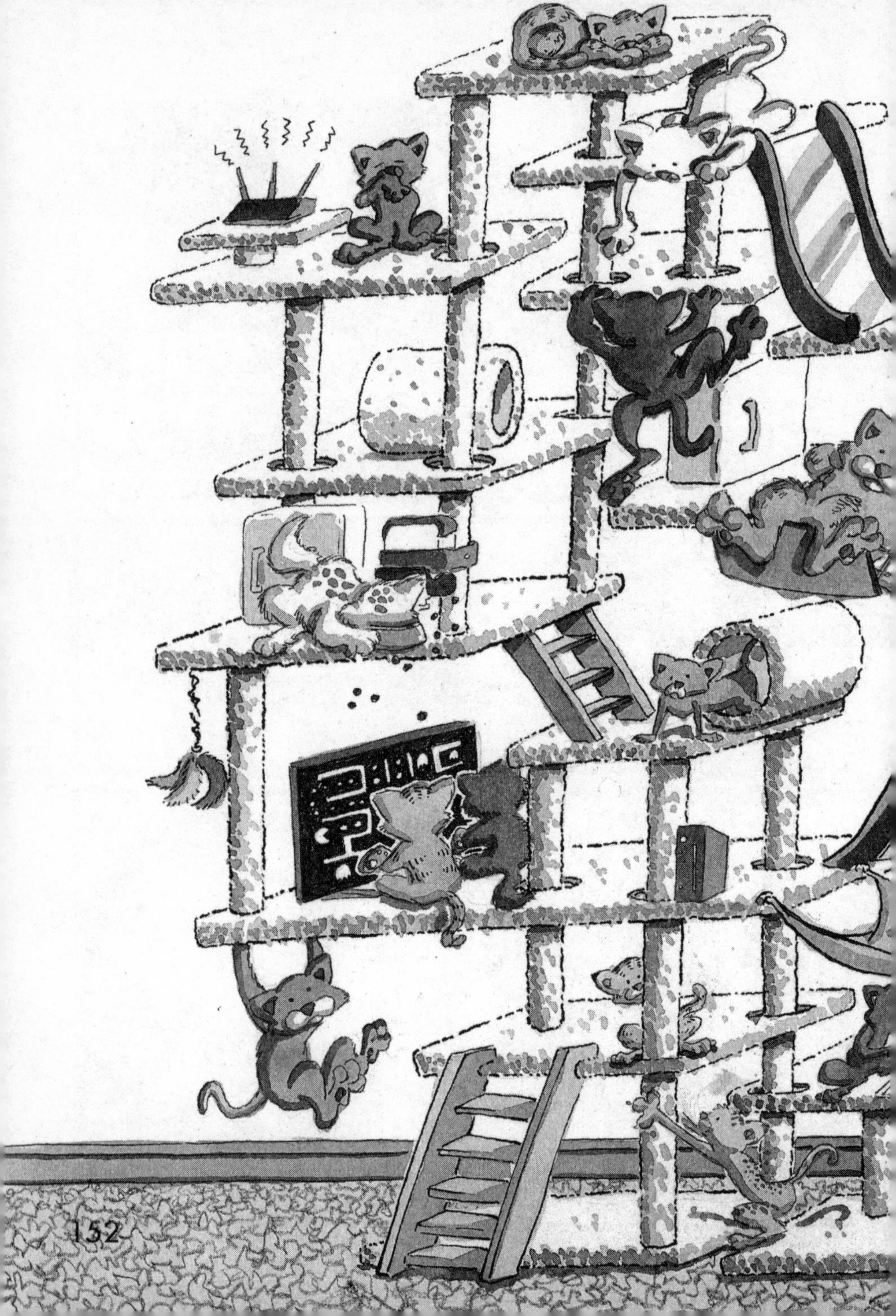

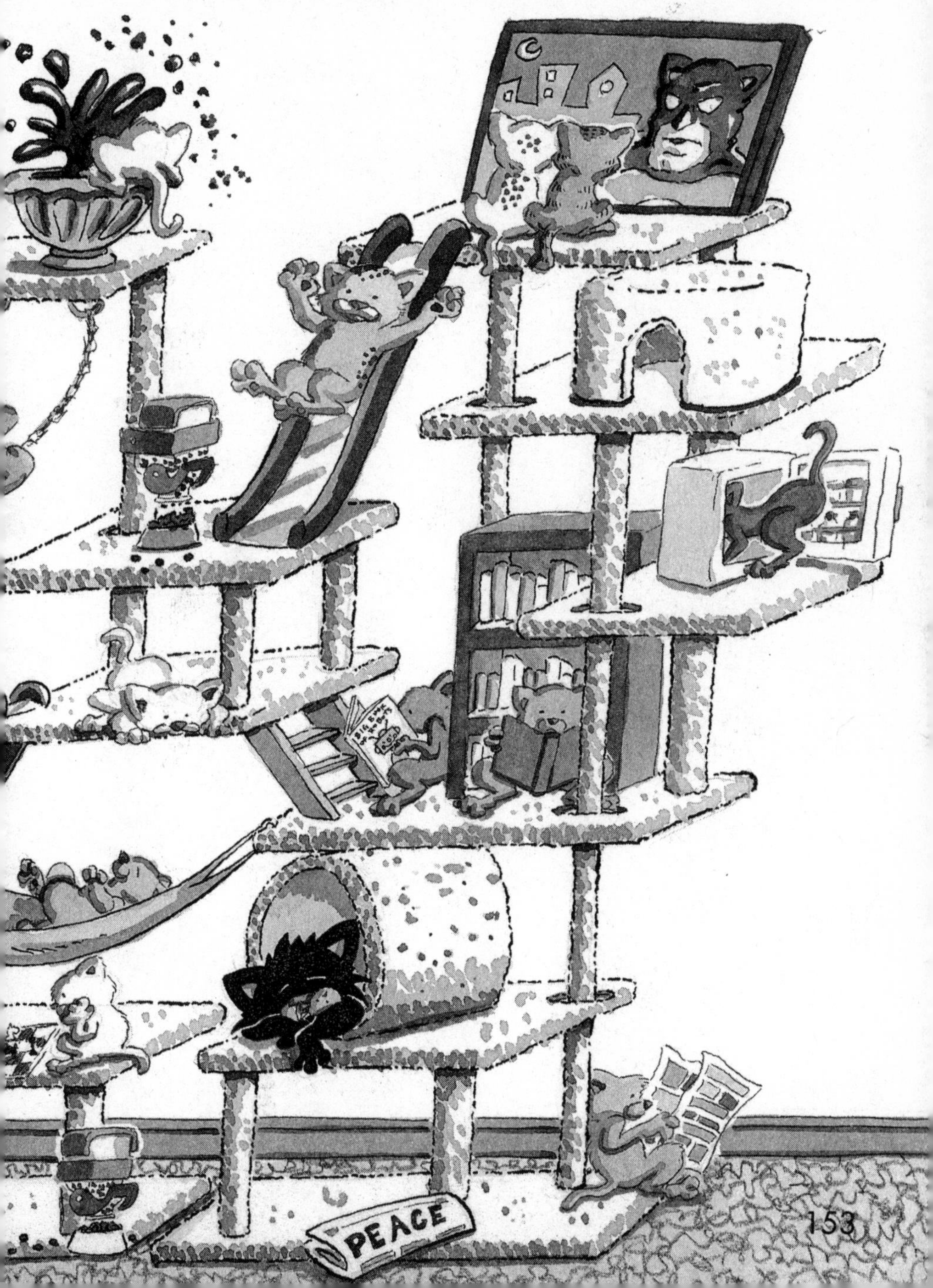
PEACE

•GLOSSARY•

The following is a list that translates one of the kitten's dialogue from French to English in the order in which it appears.

Bonjour *(bon-joor)*—Hello

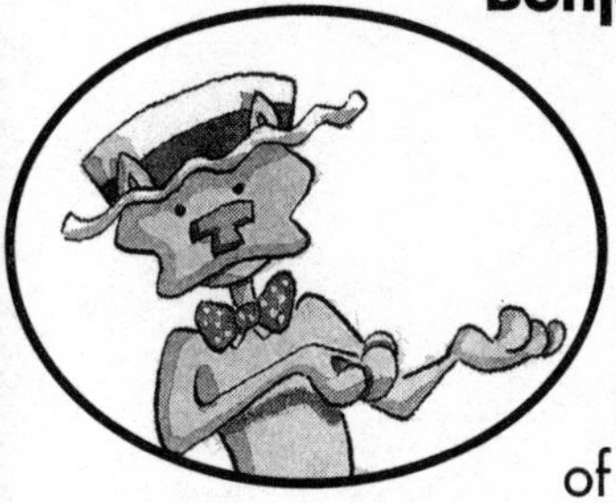

J'aime votre chapeau *(jhem vo-tra sha-po)*—I like your hat

Sacre bleu *(sa-kra bluh)*—Sacred blue (an uncommon expression of surprise)

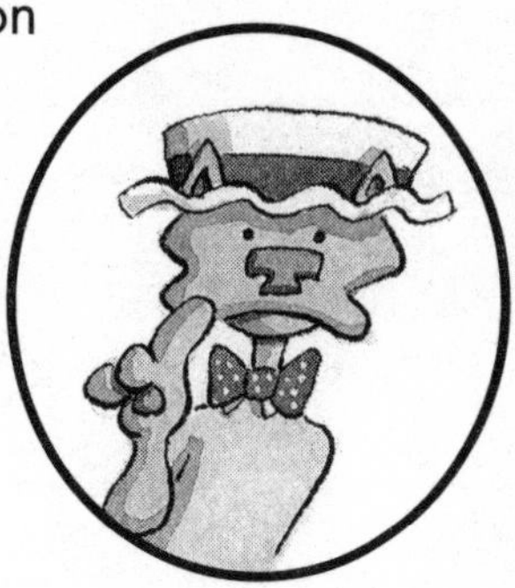

Un monstre *(uhn mon-stra)*—A monster

Petite souris *(pe-tee soo-ree)*—Little mouse

Zut Alors *(zoot a-lor)*—Darn (another uncommon expression of surprise)

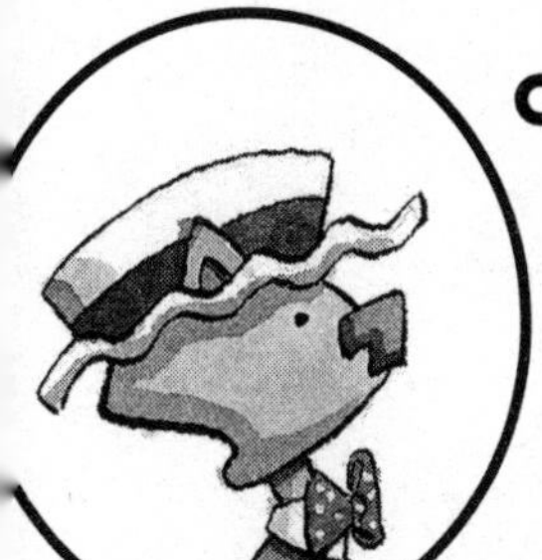

Oh, la vache *(o la vash)*—Holy cow (a slightly more common expression of surprise)

Belles fleurs *(bell flurs)*—Pretty flowers

Merci *(maer-see)*—Thank you

Mon Dieu *(mon dee-u)*—My God

Au revoir, Cher Kitty *(o rev-wahr cher Kit-ee)*—Goodbye, dear Kitty

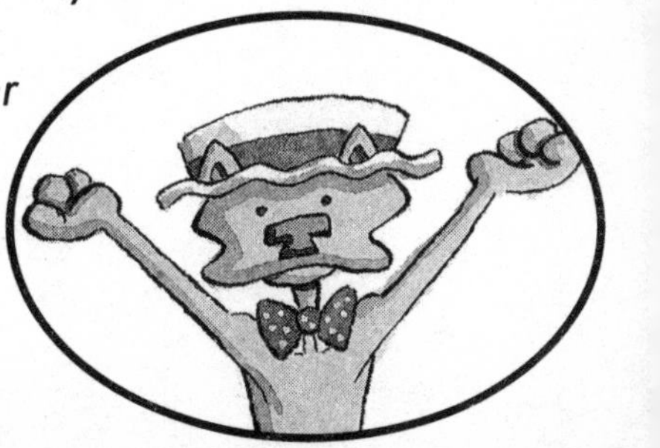

20 percent of the author's proceeds from this book
will be donated evenly between
The International Rescue Committee,
UNICEF,
and **Doctors Without Borders**.

rescue.org
unicef.org
doctorswithoutborders.org

Can't get enough of BAD KITTY?

NICK BRUEL
BAD KITTY
Gets a BATH
The New York Times Bestselling Series

Bad Kitty Gets a Bath

ISBN 978-1-59643-341-0 (hc)
ISBN 978-0-312-58138-1 (pb)

NICK BRUEL
BAD KITTY
Happy Birthday, BAD KITTY
The New York Times Bestselling Series

Happy Birthday Bad Kitty

ISBN 978-1-59643-342-7 (hc)
ISBN 978-0-312-62902-1 (pb)

NICK BRUEL
BAD KITTY
VS Uncle MURRAY
The New York Times Bestselling Series

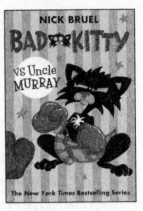

Bad Kitty vs Uncle Murray

ISBN 978-1-59643-596-4 (hc)
ISBN 978-0-312-67483-0 (pb)

NICK BRUEL
BAD KITTY
Drawn to TROUBLE
The New York Times Bestselling Series

Bad Kitty Drawn to Trouble

ISBN 978-1-59643-671-8 (hc)
ISBN 978-1-250-05679-5 (pb)

NICK BRUEL
BAD KITTY
Puppy's BIG DAY
The New York Times Bestselling Series

Bad Kitty: Puppy's Big Day

ISBN 978-1-59643-976-4 (hc)
ISBN 978-1-250-07330-3 (pb)

NICK BRUEL
BAD KITTY
Goes to the VET
The New York Times Bestselling Series

Bad Kitty Goes to the Vet

ISBN 978-1-59643-977-1 (hc)
ISBN 978-1-250-10380-2 (pb)

badkittybooks.com

Read these hilarious companion books!

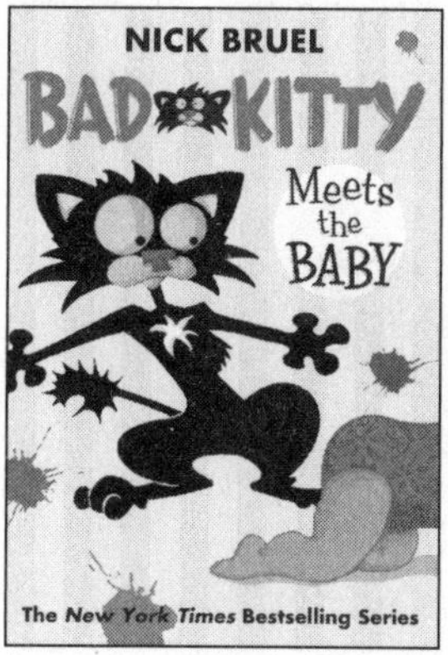
NICK BRUEL
BAD KITTY
Meets the BABY
The New York Times Bestselling Series

Bad Kitty Meets the Baby

ISBN 978-1-59643-597-1 (hc)
ISBN 978-0-312-64121-4 (pb)

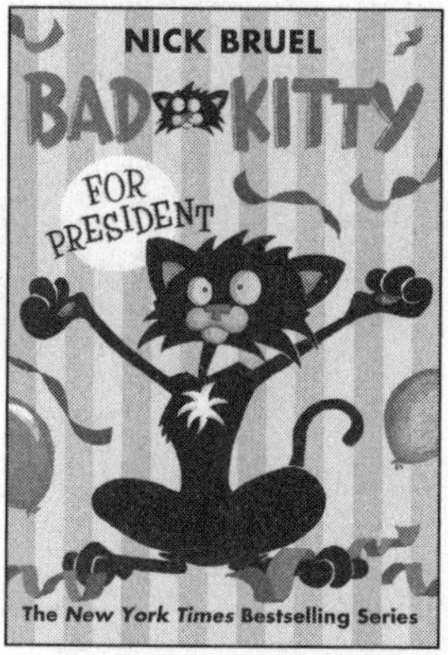
NICK BRUEL
BAD KITTY
FOR PRESIDENT
The New York Times Bestselling Series

Bad Kitty for President

ISBN 978-1-59643-669-5 (hc)
ISBN 978-1-250-07962-6 (pb)

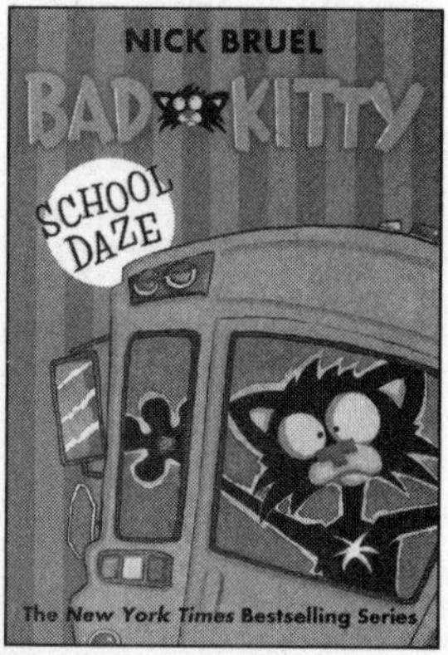
NICK BRUEL
BAD KITTY
SCHOOL DAZE
The New York Times Bestselling Series

Bad Kitty School Daze

ISBN 978-1-59643-670-1 (hc)
ISBN 978-1-250-03947-7 (pb)

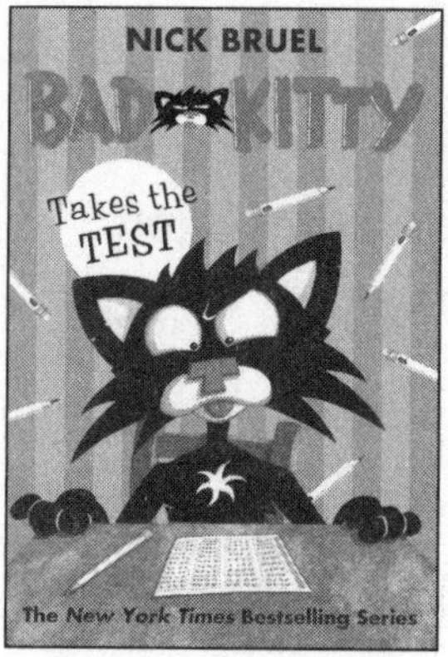
NICK BRUEL
BAD KITTY
Takes the TEST
The New York Times Bestselling Series

Bad Kitty Takes The Test

ISBN 978-1-62672-589-8 (hc)
ISBN 978-1-250-14354-9 (pb)

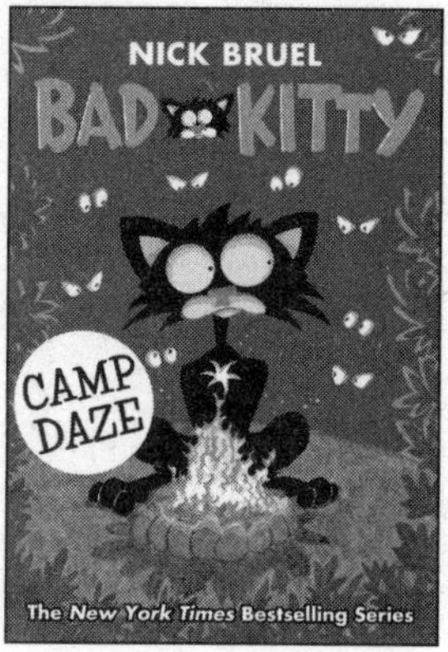
NICK BRUEL
BAD KITTY
CAMP DAZE
The New York Times Bestselling Series

Bad Kitty Camp Daze

ISBN 978-1-62672-885-1 (hc)
ISBN 978-1-250-29409-8 (pb)

mackids.com

NICK BRUEL is the author and illustrator of the phe-
nomenally successful Bad Kitty series, including the 2012
and 2013 CBC Children's Choice Book Award winners *Bad
Kitty Meets the Baby* and *Bad Kitty for President*. Nick has
also written and illustrated popular picture books including
A Wonderful Year and his most recent, *Bad Kitty: Scaredy-
Cat*. Nick lives with his wife and daughter in Westchester,
New York. Visit him at nickbruelbooks.com.

badkittybooks.com

A CONVERSATION WITH NICK BRUEL

INTERVIEWED BY UNCLE MURRAY

Hi, Gang! It's me! Everyone's favorite uncle: Uncle Murray! And it's time once again for me to interview the one and only Nick Bruel. Today we're going to talk about his book *Bad Kitty: Kitten Trouble*. But first, I have to call him. Let's hope he's available to talk.

NICK: Uncle Murray, I'm right here.

UNCLE MURRAY: Shhh. I'm trying to dial your number.

NICK: But I'm sitting right in front of you. You're the one who asked me to come here today.

UNCLE MURRAY: Hold that thought. It's ringing.

[SOUND OF CELL PHONE RINGING.]

UNCLE MURRAY: Well? Aren't you going to answer it?

NICK: Why would I . . . ? Fine. Hello?

UNCLE MURRAY: Hi, Nick Bruel! It's me! Uncle Murray!

NICK: Yes, I know that. I'm looking right at you.

UNCLE MURRAY: Is this a good time to talk?

NICK: Well, no, actually. I'm just about to be interviewed by a big goofball named Uncle Murray.

UNCLE MURRAY: I see. Maybe I'll call you back later when you're not so busy.

NICK: Uhhhh . . . That would be good. I think.

UNCLE MURRAY: Goodbye.

NICK: Bye. [Ends call. Puts phone in pocket.]

UNCLE MURRAY: Thank you for letting me interview you today, Nick Bruel. So tell me why you wrote *Bad Kitty: Kitten Trouble*.

NICK: What just happened here?

UNCLE MURRAY: What inspired you? What made you want to write this book?

NICK: The idea for this book came to me a few years back while I was driving to pick up my daughter from school and a fascinating story came on the radio. It was about a man in New York City who owned and operated a tourism agency. His company created special tours for people who were visiting his city. At the time, he was very concerned about refugees who were moving into the city that he loved so much.

UNCLE MURRAY: What's a refugee?

NICK: I'm glad you asked. A refugee is a person

who has to leave his or her home to find safety. Sometimes they have to leave because of a disaster, like a flood or an earthquake, or because of war or violence.

UNCLE MURRAY: That sounds rough.

NICK: It is. And leaving is only half the problem. Next they have to find a place where they can live until they can go home again—IF they can go home again.

UNCLE MURRAY: So what did this guy on the radio do?

NICK: He asked himself a very important question. He asked, "What can I do to help?"

UNCLE MURRAY: That is an excellent question. It's one of those questions I like to ask myself every day. "What can I do to help?"

NICK: Do you really?

UNCLE MURRAY: Sure! I asked myself that question just before we started this interview. I asked, "What can I do to help?" And I decided there and then to brush my teeth after having eaten a tuna salad sandwich with extra salami.

NICK: Uhh . . . How is that helping?

UNCLE MURRAY: Can you smell my breath?

NICK: No.

UNCLE MURRAY: You're welcome.

NICK: So, anyway, this man who owned a tourism agency in New York City realized that he could help refugees who moved into his city by giving them free tours so they could learn more about the city in which they now lived. I found this inspiring, so I decided to ask myself that same question. "What can I do to help?"

UNCLE MURRAY: And what answer did you come up with?

NICK: Well, this book, *Bad Kitty: Kitten Trouble*. It's my take on how Kitty learns to respect the plight of others. She learns to see these kittens as cats who need a little help and not as cats who are there to make life difficult for her.

UNCLE MURRAY: I feel kind of bad about how I treated those kittens at first. I think I was a little mean.

NICK: Yes, you were. But you learned, and that's what's important. Plus, you set an example for Kitty to see the newspaper kid as a human being and not as some malevolent force who only exists to torment her.

UNCLE MURRAY: I did?

NICK: Sure! You showed Kitty how to be kind to a stranger just by saying nice things and giving him money for a soda every now and then.

UNCLE MURRAY: Shhh! Not so loud! I'm going to get in trouble with his mom!

NICK: Sorry. Still, your simple act of kindness helped Kitty see him in a different light, and that's what helped her find a way to end their conflict.

UNCLE MURRAY: So, you're saying that I'm like the hero of the story.

NICK: Well, not exactly . . .

UNCLE MURRAY: I'm the hero of the story! I'm the guy who saved the day!

NICK: Ummmm . . .

UNCLE MURRAY: I'm like Superman and Batman and Captain FantastiCat all rolled into one!

NICK: That's not really what I was saying.

UNCLE MURRAY: [Climbs onto table.] Call me Captain Marvelous MurrayMan!

NICK: I'm not going to call you that.

UNCLE MURRAY: [Climbs down from table.] That's okay. It's not really official until I print it on a business card. Anyway, I think we're done here. Thanks for the interview. I have an important call to make now.

NICK: You're welcome, Uncle Murray. As usual, it's

been a fun and surreal experience. Maybe next time we . . . [Cell phone rings.]

UNCLE MURRAY: [Whispering] Answer your phone.

NICK: Hello?

UNCLE MURRAY: Hi! It's me! Everyone's favorite uncle: Uncle Murray! I'm finally done with this other guy. Boy, could he talk. Yak, yak, yak. Anyway, you want to sit down for this interview now?

NICK: Sigh.

Kitty hits it out of the park in the next installment of your favorite chapter book series!

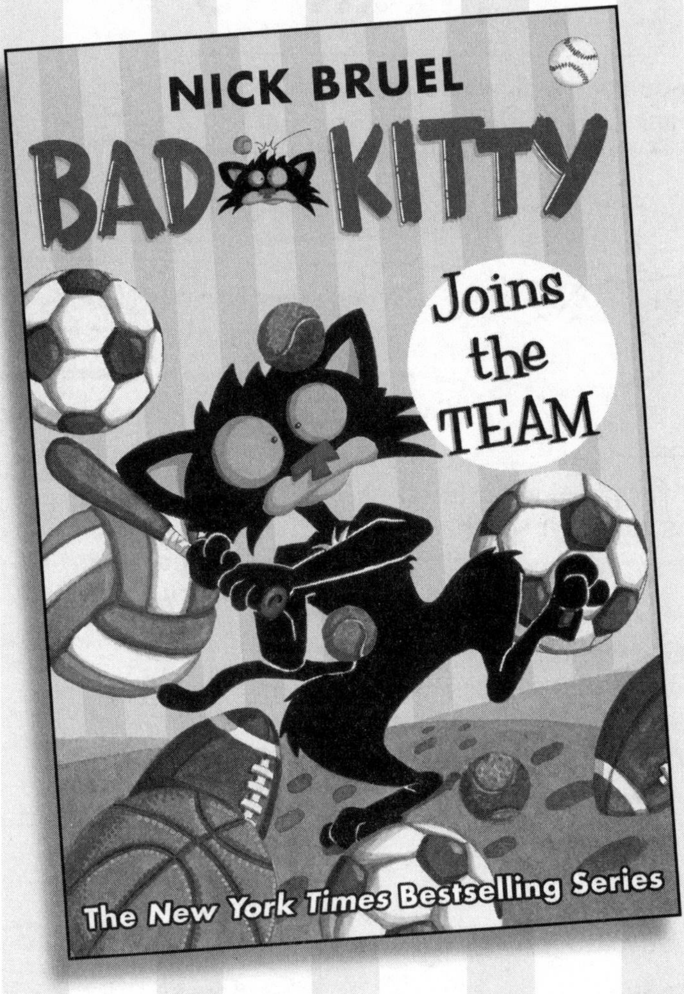
NICK BRUEL
BAD KITTY
Joins the TEAM
The New York Times Bestselling Series

Keep reading for more Bad Kitty!

•CHAPTER ONE•

SUCH A CALM, QUIET MORNING

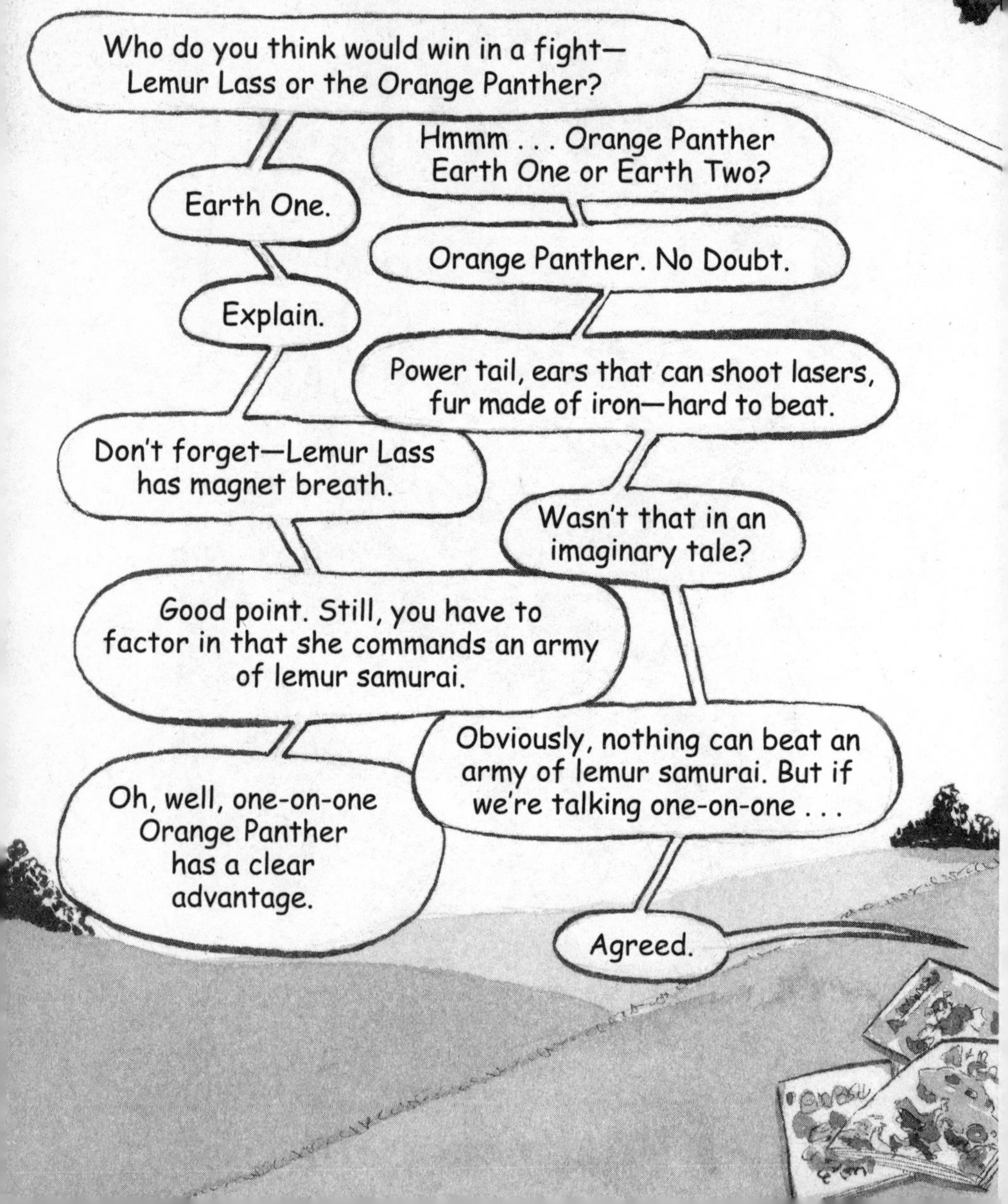
Who do you think would win in a fight— Lemur Lass or the Orange Panther?
Hmmm . . . Orange Panther Earth One or Earth Two?
Earth One.
Orange Panther. No Doubt.
Explain.
Power tail, ears that can shoot lasers, fur made of iron—hard to beat.
Don't forget—Lemur Lass has magnet breath.
Wasn't that in an imaginary tale?
Good point. Still, you have to factor in that she commands an army of lemur samurai.
Obviously, nothing can beat an army of lemur samurai. But if we're talking one-on-one . . .
Oh, well, one-on-one Orange Panther has a clear advantage.
Agreed.

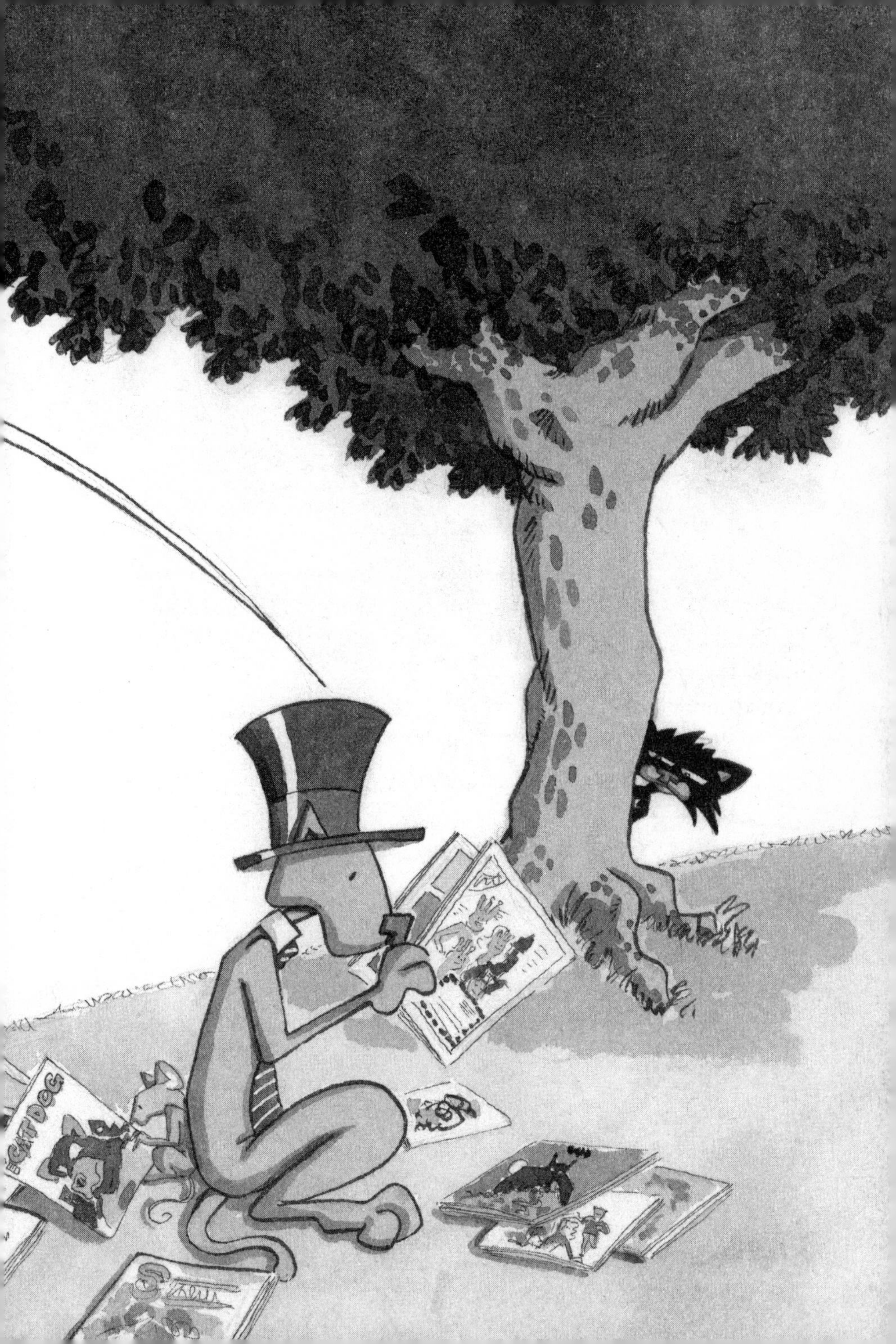
CAT DOG

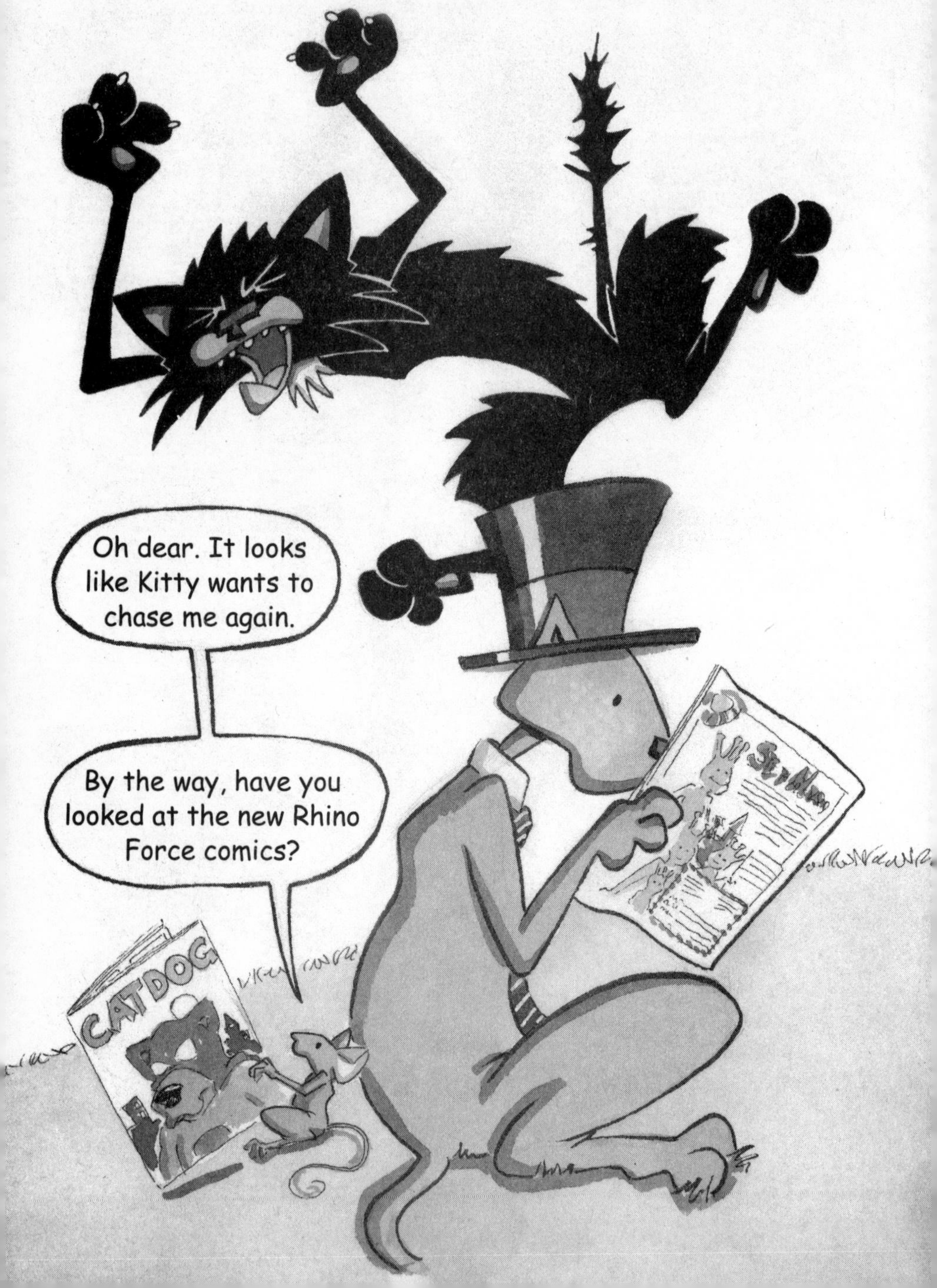
Oh dear. It looks like Kitty wants to chase me again.
By the way, have you looked at the new Rhino Force comics?
CATDOG

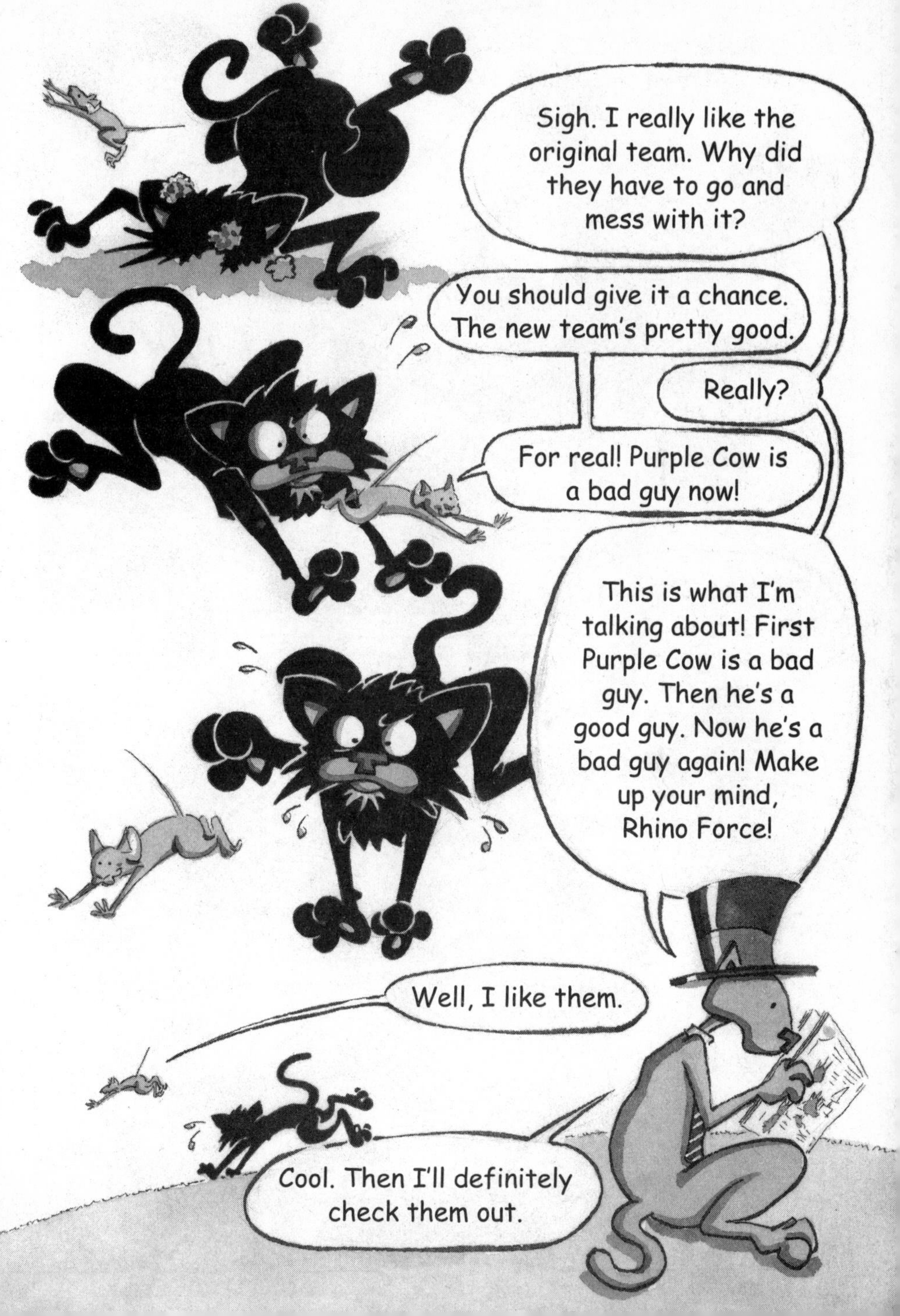
Sigh. I really like the original team. Why did they have to go and mess with it?
You should give it a chance. The new team's pretty good.
Really?
For real! Purple Cow is a bad guy now!
This is what I'm talking about! First Purple Cow is a bad guy. Then he's a good guy. Now he's a bad guy again! Make up your mind, Rhino Force!
Well, I like them.
Cool. Then I'll definitely check them out.

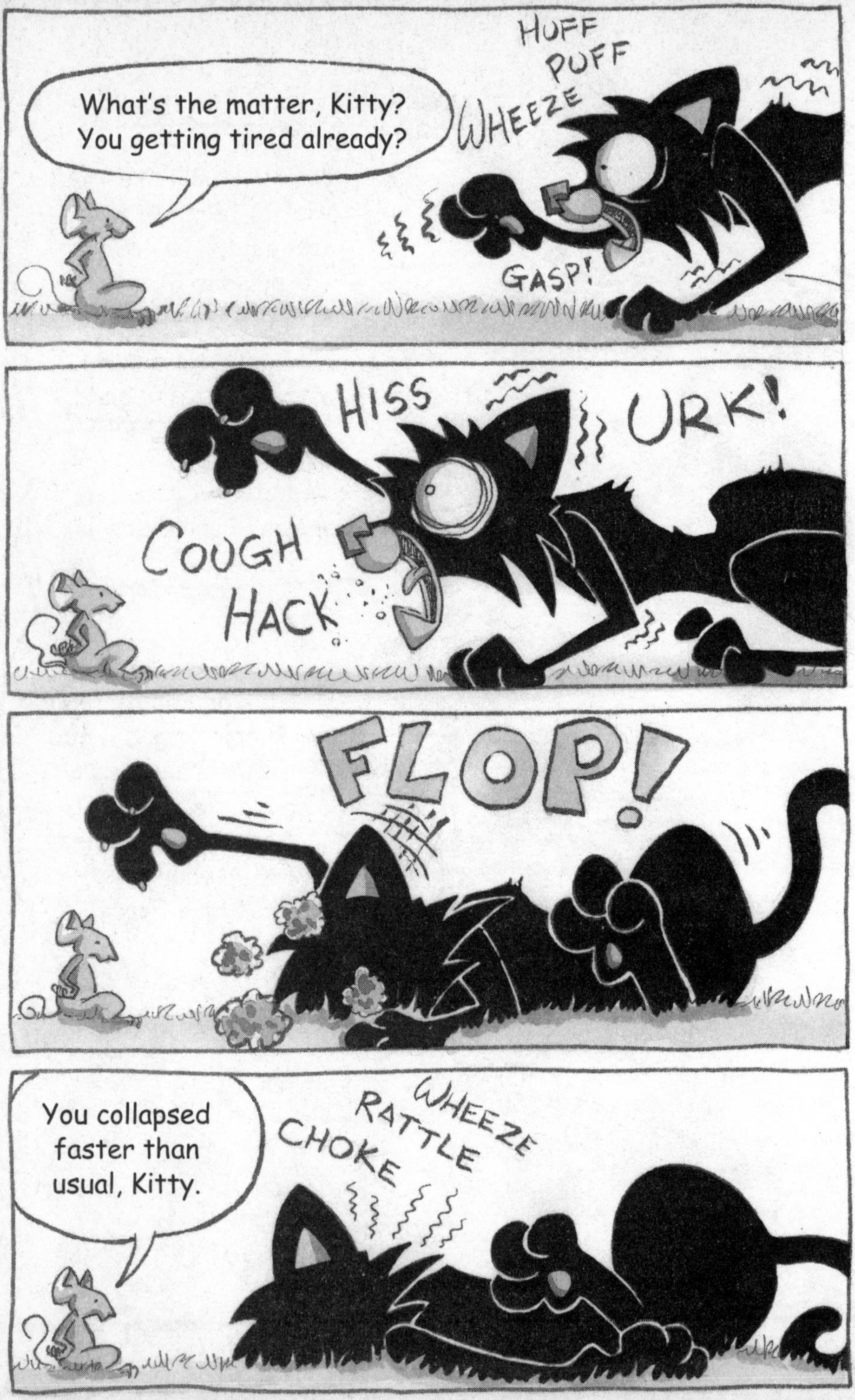
What's the matter, Kitty? You getting tired already?
HUFF
PUFF
WHEEZE
GASP!
HISS
URK!
COUGH
HACK
FLOP!
You collapsed faster than usual, Kitty.
WHEEZE
RATTLE
CHOKE

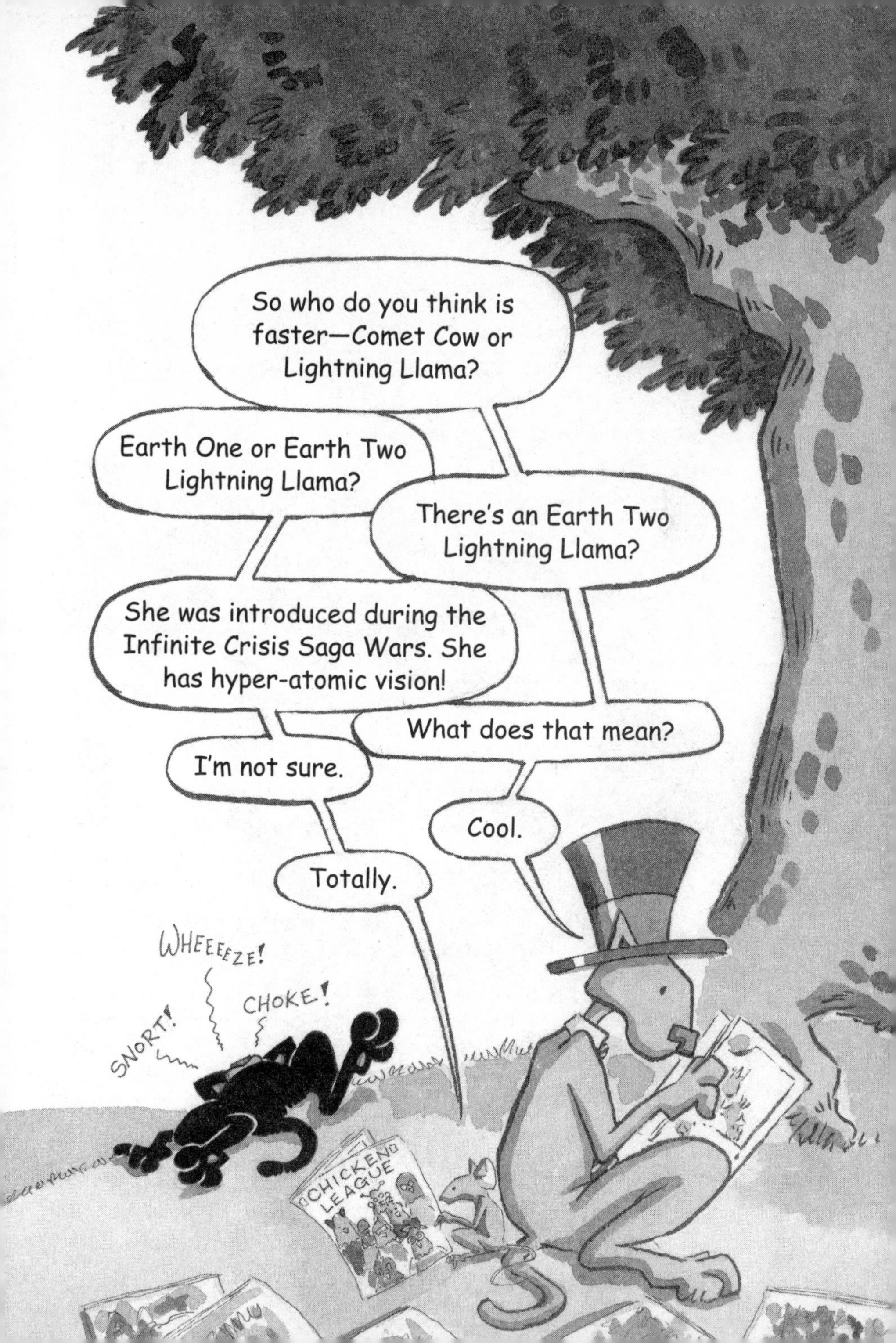
So who do you think is faster—Comet Cow or Lightning Llama?
Earth One or Earth Two Lightning Llama?
There's an Earth Two Lightning Llama?
She was introduced during the Infinite Crisis Saga Wars. She has hyper-atomic vision!
What does that mean?
I'm not sure.
Cool.
Totally.
WHEEEEZE!
CHOKE!
SNORT!
CHICKEN LEAGUE

•CHAPTER TWO•

JUST A LITTLE OUT OF SHAPE

Hi, Kitty.

Let me guess—you were chasing Mouse again, weren't you? You'll never catch him. You know that, don't you?

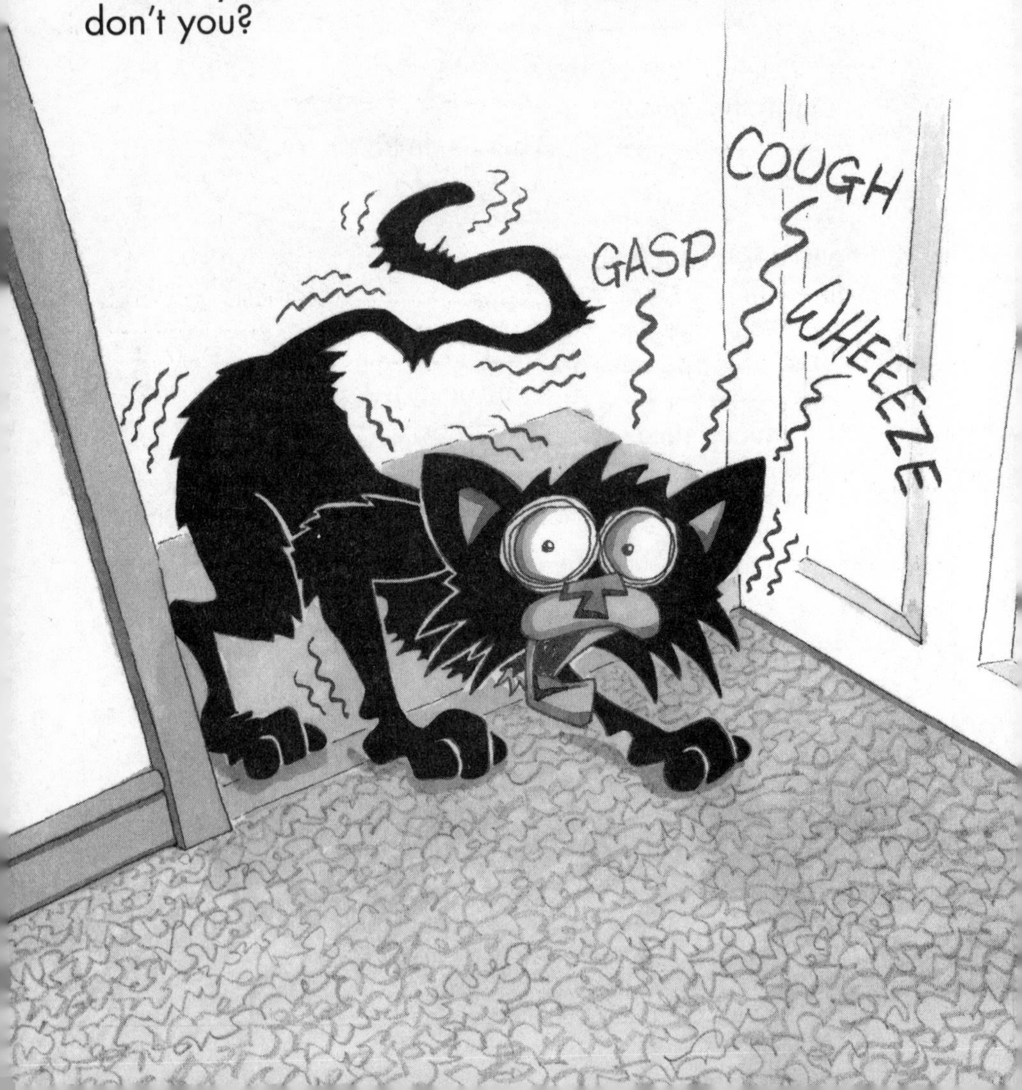
GASP
COUGH
WHEEEZE

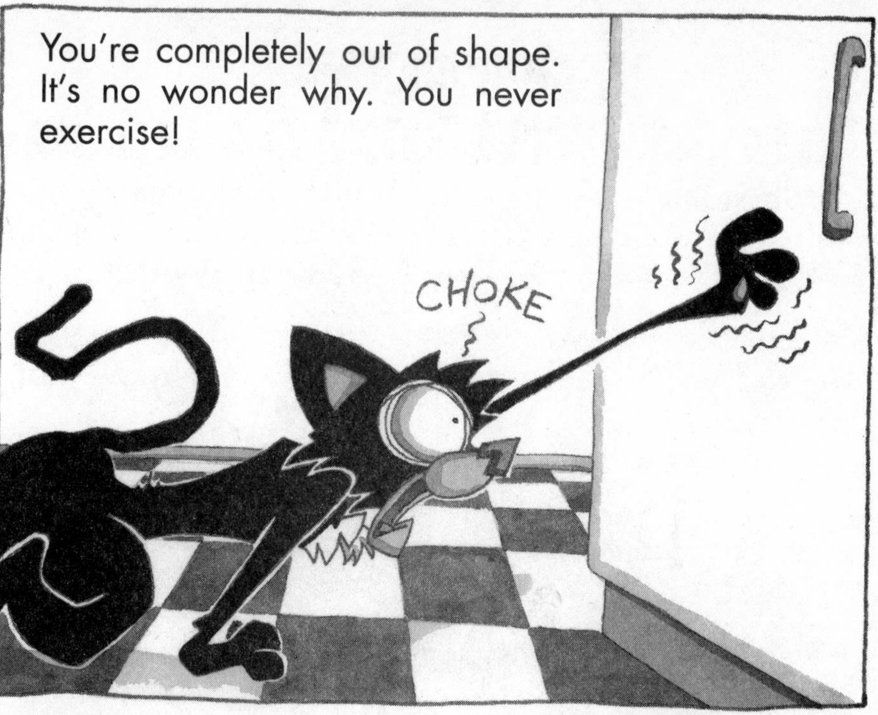
You're completely out of shape. It's no wonder why. You never exercise!
CHOKE

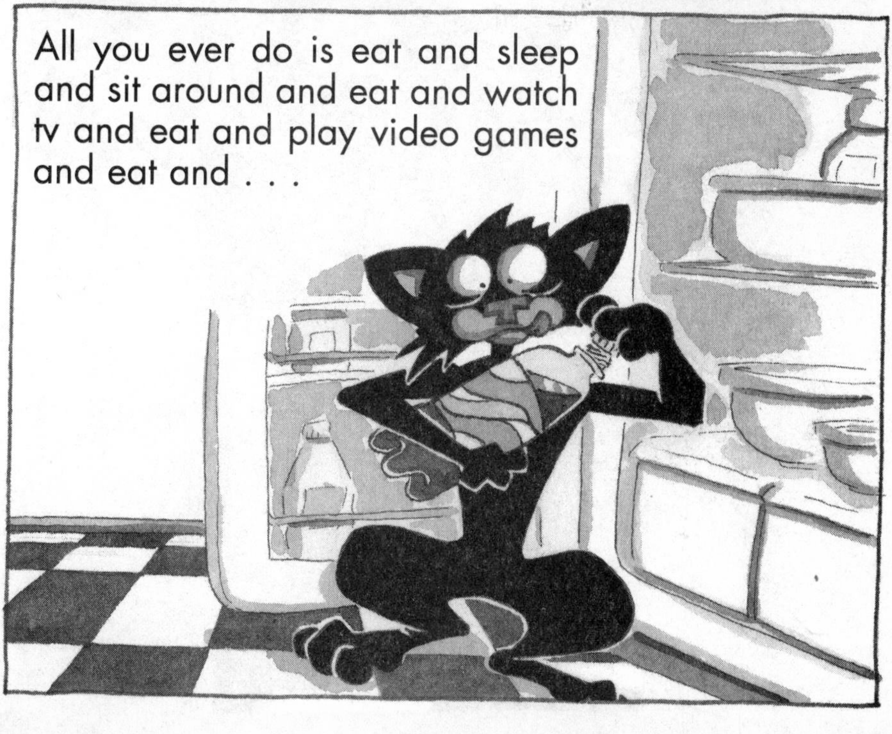
All you ever do is eat and sleep and sit around and eat and watch tv and eat and play video games and eat and . . .

KITTY!

Soda is the worst thing for you to drink when you're thirsty! You're dehydrated. Do you know what that means? It means that your body needs WATER.

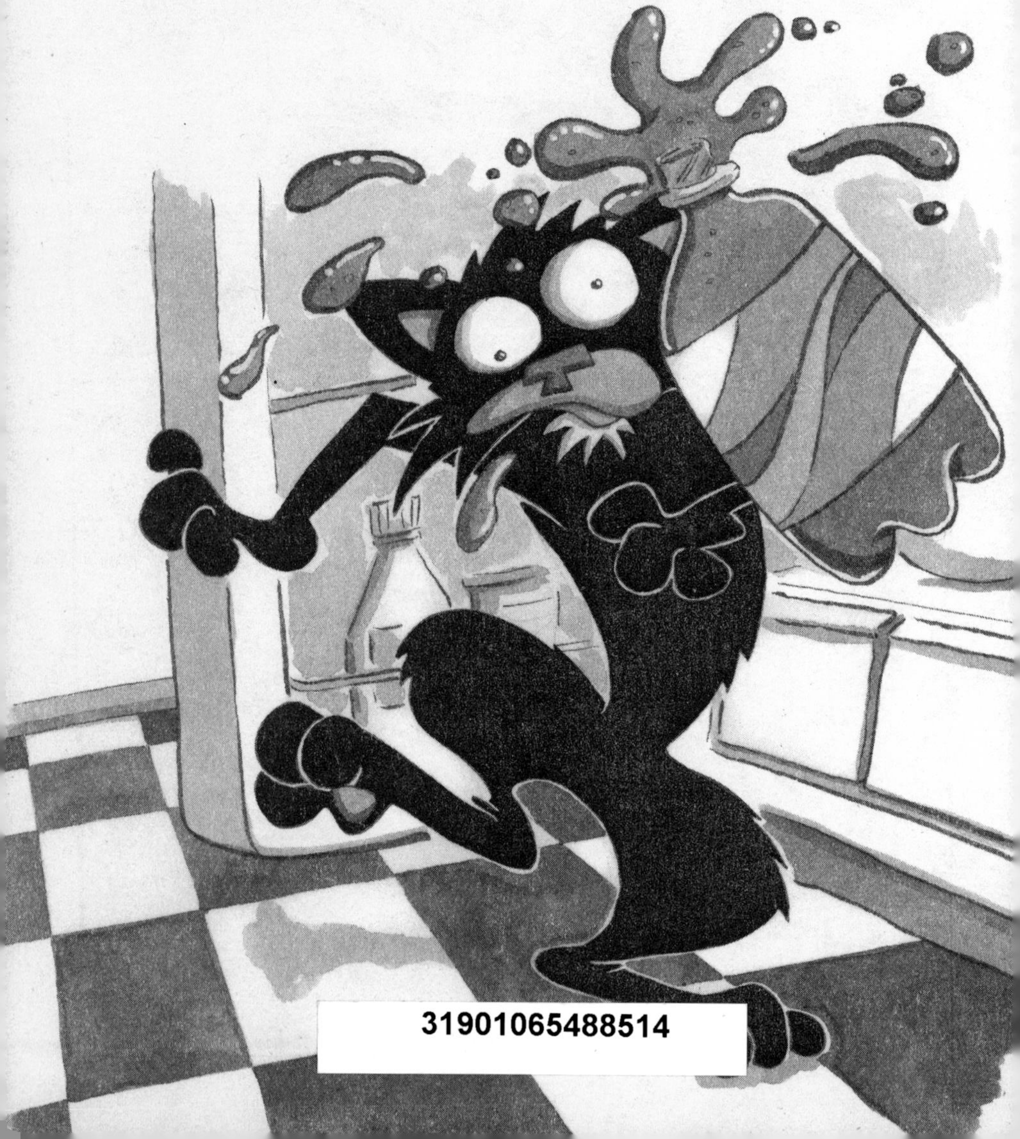